Paul A. Myers - what critics are saying

Betrayal in Europe: Paris 1938

Explores Parisian politics on the eve of the Second World War...Myers has done his research and impeccably draws the month-to-month social and political situations.

An intriguing, historically grounded imagining of behind-the-scenes machinations during a crucial moment in European history.
—Kirkus Reviews

Greek Bonds and French Ladies

Love and money are both at risk in Myers' politically driven novel of intrigue and betrayal...told with humor and sophistication.
—Kirkus Reviews

It has French charm and romance intertwined with a feeling of extravagance and elegance.
—Jennie, Goodreads review

A Farewell in Paris

Few places evoke nostalgia like the City of Light in the 1920s, and Myers doesn't skimp on the literary and historical details in his latest novel.
—Kirkus Reviews

In this lively novel, Myers clearly demonstrates his familiarity with the intellectual culture of Paris in the 1920s.
— Publishers Weekly

Paris 1935: Destiny's Crossroads

...takes us into the back rooms of high-level officials, writers, and media stars in order to understand why events happened as they did...involved and intriguing, Myers' work definitely is worth reading.
—Historical Novel Society Online Review

What were the diplomatic and political actions in France leading up to the start of WWII? What treaties and alliances in Europe set the wheels in motion for Hitler to get Germany moving? ...the true story is the political intrigue ...
—Barbara Ell, Goodreads review

Paris 1934: Victory in Retreat

...descriptive and thoroughly researched narrative feels true to the era; the "City of Light" shines through the page.
—Historical Novel Society Online Review

I fell in love with this book as I was reading it. First of all I love historical fiction and the author was amazing with the plot and the details...
—Brittany Tedder-Bixlar, Goodreads review

Vienna 1934: Betrayal at the Ballplatz

Myers' characters feel true to the era...an excellent job of making the story real due to his good research and fine storytelling. The interweaving of fact, fiction, real, and fictional people makes this book exciting and romantic.
—Historical Novel Society Online Review

Betrayal in Europe

Paris 1938 – a novel

Paul A. Myers

CreateSpace edition
Imprint: CreateSpace Independent Publishing Platform

Produced by Paul A. Myers Books
Copyright © Paul A. Myers 2015

Revision 03
ISBN 15:   978-1514364604
ISBN 10:   1514364603

Cover image: Quai a la Seine, Paris, au Clair de Lune. Frank
Myers Boggs, 1898. Cropped image.

Cover by Paul A. Myers.

Contents

Cast of Characters

Fictional

Marie Hélène ("Mimi") de Villars-Brancas, comtesse de Villars-Brancas. Daughter of a wealthy industrialist who owns the Compagnie de Marne, the constructor of the Maginot Line. She works as a lobbyist for the association of heavy industries, the Comité des Forges.

Thérèse Mathilde de Roncée, baroness de Roncée. Wife of a wealthy industrialist who also works as a lobbyist for the Comité des Forges.

Jules Dugas, a notional aide to historical character Georges Bonnet, finance minister and later foreign minister in the French government.

Captain Jacques Morel, a counterintelligence specialist with the Deuxième Bureau, the military's intelligence arm.

Carl Friedrich von Dinckler. Second secretary at the German embassy in Paris.

Le chef and *l'inspecteur*. Counterintelligence specialists for the Sûreté Nationale, the French national police.

Historical

Geneviève Tabouis. Diplomatic columnist for the Paris daily newspaper *L'Oeuvre* who was widely followed in newspapers across Europe. Excerpts from her column were page one in British newspapers across the United Kingdom in the late 1930s. She wrote her memoir *They Called Me Cassandra* in 1942 while exiled in New York.

Georges Bonnet. Finance minister and later foreign minister in the French government where he was a leading appeaser in the late 1930s. The French foreign ministry is popularly referred to as the Quai d'Orsay. His wife, Odette, was extremely ambitious for him.

Alexis Léger. Secretary general (senior civil servant) of the French foreign service at the foreign ministry. A favorite of some of the leading ladies of French society.

Édouard Daladier. Defense minister and later simultaneously defense minister and premier in the French government with offices as premier at the Hôtel Matignon. The premier is formally called President of the Council and is addressed as Monsieur le Président, which is distinct from the President of the Republic, a largely ceremonial office in the Third Republic. Daladier's mistress was the sweet-tempered Marquise de Crussol.

Paul Reynaud. A député and former finance minister who was a member of a center-right political party with personally progressive views on national finance and defense policy. Entered the cabinet in 1938 as justice minister and soon became finance minister. His mistress was the waspish Comtesse Hélène de Portes.

Ernst Freiherr von Weizsäcker. State secretary (senior civil servant) in the German foreign ministry, popularly referred to as the Wilhelmstrasse.

Neville Chamberlain. British prime minister (1937–40) who occupied Number 10 Downing Street, the name of the prime minister's office and residence.

Lord Halifax. British foreign secretary (1938–41) and a major architect of Britain's appeasement policy.

Abel Bonnard. A French poet, novelist, and politician. The characterization in the novel is derived from Geneviève Tabouis's memoir. Bonnard was later a minister in the Vichy regime (1942–44). A satirist during the war gave him the nickname "la Gestapette," a play on *gestapo* and *tapette*, the latter a French slang word for a homosexual. Bonnard's homosexual inclinations were well known.

Epigraphs

England has been offered a choice between war and shame. She has chosen shame, and will get war.
　　—Winston Churchill on October 3, 1938

But there was a "traitor" of another sort in the French cabinet—a minister whose identity was never established—who promptly informed the German ambassador of the details of the proposed French aid to Spain. The envoy immediately got on the wire to Berlin. [Describing a leak in July 1936.]

　　—William L. Shirer
　　The Collapse of the Third Republic

1. Rue Boissière

September 1937. The two women walked down the sidewalk of Rue Boissière near Place Victor Hugo, a residential neighborhood of luxurious apartments in the wealthy Étoile district of Paris. They wore the best Parisian couture. Above the sidewalk, the morning sun reflected off the smooth facades of the nineteenth-century apartment buildings while sunlight flashed off glass panes in the tall windows. This was not only the women's neighborhood; it was their world. They each walked with their thoughts this morning. They had heard it had been a big explosion—unnerving even. They wanted to see for themselves.

"Here we are," said one as she stopped by the curb, a woman in her midthirties, slender with an understated but pleasing figure just hinted at under a tailored outfit. "Yes," she said as she looked across the street, "this is where we were going to meet." The meeting was to have been in the little conference room off the executive director's office.

"Yes," said the other woman with the distracted air of someone who had something else on her mind. She was a bosomy, well-presented lady in her midforties, elegant of carriage and possessed of well-bred aristocratic bearing. She didn't try to hide her edgy expectation. Mostly she wanted to put this distasteful item of business behind her. "Imagine, we had a meeting here with the executive director this morning," she said. A shiver went up her spine. The meeting would have been boringly routine—they all were. But then she had been planning on lunch, and from there to an exciting afternoon—her friend from Berlin was here for a short visit. Just touching base with the embassy, he had said. Indeed, that was still her plan for today; her limousine was trailing behind her on the avenue, an unobtrusive hundred meters back, ready to whisk her off to the restaurant. Her mind brightened at the thought.

"Yes, I wonder who would want to do this?" said the younger woman.

Both women stared across the street at the partially wrecked office building of the Metallurgical Trades Association, the entranceway blown apart by an explosion, all the windows in the building shattered. The explosion had occurred late the night before. An even larger explosion at the same time had destroyed the General Employers Confederation building several blocks away.

The two women, members of wealthy industrial families, were active in a third organization, the Comité des Forges. Their organization represented the iron and steel manufacturers. The women had been planning on meeting this morning with the Metallurgical Association to arrange a series of lectures for a common political program. Neither liked the idea of their business appointment having been scheduled in a building that got blown up by a shadowy terrorist group.

"My husband," said the older woman, referring to the industrial magnate to whom she was married, "has good sources in the ministry of the interior." The ministry of the interior was the principal law enforcement ministry in France. "According to Claude, they think it is the work of the Far Right group the Cagoulards." The Hooded Ones, named after the group's secret initiation ceremony.

"Not the Communists?"

"No," said the older woman firmly.

"The Cagoulards?" asked the younger woman, somewhat perplexed. "I thought they were running guns to Spain?"

"They are."

"Then why this?"

"Claude says the Cagoulards thought the Communists would be blamed for the bombings. They wanted to precipitate a police crackdown on the Left," said the older woman.

"What would that accomplish?"

"End what is left of the Popular Front government. Put the conservative wing of the Radical Party at the top of the cabinet table."

"So, politics."

"Yes, politics," said the older woman with mild distaste.

"Could they do this to the Comité des Forges?" asked the younger woman, the thought of being blown up by terrorists discomfiting to say the least.

"Claude says they wouldn't dare cross him," said the older woman.

"Really?"

"Yes, he says they're just a bunch of perfumers and hair color chemists. Calls them pretty boys."

Yes, Claude would, thought the younger woman. He was as rough-hewn as an iron girder.

The older woman watched and made a small laugh. Changing subjects, she said, "Mimi, I have to take off. I have a lunch date. I'll catch up with you later."

"Fine, Thérèse. I'll see you *chez duchesse.*" At the duchess's place.

"Yes," agreed the older woman. She waved her limousine forward and turned to the younger woman and asked, "Can I drop you somewhere?"

"No, I want to walk down to the river." The younger woman believed long walks and good legs went together.

"*Au revoir.*" Until later.

Sûreté Nationale

On Rue de Miromesnil, a block away from the ministry of interior, in an anonymous office building, discreetly guarded, there was at the end of a long hallway on the fifth floor, behind a door with no nameplate, a quiet office with one secretary sitting in a reception area that rarely received visitors. Behind another closed door—it was a building of closed doors—was the office of *le chef.* Dossiers were stacked across his broad desk with more files piled high on a credenza behind him. *Le chef* was sitting behind his desk, head back in contemplation, slowly blowing smoke toward the ceiling, listening to the man sitting across from him. The man was his principal agent, *l'inspecteur.* Counterespionage was their mission, a small operation that worked quietly behind the scenes.

"And our friends, the Cagoulards. What are the developments?" asked *le chef.*

3

"Nationwide raids and arrests are underway. The Sûreté has names, addresses of safe houses. One of our agents cracked their code."

"But not all the safe houses?"

"No, not all the safe houses."

Le chef now bolted upright and leaned across his desk toward *l'inspecteur* and asked in a demanding tone, "And the assassins?" He was referring to two suspected Cagoulard assassins responsible for the vicious stabbing death of a young woman the previous spring. The young woman was reputed to be a spy for the Paris police. She had been found with her throat slit in a metro car in a working-class section of Paris.

"No connection."

"Of course not. Those operatives are still too hot for anything in Paris," said *le chef*. He sighed and confided, "One hates to see them sitting in some hidden safe house in the south of France beyond the reach of justice."

"Yes," said *l'inspecteur*. "Always a chance for more political murder when they're out there."

"Or worse," said *le chef* with weary disgust.

Changing the subject from the painful memory of the murdered young woman that lingered in his mind longer than it should have, *le chef* asked, "The Germans?"

"They use the Cagoulards for gunrunning to Spain. Controlled from Berlin. Göring gets a cut."

"Of course," said *le chef,* returning to the daily reality of Europe in 1937. "And the Germans in Paris?"

"Propaganda for now. Although it's hard not to believe someone isn't running something deeper, some hidden ring…behind the scenes…"

"Yes, so much surface activity—all the propaganda operations around Abetz and his Comité France-Allemagne," he said, mentioning the French-German friendship committee headed by Otto Abetz. He blew smoke toward the ceiling and collected his thoughts, running through the checklist. "The politicians? The newspapers?"

"Business as usual. The Radicals in the government are taking money from the industrialists. The newspapers are taking money from everyone—Germans, Italians, industrialists."

Le chef sat straight in his chair and summarized the meeting. "We'll keep watching."

"We always do," said *l'inspecteur* as he stood up to depart.

2. Chez Duchesse

The well-polished limousine proceeded up the Cours la Reine, the wide avenue on the Right Bank bordering the Seine River. Beyond the stone parapet running along the walkway, slowly swirling currents wound their way down the river through the center of Paris. Trees bordered the sides of the roadway, their long limbs bending in the brisk autumn wind. As the limbs swayed, tawny leaves shook free and whisked in whorls across the street and lost themselves in the shrubbery of a nearby park. In the backseat of the limousine, a well-dressed woman wondered about this afternoon's salon—*chez duchesse*—a gathering of the fashionable and well connected. Her hostess had told her that a senior aide working for the new finance minister would be there. Business for sure, something else possibly.

For the woman sitting in the back of the limousine, attending social events was part of her job in Paris—she represented the interests of powerful industrialists in the corridors of the government. She worked for the Comité des Forges, an association of heavy metal industries that also had close relationships with her family's construction business. She had taken to the work, finding it much more engaging than helping her husband manage his estate in eastern France—it was always his, a fact cemented by a couple of centuries of family ownership. Furthermore, working in Paris allowed her to maintain her hard-won independence from having to work with her overbearing father in the family business, the giant Compagnie de Marne, a major constructor of the mighty Maginot Line. Her father, Joseph Montciel, had gone from small-time building contractor in Nancy to majority owner of a large public works company during the Great War. The war had made him, an arc of good fortune taking him from *paysan* to *patron*.

In Paris, to her delight, she had found the politicians intriguing in their own right: she liked the sharp-edged, dark-suited élan they brought to the pursuit of the decadent temptations of Parisian life at the top, the world of *Tout-Paris*. The salons and receptions offered an enticing brew of once forbidden pleasures for those with a taste for adventure and who enjoyed the deep-down tingling of expectation that arose in the presence of temptation.

She sat and idly watched as the grand riverfront town houses lining the broad avenue passed by. And Thérèse would be there. The driver pulled over to the curb in front of one of the limestone town houses, an edifice rising five stories and fronted by tall windows and wrought iron grillwork. The building was topped by a row of dormer windows peeking out from the servants' quarters as if on a child's toy house.

The uniformed driver got out, walked around to the right rear door, opened it, and offered a hand to the woman as she stepped out onto the sidewalk. She was in her midthirties and had flaxen hair coiffed into fashionable waves. She wore a dark wool skirt coming down to midcalf with a warm-looking, cream-colored jacket. A fox fur was draped around her neck; on her head was perched a small black hat almost like a béret. Large bracelets danced on her wrists. She smoothed the gray calfskin gloves over her hands. The chauffeur tipped his fingers to his cap and mumbled, "Madame."

"*Merci*, Javier," said the lady. "I'll be about two hours." She walked across the sidewalk, then up some steps. A large front door opened, and a white-aproned maid welcomed her in. The maid took her coat, umbrella, and bag. From the foyer, she walked up the sweeping marble staircase to the drawing room. The butler welcomed her and then stepped forward to announce her presence.

"*Comtesse* Marie Hélène de Villars-Brancas," the butler called out. He motioned the lady into the room. A few of the people clustered in groups across the high-ceilinged drawing room turned their heads to look at the new arrival. A few gave her a brief nod of welcome. Social distinction was a common currency in the room.

A pretty young woman, the hostess, left a group of guests and walked over toward Marie Hélène.

"Mimi, so nice of you to come," said the young woman.

"Catherine, your afternoons are always a fascination to me," said the comtesse to the hostess, the fashionable young duchess de Chasse-Barrois, daughter of Eugène Schraeder, the steel magnate and captain of French industry.

The duchess stepped back and looked over her guest's ensemble, the dress and jacket so complementary, and exclaimed, "Mimi, you are always so well presented. A delightful outfit for an autumn day. Chanel, of course."

"Yes," said Marie Hélène, "only Chanel can put you into something both fashionable and elegant for going about the business of the day. Others can do the evening, but Coco owns the day." And going to late-afternoon salons was a business for Marie Hélène de Villars-Brancas.

"So true," said the duchess, who was wearing a high-waisted, floor-length dress, possibly by Molyneux, well suited for hosting an afternoon salon at home. She leaned forward and lightly whispered, "I can start you off with that circle over there. It includes the politician I told you about—rather interesting. And a journalist and a novelist for good measure."

"Yes, the politician," said the comtesse. "I always find them fascinating...the moves on the chessboard of power...the rivalries...the intrigues...like life in a novel..."

"Well," laughed the duchess. "You must see something in them beyond the self-importance...the pondering pontificating of middle-aged men...it mostly bores me..."

"Just who is the politician? Hopefully he's not that middle-aged?"

"Oh, he's Jules Dugas, an aide to the finance minister," said the duchess. "Midthirties I would say. One of the bright young men that hover around the edges of ministerial power."

"Yes, I know them well. Which minister?"

"Let me see now," said the duchess, turning thoughtful as if trying to remember a long-lost uncle, "his name is...they change so fast. Yes, Georges Bonnet."

"Yes, he's the new finance minister, but he's rumored to be the next premier if Chautemps falls," said the comtesse, mentioning the current prime minister. "They all fall, of course. It's just a matter of time. I love to follow the intrigues."

"In that case, maybe the journalist can tell you more. Geneviève Tabouis is here."

"Ah, Madame Tata," said the comtesse with relish. "I know her well."

"Well, you know so much more about the political world than I," said the duchess. "And we have Abel Bonnard here, the bee that spreads the pollen of gossip from flower to flower."

The comtesse rolled her eyes and said, "My many thanks…but if you're a flower, you don't always like the sting." She remembered that the last roman à clef from Bonnard's dark pen put knowing smiles on the faces of Tout-Paris. Many thought she was the inspiration for the coquette in the tawdry novel.

The duchess made a light giggle and covered her mouth with two fingers. "It would not be a salon if…the gossip…particularly the delicious…" She took the comtesse by the arm and led her across the drawing room toward a group of men and women. The circle opened up, and the duchess made her introduction: "May I introduce my good friend, Marie Hélène, comtesse de Villars-Brancas. Our families go way back…" The duchess held out her arm and ushered Marie Hélène into the circle and added, "Mimi to her friends." Then the duchess smiled, made a small bow, and returned to the group with whom she had originally been talking.

"Mimi, so nice to see you again," said Geneviève Tabouis, the diplomatic correspondent for the major Parisian daily *L'Oeuvre.* The Madame Tata sobriquet had been hung on her by one of the writers at *Action Française,* the leading right-wing rabble-rousing tabloid, because of the remarkable clairvoyance of predictions appearing in her diplomatic column. She had inside sources in every capital of Europe.

"Yes, Geneviève, my father always says that France never had two better ambassadors than your uncles," she said, referring to Jules and Paul Cambon, who served as ambassadors to Washington and London before and during the Great War. Indeed, Geneviève came from one of France's great families. Marie Hélène admired the spirited independence of the well-dressed, midforties journalist. Madame Tabouis's light blue eyes were both friendly and inquisitive. Her slender figure was topped by dark honey-blond hair, a stray wisp of white here and there adding just the right touch of *je ne sais quoi* to her aristocratic bearing. Marie Hélène hoped a compliment or two at the beginning would soften the barbs surely to come from the sharp-tongued journalist, rarely a friend of the industrialists even though her family included one or two. Geneviève Tabouis was the only woman in Paris who Marie Hélène found socially intimidating. Her piercing intelligence was both formidable and unusual among this social set, thought Marie Hélène, who was brought up in the street-smart household of a self-made man.

"Merci, comtesse," said Geneviève with a dip of her head. "Your father became a power during the war. So many hands contributed to the victory." A compliment returned.

A light falsetto voice piped up from an elfin presence at the edge of the circle. The writer Abel Bonnard, a literary lion—or at least a well-petted kitten—of the salon circuit, took charge of the conversation. He explained to Marie Hélène, "We were just telling Geneviève that her continued attachment—and that of the government, of course—to the Franco-Russian pact is the greatest impediment to our coming to an understanding with Hitler and Mussolini."

"I plead guilty to being an impediment," said Geneviève, characteristically defiant.

"The worst of the pact is not that it's criminal," said another gentleman in the circle, "but that it's silly. Could anything be more absurd than the idea of our going to war to help Russia?"

Heads around the circle nodded in agreement. To go to war for the benefit of the Bolsheviks was unthinkable.

"We can only come to an understanding with Hitler," Geneviève said dryly, "by giving him France, our empire, and the rest of Europe as well. Otherwise, we had better prepare to resist Herr Hitler."

"Resist Hitler?" said another gentleman, incredulously with a tone of dismay, if not defeat, in his voice. "Sounds like *bellicisme* to me." Warmongering.

Geneviève looked down her aquiline nose at the gentleman with mild disdain. "We have now let pass three opportunities to win a war without fighting," said the outspoken journalist.

"Three? When did this happen? Please tell us, you who are called the Gypsy Fortune-Teller," said another gentleman, referring to yet another sobriquet attached to Geneviève by the right-wing press.

"Ethiopia was the first lost opportunity. Remember, rather than work to check the aggression of Mussolini, Laval throttled the League of Nations." Geneviève could never say the word *Laval* without disgust coloring her expression.

"But Laval took the only sensible course," protested the gentleman. "Mussolini was engaged in a civilizing mission in Ethiopia. It would have been good for the Ethiopians."

Geneviève rolled her eyes in disbelief at this widely repeated canard. "It was a two-faced policy. I remember at Geneva one night Anthony told me," she said, referring to Anthony Eden, the British foreign minister, "that his foreign office colleagues said you could not trust a man whose name can be read both ways—L-A-V-A-L." Geneviève always relished telling the anecdote, her dislike of Laval legendary.

Voices chuckled around the circle, but one voice asked, "And can we trust the British to be there when we need them?"

"And who wanted to intervene on behalf of Ethiopia?" said another man. "Who wanted their sons and brothers to die for Ethiopia? Are not our cemeteries filled with enough graves?" Heads nodded in agreement around the circle.

"The second lost opportunity was the Rhineland," continued Geneviève. "Flandin and the cabinet did not respond to this serious military breach of the Versailles Treaty by Hitler. A firm response would have changed the course of events."

"But the British were not with us, Geneviève," said the gentleman plaintively.

"If we would have acted..." said Geneviève, letting her words trail off. Continuing on another tack, she said, "Alexis Léger said that if France would not act, then Germany would be top dog and France nothing. So it is turning out." Léger was the secretary general at the French foreign ministry at the Quai d'Orsay and a close confidant of Madame Tabouis.

"I remember," interjected another member of the circle, "the other Paris papers shouting that you were a warmonger—*une belliciste*. France does not want war."

"Yes, so said the prime minister of France at the time." She made another look of disgust. "Monsieur Flandin was the spokesman for the appeasers and financiers," she said as she punched her hand forward toward the gentleman to drive the point home in reference to Pierre-Étienne Flandin, a former premier and foreign minister.

Geneviève gave the man an icy glare and continued. "The third lost opportunity occurred when France did not go to the aide of the legitimate government in Spain in the summer of '36."

"But they are Communists and Marxists," said the gentleman. "You cannot expect us to support a Russian outpost in the western Mediterranean?"

"So instead we are giving Spain to the dictators. Germany and Italy bullied France into the Neutrality Pact."

"Britain made us do it," said the gentleman. "They thought the French government was carrying out the Moscow agenda."

"Yes, you must remember, Geneviève," said another voice, "that the British are never with us."

"Yes, sadly that is true," said Geneviève. Britain had coerced France into abandoning the Spanish Republic and going with the Neutrality Pact. "Nevertheless, that makes three times France has backed down in the face of threats from Germany. The bad shepherds are leading France to a future of great difficulty, a meadow of poisoned water."

"How can that be, Madame Tabouis? We have much in common with Hitler. Why it was Hitler who said at Nuremberg that Bolshevism was public enemy number one. Surely we can all agree on that. We have an overarching common interest with Germany. Bolshevism." The gentleman shuddered at the word *Bolshevism*.

Another voice added, "Yes, the Germans are right. Judeo-Bolshevism is the number one threat to Europe."

"Yes, Jewish finance," said someone else, shaking his head in disgust.

"And the Masons," said another with tremulous fear in his voice.

Heads around the circle nodded in enthusiastic agreement with this understood wisdom.

Sensing the arguments were turning tiresome, the writer Bonnard gaily returned to the conversation, pronouncing in his prancing way, "Oh, all these troubles spring from being a republic." With a flutter of his hands, he sang forth like a child in a choir, "Only the monarchy can grasp the whole of France in its embrace." Most of the guests smiled, a few nodded with amusement. Serious Royalist sentiment had long been relegated to the sidelines. Even the most ardent of Royalists made jokes of the leading Royalist pretender.

Geneviève made a long, dismissive glance at Bonnard; she knew the fluttering butterfly persona of the homosexual salon gadfly covered up a virulent set of right-wing beliefs. Beneath the wings of the butterfly were the grasping black claws of a fascist tarantula. Bonnard's playful discrediting of the powerful was one of the manifestations of his many resentments, a well-aimed needle at the cosmopolitan sophistication of Tout-Paris, the Parisian upper crust of the social swirl. Geneviève swung her glance from Bonnard to Marie Hélène and arched an eyebrow at the comtesse as an invitation to say something.

"Well, I suppose you are asking about how the Comité des Forges," the comtesse said in reference to the powerful industrial confederation of steel companies she represented, "feels about the issue?"

"Well, yes," said Geneviève, "you are at least one of the prettiest faces at their receptions, I recall."

"A pretty face maybe," said the comtesse as she smiled at Geneviève. "But hardly its voice. But I can say that the Compagnie de Marne is a large customer of the industrialists," she said in reference to her father's company. "So we of course participate."

"If not share their politics," added Geneviève.

"Sometimes," said Marie Hélène noncommittally. "We do express skepticism about an alliance with Russia; capitalism does not easily sleep in the same bed as Communism."

"It's really about geography," said Geneviève. "France needs allies in the East to contain German power."

"Yes, but Russia is on the complete other side of Europe from France," replied Marie Hélène. Most of the heads in the circle nodded yet again in agreement. A Russian alliance sat uneasy in the minds of most members of the *haute bourgeoisie*—the upper class.

"Yes, but an understanding with Germany, if possible, might be even better," said another man in the circle, returning to a favorite them of the haute bourgeoisie.

"Yes, a Franco-German pact. That's the answer," said another. "A Berlin-Paris agreement."

The younger man that Marie Hélène took to be the politician nodded slightly in agreement at the pro-German sentiments. In the break in conversation, he looked over at Marie Hélène and held out his hand and introduced himself. "Jules Dugas. I'm an aide to Finance Minister Bonnet."

"*Enchantée*," said Marie Hélène with a warm smile. She found Dugas attractive and his voice authoritative. "What do you think?" she asked him.

"Any agreement that can be reached with Germany would of course be helpful."

"Why?" asked Marie Hélène.

"We in finance find the current defense budget ruinously expensive while cutbacks are bitterly, and often successfully, resisted."

"Yes, the deficits…then the devaluations…" said another gentleman in the circle. "What will become of France?" The forlornness of his statement met with sad agreement among the group.

"It is not just Russia," said Dugas. "It is also the alliance system in eastern Europe, the *cordon sanitaire*, which looked so promising in the 1920s and now seems like a millstone around France's neck. A new understanding with Germany about Europe might ease the security system…and the financial burdens that go with it."

"Since when was the finance ministry responsible for foreign affairs," said Geneviève, sarcasm lacing her words.

"Foreign policy is ultimately a cabinet responsibility," said Dugas with a touch of authority. "A policy that exceeds the means of a country ultimately becomes a financial problem." Again, heads nodded. Everyone knew that budgets were breaking the treasury of the republic.

"I've known Georges Bonnet since I was a young woman," said Geneviève, referring to the finance minister. "I used to go dancing with him at all the brilliant parties before the war. He married one of my friends. For as long as I can remember, he has been a stalwart supporter of French policy. Is there a wavering of purpose occurring here? Something I haven't seen?"

"Of course not, Madame Tabouis," said Dugas. "I'm just saying there must be a search for alternatives, a willingness to enter into new discussions. Yes, new discussions…possibly realistic accommodations…"

Geneviève looked at Dugas, tilted her head, and studied him some more. *Possibly he knows something*, she thought. The other guests sensed her interest; no one could smell out a deep secret, the hidden scoop, like Madame Tata; they all knew that.

"Oh, Georges Bonnet, my favorite minister," said Bonnard, jumping back into the conversation with relish. "Geneviève, I did not know you knew Odette," he said with a flutter of his hands. "She's my favorite. What can one say about a minister's wife nicknamed Madame Soutiene-Georges," he said, eyelashes batting, playing on the well-known pun on the French word for brassiere *soutien-gorge* that had attached itself to the finance minister's wife, adding, "when she so amply fills the nickname." Bonnard twisted and writhed in delight at his witticism as the group laughed at his humor.

"But enough of politics," said Bonnard, his eye keen on finding out those gossipy little tidbits that tantalize and his function as a conversational adornment coming to the fore. He looked askance at Marie Hélène and, with an abashed look, asked, "Mimi, just how is your husband, *le comte*?"

"Oh, I thought you would never ask," said the comtesse as the group laughed heartily at her riposte. Bonnard was renowned for writing thinly disguised tell-all scandal novels of Tout-Paris, the fashionable café society of Paris—stories of aging aristocrats and striving politicos and beautiful young actresses at the Comédie-Française.

"Well, yes, just how is he?" Bonnard said again in his chirping little voice, now with an edge of insistence.

"Oh, he has his duties on the company board, watching over the wine harvest at the chateau, and of course the hunt is coming up," recited Marie Hélène with well-practiced ease. "So life out in Moselle keeps him busy."

"And your life here in Paris?" said Bonnard with a crooked smile, his expression now one of expectation. "Lonely?"

"Well, no. I have my friends. Luncheons and such. And the Compagnie de Marne has many interests to be tended to here in

Paris. So, lonely? No, hardly." And she smiled at Bonnard, thin and sweet. The other guests smiled at her elegant brush-off; she was rumored to be skilled at the discreet rendezvous.

"Well, I have a column to write," said Geneviève. "I better depart." Other guests nodded agreement and headed across the room.

Hélène Marie looked across the circle and caught the eye of Jules Dugas. She nodded toward the windows and walked over and took Jules's arm and walked with him over to the tall windows where they stood together and looked out at the gray Paris afternoon. Marie Hélène looked back and saw Bonnard staring at them with singular interest; she gave him a slow crosswise nod of disapproval and dismissal. She turned back and said to Dugas, "I would like to hear more about your views on government finance. It is a fresh viewpoint, and possibly you are better informed than you let on."

"Thank you. Yes, I can give you a deeper appreciation of the new thinking in the cabinet," said Dugas, showing a deep interest in her. He had read Bonnard's novel, too.

"Yes, the government has changed," she said, alluding to the fall of the Popular Front government of the Socialist prime minister, Léon Blum, in June. The Blum government fell when the Senate refused to grant Blum decree powers necessary to save the franc. Its successor, though still technically a Popular Front coalition, was led by the Radicals. A half-empty balloon most observers thought. "I would like to understand the changes."

"Luncheon perhaps?"

Her eyes brightened at the invitation. "Yes, that would be fine."

"Rue du Bac. Bistro Les Ministres." He looked at her. She seemed agreeable. "Next Tuesday at one?"

She smiled. "I know it well. Yes, next Tuesday at one," she repeated. She gave him her hand for a polite good-bye and turned and walked across the drawing room. She saw Thérèse standing among a circle of mostly men and a few women chatting about who was with whom, and of course Thérèse boring in on just who was in whose bed. Marie Hélène observed that Thérèse's buxomly stylishness attracted even the dullest of salon climbers. Marie Hélène whispered over her shoulder, "Thérèse, so nice to see you."

"You, too, Mimi. I see you're making new friends."

"Yes, do you think he's promising?"

"Until they...you never know," said Thérèse lightly. She winked at Marie Hélène. Thérèse was like an older sister to Marie Hélène. She had given her one piece of great advice when she had first entered the social swirl of life in the Paris salons: never embarrass an older husband. Everything else was OK.

Marie Hélène squeezed Thérèse's arm. "So true. I have to run. We'll get together on the next program."

"Of course," said Thérèse. She turned back to her conversation partners, asking, "*La marquise* was with whom...and the husband was where...away on business, you say..."

Marie Hélène smiled and resumed walking toward the stairwell, waving good-bye to the duchess as she went. Dugas nodded at Marie Hélène and then went over and took a more formal leave of the hostess. He had enjoyed the salon and would like future invitations; he wanted to hear all the sentiments of Tout-Paris as he helped his minister plot the intrigues through the political crosscurrents of what he thought were the last months of the Popular Front government. Getting Blum out would of course set the stage for an eventual restoration by the Radical Party, of which Georges Bonnet was one of the leading pretenders to top political power. Everything was on track.

"We so much enjoyed having you," said the duchess. Jules was pleased. She told him she looked forward to seeing him again. With that as a lift, he, too, departed.

Bonnard stood near a fireplace, its flames lightly flickering, and watched the comtesse and the politician depart. Yes. Right before his eyes. The arrangement. But where? He smiled to himself. Ultimately, no secrets in Tout-Paris.

3. Lunch at Rothschild's

Geneviève Tabouis sat down past the salt at a long table, sparkling chandeliers above the table, flashes of light from the dangling crystal dancing on the white linen tablecloth. A delightful pastry sat on an enameled hand-painted plate in front of her place setting accompanied by a polished silver fork and spoon to one side, a cup of coffee on the other. The man to her right passed some cream, which she poured into her cup. Then she ladled in a heaping teaspoon of sugar and stirred the brownish brew as she looked up to the head of the table where Maurice de Rothschild sat, the distinguished head of the Rothschild bank in Paris. On his left sat his great friend, the pretty Princess Emma d'Aremberg, his frequent hostess. Around the table were arranged half a dozen diplomats from the corners of Europe. The luxurious opulence of the Rothschild dining room was impressive even to men long conditioned to lunching in the most distinguished of continental dining rooms.

Rothschild turned to the Russian diplomat and asked in his blunt, straightforward way, "Why if you have a pact with France do you still flirt around with Germany?"

The Russian, smooth and smart, replied, "France and Great Britain are like two eminently respectable old ladies at a tea dance. But there is only one country that we fear, and that is Germany."

Heads around the table nodded at the forthrightness of the statement.

"Now we hate Germany so much that we perfectly capable of engaging in a dalliance with Germany to rouse the respectable old ladies of France and Great Britain to our need. We very much worry about being forsaken by our elderly lovers in the West."

The comment drew hearty laughs from around the table.

The Russian diplomat solemnly intoned, "We are also not going to let the West entice us into fighting Germany on their behalf—alone. Against Germany, one must have allies."

Heads nodded in solemn agreement at this conclusion. A diplomat leaned over and whispered to Geneviève, "That was funny, but it was no joke. And, if we are wise, we will keep the Soviet delegate's words in mind."

Geneviève looked at him and nodded in agreement. Then she looked up the table and spoke, "We have the Franco-Russian pact. It was signed in 1934. We have only to implement it…the military provisions."

The Russian diplomat looked over at her and said, "But France drags its heels on implementing the military collaboration. And then there is the criticism from the French press in the Paris papers…all the shouting about Bolshevism."

"Yes," said another diplomat at the table, "but the Russians never seem to be in a hurry to implement it, either."

"Well, yes," said the Russian, a sly smile crossing his face, "but after all, you need us more than we need you."

Geneviève nodded in silent agreement. She had known for years that Russia was the only power that the Germans feared, and therefore respected.

"Thank you, gentlemen, for the good conversation at lunch," said Rothschild in conclusion. "And as always, Geneviève moves the gentlemen's conversation along."

The men laughed; Geneviève made a polite blush. They all stood up, and after a round of handshaking, they left for the hallway. On the way out, a diplomat from one of the eastern European countries asked Geneviève, "Why does Paris resist the Franco-Russian pact? Collective defense should be good for France. For all of us."

"Agreed," said Geneviève. "But the bankers and industrialists believe that a Franco-German pact would be more advantageous to their interests."

"Get along with the Germans?" said the diplomat in wide-eyed disbelief. "With the Nazis?"

"That's what they think. That the Franco-Russian pact stands in the way of a Paris-Berlin agreement."

"Incredible," said the diplomat, shaking his head in disbelief. "A Paris-Berlin agreement."

"They think an amicable deal can be reached with Hitler."

"The bankers and industrialists think this, here in Paris?"

"Yes, and they have powerful friends high up the cabinet table."

"Yes, sometimes democracies…the money…purchased loyalties…"

"Yes, sometimes a trial…by temptation…there are many temptations in Paris…money buys most of them."

"Madame, as always, a very enlightening conversation. I have a limousine. May I give you a lift to your offices?"

"Why yes. Thank you," replied Geneviève

.

4. Les Ministres

Marie Hélène walked down Rue du Bac and into the bistro Les Ministres in the faint sunlight of an overcast day. She was wearing a midcalf navy-blue overcoat with a blue-and-gold scarf wrapped snugly about her neck. Her hair bounced on the wide flat collar of the overcoat. A large hat swooped rakishly down toward her left shoulder giving her an air of detached sophistication.

She entered the restaurant and stood near the pedestal desk used by the maître d' as she scanned the tables. She saw Jules Dugas and made a small wave. He stood up behind the table as she walked over, the maître d' coming from across the room at an angle to meet her. The maître d' helped her out of her coat, and then she handed him her scarf and hat; he seated her and walked back to the front and hung the coat, scarf, and hat on a rack near the door.

"*Bonjour, madame,*" said Jules as he reached across the table and grasped her hands in both of his before sitting down.

"*Bonjour, Monsieur le Politique,*" she said, playfully addressing him as Mister Politics. "But someday it will be *Monsieur le Ministre, n'est-ce pas?*"

"Perhaps," he replied and then turned the word play around, "or possibly managing director of Compagnie de…" He paused.

"Compagnie de Marne?" she said, completing the phrase with a laugh.

He smiled with amusement.

"You wear your ambition lightly," she said, eyes sparkling.

"I started as an *inspecteur des finances,*" he said, mentioning a prestigious position in the finance ministry. "I like business."

"But not as much as politics?"

"You read my mind."

"If you ever come to the Compagnie de Marne, you could work with my husband on the board."

"A delight I'm sure."

"Only if you share an interest in vineyards…he knows nothing of construction…which is why my father chose him for the board."

"Vineyards? Where may I ask?"

"His—our—estate is in the Moselle region. The Chateau de Villars-Brancas sits on a beautiful rolling hill, surrounded by vineyards. It's been in his family for centuries...while my ancestors, the Montciels, were blacksmiths, I'm afraid," she said good-humoredly.

"You wear your prominence lightly."

"We are two of a kind?" she said with an inquisitive glance.

"Possibly."

"And your current position? You are *chef du cabinet* for Monsieur Bonnet?"

"I soon will be."

"You have been with him long?"

"I was with him when he was ambassador to the United States. Blum wanted to get him out of Paris," he said, referring to Léon Blum, the former Popular Front premier.

"And you're both back in Paris in high office."

"When Blum's government fell in June and Chautemps followed as premier, the precipitating event was a financial crisis. Monsieur Bonnet is recognized in the Radical Party as its preeminent finance and economics leader. So Chautemps brought him back to Paris. The Chamber of Députés and the Senate approved the financial emergency measures drafted by Monsieur Bonnet."

"And the day was saved?"

"I wish it were so. A day of reckoning was, at best, put off. The public debt weighs heavily on the value of the franc."

"And so your comments at the salon of my good friend, *la duchesse*?"

"Defense expenditures consume the budget."

"But my family's company has been a big constructor on the Maginot Line," she said, mentioning the long fortified defensive line running along France's eastern border with Germany. "That has not been a good investment?"

"It has been an important investment, for sure," said Jules. "But the navy needs to defend the empire—the sea lanes to Algeria are crucially important. And now airplanes. Never enough airplanes. And Paris is closer to Germany than London, and the British worry about German air attacks incessantly. So it is a real threat."

"Cause for concern?"

"Yes. You grasp the essentials."

"The Compagnie de Marne thinks the Maginot Line should be extended along the Belgian border."

"Yes, but its extension poses diplomatic problems with Belgium," said Jules with a clouded expression. "We must proceed carefully."

Marie Hélène shifted the conversation back to diplomacy. "So some sort of understanding with the Germans? Ease the financial burden?"

"Exactly. France cannot afford to defend itself in the West while subsidizing the alliances and so-called allies in the East—Poland, Czechoslovakia, Romania, all the others. A constant drain..."

"So a rapprochement with Germany...for money reasons?"

"Yes."

"Most of my friends cannot imagine an alliance with Communists..."

"Monsieur Bonnet's anti-Communist credentials are solid. He was one of only eighteen Radicals not to support the Popular Front," said Jules.

"Yes, we all remember...the closed factories...the Red flags flying from all the department stores in Paris...the sound of 'L'Internationale' drowning out 'La Marseillaise' on the streets of Paris...the summer of 1936 was indeed frightening..." she said, her face clouded at the memory of the massive demonstrations of the Left.

"Premier Chautemps has France back on the right course," said Jules.

The waiter came and cleared away the plates.

"*Du café,* monsieur?" asked the waiter. He looked at Marie Hélène. "And, madame?"

Jules sighed. "I'm afraid I can't. I must get back to the office."

"I understand."

"If we could meet again..."

"Yes, I would like that...we could have some more time...perhaps?"

"Yes, may I suggest late in the afternoon..."

She hesitated before saying, "Fine." She looked at him expectantly.

"Perhaps we could meet at my flat." He looked at her under an upraised, questioning eyebrow. Nothing ventured, nothing gained.

She was momentarily taken aback. So sudden. But isn't that why she came to lunch? She leaned back in her chair, let her shoulders relax, and smiled across the table at him as she nodded in acquiescence.

"Quai de la Tournelle. Here, let me write down the address." He pulled out a business card and wrote on the back and pushed it across the table. "The concierge will let you in."

"She does this often?"

"Not so often. Remember, I've been away."

"Yes, with the Americans. You will have to tell me about them. In particular, the women...in Washington..."

"Not possibly as exciting as you think..."

"And you, are you exciting?"

"Next Tuesday," he said and let a smile burn across his face.

"Fine."

"Good. Let me walk you to the door, but then I do have to leave." They stood up, and he took her hand and walked her over near the door. He took the coat and scarf off the hook and handed them to her. She put them on and then reached up and took the hat off its peg and placed it on her head. She looked in a mirror and adjusted it, getting the angle just right. They went outside and stood on the sidewalk and looked at each other. She smiled and squeezed his hand.

"I look forward to it," she said. She squeezed his hand one more time, seeming to wish the intimacy to start now, before letting the hand go. She turned and walked up the sidewalk, her hips swaying to and fro. She knew the effect. He watched in appreciation and then turned and walked back to his office.

5. Wilhelmstrasse

Berlin, October 1937. Carl Friedrich von Dinckler stood in the anteroom to the office of State Secretary Ernst Freiherr von Weizsäcker. The office was in the massive stone building of the German foreign ministry on the Wilhelmstrasse, the seat of power of the resurgent German Reich. The door opened, and a trim secretary in a long skirt and a starched blouse came out and said, "The state secretary will see you now." She held her hand out to escort him in. She closed the door behind him.

Weizsäcker stood behind his desk and held his hand out. Dinckler shook the outstretched hand. The secretary pointed for Dinckler to take a seat. He did, and the secretary resumed her seat.

"I have spoken with the foreign minister," said Weizsäcker, referring to Foreign Minister Konstantin von Neurath. "We are sending you back to Paris as second secretary."

"Yes, sir," said Dinckler. "That is a promising promotion to build on previous efforts." Dinckler had been an attaché in Paris up until last summer when he came back to the Wilhelmstrasse for a round of staff planning. He had been back to Paris briefly in September tending his contacts and keeping the money flowing in his network.

"Exactly, we want you to build on your previous political work there. Aim at the French cabinet. We need to know what they are thinking with regard to Austria and Czechoslovakia. The Führer is moving these to the top of the agenda."

"I believe our clandestine financing of French newspapers provides a path to gain further influence at the highest French political levels. Through the newspaper channel, we are providing surreptitious funding to the pacifist wing of the Radical Party."

"Good. And you propose to expand upon this?"

"Yes, we will ask for more detailed reports on cabinet deliberations to come back to us through this channel. We want to mask the ultimate destination from the French politicians. Supposedly it will be 'background' information for our journalist informants that will not be used for publication."

"A lot of confidential information is already published in the French papers."

"Yes, that is why it should be easy for our sources to get even more information out of the Matignon," said Dinckler in conclusion. The Matignon is the office of the premier and normal meeting place for the cabinet.

"Have you seen our military friends?" asked the secretary.

"Yes," sighed Dinckler, referring to his recent training sessions with the Abwehr, the German military intelligence agency. "They want me to try to widen the intelligence net out from the Comité France-Allemagne," he said, doubt in his voice. He was referring to the Franco-German Friendship Society, a Paris-based organization founded by master propagandist Otto Abetz, which included many prominent and highly conservative aristocrats and industrialists.

"You have doubts?"

"Yes, I think at this time we should build on what we have and get to individuals close to the cabinet. You're not going to get the truly good information over champagne glasses at a reception, no matter how charming Otto is."

"The foreign minister completely agrees with you, as do I."

"In that case, I will keep my distance."

Weizsäcker laughed. "Most likely the Deuxième Bureau knows more about the Abwehr's Paris spy rings than the admiral himself. I'll clear it with the Abwehr." The Deuxième Bureau was France's military intelligence agency. Admiral Wilhelm Canaris was the head of the Abwehr, the German military's intelligence arm. "Let the embassy press attaché deal with Abetz."

The secretary pulled a file across his desk and opened it. "Let me give you a little more background. We want you to try to get good information on how the upper rungs of the French cabinet perceive German power. Your work during your first tour in Paris was exceptional for one so young."

Dinckler had tracked down statements made by the French army chief of staff, General Maurice Gamelin, that France would not fight the remilitarization of the Rhineland. No French troops would cross the border and evict the offending German regiments. He verified this key finding through multiple sources. Gamelin's thinking was repeated by leading politicians over late afternoon refreshments at some of Paris's leading salons. The French politicos were a very talkative bunch, particularly when pretty women were about.

Under General Gamelin's thinking, by avoiding fighting in the West, the French would shift the Germans' attention toward the East. In the East, France would then support its allies in Poland and the Little Entente countries of Czechoslovakia, Romania, and Yugoslavia. The French would shelter behind the Maginot Line while helping the eastern allies by sending an expeditionary force. Of course, when Italy broke off its alliance with France and Britain in 1936, the door to the East was slammed shut.

"Yes," continued the secretary, "finding out that an opposing general will not fight is always of the greatest strategic value. The Führer used that information to great effect in March 1936." Hitler, against the advice of his generals, had sent the German army into the Rhineland in March 1936. The French stood by and watched because the British would not contemplate an armed response across the border. The Versailles Treaty of 1919 was irreparably broken. The victory of 1918 lay on the ground like a broken reed. Dinckler's intelligence had been spot on.

"We are rearming," continued the secretary, "but it is going more slowly than thought and will take longer than many admit. The army may not be fully ready until the early 1940s."

"So we can't risk war?" asked Dinckler.

"Not exactly. We must minimize the risk of war. In the Great War, we had the best military in the world and still lost the war. We have many enemies."

Dinckler sighed. The defeat had weighed heavily on his early manhood; he had been sixteen when the armistice was signed, seventeen when the hated Versailles Treaty was ratified. The bitter taste of victors' justice was remembered by all Germans. "What do we do now?"

"If France and Britain see Germany as strong, they will not risk a general war for some countries in eastern Europe for whom they have little regard anyway."

"So we want to exaggerate our strength to the French?"

"Not exactly. Our reports say that the French have already overestimated German strength. We want to make sure it stays that way."

"I see," said Dinckler.

"An easier task overall, I would think," said the secretary. "Importantly, it fits into a much grander plan, one in particular that is dear to the foreign minister."

Dinckler looked at the state secretary with interest. He was being let in on a strategic plan of the first importance.

"The foreign minister believes that Austria and Czechoslovakia can be had without a fight. German foreign policy, not the army, would be on the march, in the van."

Dinckler's mind quickly grasped the ramifications; the order of prestige in Berlin would be stood on its head.

"The foreign ministry would be first among ministries in prestige," said the state secretary.

Dinckler nodded in agreement. "Where?"

"The Führer is going to move aggressively on bringing all Germans back into the Reich—one people—one Reich—one leader."

"Yes," said Dinckler. "Then?"

"Austria, Czechoslovakia, Danzig, the Corridor...*Ostpolitik*." The eastern strategy.

"Poland?"

"Eventually. As you well know, we Prussians have centuries of experience living on the vast plains of eastern Europe...Poland? New solutions are required there."

Dinckler nodded in understanding. His family's estates were east of Berlin near the Vistula River. Poland was just to the east of the lands he had grown up on, and then came the vast steppes of Russia, fearful in their immensity.

"The real threats," Weizsäcker said, letting the words hang in the air, "always come from the East, on the hooves of barbarians threatening the destruction of all they find before it...the farms, the livestock...the women..."

Dinckler appreciated the chilling vision. His family had been Prussian military officers for centuries. Only the army had stood between their estates and violent chaos riding in from the East.

Weizsäcker watched the young man. Yes, he grasped everything. "The Führer will move sooner than many think."

Dinckler could sense that the first move would come soon.

"One more thing. A special mission may be coming up that will require your mastery of French. Word will come at a moment's notice."

"I will hold myself in readiness, Herr Secretary."

"Good," said the state secretary, and he stood up and held out his hand, signaling the end of the interview. Dinckler took the night train to Paris that evening.

6. Quai de la Tournelle

In the late afternoon sunshine of a brisk fall day, the taxi stopped at the intersection of Quai de Montebello and a crooked little cross street meandering out from the Latin Quarter of the Left Bank. The corner was just across from Île de la Cité, the island sitting in the middle of the Seine River. Marie Hélène got out and paid the driver. She looked across the river at the park around the massive Notre Dame Cathedral, the sunlight flashing off the shiny rust-brown leaves rustling in the breeze of the trees bordering the long nave. *A beautiful spot*, she thought.

She crossed the street and walked along the sidewalk of Quai de la Tournelle, the street running along the river. Coming to a door at the base of the high façade of a nineteenth-century apartment building, ornate iron grillwork setting off the shuttered windows, she pushed it open and stood in a tunnellike entrance leading to a small garden in the middle of the apartment building. She went up to an open door and peered inside. A stout older lady in a housedress and apron came forward and asked, "Yes, madame?"

"Monsieur Dugas?"

"*Oui, quatrième étage.*" Yes, fourth floor. She smiled. "*Allez.*" The concierge pointed to a small wire-cage *ascenseur*, an elevator, at the end of the entranceway.

Marie Hélène took the *ascenseur* to the fourth level—the fifth story. She walked over to the number on the door she had been given, knocked lightly, and heard the footfalls of someone coming to the door. The door opened, and Jules stood there smiling and welcomed her with a sweeping gesture of his arm. "*Entrez.*" He was wearing a long silk dressing gown over some sort of evening shirt with silk pajama bottoms. A man waiting for a lady. The directness did not surprise Marie Hélène. In fact, she sort of welcomed it.

"What a charming apartment," she said. She walked over to one of the tall windows and looked across the river to the Île Saint-Louis with its beautiful town houses lining the riverfront, the falling sun glinting off the glass windows. She looked at Jules and arched an eyebrow. "For someone in government?"

"It is provided for me," he said with the self-confidence of a man who knew what he was due. She turned and set her handbag on a chair; he reached out and took her coat off her shoulders and lifted her hat off her hair. He set them on the chair.

Marie Hélène smiled warmly at him while coolly thinking that like so many in the ministerial circle he overestimated his worth but not possibly his value. Those in the ministerial circle held the power while the money was outside. But money was good at getting its due.

"I'm so glad you could come. You fascinate me," said Jules. "So many of the others want the minister himself," he said in reference to the prominent women seeking the company of powerful politicians.

"An older man?" she said coquettishly under the doubtful expression of a raised eyebrow.

"They have the power."

"Yes, but the younger men, they have a certain power, too. N'est-ce pas?" She smiled seductively at him.

"Yes…" he mumbled as he looked at her with amusement. "So something different?"

"Compagnie de Marne gets what it wants. The money sees to that. Then I think I should get what I want. You don't think that is fair?"

Spoken like the true daughter of a powerful industrialist, he thought. "Just what do you want?" he asked.

She stood in front of him and twiddled with his collar between her fingers. "Some understanding…we live in an interesting time…it is all going somewhere…but where? I want to know."

"Where?" he said, glancing out the window, the unknowingness of the future now clear in his expression, his monumental self-assurance momentarily blank.

She watched his expression with keen interest. *Yes*, she thought. *He is the right one.* She stepped over toward the chair and picked up her handbag and looked at him. "*La chambre?*" The bedroom.

"There," he said, pointing with his hand.

"I'll be just a moment," she said and walked over toward the hallway and down to the bedroom.

She returned in a few minutes in bare feet—creating an almost atavistic rush for Jules—and wearing a sheer, silk dressing slip, low off the shoulder, ending just above the knee. Soft breasts pushed the front out, nipples seemingly quivering under the silk, the material resting softly on the round curve of slender thighs. Her lower stomach just pushing the material out, not too tight, not too loose. She smiled at him with a directness that was breathtakingly refreshing to him. Indeed, she was something new.

She came up to him, brushed his cheek with her fingers, and went and stood before the window, gazing out across the river at the magnificent view. He came up behind her and put his hands on top of her hips. She twisted her neck and looked up at him over her shoulder. "It's beautiful. I'm sure we will have a lovely time."

"Whatever I can do," he mumbled. He bent his head down and kissed her upturned lips. She pushed her lips into his invitingly and then dropped her head back and looked out the window. The scent of Chanel Number 5 wafted up into Jules's nostrils. *Sort of like an engraved invitation*, he thought.

He slid his hands up her torso and cupped her breasts in his hands; she rested her head back against his chest and closed her eyes. She pushed her buttocks against his pelvis and slightly swayed. He let his right hand fall down to her thigh, pulled the hem of the slip up, and put his palm around the inside of her thigh. He slowly stroked and squeezed as he moved his palm up the inside of her leg. He ran a fingernail along the crease between her thigh and pelvis, wiggling the little hairs along the way. She gasped and made a small jerk, the languid body coming suddenly taut. Then she sagged back against him, her knees seemingly weak, her thighs widening.

He moved his left arm across her chest and cupped her right breast, seemingly holding her up against his chest. He gently caressed between her thighs, different fingers going to other places, her head now arched back, her white throat stretched taut below his gaze as he surveyed a body completely in his grasp if not control.

With one swoop, he swept her body up into his arms, her arms draped around his neck. She reached her head up and

32

planted her lips hungrily on his neck. He carried her down the hall and into the bedroom. With one hand, he reached down and pulled the bedcovers away and then leaned over and laid her supine body on the satin sheets. He walked around, took his dressing gown off, and lay down beside her.

In the dove gray light of twilight, he reached over and pulled the straps off her shoulder and pulled the slip down to her waist. He leaned across and kissed her breast, his tongue playing with the nipple. She arched her back and ran her fingers through his hair. His hand pulled the bottom of the slip above her waist. He ran a finger round her navel, wiggled it playfully, then bent his head down and kissed her navel, his tongue wiggling.

Hours later, autumn starlight coming through the window, he perched up on an elbow and watched. She was standing unclothed before the window looking out, the lean thighs running up into the taut haunches, the narrow waist, the graceful curve of her back, the beautiful flaxen hair tumbling around her shoulders. *Like a diminutive Teutonic goddess,* he thought. He fell asleep watching her standing at the window. In the morning, she was gone. A silk slip hung in his closet, a faint aroma of Chanel Number 5 lingering with its presence.

7. Deuxième Bureau

Captain Jacques Morel sat at his desk at the offices of the *Service de Renseignement*, the secret intelligence service, at 2 Bis Avenue de Tourville just across from the massive military complex at the Hôtel des Invalides. He looked at the report on his desk: Carl Friedrich von Dinckler had returned to the German embassy in Paris as second secretary. He had originally come to Paris in the early 1930s. Then he came back in 1936 about the same time as the present ambassador, Count Johannes von Welczeck, a long-time German diplomat. A Prussian aristocrat, Dinckler had served in both the London and Rome embassies in the 1920s and '30s. In his most recent tour in Paris, he had been an assistant commercial attaché. He had been unusually successful at getting many of the projects in this year's Paris Expo to use German industrial products. *Boringly routine*, Morel thought.

Morel took a sip of coffee and leaned back in his chair and reflected. The German foreign service posed two espionage threats in Paris, reflecting the unusual fact that there were two German foreign ministries in Berlin. One was the traditional foreign ministry on the Wilhelmstrasse, and the other one was a shadow ministry, oriented toward Nazi propaganda initiatives, organized by Joachim von Ribbentrop, the current German ambassador to London. In Paris, the propaganda operation was run by Otto Abetz through his Comité France-Allemagne, a French-German friendship committee. The Renseignement Généraux, the counterintelligence section of the Sûreté Nationale, kept tabs on the Abetz operation.

What bothered Morel this morning was what he could not see, but that he suspected was there: some sort of espionage operation in Paris that he didn't know about. Possibly in the embassy, possibly not.

Morel got up and walked over to a cabinet and pulled out the Dinckler file and placed it on his desk. Morel paged through it. Very routine. He pushed the file aside. He turned around and took a large dossier off his credenza. The dossier had a red tab on it denoting an important open case. He placed it front and center on his desk and paged through it; he almost knew it by heart. He leaned back and ran through the details in his mind.

In late July 1936, a rare successful decrypt of a German embassy message to Berlin had revealed startling information: someone had given the Germans a complete list of the armaments the French ministry of defense was preparing to ship to the Republican government in Spain so that it—the legitimate government—could suppress the revolt of nationalist forces under General Francisco Franco. Surprisingly, the German ambassador's report said that the information had been expressly confirmed by a member of the cabinet. Analysis of the German message indicated the information, in particular its completeness and accuracy, had originated as a leak from the highest levels of the French cabinet. Telephone taps on German embassy telephones, and some on known German agents in Paris, revealed nothing. Who had tipped off the German ambassador? That was never learned.

Subsequently, similar information was leaked by the Spanish embassy, a hotbed of Franco supporters, to the right-wing press, and in the ensuing uproar, the weapons shipments were curtailed and some suspended. Premier Blum's policy of supporting the Spanish government lay stillborn in its cradle.

For the next ten months, Morel, working with agents of the Sûreté, had shadowed German embassy personnel. But nothing came of it; the trail of the person revealing the secrets from the French cabinet had gone cold. Who had been the source of the leak? The question nagged. Time to meet with the Sûreté again.

Morel reached over and picked the telephone handset off its cradle and spoke into the mouthpiece, asking for *le chef.* He waited for a few moments as his secretary put through the call. A voice came through the earpiece.

"We must meet," said Morel.

"A new second secretary at the German embassy," he said in answer to the question coming from the other end of the line. Then he listened. He replied, "Dinckler."

"Yes, in a half hour." He put the telephone handset back in its cradle. He got up and walked over to the coat rack in the corner of the office. He was wearing mufti—civilian clothing. All the intelligence officers working in Paris did. He put on his overcoat, placed a scarf around his neck, and put a fedora on his head. He walked out, spoke briefly to the secretary, and left the office.

Sûreté

The taxicab stopped in Place Beauvau across from the ministry of the interior. Morel got out, paid the driver, and then walked up Rue de Miromesnil past the imposing ministry building, gendarmes standing guard outside the edifice. Several minutes later, he came to a door of a large apartment building; he knocked on the front door. The door opened, and he showed his identification to a plainclothes officer, who directed him down to a small elevator in the central space of the building. Morel rode the elevator up to the fifth floor, got off, and walked down the hallway. He knocked on an unmarked door and listened.

"*Entrez*," said a woman's voice from inside.

Morel entered and, in response to the secretary's questioning look, said, "*Le chef.*"

She walked over and opened a door and held her hand out for Morel to enter. She closed the door behind him.

A middle-aged man with thinning brown hair was standing behind the desk, a cigarette burning lazily in the ashtray. The two men shook hands. The older man, who was *le chef de bureau* of a small counterintelligence section of the Sûreté Nationale, said, "*Eh, bien.*"

Le chef sat down. He picked up his cigarette, took a long drag, blew a plume of smoke up toward the ceiling, looked at Morel, and asked, "The German embassy again?"

"Yes, another change in embassy staff. A new second secretary. But he was previously a commercial attaché at the embassy."

"Are we not chasing straws here?" asked *le chef* with a touch of weariness.

"The missing piece, I would say."

"OK, I have asked *l'inspecteur* to join us. He oversees the surveillance of the embassy. He has a sense of the place."

There was a light knock on the door, and it opened. A heavyset man came in and took a seat next to Morel. He reached over and casually shook Morel's hand. "Nice to see you again."

Le chef quickly put *l'inspecteur* in the picture and then asked for a rundown.

L'inspecteur began: "Dinckler? Well, he stuck pretty closely to his commercial attaché duties. Attended lots of trade fairs, industrial talks…things like that. When he was at Abetz's receptions, he stuck to his assistant attaché persona. Very deferential, unlike the other peacocks. Nonpolitical. Very charming with the ladies."

"Any affairs?" asked Morel.

"A few. The bored older wives of aging industrialists…that sort of thing."

"A drawing room ornament?"

"Not quite. Just whatever came his way…"

"The industrialists…"

"He regularly attended Comité des Forges," said *l'inspecteur,* mentioning the committee of the big industrial companies. "A lot of elite personages attend. The champagne is always good."

"Well, lots of *députés*, senators, and political people also attend those receptions," said *le chef.* And then with a look of distaste, he added, "And the salons."

Morel nodded in agreement. Paris was a sieve of leaking information.

"What else do we know?" asked Morel. "Are we missing something?"

"As an attaché, he met frequently with the French subsidiaries of important German industrial firms, such as Bayer and IG Farben," said *l'inspecteur.*

"And they…"

"Provide substantial advertising contracts to many of the Paris newspapers that support the pacifist line and various pro-German sentiments," said *le chef.*

"Political influence?" asked Morel, now very intrigued.

"We believe money flows to pacifist politicians in the Radical Party, but we're not quite sure how," explained *le chef.*

"Any guesses?"

"Money comes through corporate accounts to Banque Paris et Londres and gets distributed from there," said *l'inspecteur.*

"By a paymaster named Hirsch," said *le chef*.

"A Jew?" asked Morel incredulously.

"Yes," said *le chef*. "The Nazis work a number of refugees like this. Hope to get a relative out or something like that."

"Cynical but effective," said Morel. "Dinckler may play a much larger role than his second secretary title indicates."

"As second secretary, he would have lots of time for espionage. And anonymity," said *le chef*.

"So if someone near the cabinet wanted a high level contact with Berlin, they would follow the money trail back up the line, not go to the Abetz crowd?" said Morel.

"That would be logical," pronounced *le chef*.

"So it is the embassy," said *l'inspecteur*.

"It worked before for someone," said Morel.

"Yes," said *l'inspecteur*. He turned and looked at Morel. "What is it the Germans want to know?"

"On the German side," explained Morel, "we think they are going to move on Austria…"

"What is the military significance of that?" asked *le chef*, breaking in.

"If the Germans hold Austria, they have Czechoslovakia surrounded on three sides. Importantly, the Germans can flank the Czech-fortified line facing Germany."

"So the first domino guarantees the fall of the second," said *l'inspecteur*.

"Precisely. From Austria Hitler will move to bring the Sudetenland Germans in Czechoslovakia back into the Reich. Berlin will focus its espionage efforts on finding out whether France will honor its treaty with Czechoslovakia…"

"Yes, but why would someone in the French cabinet tell the Germans this vital fact?" asked *l'inspecteur,* his mind turning back to the analytical.

"A deep commitment to peace, a belief that France cannot win a war against Germany," said Morel. "It could be a very sincere belief. But misplaced."

"If France went to the aide of Czechoslovakia, that would mean war," said an astonished *l'inspecteur*, a tone of shock in his voice. He knew Morel had the best information in Paris.

What had been an abstract possibility now moved to the concrete in *l'inspecteur*'s mind. War.

"So the question of the hour in Berlin will be—how will the French cabinet respond?" said *le chef*.

"Or?" asked *l'inspecteur*.

"Let Czechoslovakia go the way of Spain, the Rhineland..." said Morel.

"I see," said *l'inspecteur*. "A hard game."

"Yes," said *le chef* in agreement, taking a long draw on his cigarette in contemplation. "It might be like Spain." They all knew that Britain had prevented the French government, a Popular Front coalition, from going to the aid of the elected Popular Front government of Spain just a year ago. France, confronted by British demands for neutrality, decided it couldn't risk its relationship with Britain. So it, too, went into a halfhearted state of neutrality. "If Britain doesn't support France, then France will have to stand back. It will not face war with Germany alone," concluded *le chef*. That was the stark fact facing the French government in the late 1930s.

"Yes, just like Spain," sighed *l'inspecteur*. His shoulders sagged.

"Precisely," said Morel.

"Yes, even the charwomen at the Quai d'Orsay know that," said *le chef*, mentioning the French foreign ministry. Everyone in Paris knew that the French foreign ministry placed its alliance with Britain above all else.

"So we want to see if the Germans succeed at getting an ear into the cabinet?" said *l'inspecteur*.

"Exactly," said Morel. "And what that ear hears."

"Either way the Germans win," said *le chef*. "They can always wait for next time."

The three men nodded in mutual understanding and then sat in silence as they contemplated their thoughts. *Le chef* leaned back in his chair and blew cigarette smoke up toward the ceiling; he watched the plume billow and unfold in long tendrils. "The Germans will want to know if the French will go to war," pronounced *le chef*, breaking the silence and nailing the conclusion.

"*C'est ça*," said Morel. That's it.

"I know what to do," said *l'inspecteur*. "More of the same." Lots of surveillance. "Look for a contact, a link."

"*Cherchez la femme,*" said *le chef* with a smile. Look for the woman.

They all laughed. Morel stood up and shook hands with both men. Then he departed.

8. Faubourg Saint-Germain

Marie Hélène sat at her escritoire, an eighteenth-century antique writing desk with carefully carved spindly legs. She worked at her correspondence in her study, an upstairs room in the *hôtel particulier*—mansion—in the Faubourg Saint-Germain that her family had picked up for a song toward the end of the war. The morning sunlight came through the tall windows from the small garden outside, making it almost the aerie of a fairy-tale princess, she thought. A maid, wearing a black dress and white apron with a white cap in her shiny black hair, came in bearing a tray with a letter on it. In the maid's left hand was a bouquet of flowers. She handed the flowers to Marie Hélène, who took them, smelled their fragrance, and then set them aside. The maid held the tray in front of her so she could take the letter.

"This came for you, madame," said the maid. "A government messenger." She was mildly impressed, but then madame traveled in high circles.

"Thank you, Delphine," said Marie Hélène politely. She opened the scented envelope and pulled out a small card and read the script: *Tuesdays?*

She smiled and whispered, "So sweet." She reached across the desk and took a fountain pen from a small nook, tested it on her writing pad, and then wrote on the card: *Mais oui.* Yes.

She put the card back in the envelope, sealed it, looked to see that there was an appropriate return address, and handed it back to the maid. "See that it is delivered."

"Yes, madame." The maid turned and departed, closing the door softly behind her.

Marie Hélène took a sip of tea from a cup, put it back on its saucer, and leaned back in her chair. She thought about the night before. *A delicious experience. Everything she could imagine…and then more…too bad he was a politician…but she would see…so hard to get great pleasure and real commitment in one man…Thérèse makes this complaint endlessly.* She sighed and made a bleak look. There was also the other reality. He was indeed a politician, and for a politician, a married woman with a great fortune was the golden pheasant of Parisian society. Yes, she was a golden pheasant. *Maybe she always would be*, she thought.

She turned back to her desk, took another sip of tea, and turned to her correspondence. Indeed, here was a letter from Thérèse, her friend at Comité des Forges. They worked together on refreshments and other tasks related to the committee's receptions. She opened it and read. Carl von Dinckler was back as the second secretary of the German embassy. Yes, she remembered him well. Thérèse was quite taken with him; she said the most indelicate things about him. Marie Hélène smiled at the recollection. Surprising considering how low key the diplomat was in social settings.

Thérèse said Dinckler was going to give a little talk on developments in Germany at the next reception of the Comité des Forges. Would it be possible for Marie Hélène to give a short introduction? Marie Hélène understood that Thérèse wanted to stay out of the limelight; she would not want any more talk than there already was. The three of them could meet for lunch and go over the details. Next Wednesday. Chez L'Ami Louis over on the Right Bank. Small place, out of the way.

Marie Hélène picked up her fountain pen and wrote on the bottom of the note that lunch would be fine. Yes, next Wednesday. She knew the bistro. *Perfect for a discreet rendezvous*, thought Marie Hélène. Undoubtedly Thérèse would go on from there. She had a little hideaway apartment nearby. Indeed, it had inspired her to get her own. Marie Hélène found all the little intrigues swirling around the luncheon fascinating.

She got up and took the letter down to the maid to post.

The telephone in the parlor rang. The maid answered, then held the receiver and said to Marie Hélène in a whisper, her hand over the speaking end, "Your father."

"I'll take it," said Marie Hélène as she walked over and took the receiver from the maid's hand.

"Father, how nice of you to call." She nodded to dismiss the maid. She listened to the receiver.

"Yes, I'm of course staying very close to Daladier and his circle." She listened some more to the receiver.

"Yes, I'm urging the extension of Maginot Line up along the Belgium border every chance I get." She listened.

"Difficulties? No, everyone agrees on the extension. Money is just very tight." She listened some more.

"Yes, of course I'm extending my influence. Every chance I get." She sighed and listened. This was part of the weekly phone call.

"Remember, we hosted a reception for Georges and Odette Bonnet when they came back from America. They are very grateful for everything we do for them." She listened some more, minor impatience spreading across her face.

"If you really want to know, I'm in the process of conquering the finance ministry," she said rather forthrightly. "One of the men is quite interested in me." She held the receiver away from her ear as the fatherly reprimand came down the line.

"That's one of the things I do here," she said, a droll smirk on her face.

"I am not seeking my mother's approval," she said with minor annoyance.

"My husband? What's he got to do with it?" she said with a look of consternation on her face.

"He's on your board of directors, not mine," she said as if instructing a schoolboy.

"Yes, thank you. Always nice to speak with you, Poppa." She placed the receiver back on its cradle, ending the call. She walked out into the hallway, found her maid, and put in a request for lunch. She asked the maid, "Is my bath ready?"

"Yes, madame."

"Thank you," replied Marie Hélène, and she started up the stairs to the second floor for a nice soak and the remembrance of delicious thoughts from the previous night. There was a rough edge to Jules that she found exciting. She looked forward to the future. After her bath would come lunch on the *terrasse* overlooking the garden; the sunny days were getting rarer.

9. Île Saint-Louis

The candlelight threw a flickering light on the dark boiserie on the wall adjacent to the little table in the restaurant, a small establishment of long standing situated in the middle of Île Saint-Louis, the almost magical island sitting in the middle of the Seine River. Convenient because it was a short walk to Jules Dugas's apartment.

"Thank you for agreeing to this late rendezvous. A very busy Tuesday. I simply could not get away from the ministry," said Jules. He swirled some wine around in its glass and took a sip.

"I understand completely," said Marie Hélène. "I've never really known anyone this close to the center of political power. What is it really like?"

"Constant intrigue," said Jules.

Marie Hélène leaned forward and whispered, "You will have to tell me more. Sounds exciting." She sat back up and took a sip from her wineglass, enchanted by the dark candlelit ambiance, the handsome man sitting across from her, and an evening promising to be both interesting and exciting.

"The priorities of the various factions are in constant conflict, thus the intrigue."

"Which faction is which?"

"Collected around Daladier," he said, referring to the minister of defense, "are those who see rearmament as paramount."

"Yes, I see them at Madame de Crussol's salon."

"You attend that salon?"

"Sometimes."

"You must keep me informed. I need to know what goes on around Daladier," said Jules. He was Bonnet's principal rival to replace Chautemps as premier someday.

"I will."

"Then there are those gathered around my boss, Monsieur le Minister," he said, referring to Georges Bonnet, the finance minister. "Bringing the budget into balance is a crucial goal."

"Why?"

"Why?" Jules asked, somewhat astonished that the question was even being asked. "If the budget cannot be stabilized, then there will be endless speculative attacks, and gold will leave the country. The franc will become a gypsy currency, traded this way and that by hidden hands, a plaything for foreign speculators. It will be like a fallen woman. Any and all can have their way with her."

"I didn't realize."

"It is the great legacy of the Popular Front," he said bitterly, "a gift from Monsieur Blum to the bourgeoisie. It robs their wealth."

"Yes. The devaluations. What is needed?"

"Balance the budget so that the Bank of France can once again hold the value of the franc steady against gold, the central virtue in state finance, and restore the franc to its rightful place as queen among currencies."

"Sort of the Royalist position in finance?"

"Well said," said Jules, smiling at Marie Hélène and pleased with her understanding of the complicated issue.

"And the premier?" asked Marie Hélène. "Where does he stand?"

"He stands in the middle, conciliating each faction as best he can."

"And if we could come to an understanding with Germany?"

"We could lower our defense expenditures."

"What would bring that about?"

"A new understanding," said Jules. He took a sip from his wineglass. "There is a growing school of thought that Germany is preoccupied with eastern Europe. In Russia, a powerful and sinister new ideology, Communism, has merged with the largest state in Europe…a powerful combination…very threatening to Germany…Germany's eyes are looking east…"

"Yes, I understand. Bolshevism is the number one threat to all European civilization, not just Germany."

"Yes, we almost had a Communist revolution right here in France in 1936 with the Popular Front," said Jules. "We don't need red flags flying from the department stores of Paris."

"A new peace? How would it work?"

"Britain and France would reach an understanding with Germany. The western powers would maintain their security behind the Maginot Line and the protective wings of air power. In exchange, Germany could arrange a new and more secure order in eastern Europe."

"And the treaties with Czechoslovakia, Poland, and Russia?"

"New understandings will have to be arrived at."

"That will require a new foreign policy," said Marie Hélène, grasping the significance of what Jules said.

"Yes, and possibly a new foreign minister," said Jules, a low smile breaking across his face.

"And the goal of the new foreign minister?"

"A Franco-German pact."

Marie Hélène leaned back, her understanding now putting a sparkle in her eyes. "The centerpiece?"

"Yes," said Jules.

"I understand," she said as a glow of self-satisfaction came over her face. "The Maginot Line would be a cornerstone of the policy."

"Yes."

This is exciting, she thought. She had made a good choice. A strong horse. She smiled seductively and extended her wineglass out into the middle of the table and proposed, "To a new foreign minister."

"To a new peace," said Jules as lifted his glass up and clinked hers.

The waiter came and cleared the dishes away. Jules arched an eyebrow and asked, "Cognac? *Chez moi?*" My place.

"Only if we skip the cognac."

"We'll sacrifice."

"Good."

He stood up and offered her his hand. They went to the front of the little restaurant. The maître d' helped Marie Hélène into her overcoat. She wrapped a soft wool muffler around her neck and put on a small, round, béret-like hat. Jules took her arm, and they departed. They walked down a small street, crossed the Pont de la Tournelle, and walked up the quay to

Jules's apartment house. They ascended the elevator and went in. He took her coat and hat and hung them up. She threw her muffler on a chair. He put his own overcoat away, tossed his jacket on top of her muffler, and walked over to a small fireplace. He kindled a fire and stood back. The fire blazed. She came up to him.

"I can take you home in the early morning?" he said.

"That will be fine," she said. "I'm not expected."

"Good." He reached out and held her shoulders in his hands. He leaned over and kissed her on her forehead. Then he rotated her around until she was standing in front of the fireplace, her back to the small flames, the firelight radiating around her torso, the light coming through the sheer silk of her blouse.

He slowly unbuttoned her blouse, button by button, and pulled it out of her skirt. He tossed the blouse on the chair. Next, he reached around and unbuttoned the back of her skirt and pulled the small zipper down. She stepped out of the skirt; he threw it over on the chair, watching to see that it landed on top of the other clothes. He stood up, gathering the hem of her slip as he went.

"Hands up," he softly ordered. Her hands went up over her head as if to dive into a pool. He whisked the slip over her head. She let her arms fall down to her side. He reached over and removed her brassiere.

He stood back and let the firelight play on her now naked torso, the flickering light making shadows and ripples on the smooth white flesh. "Beautiful," he whispered. She basked in his admiration and pushed her breasts slightly forward. He bent down and kissed each nipple in turn as he reached down and untied the tiny drawstrings holding her drawers around her waist. Finished, he hooked his thumbs inside the waistband and pulled it open. The newly freed drawers slid down to her ankles in one smooth motion. He kneeled down and held the silk material as she stepped out of them. The smell of her perfume intoxicated him. He tossed the drawers onto the chair.

He reached up and rolled her stockings down, one leg at a time, his fingertips playing with the inside of her thighs as he did so. Her breath quickened. He was pleased, his excitement mounting. Throwing the last stocking over onto the chair, he looked up, unhooked her garter belt in the front and threw it over on the chair, like a small bow on top of a package, he thought.

He reached around and gripped her buttocks in his hands and pulled her forward, planting his lips on the soft white belly below her navel. He dug his fingers in and made slow sucking kisses down her belly. She planted her fingers in his hair and caressed his scalp with her fingers, and then she gripped the back of his head suddenly, her fingernails biting into the back of his neck. He heard her gasp.

He awoke in the morning, darkness still coming through the window. The smell of coffee wafted in from the other room. She was up. He got up and put on a robe and went into the dining area. The gray approach of dawn was in the window. She was standing in the kitchen in an oversize kimono, pouring café au lait into two small cups. She brought some slices of a baguette with some butter over and set them on the table. She set one of the small coffee cups in front of him. She looked at him and smiled. "Monsieur, anything else?"

"Nothing that I could possibly imagine."

"A real compliment from such a grand Parisian man about town."

"The inner essence of the woman...makes all else...pale..." he mumbled.

She smiled. She knew her talents. She also thought she would never forget the touch of last night's fingers, the exquisite feeling of silk sliding over skin...what followed...

They took a cab back to the quarter, and he dropped her off, mentioning that except for the occasional late running meeting he was at her service. He kissed her good-bye inside the cab, and she stepped out onto the sidewalk and walked over to the large wooden door to the courtyard and rang a buzzer. The door opened, and she was gone.

10. Chez L'Ami Louis

Marie Hélène walked down the street in a working-class district near Place de la République, just a short cab ride away from the fashionable Right Bank shopping districts. She entered the bistro. Yes, it was in an out-of-the-way place, but Thérèse said it had some of the best traditional cooking in Paris. Thérèse was standing inside looking at the menu pinned to the wall.

"Well, you have the color in your cheeks this morning, Mimi," said Thérèse.

"Yes," said Marie Hélène, her mind flashing back to the previous night's pleasures. She mumbled an explanation, "A relaxing bath this morning."

"He'll be here in just a minute," said Thérèse, an edge of excitement in her voice at seeing Carl von Dinckler again. "He's been in Germany on some sort of business since last May…he's only been back once." Marie Hélène could see that Thérèse felt Carl's absence was an eternity. "I'm so glad you're helping out," added Thérèse.

"My pleasure," said Marie Hélène. She had always admired Dinckler's immaculate manners. What woman would not be impressed?

"There are always two sides to every question," said Thérèse. "Carl will be able to explain the German side of these controversies. So much of the French press is biased."

Just then Carl von Dinckler came through the door, taking off his hat as he did. He took off his overcoat and hung it on a hook just past the door. He leaned over and kissed Thérèse on the cheek. She beamed. He looked over at Marie Hélène and said, "Comtesse, what a pleasure to see you again."

"Thank you," said Marie Hélène, holding out her hand, palm down. Dinckler swept it up and gave it a light kiss. Marie Hélène could hear the click of his heels.

The owner came up and asked, "All present?"

"Yes," said Dinckler, taking command of the situation.

The owner swept them into the small dining room with a dozen tables irregularly spotted here and there. He seated them at a small table against the wall near the rear of the restaurant with three chairs. Dinckler took the outside seat, the two women facing each other across the table next to the wall.

"Ah, comtesse," said Dinckler.

"Please, Mimi."

"Yes, at the receptions...I remember your husband...*le comte*...he provided very good wines, I believe. From the Moselle region?"

"Yes," said Marie Hélène, "in fact, he is out at the estate supervising the pressing of the grapes as we speak. I'm of course trapped here in Paris finagling paperwork on contracts for my father's company."

"Compagnie de Marne, I recall?"

"Yes."

The waiter came up and asked if they would like to start with some wine.

"How about a bottle of Moselle?" ventured Dinckler. The women smiled in agreement.

"Perhaps you can name one for us, Mimi?" asked Dinckler. He looked at the waiter and said, "The lady will choose."

The waiter started to read off the wine list.

"There, that one," said Marie Hélène. "The estate is right next door. It overlooks the river."

"So it will be," pronounced Dinckler as he nodded at the waiter.

"An excellent vintage," replied the waiter as he departed to get the wine.

Thérèse moved to change the conversation. "We want to go over Carl's background, Mimi, so you can give a proper introduction."

"Let's get the details," said Marie Hélène as she took out a small notebook and pencil from her handbag.

The waiter returned, showed the bottle to Dinckler, and then poured a small sample in his glass. He took a sip and pronounced it excellent. The waiter filled the two women's glasses and then topped off Dinckler's.

"Yes, now," said Dinckler, beginning to recount his career. "I was a military cadet and then served two years with an infantry regiment in the early 1920s, near Berlin. I left and resumed my studies, receiving a doctor of laws degree, and entered the foreign service."

"Where have you served?" asked Marie Hélène.

"Rome, London, but mostly Paris with brief stints back in Berlin."

"And you have returned here to Paris as second secretary? Before you were a commercial attaché."

"An assistant attaché," he corrected. "But, yes, as an attaché, you get out and about. See the country, the industries. Meet the business leaders. Now as a secretary, probably lots of dull diplomatic chores." He made a good-natured laugh.

"Not so many receptions?" asked Marie Hélène.

"True," said Dinckler, and he looked at Thérèse. "But more time for my friends."

Thérèse beamed. Then with heartfelt sincerity, she said, "I do hope French-German friendship can be improved. So much good could come of it."

Marie Hélène looked across the table at her friend, reached across with her hand and took Thérèse's in hers, and said, "I do, too. Real friendship would do so much for Europe." Dinckler watched with fascination, the deep sincerity of each woman touching him. He would not forget.

"Tell me some of the highlights from your talk," said Marie Hélène.

"Of course, I want to discuss eastern Europe. That is the number one area of concern to Germany. Germany won important military victories over Russia in the last war and concluded a peace treaty that would have brought long-term stability to eastern Europe."

"What happened in the East?" asked Marie Hélène.

"The lost territories…in the East…Prussian for centuries…"

Marie Hélène wrote this down on her pad. *Fascinating,* she thought. *I get to hear the story from the other side.*

"But the Versailles Treaty took these lands, these protections away from Germany and substituted a difficult situation in eastern Europe—a bunch of troublesome neighbors, not the least of which was Russia, which had gone Communist and posed a major threat to Germany, indeed, to all of Europe."

Both Thérèse and Marie Hélène nodded in agreement to this piece of wisdom, which all knew to be true. Russian-based Bolshevism was the biggest threat to Europe today.

"Yes, red flags over the department stores of Paris," said Thérèse. "Why even Coco's shopgirls and seamstresses went out on strike. Was nothing safe? Where would it end?" One could hear the remembered distress in Thérèse's plaintive statement. Marie Hélène nodded in sympathetic agreement.

"Yes, but Germany—like all countries—has both good angels and bad angels in its midst. The peace treaty gave too much fuel to the bad angels and not enough to the good angels. So there is a deep tension inside Germany."

"Yes, we see that," said Marie Hélène, "and fear it. My family's business is building the Maginot Line—keeping any bad angels out of France is the hope."

"For somewhat similar reasons," said Dinckler, "that is why Germany is building the West Wall in the Rhineland. To ensure that it has a secure and safe border with the West so that it will be able to address the challenges from the East."

Marie Hélène instantly saw the correctness of what she heard. Dinckler was mildly astonished; he could see that she grasped the point immediately. *Such quickness is sort of rare for a French aristocrat,* he thought. But then she had married into the title, he remembered.

Marie Hélène now saw the Maginot Line in a new light. Like so many French, she had always seen the Maginot as a bulwark against a new invasion from Germany—but the Germans weren't coming, she now realized. Now it made so much more sense; the Germans were facing the East. So they were building their own West Wall, further confirmation of the truth that Jules and Dinckler both had said was the new reality. Germany's defensive line on its side of the border would guard against an invasion from the West while the Germans pursued their interests in the East. *Although it beggars belief that the French and British will ever launch an invasion of Germany,* she thought. So the future might not be a rerun of the Great War. That would be a huge relief to everyone in France.

And possibly more exciting, she realized, that once again she would have a box seat to the great European opera through her relationship with Jules; she would be close to a powerful player.

Dinckler watched and saw that the women grasped the point. He continued, "That is what I want to do with this talk. Stress the interests that France and Germany have in common, not the differences."

"I'm sure our membership will be captivated by your explanation," said Marie Hélène.

"Yes, differences can always be bridged," said Dinckler. He reached across and took one of Thérèse's hands in his and lovingly caressed it with his other. He looked deeply into her eyes. Marie Hélène could see Thérèse's shoulders ease, a look of expectation cross her face—she was looking forward to the afternoon.

Dinckler turned to Marie Hélène and said, "Like in France, in Germany there is the old aristocracy, the land-owning Prussian Junkers, in alliance with the industrialists, the new nobility of our age. Both parties are joined by their deep interests in the security and well-being of the state."

"And you're part of that?" asked Marie Hélène.

"Yes, my family goes back centuries in service to the Prussian state and now the new German state. I share a deep sense of tradition."

"Yes, Carl and I have so much in common," said Thérèse. "We share rituals of an ancient class rooted in the land and respect for aristocratic tradition passed down over the centuries in our families—bonds of respect to the old order that span borders. The new industrialism mostly bores me."

Dinckler patted the top of her hand with his and smiled benignly at her.

"Yes, that's true of my husband's family," said Marie Hélène, "the family chateau is a temple to centuries gone by."

"It's nice when you can share in the tradition," said Dinckler in a very neutral tone. New money marrying into the aristocracy can always be a bit touchy about that, he knew from experience. But Marie Hélène seemed unusually comfortable in her social position.

Marie Hélène smiled at Dinckler, took a sip of wine, then set her glass down, and said, "It's been very nice, but I will leave you two to your lunch. I have another appointment...the work of a businesswoman never ends." She stood up and looked at Dinckler. "I'm sorry that I have to leave so soon…"

Dinckler stood up. "I completely understand. I look forward to giving this little talk. If the other guests grasp the points as well as you have today, the talk will be a great success."

"I will see that we have some good Moselle on hand," said Marie Hélène.

"Excellent," said Dinckler with a broad smile. "If you need anything else, just contact Thérèse. I am at your service." He bowed his head and clicked his heels.

Thérèse stood up, pleasure with her friend spreading across her face. "Thank you so much, Mimi. You are a true friend."

Marie Hélène turned and walked around a couple of closely placed tables and was soon out on the afternoon sidewalk. She hailed a cab and headed back to the Left Bank. And a well-deserved nap after last night's delights.

11. Hôtel Matignon

November 1937. On an autumn day, cold and damp with a misty rain wetting the streets, a long black Mercedes limousine moved up Rue de Varenne on the Left Bank, its passenger salon curtained off from outside view. It turned through the gates, tall stone pylons standing like sentinels on either side of the entrance, and drove across the courtyard and made a swinging turn in front of the steps of the entrance to the Hôtel Matignon, the office of the premier. Uniformed guards came out, holding umbrellas up, and opened the rear door and shielded two men as they got out and ascended the steps and walked through the tall doors. They were wearing long dark overcoats and homburg hats. One man carried a briefcase. The two men were ushered into a foyer where the men pulled black gloves off their hands; a formally attired usher took their hats and overcoats.

The men were escorted down a hall and into a sumptuous book-lined study, a warm fire crackling in a large fireplace. The French premier, Camille Chautemps, stood behind the desk waiting to welcome the guests. As they came up to the desk, he addressed the one on the right, "Your Excellency, so nice you could come and talk." He reached out and shook Fritz von Papen's hand. Papen was German ambassador to Austria.

"Our pleasure, Monsieur le Président," said Papen.

Papen turned and introduced his companion to the premier. "May I introduce Carl von Dinckler. He is second secretary here in the German embassy. He can help me with any translation difficulties."

Chautemps shook the young German's hand.

Papen then turned to the Frenchman standing to one side of the premier's desk. "I don't believe we have had the pleasure of meeting before, Monsieur Bonnet. I so seldom get to meet a finance minister."

"My pleasure, Your Excellency. As you know, finance is an important dimension in modern diplomacy," said Georges Bonnet.

Papen nodded in agreement and then looked at the third man, a younger man. Bonnet said, "Let me introduce my aide, Monsieur Jules Dugas. Like Monsieur Dinckler, he is here to assist the premier and me with any difficulties we encounter with the language."

"Excellent," said Chautemps, "we all want to be clear."

"Did you enjoy your visit to the expo, Your Excellency?" asked the premier, mentioning the big Paris expo that had attracted millions of visitors to Paris in the preceding months.

"Yes," said Papen, "the exhibits were fascinating to see. Modern technology is such a marvel. Carl was able to point out the many German products present in the exhibitions."

"Let us sit over at the conference table," said Chautemps, pointing to a long conference table just to one side of the heat-giving hearth. The men all walked over and took seats, Chautemps at the head of the table while Papen took a seat at the other end. Bonnet sat on Chautemps's right and Dugas next to Bonnet where he could quietly advise. On the other side of the table and at the other end near Papen sat Dinckler. Dugas looked at Dinckler; he faintly recalled seeing him at receptions and minor public events. Odd that he was chosen for this meeting since the discussions could be quite significant. Possibly he played a larger role in the embassy than Jules thought.

Chautemps opened the discussion: "France of course recognizes Germany's influence in southeast Europe."

Papen smoothly replied, "That has been a traditional sphere of influence for Germany for a long time…"

"As it has been for France," responded Chautemps.

"Yes, but your formal alliance system in eastern Europe, particularly with Russia, has often been seen as a threat in Berlin."

Chautemps listened and then shifted to a new line: "Let us get straight to our concerns. France is concerned about Austria and Czechoslovak in particular and eastern Europe in general."

"Well," said Papen, "I can assure you that the Führer is clear on his overall goal: all Germans must be part of the German Reich. The details of the arrangements are of course quite open."

"Austria is an independent country, its status guaranteed by international treaty. Germany agreed to that treaty," said Chautemps.

"Possibly that German government had no choice..." said Papen. "If the Austrian people want a closer affiliation with Germany, is not that their right?"

"Well, yes and no. The treaty was for their benefit," said the premier.

"A customs union seems hardly a threat," countered Papen.

"If it remains simply a customs union," replied Chautemps.

"But there are threats from the East," said Papen. "Russia, and its international wing, the Comintern, threaten many of the countries in eastern Europe with Communist subversion, not the least being Austria and Czechoslovakia. They have a right to seek any safety..."

"Possibly their safety and independence could be strengthened by international treaties," said Chautemps.

"Then there is the matter of the three million Germans living in the Sudetenland of Czechoslovakia, separated from their Fatherland, often mercilessly exploited..."

"We believe negotiation could resolve many of these issues," said Chautemps. "Some sort of looser federation of the provinces might be possible."

Papen nodded silently in understanding.

"France would accept the peaceful extension of German influence in Austria and Czechoslovakia," Chautemps continued, "as long as German aims were limited and there were not any surprises."

"Perhaps, Monsieur le Président...further discussions would...yield many benefits..."

"Yes, we would consider a reorientation of French policy in central Europe as entirely open to discussion," replied Chautemps.

Papen again made a nod in agreement. He looked at Dinckler to make sure the young aide was keeping notes.

"We think," said Bonnet, entering the discussion, "that as Germany enhances its western security by constructing the West Wall, it has much less to fear from that direction. A system of mutual defense treaties in the East would—with a set of new understandings—ease the burden of armaments expenditures for all concerned."

"Yes," agreed Papen, "but we in Germany are never sure what threats the military assistance and mutual defense promises made under your system of eastern treaties—the so called *cordon sanitaire*—means. Is it to protect these countries from Russia and Communist invasion, or is it a giant military encircling movement of Germany, all directed from Paris?"

"If we could restart disarmament discussions, possibly within the context of new arrangements for eastern Europe..." said Bonnet.

"Yes, more Geneva," said Papen, somewhat dismissively.

"France believes," said Chautemps, breaking back in, "that the grounds for mutually beneficial talks are many." He didn't want to argue the merits of individual issues with Papen.

"I have been instructed by Berlin," said Papen, "to encourage further talks. After the security of Germans outside the Reich is provided for, the Führer feels there are many possibilities for accommodation, possibly even a return to Geneva." Papen looked at Bonnet and said, "A return to the League of Nations might be possible," dangling the ever-present promise of grand international bargains before the French leaders.

Chautemps stood up, signaling that the meeting was over. "We have much appreciated this opportunity to speak frankly about important issues between our two countries."

Papen, now standing, said, "I will make a favorable report to Berlin. Your constructive attitude will not go unnoticed."

The two Germans stood and left the study, heading back to the foyer to collect their overcoats and hats, before making the short trip back to the embassy.

In the rear of the limousine, Papen asked Dinckler, "Did you take notes?"

"Yes, Your Excellency. I will get them typed up."

"Good. What do you think?"

"The French are unlikely to challenge Germany on Austria..."

"Yes, that apple is ready to fall from the tree."

"Czechoslovakia is less sure. The French have a solid treaty of mutual defense with Czechoslovakia...dating from 1924. If they walk away from it..."

"The French walked away from the Rhineland, from Spain.... Are you telling me they might find their spines in Czechoslovakia, a country not one in ten Frenchmen could find on a map?"

"Possibly," said Dinckler. "In each of the cases you mention, Britain was the key. They did not stand behind the French."

"Yes, perfidious Albion."

"Britain is still the key to any French display of resolve."

"No Britain, no resolve?"

"Yes, Your Excellency."

"You're quite right, Dinckler." Papen leaned back. "The French won't move without the promise of British divisions in Flanders."

"Yes, we learned that with Spain," said Dinckler. "The Quai d'Orsay was our greatest ally."

"Yes, a wavering Frenchman is worth ten resolute Italians," said Papen with a derisory sneer.

"We just need to keep Mussolini in Rome, not up on the Brenner Pass protecting Austria," said Dinckler.

"Yes, the Führer will not repeat the mistakes of 1934," said Papen, referring to the summer when Mussolini rushed Italian troops up to the Austrian border to keep Hitler out of Austria. Back before Berlin had arranged a proper understanding with Rome.

"Nevertheless, the French have wavered each time they have been challenged," said Dinckler.

"Yes," snorted Papen, a smile coming to his face as he remembered how the French Popular Front, the almost Jewish, almost Communist French government, backed away from Spain because the English aristocrats didn't want to risk war for a dirty rabble of Spanish Leftists celebrating free love on the streets of Barcelona.

Dinckler sensed an opening, an opportunity to add a point. "The British have worldwide interests...and few of them are in eastern Europe."

"Right again." Papen looked approvingly at Dinckler. "You have good strategic sense."

"Thank you, Your Excellency."

"Anything else?"

"Interesting that their finance minister was present for a meeting about foreign policy. Possibly Monsieur Bonnet is some sort of shadow foreign minister, waiting to replace Delbos."

"If Bonnet replaces Delbos, what does that mean? You're the expert on French government."

"Bonnet is very appeasement minded. Wants desperately to reach an accommodation with Germany."

"Desperately?"

"Yes, very much so."

"So the French cabinet is split on foreign policy. That's what you're telling me?"

"Deeply."

"Good. Be sure to stress that in the report. The Führer has a sixth sense about these weaknesses, the failings of the decadent states. He knows when to strike."

"Yes, the remilitarization of the Rhineland was a brilliant stroke."

"At the embassy, we must get a report back to the Führer immediately," concluded Papen.

"Yes, Your Excellency."

New Understandings

After shaking hands with the departing Germans, the three Frenchmen sat back down. A steward entered the study and asked them if they wanted something to drink. The premier and finance minister asked for whiskeys while Dugas asked for a glass of Moselle.

The steward brought the two whiskeys and the glass of wine.

Bonnet looked at Dugas and asked, "What do you think?"

"They are amendable to new understandings, possibly written agreements at some point," said Dugas with a troubled look on his face. "But I don't know what the price will be?"

"Pay something?" said Bonnet quizzically. "I'm not sure we can afford more than what we are doing now. Our resources are stretched. We need to do less."

"Yes, we get weaker and Germany gets stronger," said Chautemps. "The reality of our times."

"I think at each step we should get what we can," said Bonnet, "but we can't risk general war. We simply can't tax and devalue our way to security."

"Agreed," said Chautemps. "The French people don't want it. Leastwise the people who count."

"We must keep our alliance with Britain intact no matter what," said Bonnet. "We must organize an effective defense with Britain along our eastern border. Only the Maginot Line can provide France with the security it needs. Chasing alliances in the East is a chimera—a fatal delusion."

"Yes, that should be our core organizing principle," said Chautemps.

"We need to consider extending the Maginot Line so the Germans cannot come through Belgium. Like last time," said Dugas.

"Do they even want to come west?" asked Bonnet. "They are building a West Wall. Possibly the Germans have a defensive orientation in the West?"

"Yes, but keeping Belgium secure is an important point," said Chautemps, making a nod of approbation to Dugas.

"Britain remains the key," said Bonnet.

"Everyone agrees on that," said Chautemps. "Even Blum and those people."

Bonnet and Dugas nodded in agreement. Chautemps looked at them. *Yes, they seem to really believe there is a future with Germany,* he thought. They thought it could all be worked out. But the premier wondered if that were true.

"I think we should regard our meeting with Monsieur von Papen as a minor affair. No need to mention it beyond this room."

"*Oui,* Monsieur le Président," said Bonnet. "Particularly with the British."

"Yes, the upcoming meeting," said the premier.

12. Sûreté

The door to the office opened and *le chef* watched as *l'inspecteur* walked in and sat down and said, "I have further news on the Cagoulards."

"Did they find who set off those bombs at the trade association offices?"

"No, but the dragnet is proceeding across France. Four hundred and fifty warrants have been issued."

"Results?"

"So far, machine guns, antiaircraft guns, cartridges, cases of hand grenades."

"From where?"

"The weapons are German, French, and British."

"Leaders?"

"The police are moving to arrest Eugene Deloncle, an engineer who consults for the naval shipyards, a suspected ring leader…"

"What was the plan?"

"Paramilitary squads were going to deploy through the Paris sewers and then seize the Palais Bourbon and other public buildings and declare a Royalist dictatorship."

"Audacious."

"Very."

"And the various kings in exile?"

"They deny everything."

"Foreign agents?"

"At least two are on the run…but they're probably back in Rome by now."

"Not the Germans?"

"No, they just use the Cagoulards to smuggle arms to Spain…. They have no interest in supporting insurrection in France at this time—the propaganda campaign is doing their work for them."

"And the assassins?" asked *le chef*. The grisly stabbing of the woman in the metro car last spring still bothered *le chef*.

"They slipped through the dragnet…stashed somewhere in the south of France."

"Yes, they are going to be harder to capture than we initially thought."

"Possibly they're being held back for some special assignment."

"Yes, and their calling card will be a dead body," said *le chef* with real sadness in his voice, hoping that it would not be a woman. The intercom buzzed and his secretary said there was a telephone call from a man who refused to identify himself. Said he had information.

"They all say that," said *le chef*. "Oh, well, put him on the line." He picked up his telephone and held it out into the middle of the desk with the earpiece turned up so *l'inspecteur* could also hear.

"May I help you, monsieur?" said *le chef* with a distracted air.

"I have information on the assassins you're looking for," said a gravelly voice, hard with experience.

"You do?" said *le chef,* and he straightened up and stared at the telephone hand piece.

L'inspecteur put his finger to his lips and mouthed the words that he knew who the voice was. His eyes were bright with expectation.

"Are you a police informant?"

"Lord no, besides, I use better informants than the police. Deeper inside, higher up."

"You pay more?"

"Of course."

"I'm listening, monsieur."

"The knife was OVRA," said the voice, referring to the Italian secret police. "He's back in Rome. The finger was a Frenchman; he's over the border in Spain, in San Sebastian."

"Any others?"

"You're rolling them up." The line clicked dead.

Le chef put the telephone handset back on its cradle and looked at *l'inspecteur*.

"Claude de Roncée," said *l'inspecteur*.

"The industrialist?"

"Yes. And the husband of Thérèse, one of the influence peddlers at the Comité des Forges that we're watching. We have a tap on the committee's phones."

"And?"

"She's one of the wives that Dinckler has had affairs with."

"Over?"

"We don't think so. On going."

"A telephone tap?"

"On her residence. But nothing's come up. As I said, Dinckler is very elusive. Shadows leave more footprints."

"But nevertheless some sheets get rumpled up?"

"Yes, but where is not clear. But the telephone tap, that's how I know Claude's voice."

"Is the tap disclosed to the ministry of the interior?"

"No, just the tap on the Comité des Forges. We don't always follow the standard procedure with the ministry."

"Yes, they share too much with their friends."

L'inspecteur laughed. "Why do you ask?"

"A lot of the industrialists didn't like the Étoile bombings. Too close to home," said *le chef*. "Don't like blowing up the neighborhood."

"That's probably why Claude called. Make sure we keep the pressure on."

13. London

Tuesday, November 30. In the afternoon twilight of a gray London day, a cluster of British and French statesmen stood on the long concrete landing in Victoria Station next to the brown-and-cream Pullmans of the Continental Express. They were bidding farewell to one another after three days of diplomatic meetings concerning the great issues of European high politics. All the men were holding black silk toppers at their breasts and bending over in polite bows and making congratulatory handshakes among the farewells and beaming smiles.

A reporter for a big New York daily stood to one side with other journalists and watched the diplomatic theater, now and again writing something down in his notebook. *Just what commitments had the French gotten out of their British counterparts in these talks*, he wondered.

Train whistles blew, and Premier Camille Chautemps stepped aboard the coach followed by Foreign Minister Yvon Delbos and Secretary General Alexis Léger. On the landing, British prime minister Neville Chamberlain called out, "Good-bye," under flashing dark eyes, raised eyebrows, and an expression of bright good cheer that always seemed to mask some deeper skepticism.

"*Au revoir*," added British foreign secretary Anthony Eden, handsome and debonair.

The Frenchmen returned the farewells and waved. The train moved out with the British delegation standing on the landing waving their top hats. As the train pulled away into the distance, the British statesmen put on their top hats, adjusted them just so, and walked down the landing toward the waiting limousines with the dignified insouciance of aging public schoolboys having gotten the lesson well and truly done.

The reporter from the big New York daily made some more notes in his notebook, tucked a copy of the communiqué issued by the His Majesty's Foreign Office between its pages, and put both in his pocket. He glanced at the train, now in the distance. The French foreign minister was leaving for a tour of eastern Europe in a couple of days. What would he say? Did he really have a solid guarantee from the British about eastern European security?

The reporter walked over to the station café, bought a cup of coffee, and sat down at a table and started to write his story.

He read over his notes: "the common interests of the British and French governments in the maintenance of peaceful conditions in central and eastern Europe...a marked harmony of views, particularly on the prospects of appeasement and disarmament in Europe...the need for 'extended study' of other difficult international subjects..."

The overall theme of the conference was summarized by Premier Chautemps: "perfect and total agreement." In particular, the French were pleased that the British were in complete sympathy to the French formula that any concessions to Germany must be part of a general settlement. The idea of a free hand for Germany in the East was never suggested.

On a negative side, several French insiders mentioned an imperceptible shift in British attitudes on Austria: the British pin current hopes on the belief that Italy may play a decisive role in preventing Austria's incorporation into Germany as it did in 1934. But observers in the know completely doubt this eventuality.

What's missing from the narrative? the reporter thought. He decided to start filling in the blanks. First, there were the reports that the British would add in the near future three motorized divisions to the single one they had recently reorganized. So, at least some officials in Britain foresaw difficulties ahead.

What about central Europe? the reporter thought, chewing on the end of his pencil. Officials on background had told him that the French requested a firm British declaration, a statement that Foreign Minister Delbos could use as evidence of Franco-British unity during his forthcoming trip to eastern European capitals slated to start at the end of the current week. Nevertheless, the British advised Delbos to warn Czechoslovakia to do everything possible to avoid incidents that might provoke Germany. The whispers in the corridors were riven with a sense of weakness.

The reporter wrote out his assessment that the British and French would continue to try to appease German demands, but that both countries were shocked by the bluntness of German demands conveyed to Lord Halifax at his unofficial meeting last month with Hitler at Berchtesgaden where he had gone to sound out the German leader on behalf of the cabinet.

On a happier note, the reporter noted that the French delegation was greatly pleased with the luncheon at Buckingham Palace hosted by the king and queen.

14. Café de la Paix

In the back corner of the restaurant, walls resplendent with red damask wall covering in the Belle Epoque style, sat Geneviève Tabouis in a leathered banquette. She idly stirred her tea and looked across the vacant restaurant and out the windows to the gray wintry day on Place de l'Opéra, a light mist in the air. Her newspaper's Paris offices were just across the square. A trip to eastern Europe was coming up; it sat uneasy on her mind.

She watched as André Géraud, the widely read foreign policy columnist for *L'Echo de Paris*, came through the front door. He wrote under the name Pertinax. She watched as he made a hushed inquiry of the maître d', who turned and nodded toward the corner where Geneviève was sitting. Pertinax followed his eyes, his face lighting up as he spotted Geneviève, and then he wove his way through the tables and over toward her. She stood up as he approached the table and welcomed him. "*Bonjour*, André."

"*Bonjour*, Geneviève," he replied. She sat back down and pulled a notebook out of her handbag and opened it, characteristically ready for business. She gave an order for a coffee to the hovering waiter and turned to Pertinax. "Give me your views on the London conference? Was it the success the papers say it was?"

"Well, yes, the London meeting was a great success because complete solidarity was achieved by the careful avoidance of talking about any differences," said Pertinax with dry understatement.

Geneviève laughed. "What was there agreement on?"

"On all the vague generalities. Britain expressed support for the French position on maintaining the status quo in central and eastern Europe in the face of German demands."

"Good, Delbos can use that to reassure the eastern allies on his coming tour of the eastern capitals?"

"He's leaving tomorrow. Are you going with him, Geneviève?"

"No, I am persona non grata everywhere except Czechoslovakia."

"Why?"

"Because my columns these past six months criticized Poland's and Romania's attempted rapprochements with Hitler."

"Yes, they were clear and sharp. Couldn't Delbos help you with the visas? You are an important French journalist."

"Delbos help me? Heavens no, why he's barred me from the Quai d'Orsay ever since January because of my column on Morocco," she said, mentioning her sensational column about German troops heading to Spanish Morocco to reinforce Franco's insurgent forces in complete violation of the nonintervention pact.

"He didn't like the column?" asked Pertinax, his eyes dancing with delight at the delicious understatement.

"The Bourse went down. A new first for me," said Geneviève with a warm glow of recollection. "The board of directors of the paper tried to get me fired!" She smiled thinly.

"Truth to power. The elect never like that."

"No, they fear the truth."

"Yes, the truth does seem to have a horrible inevitability," said André. "What will you do now?"

"I will go to Prague the following week and catch up with the French delegation there. I'm still welcome in Prague."

"Do you foresee problems for Delbos on this trip?"

"Plenty. That editorial in the London *Times* two days ago completely undercut Britain's public reassurances to Chautemps and Delbos at the London meeting. They weren't even on the train heading back for Paris before the ground was cut out from under them."

"Yes, the Czechoslovakian press caught it right away. The editorial policy of the *Times* is now dictated by a small but influential clique of wealthy men, they said. Called the paper a mouthpiece; so much for England's most venerable newspaper."

"Just like in Paris, a reactionary elite," said Geneviève with scorn in her voice, thinking of the Comité des Forges and other groups representing the Two Hundred Families.

"What do you think the real British policy is?"

"I spoke with someone close to Anthony," said Geneviève in a low and conspiratorial voice, referring to Anthony Eden, "and this person quoted Anthony as saying if we do not get, we shall not give." Britain would demand trade-offs in any general European settlement.

"Yes, he has principles."

Geneviève nodded and then asked, "What about Austria?"

"They feel abandoned by world opinion."

"Yes, Austria's independence is precarious," said Geneviève, "but Austria is the keystone in the arch of keeping freedom alive in eastern Europe. Lose it and…"

"Yes, Austria goes, and Czechoslovakia will be surrounded on three sides."

"That leaves the central question," said Geneviève. "What about Hitler's demand that Germany be given a free hand in central Europe?"

"Yes, the elephant in the room," said Pertinax ruefully. "No, it wasn't brought up in London. But it's out there."

Geneviève laughed. "Probably hiding under the table!"

"Or under the rug."

Geneviève laughed again—brittle and regretful. Then she scowled and said, "Now begins the season of drawing room talk about understandings with Hitler…. Why it's even in the best papers in London…"

"Ultimately leading to a bitter season of regret and morbid fancies about the poor, trampled Austrians and bartered Czechs if those countries go under the Nazi heel," said Pertinax.

15. Hôtel de Crillon

Deep red carpet stretched from one end of the long meeting room to the other; golden yellow damask wall coverings with intricate royal patterns were woven into the rich fabric and provided an aristocratic élan. Large spreading chandeliers illuminated the room with bright light. Underneath the sparkling crystal, small groups of well-dressed men and women chatted while drinking champagne in long flutes. The men wore black dinner dress, starched white shirtfronts, all topped off with crisp black ties. The women were in long gowns, the hems sweeping the carpet.

Thérèse stood next to Carl von Dinckler, beaming with adoration at the German diplomat. Marie Hélène stood at the other side of the small conversation circle and watched as Dinckler spoke earnestly and seriously to some of the French industrialists asking him questions about Germany. Just then a striking blond man with a round face approached the circle with an elegant woman at his side. It was Otto Abetz, head of the Comité France-Allemagne. The jovial Abetz smiled at everyone and waited for a break in the conversation, then said, "Thérèse, you are to be congratulated on getting Monsieur Dinckler to speak. I have tried for months to get him to address our group, and he always begs off about having to attend a trade show."

"Oh, Otto, our group is a business group, so someone with an attaché background is just right," said Thérèse, simply beaming with pride.

Abetz nodded to familiar figures in the circle and then looked at Marie Hélène and said, "Comtesse, so nice to see you again. May I introduce my companion." Abetz held his arm out to the woman accompanying him. "May I present Baroness Reissa von Einem."

"Enchantée," replied Marie Hélène as she held out her hand.

The baroness politely shook hands and then stepped back next to Abetz.

"Comtesse, we never seem to get you over to our committee. You should come with Thérèse some evening."

71

"Ah, my dear Otto, I have a hectic life just maintaining my company's many relationships in Paris as it is. I hardly even have time for my old friends."

Abetz smiled politely and turned to a gentleman standing next to Dinckler and asked a question.

In the front of the room, a man stepped forward near the lectern. In front of him were rows of chairs spread out to seat the audience. He tapped a spoon on a wineglass and said in a voice that would carry to the rear of the room, "Please come take a seat and we will start out program." The man watched as men and women came forward and took seats. As people sat down, the man said, "Let me introduce Thérèse Mathilde de Roncée, baroness de Roncée, of the reception committee who will tell us more about tonight's program." The man walked over to the side of the room.

Thérèse walked up to the front. She was wearing a dark blue gown with a bolero jacket; the bodice of the gown featured finely embroidered edges to a formal décolletage setting off her still alluring figure. She stood facing the audience and said, "Let me welcome you to the Hôtel de Crillon tonight for our holiday reception. Let us have a round of applause for the Taittinger organization for once again providing us with the sumptuous hall to host our meeting." She started to politely clap and all the guests joined in.

"I would like to introduce another member of our committee who will introduce tonight's special guest," said Thérèse as she held out a welcoming hand. "May I present Marie Hélène, la comtesse de Villars-Brancas."

As the guests politely clapped, Marie Hélène came forward, dipped her head in acknowledgment of the applause, and stood standing next to Thérèse, who smiled at her and then departed, moving over to the far wall.

"Thank you very much," began Marie Hélène, "tonight it is the pleasure of the Comité des Forges and our guests to have Monsieur Carl Friedrich von Dinckler, the second secretary of the German embassy here in Paris, speak to us about how the diplomatic outlook appears from a German perspective." Marie Hélène held her hand out toward Dinckler, who was standing off to one side. He took one step forward and dipped his head in acknowledgment. Marie Hélène glanced over at Thérèse; she was rapturous with expectation.

"Monsieur Dinckler was born in eastern Germany into a long established Prussian family with estates along the Vistula River in 1902. After military service in a Potsdam infantry regiment in the early 1920s, he took up his studies and received a doctor of laws degree. He then entered the foreign service, as had his father and grandfather before him. He has served in the embassies of Rome, London, and Paris with stints at the foreign ministry in Berlin. If he looks familiar to some of you, that is because he served as an assistant commercial attaché from the early 1930s up until June of this year. He has just arrived from Berlin, so we will all be privy to the newest information from Germany. Let us welcome Carl Friedrich von Dinckler." She started politely clapping, and Dinckler came walking over and held out his hand. Marie Hélène made a polite shake, a warm smile, and then walked over and stood next to Thérèse.

In front of the audience, Dinckler began his little talk: "I would like to explain the many common interests between France and Germany tonight so that I might further explain how current differences could be resolved and turned into points of common interest and solid relationship." He looked out at the audience; more than a few faces betrayed skepticism. Just as he thought.

"Like France, Germany is indeed fortunate to have its major industrial areas along the Rhine River and in the Ruhr near the French border. These strategic industrial sectors are far away from the East where traditionally the greatest threats to Germany arise." Many of the faces in the audience turned deeply interested; people had thought of that as a strategic weakness, not a strength.

"As the comtesse de Villars-Brancas pointed out, I come from a Prussian family. We have faced horrific and often barbarian assaults from the steppes of Russia for over half a millennia." Marie Hélène was pleased to note that Dinckler's pronunciation of her name was impeccable.

"And today, with a powerful and fearsome new ideology— Bolshevism—in complete control of Europe's largest state— Russia—all of Europe faces new perils." Heads all across the room nodded in agreement, and murmurs of assent trickled up. Dinckler was momentarily startled as he saw Jules Dugas enter the room and take a seat. Well, maybe Dugas wanted to see the public face of what had been discussed privately at the Matignon. *No harm in that,* thought Dinckler.

"In March 1936, Germany reoccupied the Rhineland. Germany immediately began to construct the West Wall—which is very similar to France's Maginot Line and built with the same end in mind—to prevent invasion from across the western border. A strong defensive line in the West gives Germany the freedom to organize its security in the East. Germany learned the lesson of the Great War; no more Western Fronts." Heads turned to one another with smiles of agreement and more murmurs of assent. Yes, lots of common ground.

Over at the side of the room, Thérèse lightly bumped Marie Hélène with her elbow and leaned over and whispered in her ear, "Your new friend is here." Marie Hélène looked out over the audience and saw Jules Dugas sitting toward the rear with an empty chair next to him. She squeezed Thérèse's arm as a thank-you and then walked over and sat down next to Jules, giving him a silent but warm smile of welcome.

"With regard to the East, Germany observes that previous French administrations have tried to hem Germany in with a series of treaties with eastern European countries. This system of treaties—the *cordon sanitaire*—leaves Berlin confused. Is this defense or is it offense? Is it a dagger aimed at Germany's heart?" The audience listened transfixed. A good question.

Dinckler looked out over the audience and was surprised a second time: Marie Hélène was sitting next to Dugas; they seemed to know each other. Rather well. *Very interesting,* thought Dinckler.

Dinckler continued: "So Germany has been trying through various diplomatic approaches to reach new understandings with France and Germany with regard to eastern Europe. The Führer believes he needs a free hand in the East to counter the horrific threats emanating from that troubled and uncivilized region." Yes, Russia and Communism are the big threats facing Europe. Everyone in the room understood that.

"With regard to Austria, Germany feels that German-speaking people everywhere have need for common security arrangements and that they deserve to share prosperity through customs unions and other arrangements." Nothing controversial here. Very hard to stop the Austrians from joining Germany if they want to.

"With regard to Czechoslovakia, there are two concerns. First, there are three million German-speaking citizens in the Sudetenland, second-class citizens often exploited by their Czech masters." The distaste in Dinckler's remarks was palpable. "Second, is Czechoslovakia really its own country, or is it an outpost of Russian Communism right on Germany's border?" Many of the members of the audience leaned back in their chairs. The Communist outpost theory was new and troubling. Very confrontational. Well, thank God, Czechoslovakia was far away. Not like throwing Belgium to the wolves, for example.

"In summary, Germany expects to reach new understandings with France and Great Britain on issues of mutual security in the West in its coming diplomatic initiatives. Understandings that could profoundly affect the establishment of a durable peace in the West." Dinckler watched the audience; they were accepting of his conclusion. Many were obviously relieved. *The French are just not up for more war*, he thought.

"Thank you for having me here this evening. Good night." Dinckler stood and smiled as the audience politely clapped. Thérèse came out and shook Dinckler's hand and said thank you. Then she took Dinckler by the arm and walked him over to an hors d'oeuvre table behind the seats and presented him with a flute of champagne.

"I'm so pleased. Your talk was well received. I'm sure we're at the beginning of a new era in friendship," said Thérèse. The last thing she needed was another war destroying a romance in her life.

"I'm very pleased you feel that way, Thérèse," said Dinckler.

He watched as Marie Hélène came up and held out her hand and said, "Thank you very much, Carl. It was a fascinating talk, full of fresh insights."

"Thank you, Mimi." He looked over her shoulder and saw Dugas chatting with Odette Bonnet, the finance minister's wife, across the room. Presently he saw Abetz come up and take Odette's hand in his and give it a well-mannered kiss, then stand up and reach around and give her a good-natured hug and murmur good evening. He turned to Dugas, shook his hand, and slapped Dugas on the shoulder and bade a hearty good evening. The three chatted amiably with Dugas periodically nodding in agreement. Odette would frequently beam under some light compliment given by Abetz.

Dugas then declared in a voice easily heard by others, "The speaker confirms so many of the things that you have been telling me. It is very reassuring."

"Yes, I trust all the right people will get the message, *mon cher*?" said Abetz.

"I'm sure they will," said Odette. "Jules knows how to work the cabinet room."

"Of course. You can count on me for that. Monsieur Bonnet feels strongly this is the proper course for France to take. Peace counts a lot for him."

"And for Odette, too," smoothly said Abetz, smiling at the bejeweled and gowned middle-aged woman.

"Women hate the war, the entire memory of it," said Odette. "George vividly remembers his front line service during the Great War."

"Yes, so many suffered," said Abetz sympathetically. "That is why we must overturn the lingering injustices from the war, the poisoned legacies from the treaty."

Dugas nodded and said agreeably, "Yes."

Dinckler watched the conversation at a distance out of the corner of his eye as he bantered with Thérèse and Marie Hélène. He noticed that Marie Hélène also kept a discreet eye on the conversation involving Jules. Interesting.

Presently, the Baroness von Einem came up and held Jules by the arm and said, "Germany has no claims on France. It's Bolshevism that's the threat." She looked at Jules with deep sincerity.

"I appreciate that, as do so many in the French government. But not everyone." He smiled agreeably at the baroness and then turned and faced Abetz, adding, "I'd better be taking my departure." He shook hands with Abetz and made a small bow to Odette and the baroness. He turned and headed for the door, taking a quick sidelong glance at Marie Hélène. Then he was out the door.

Marie Hélène watched out of the corner of her eye as Jules was leaving. She waited a couple of minutes and then walked over and held Thérèse by the arm and said, "I'd better be taking my leave. Let's have lunch tomorrow?"

"Yes, by all means," said Thérèse absently, her interest all on Dinckler.

"Good night, Mimi," said Dinckler good-naturedly. He watched her depart. He turned to Thérèse and asked casually, "Your friend, Mimi, she has many gentlemen friends?"

"Very few I would say," said Thérèse. "Always French, usually older. As you know, she has a husband who lives on his estate out on the Moselle River."

"Yes, the absent husband," said Carl as he turned and smirked at Thérèse.

"And the gentleman speaking with Abetz just now?"

"Jules Dugas?"

"Yes, is he a friend of Mimi's, too?"

"You seem to be unusually interested in my friend Mimi?"

"I'm interested in him, not her," crisply replied Carl.

"Oh, in that case, I believe Mimi has dealings with him. He's an aide to the finance minister. She represents the Comité on various issues to the government. She does that for her family company, Compagnie de Marne, also."

"So if I wanted to get a discreet message to the finance minister, I could have you arrange"—he looked at Thérèse with a glowing smile—"to have it delivered through Mimi to Jules Dugas?"

"Of course," said Thérèse.

"And if Dugas wanted to get information to me," asked Carl, "he could deliver it through Mimi to you and ultimately to me?"

"Of course," said Thérèse, a warm smile breaking over her face at the thought of being of valuable assistance to Carl. She so wanted to earn his loyalty. She was meeting Marie Hélène for lunch tomorrow; an excellent opportunity to broach setting up a secret communication channel. She shivered at the excitement of the new adventure.

In a far corner of the room, *l'inspecteur*, dressed like a hotel supervisor, took it all in. His practiced eye saw Dinckler trace the connection between Marie Hélène de Villars-Brancas and Dugas, and he presumed his inquiry to Thérèse de Roncée had something to do with establishing communication through Marie Hélène to Dugas. Maybe here was the beginning of something?

A Betrayal in Europe

16. Prague

The French trimotor aircraft flew several thousand feet above the tiled rooftops of the *Mitteleuropa* city of Prague, capital of Czechoslovakia. Great castles crowned the hilltops; tall spires of a magnificent cathedral reached into the winter sky. Inside the plane, Geneviève Tabouis looked outside with fascination as the plane slowly descended toward the new airport just outside the city. As the plane prepared to land, she tightened her seat belt upon instructions from the pretty Air France stewardess and sat looking straight ahead as the wheels touched down on the new concrete runway. Once on the ground, the plane taxied up toward the long sleek art deco terminal with its new control tower bristling with antennas protruding into the sky. *It is all a marvel*, she thought.

"Will you be continuing on to Dresden with us today?" asked the stewardess, mentioning the nearby city in southern Germany.

"No, I don't think so. I am persona non grata there, to say the least," replied Geneviève with a chuckle. "They'd throw me in a dungeon for sure."

The stewardess looked at her quizzically and changed the subject. "You have business in Prague today?"

"Yes, I'm having dinner with a charming couple, and we will discuss the events of the day. I'm a journalist."

"Well, so much better than a dungeon. Welcome to Prague, madame." The stewardess continued up the aisle.

Hradčany Palace

In the evening, a long black limousine pulled in front of the Hotel Esplanade and stopped. The doorman opened the door and escorted Geneviève across the sidewalk and opened the rear door, and she gracefully slid into the rear seat, pulling her overcoat up close around her in the chill night air. The door closed, and the limousine pulled away and drove through the dark streets of Prague and up to the entrance to the apartments of the Président of the Czechoslovakian Republic at Hradčany Palace. Another doorman stepped forward and opened the door. Geneviève slid out with practiced ease, and the doorman said, "Follow me, madame."

They entered the foyer of the palace, and a tail-coated usher took over and escorted Geneviève toward a drawing room. As they entered, she saw a massive hearth with a great fire blazing away, giving the room a feeling of sumptuous warmth. Tapestries hung on the wall, thick carpets lay on top of deeply shined wood floors, golden yellow light flooded out from white linen lampshades, and deep leather sofas and chairs spread out from the hearth. A middle-aged man approached holding both hands out and said, "Geneviève, so nice of you to come."

"Monsieur le Président," she said deferentially, addressing the Président of the Czech Republic, Edvard Beneš.

"Let's have none of that tonight. Edvard, please."

A middle-aged woman in a long broad skirt approached, neat gray hair in permanent waves, beaming and holding out her hands. "Geneviève, so nice to see you again."

"Madame," said Geneviève in formal reply, holding out her hand.

The woman swept around the outstretched hand and gave Geneviève a big hug. "Geneviève, none of that tonight."

"Yes, Hana," said Geneviève. "It's so nice to see a friendly face."

"You must tell us everything about Paris," said Edvard. "And London. Your impressions about where things stand. Will the English really be with us?"

A black-suited butler approached and nodded at the président.

"Ah, dinner is ready. Let's go into the dining room, Geneviève, and you can tell us all about it."

"My pleasure."

The butler led the way into the grand dining room with a long table. Underneath the far chandelier, three place settings were arranged. The président held the chair and seated Geneviève while the butler seated Mrs. Beneš across the table. The président moved to the head of the table and sat down. A waiter came and poured cool Riesling wine into the tall goblets.

"Now tell us all about Paris? And London?" said Edvard.

"The French got the British to agree that they cannot disinterest themselves in eastern Europe," said Geneviève.

"But not a hard commitment?" asked Edvard.

"Never from the British," said Geneviève. "Except I believe Anthony has a real commitment to collective security."

"Yes, Eden is a good man," said Edvard thoughtfully. "But Lord Halifax's unofficial trip to meet Hitler at Berchtesgaden weakened Eden's position in the cabinet."

"Most likely," agreed Geneviève.

"What about Austria?" continued Edvard.

"Some sort of customs union for sure. Talk about maintaining Austria's independence, but a lot of observers noticed some hidden shift in attitude."

Edvard sighed. "A test is coming. After the Rhineland it was just a question of where." He turned and stared at Geneviève. "Austria is a hard case."

Geneviève calmly waited. Edvard Beneš was regarded as one of the most skilled diplomats in Europe. She sensed the question was coming.

"What about Czechoslovakia?"

"Delbos is going to ask for modifications to the Czech constitution to give satisfaction to the German minority."

"That's what my diplomats report."

"My understanding is that Delbos clearly understands that Hitler wants territory, not better treatment for the Sudetenland Germans."

"Good. That gives me a leverage point in my discussions with your foreign minister."

"And Anthony said that if we do not get, we don't give."

"Good. Another bargaining point."

"Well, you're pretty optimistic tonight," said Geneviève.

"Yes," replied Edvard, leaning back in his chair, a smile of both satisfaction and expectation crossing his face. "When the Germans send me their ultimatum at the end of this summer," he said, "France will come to our rescue."

"Yes, but I would feel better if the Franco-Russian pact were nailed down," said Geneviève. "Russia is the only power in eastern Europe that can truly awe the Germans."

"Yes, but if we can stick together…" The président took a sip of wine and set his glass down to make the point.

"They all say that except—" said Geneviève.

"They?"

"The east Europeans."

"Except?" asked Beneš with an inquisitive look.

"The English."

"Yes, the English," said Beneš with a slightly crestfallen look. *Always the enigma.*

Three waiters came in bearing dinner plates. Other waiters appeared and placed serving dishes on the table. Portions were ladled out. Napkins were unfolded and placed on laps. Forks and knives were taken in hand.

"Now, you must tell us all about what is going on in Paris," said Madame Beneš.

"Well, yes, now, Hana, with regard to fashion…"

Cheb

The train carrying the French foreign minister from Prague for his return journey pulled into the small Czech town of Cheb on the frontier. A large crowd from the small village gathered along the station quay. Geneviève Tabouis slipped off the train and stood among the crowd. Delbos soon appeared on the rear platform of his coach and delivered some remarks to the waiting townsfolk. An interpreter stood next to him.

"There are no two peoples in the world more happily and completely united than are the French and the Czechoslovakians," shouted out the foreign minister.

The crowd applauded, and some whistled in appreciation. *Surely France would stand by Czechoslovakia*, they thought.

"Czechoslovakia is an extension of France. France and Czechoslovakia are one, united and indissoluble," said the foreign minister, his hands slashing at the air to make his points.

The audience members looked at one another: there is a marriage, the union of the two peoples, consecrated by solemn vows. They smiled at one another, their confidence in their security strengthened by the infectious enthusiasm of the French foreign minister.

After some further remarks, Delbos waved to the crowd, beamed a wide smile of benediction, turned around, and stepped back into the carriage. Down in the audience, Geneviève turned and pushed her way through the crowd to the train. She reached up to the handrails with her gloved hands and pulled herself up onto the first step of the four steps leading to the landing. She entered the carriage and made her way to her seat in the comfortable Pullman car.

Geneviève watched as Delbos's *chef de cabinet* came up the aisle, eyes fixed on her.

"Madame Tabouis, the foreign minister sends his compliments and asks if you would like to have dinner with him in his car."

"Of course, I would be delighted." She stood up and followed the aide back to the foreign minister's traveling coach. She walked up the aisle and found Delbos standing up on one side of his dining table waiting to greet her. He held out his hand and said, "Geneviève, so pleased that you could join me."

"My pleasure, Monsieur le Minister," replied Geneviève. She sat down followed by Delbos.

"Yvon, please," said Delbos. "We've been friends a long time, Geneviève."

"Yes, but friendship must accommodate differing points of view."

"Of course," said Delbos.

"Your trip, how has it gone?" asked Geneviève.

Delbos's shoulders sagged. "Warsaw, Belgrade, Bucharest," he recounted, his expression turning bleak as he referred to the first three capitals of his eastern European trip. "I can see now that France is alone. And danger is near at hand."

"Yes," agreed Geneviève. "But Russia is still in play. The Franco-Russian pact takes on new significance," she added. "Even the Germans have to hesitate before taking on the Russians."

"Yes, but everyone but the Communists and the Socialists in Paris hates the idea. They scream 'Bolsheviks! Bolsheviks!' Some of the older conservative Radicals around Bonnet think some sort of agreement can be reached with Germany instead."

"Possibly a fatal miscalculation."

Delbos's face shrank. He shrugged his shoulders fatalistically and then looked at Geneviève. "Who did you see in Prague?"

"First, I met some of the Sudeten German leaders including the infamous Kundt. A real rabble-rouser."

Delbos winced.

"Very Nazi. Blunt and brutal in his replies to my questions," said Geneviève. "I left the interview extremely apprehensive."

"Yes," said Delbos. "First the Fifth Column, then the table pounding, followed up by demands from Berlin about the mistreatment of the poor, exploited Germans."

Geneviève nodded in agreement. "Then I went to the parliament. I spoke with some of the German deputies," she said. "They assured me they were ready to die for

Czechoslovakia, that they were democrats first and Czech patriots above all."

"We'll see," said Delbos. "Democratic sentiment is the first thing to go when times get tough."

"Yes, the Germans will never vote against their blood and their race," said Geneviève.

The two of them talked through dinner, the dark night rushing past the black windows of the Pullman car. They reminisced about earlier and happier times when it looked like collective security and the League of Nations would meet the challenges of modern Europe. There had been such high hopes that first decade after the war.

17. Deuxième Bureau

January 1938. Captain Jacques Morel sat at this desk. He paged through the report from the *secrétariat général* of the High Command. The report concluded that Germany would soon launch a *coup de force* against Austria. A top German general had been in Rome in the previous month making sure there would be no Italian interference with the *Anschluss.* The green light was in place.

Morel pulled another document from a corner of his desk. The document was from a trusted source, a major in the German Abwehr working for Czech intelligence. It was a staff exercise prepared for the German General Staff for an invasion of Czechoslovakia. Interestingly, it planned for defensive operations along the West Wall facing France. The document confirmed a major premise of French strategic thinking: the Germans would maintain a defensive posture in the West as they pursued strategic expansion in the East. So the French generals hoped.

Morel sat at his desk and sipped his coffee. He knew the Deuxième Bureau had been warning since late last year that Germany's next moves would be against Austria and Czechoslovakia. Which one? The report from the *secrétariat général* said Austria.

Austria made sense. Take Austria, and the Germans would flank the Czech Maginot Line, the most formidable obstacle between Germany and Prague. The Czechs would be facing Germans on three sides; never a pleasant prospect.

When? Possibly soon said the report.

Morel picked up the phone and placed two telephone calls. He stood up and left his office and walked along the vast Esplanade des Invalides to the Quai d'Orsay, home of the French foreign ministry.

Upstairs at the Quai d'Orsay

Inside the Quai d'Orsay, Morel walked up the *grand escalier*—the great stairway—always a moving reminder of France's greatness, and then down a long hallway to the Department of Political and Commercial Affairs, the liaison office with the Deuxième Bureau. He nodded a familiar good morning to a secretary and proceeded to the office of Thierry Pruneau, who prepared the daily intelligence summary for the foreign ministry.

"Hello, Thierry," said Morel as he walked in and sat down across from Pruneau's desk.

"Got your phone call," said Pruneau. "What's on your mind?"

"What word does the foreign ministry have on German intentions toward Austria?"

"The Berlin embassy has sent a message that movement against Austria is rumored, but not imminent. Most likely the Bendlerstrasse is not on board yet," said Pruneau, mentioning the headquarters of the German army.

"Who in our embassy?"

"I better not say."

"Of course not," said Morel. Obviously it was from Ambassador François-Poncet. "I won't keep you. I have an appointment across the river." Morel stood up and departed.

Outside, Morel walked along the sidewalk above the River Seine to the Pont de Alexandre III and crossed the river. He walked up to Place Beauvau, past the ministry of the interior, and made his way to the office of *le chef* in the anonymous building of the Sûreté Nationale. *L'inspecteur* was already present.

"We believe," began Morel as he sat down, "that Hitler is going to move against Austria. And soon."

"Yes," said *le chef*. "What else?"

"The Quai d'Orsay confirms this."

"Yes, the dispatch from the ambassador, Francois-Poncet," said *le chef* authoritatively.

"How do you know that?" asked Morel, somewhat surprised.

"From the Quai d'Orsay," said *le chef*.

"We have a tap on the journalist Geneviève Tabouis's telephone," said *l'inspecteur*. "Someone high up in the foreign ministry called her. Probably Léger."

"The secretary general?"

87

"Yes, that's her normal contact. There are others. She knows the whole building."

"Well, the lady is ahead of you again, Jacques," said *le chef* with a chuckle.

"She has better sources than me," said Morel with a laugh. The other two men joined in the laughter. "In Berlin, she seems to know the entire diplomatic community." Tabouis frequently sourced her sensational inside scoops on what was going on in Berlin to various foreign diplomats stationed in the German capital.

"In Berlin, we believe," said *l'inspecteur* gravely, "those are often Germans, high up in the ministries. Not all Germans are Nazis. All this talk about diplomats is to disguise the true sources deep inside the German ministries."

"She really frustrates the Nazis," said *le chef.* "Anyway, when something big is brewing in Berlin, the telephones from Switzerland to Place Malesherbes start buzzing," he said, mentioning the beautiful square in northeast Paris where Tabouis lived.

"And our men start listening," added *l'inspecteur*. "Other sources, other conversations are whispering Austria."

"And our other project?" asked Morel.

"The Führer's social brigade is sipping champagne at the best salons in Paris," said *le chef.*

"And Dinckler?"

"He spoke at a meeting of Comité des Forges last month. He stresses German desire for peace in the West while having a free hand in the East to restore security arrangements lost in the Versailles peace treaty."

"That would have great appeal with that audience."

"It does."

"Personal alliances?"

"Dinckler is carrying on an affair with Thérèse Mathilde de Roncée, baroness de Roncée. She is almost completely apolitical. She's simply smitten."

"Any connections with the French government?"

"With Thérèse, no. But the woman who arranged the talk was Marie Hélène de Villars-Brancas, comtesse de Villars-

Brancas, and daughter of the owner of the Compagnie de Marne."

"That would give her many contacts with the French government."

"Yes, she is close to the Daladier circle at the ministry of defense."

"Of course. The ministry funds the Maginot Line, her family's lifeblood."

"True, but she has now widened her circle of contacts across all of Tout-Paris. She held a reception for Georges and Odette Bonnet when he arrived back from America to be the finance minister. Later she started an affair with Jules Dugas, the *chef de cabinet* to Bonnet. We're not sure whether she just met and liked him or whether she angled for the relationship."

"Ah, boudoir intrigues," said *le chef*, relishing this new information.

"Politics?" asked Morel.

"She's very political. Been in and out of various cabinet beds over the years. Likes the game. Now and again something younger, more exciting, takes her fancy."

"And?"

"She's a close friend of Thérèse."

"Voilà. The connection." The excitement in Morel's voice leaped. "Have we been able to follow a link from Dugas through Marie Hélène and Thérèse to Dinckler?"

"Not directly. We see Dinckler's assignations with Thérèse and Dugas's with Madame de Villars-Brancas, but we do not keep a complete surveillance on all of them all the time. Dinckler is very good at escaping surveillance when he wants to."

"How often is that?" asked Morel.

"Now and again," replied *l'inspecteur.*

"Yes, he could meet people we don't know about," said Morel.

"Yes," agreed *l'inspecteur*. "Dinckler is very elusive. We think he orchestrates the funding of right-wing Paris newspapers through the French subsidiaries of German companies. We know the bank, the banker, the recipients, the papers—everything but the mastermind behind it. And no fingerprints."

"Well, tensions between Berlin and Paris are sure to rise with any move on Austria," said Morel. "The Germans can use the back channel to tell Paris to stay calm."

"Bonnet will lap that up like mother's milk," said *le chef*. He shook his head in disgust.

"There's more," said *l'inspecteur*.

Morel leaned forward and put his elbows on his knees and clasped his hands in front of him and looked intently at *l'inspecteur*.

"The same channel that pays off the newspapers is used to funnel money to Odette Bonnet and Bonnet's personal staff…"

"Including the *chef de cabinet,* Jules Dugas," said Morel, filling in the thought.

"Yes," said *l'inspecteur*. His eyes twinkled, and Morel again looked at him with interest. Something was coming. "The Comité des Forges sends its money to Bonnet through the same channel."

"And Madame de Villars-Brancas is involved with that channel?"

"She controls it. She divvies the cash out to government ministers plus some conservative députés like Reynaud. Few people know that."

"Just who does she pay off?"

"All of them," said *l'inspecteur*. "The Radical ministers, that is. Even the Jews."

"What do they want?" asked Morel.

"Results," said *le chef*.

"Let's keep a close watch on Madame de Villars-Brancas," said Morel. "Dinckler might bypass Thérèse and make direct contact with her—when he goes dark."

"*Cherchez la femme,*" said *le chef* with a wide smile and satisfaction in his voice.

"We are," said *l'inspecteur*. "At a distance. On both women. We can't afford to tip them off that we know about them."

"And Dugas? What do you know about him?" asked Morel.

"He used to work for Chautemps before he shifted over to work for Bonnet."

"Why?" asked Morel.

"We think Chautemps put him on Bonnet's staff as a minder," said *l'inspecteur*. "Bonnet's an innocent. The old bulls of the Radical Party want to keep an eye on him."

"What's so special about Dugas's relationship to Chautemps?"

"Dugas worked for the Paris prosecutor's office back when they were protecting the notorious fraudster Stavisky from prosecution. Stavisky was paying off the whole top echelon of the Radical Party. When the scandal blew up, the prosecutor who had provided the judicial cover was found murdered on the train tracks to Dijon." Stavisky had been at the center of the biggest public corruption scandal in France during the 1930s and was popularly believed to have been murdered by the police during his arrest in early 1934 to keep him from talking.

"Yes, I remember," said Morel. "There was suspicion that people high in the government had the prosecutor killed to silence a witness to the corruption at the top of the Radical Party. He was the key witness."

"Yes, a grisly episode. The prosecutor had been drugged and tied to the rails."

Morel winced at the gruesomeness of the murder. "But what does that have to do with Chautemps? He was the premier. Surely the scandal didn't reach that high, did it?" asked Morel.

"Camille Chautemps's brother-in-law was the chief Paris prosecutor."

"Oh, my God," said Morel. "Corruption meets treason."

"Dugas knows how to play a dirty game," said *le chef*. "On the inside."

"So we have two resourceful men at either end of this espionage channel."

"Yes, it might turn into a dirty game," said *l'inspecteur*.

"I think it's about information," said Morel.

"And money," added *le chef*. "With politicians, always money."

18. Place du Palais Bourbon

Marie Hélène walked into the foyer of the spacious flat and handed her card to the butler. He nodded toward a waiting maid who took Marie Hélène's overcoat, muffler, and hat. The butler said, "They're in the drawing room."

Marie Hélène walked down the hallway and into the crowded drawing room. Spotting the hostess, the Comtesse Hélène de Portes, in the middle of a group of men and women, she walked over. The comtesse was chattering away like a magpie to the group, all seemingly spellbound by the torrent of words pouring forth. Abel Bonnard hovered on the edge of the group, all aflutter, his ear tuned to hear some unguarded gossip if he could, to provoke it if he could not. Marie Hélène saw Geneviève Tabouis standing at the edge of the group, taking it all in.

As Marie Hélène approached, she heard the comtesse's words floating across the room: "Of course Paul would be the best choice…he understands the dangers of deflation…he understands economics…why he's even read the Englishman Keynes…" And she poked the air a couple more times for good measure. She was referring to Paul Reynaud, to whom Hélène de Portes was both mistress and chief promoter. Hélène had dreams of being the power behind the throne when someday Reynaud ascended to the premiership.

Everyone knew Bonnard hung on the words of Madame de Portes because the unguarded comment was her calling card. In a similar manner, he prowled the salon of the Marquise de Crussol for juicy bits about the backbiting intrigues at the top of the Radical Party. The marquise was the consort of Minister of War Édouard Daladier.

As Marie Hélène came up, the comtesse turned and put on a smile and held out her hand and said, "Mimi, so nice you could come." The other members of the circle nodded in agreement.

"Hélène," said Marie Hélène. "Let me not interrupt. I can see you were deep into making your point. But I completely agree; Paul should be the finance minister. The country cries for it."

Hélène beamed with satisfaction. Her ambitions were playing out. "Yes, Mimi, we were talking about the finance ministry. Destiny cries."

"A new government is forming," said Marie Hélène. "His time is coming—soon."

"Yes, but the rumor is that Daladier will eventually become premier of the Radical- led government when Chautemps falls," said a gentleman in the circle.

Bonnard leaned into the circle and said with a conspiratorial whisper, eyes flashing with wit, "You know what they say? Daladier is a reed painted to look like an iron rod."

Laughs erupted around the group. Madame de Portes clapped her hands together in joyful approval. "If Abel says it…it must be true…"

Geneviève smiled benignly; she admired Daladier's honesty but felt that indecision plagued him at moments of crisis. Wanting to put a positive touch to the conversation, she said, "Yes, but the finance ministry is an important place to start."

"I completely agree with you, Geneviève," said Marie Hélène, not wanting to let an area of agreement slip by unremarked. Geneviève nodded in silent agreement.

Madame de Portes, eyes sparkling, continued, "Why I believe, Mimi, you, too, have friends at the finance ministry. The gossip wouldn't lie, would it?"

"My friends in the finance ministry view it the same as you do, Hélène, as a way station toward something grander," said Marie Hélène. "Nevertheless, business interests demand a certain liaison with that ministry for the timely payment of bills…"

"Was that what you were doing when you were arranging your rendezvous with Jules Dugas…a little bill collecting, Mimi?" asked Bonnard with sly innuendo. "Does he pay before or after?" He wanted to chart the low bedroom intrigues of high politics in his novels, rumpled sheet by rumpled sheet.

"Oh, and I thought he was interested in my views on how to pour concrete on the Maginot Line," replied Marie Hélène, and she made a flutter with her hands to imitate the gadfly's most prominent mannerism.

The other people in the circle laughed over the ironic riposte. Moving men around on the political chessboard was the pastime of these women.

Marie Hélène quickly glanced across the room and saw Paul Reynaud holding forth to another group of men and women listening in rapt attention to the former finance minister who now plotted his ascent yet a second time to the powerful ministry. He was one of the leading conservative politicians, but hard to pigeonhole. "Speaking of Paul, there he is. Let me go say hello before I get caught up in the gossip mill," said Marie Hélène, and with a twinkle in her eye, added, "that never lies." She flashed a warm smile to Madame de Portes as she stepped away. Geneviève Tabouis followed her.

Marie Hélène moved across the room. She could see that Reynaud, a quite short man, was standing in his elevator shoes, ramrod straight, his thumbs hooked into his vest, head held high, his thick hair dyed black. He was fit and energetic; he often took a bicycle ride through the Bois de Boulogne at six o'clock in the morning. As she approached, she could hear his words confidently spill forth that "deflation is not the answer...devaluation is an inevitability..."

Reynaud paused and turned toward her. "Always nice to see you, Mimi." He turned to the group and said, "Let me introduce Marie Hélène, comtesse de Villars-Brancas. Of the Compagnie de Marne."

Marie Hélène smiled at the group and then spoke directly to Reynaud, "Paul, I would like to say on behalf of the Comité des Forges that we appreciate your support on the many issues of joint concern."

"Not at all," said Reynaud, beaming.

"We strongly support a growing French economy as the backbone of a strong France," said Marie Hélène.

"We all do," said Reynaud. Geneviève nodded in agreement.

"Oh, there's my friend Thérèse," said Marie Hélène. "I need to speak with her about some committee business. Let me not keep you from your conversation." She smiled and stepped away from the group and walked over toward where Thérèse was speaking with two other women.

"So nice to see you," said Thérèse as Marie Hélène approached. She said sotto voce, "I have a few things to share with you." The other two women smiled at Thérèse and took their leave.

"Yes," said Marie Hélène expectantly. "Further to what we were talking about at tea last week?"

"Exactly. Carl is in agreement."

"Good. Jules is, too. I have the details worked out," said Marie Hélène. Jules was entrusting her with the sensitive task of setting up the back channel to Dinckler.

"Carl wants to have a direct line of communication open through Dugas to Bonnet."

"Good," said Marie Hélène. "Jules wants to keep the messages verbal. Written documents or writings should be avoided except in an emergency. The Sûreté is everywhere."

"Carl will agree with that. How do we communicate?" asked Thérèse.

"When Carl wants to deliver a message to Jules, Carl is to call my house and ask for me or my maid, Mademoiselle Dubois. He is to identify himself with the code word Frederick. She will give him an address, the name of a bistro or bar, and a time. I will meet him there."

"And if you want to contact Carl?" asked Thérèse, hoping she would be part of the chain.

"Jules suggested I either make a contact with you or someone at the German tourism office. We'll identify ourselves as friends of Frederick. Then I can make contact with either you or Carl at a bistro or bar. We need the tourism office as a backup in case of something urgent. In an emergency, Jules will call you directly."

"Fine. I'll get that arranged. I'll tell Carl we're using the code word Frederick."

"Good. And Thérèse, we're trying just to use the telephone to arrange the meetings, not deliver any of the information. It's too sensitive."

"OK."

"Where possible," said Marie Hélène, "I'd like to deliver the messages verbally to Carl. No notes."

"I understand," said Thérèse somewhat uneasily.

"So would you please meet Carl in person and tell him this, Thérèse. Do it in person, not over the telephone."

Thérèse nodded in satisfaction at the prospect of such a meeting. The last one had been sheer delight. She never quite got enough of Carl. A waiter came up with a tray of champagne. Marie Hélène picked one up and said, "I will await the opening move, so to speak."

"Fine."

Marie Hélène smiled good-bye to Thérèse and walked over toward one of the tall windows framed by heavy satin drapes. She looked out through the window panes and across the square to the Palais de Bourbon, home of the French Chamber of Députés and the powerful lower house of the parliament.

Jules had told her that the Radicals were holding a closed-door meeting today at the Palais. The government of Camille Chautemps had submitted its resignation. Chautemps had antagonized the Communists, leading the Socialist Vice Premier Léon Blum to withdraw his party's support, putting an end to the struggling, dissension-riddled Popular Front government that had limped along for the past six months. The Radicals were going to try to form an all-Radical government that would have tacit support from the Socialists.

As Marie Hélène looked across the broad square behind the parliament building, Paul Reynaud came up and stood beside her. "They're meeting over there," said Reynaud.

"Yes, that is what I understand," said Marie Hélène.

"Chautemps is playing a very clever game. As always, he's several moves ahead of the other players."

"Really? Just who are the other players?"

"For today, Bonnet. He's going to try to form a government. The président of the république has given him his opening."

"In that case, he should prevail, shouldn't he?"

Reynaud laughed. "It's all just theater. But Bonnet doesn't see it. He's blinded by ambition."

Marie Hélène stood quiet for a moment. *Well, twisting men's ambitions for other ends is my basic business,* she thought. She looked at Reynaud. "Why?"

"Bonnet is a deflationist—pure and simple."

"Well, that's what it takes to defend the franc, isn't it?"

"The franc is a goner. It needs to devalue," said Reynaud. Marie Hélène knew that Reynaud was the leading proponent of a competitive devaluation. But devaluation would depreciate the value of French government bonds in which so many members of the Comité des Forges held their wealth. Preserving wealth was a crucial property right felt Marie Hélène.

"The Radicals' political power is out in the provinces, the smaller cities and villages, the farmers. They hate deflation," said Reynaud. "On the other hand, a devaluation raises the world price of wheat. And wheat is the backbone of the French rural economy."

"Yes, the farmers," said Marie Hélène with a touch of annoyance.

Reynaud laughed again. "There's one other thing. Blum sent Bonnet a letter and said the Socialists would never support a cabinet headed by Bonnet."

"Blum has a veto then?"

"Yes. The letter's in Bonnet's pocket as we speak."

"Really? But he is going to try to form a government anyway?"

"Yes."

"Why?"

"Ambition."

"What will happen?"

"Bonnet will fail. Eventually Chautemps will form another government. That's been his plan from the beginning. Get rid of the Socialist ministers, put paid to the Popular Front, what little of it that is left. Chautemps's new government will be all Radical ministers but will have Blum's under-the-table support."

"So Bonnet stays at finance?"

"No. Chautemps will take the opportunity to kick Bonnet upstairs and make him minister of state. A grand title but no portfolio."

"Why?"

"The other Radicals will demand it."

"Yes, the farmers," said Marie Hélène with a trace of contempt.

Reynaud laughed. "Yes, the farmers."

"And you move into the finance ministry then?"

"No, I'm not a Radical. Later, most likely after another crisis or two, someone will form an all-government cabinet that will include members from other political parties. That will be my opportunity."

"Who will do that?"

"Most likely Daladier. He's the big horse on the Radical side."

"And Bonnet?"

"Foreign affairs maybe. That's his real interest."

"Interesting."

"It's always that," said Reynaud. "I better get back to the other guests." He turned and departed.

Marie Hélène watched as he walked away. She knew Reynaud was one of the sharpest minds in the Chamber, respected across the political spectrum for his acumen. But he was also besotted with the sharp-elbowed, often crude Hélène de Portes. His vanity was his great weakness. She smiled. Let others worry about the price of wheat; the vanity of men was the currency she traded in.

She walked over toward Hélène de Portes and made a silent wave of good-bye and got a polite smile in return from the busy hostess. She waved at Geneviève and took her departure. She had yet another rendezvous today.

Rendezvous

Lying in someone else's bed, covers pulled up against the chill of the flat, Marie Hélène roused herself from a drowsy half sleep when she heard the door lock open. *Jules is finally home*, she thought. She got up and pulled on a housecoat over her silk sleeping gown.

"Oh, good, you're here. I was afraid you might have left," said Jules Dugas, coming into the flat and hanging his overcoat up in the closet.

"No, I want to be with you. I miss you."

"Good," he said. "Been here long?"

"I was at the salon of Madame de Portes. I came over here right after that."

"Did you get our secret channel going?"

"Yes, Carl will contact me or my maid."

"And how do we contact them?"

"We can contact either Thérèse or a name at the German Tourist Office. She's working on that now."

"Good."

"You took a long time tonight?"

"I'm sorry to be so late. The meeting of the Radical députés went on and on."

"Paul Reynaud told me about it. He explained what he thought would happen."

"What did Paul say?"

"That Bonnet wouldn't get the premiership...too much deflation in his policies..."

"Well, he got that right. Let me get a brandy and I'll tell you about it."

"Here, let me pour the drink for you." Marie Hélène walked over to the sideboard and pulled forward a large wine goblet and pulled the cork out of a bottle of good cognac. She poured a generous amount of the golden liquid into the glass and then carried it over to where Jules had plopped into a chair.

"Thank you." He kicked his shoes off and took a long sip. "Let me tell you. Georges addressed the députés, a good speech for him. But he lacks the common touch."

"Yes, I understand," said Marie Hélène. The beaky nose, the gawky manner, the always too eager to please voice that telegraphed insincerity if not something worse—Marie Hélène had seen it many times.

"So the speaker called for a vote. Bonnet jumped up on a chair, eyes darting across the assembled députés, and he stood there on top of a chair and counted the hands as they voted, disappointment slowly creeping across his face as he saw he was falling short."

"Really. He was that anxious?"

"Yes, sometimes ambition overtakes...his other qualities..."

"That's what Paul said."

"Well, he should know. He's ambition incarnate. And the comtesse de Porte does nothing put promote his political prospects. First for finance and then she'll push for premier."

"Back to your minister. Paul thinks he'll wind up as a minister of state…that the rural members will want him out of the finance ministry."

"Right again." Jules sighed. "But that's all right. Bonnet really wants foreign affairs…and that day will come."

"Paul thought his opportunity would come with Daladier."

"Probably."

"What do you think?"

"Foreign affairs would allow us to pursue a rapprochement with Germany…keep the peace in the West…it's simply crucial to France's future…don't let other people tell you otherwise…"

"I won't…I remember the war…"

He walked over and put his arms around Marie Hélène. "And I remember you without your clothes on. So much prettier than war."

"Yes, I would like to be the goddess of peace…"

"Could I catch a couple of hours of you as the goddess of passion?"

"Aphrodite?" She smiled seductively.

"Don't turn to marble." He pulled his arms back and untied the belt of her housecoat; the front fell open. He reached in and felt the smooth silk of the gown on her hips in the cup of his palms, then slid his hands around back and dug his fingers into her buttocks as he drew her against him and turned his head and leaned down and kissed the upturned lips. She pushed her pelvis into his and let a gurgling sound rise from her throat.

She broke off and whispered, "You're overdressed and it's over late."

"Let's fix both of those," he said and led her into the bedroom. As he undressed, she took off her housecoat and then pulled her silk gown up over her head, the silk making a soft rustle. She got in bed and held the covers open as she watched him remove the last of his clothes. He walked over and slid under the covers.

He leaned over and kissed her breast; she pushed it up into his lips as he nibbled. His hands ran down her body, and he felt her rise up to his touch. She always seemed to quiver like a tuning fork when she was ready for his entrance. He pushed her knee out with his hand, making a wide V and slid over between her legs. He let himself rub between her legs as she reached down to guide him forward toward tonight's consummation.

19. Anschluss

February 1938. In the middle of the night, the telephone rang in the spacious flat of Geneviève Tabouis overlooking Place Malesherbes in a fashionable quarter of northeast Paris. She was hunched over the dining room table arranging her notes for an upcoming lecture. She walked over and picked up the receiver while taking a seat at the small desk on which rested the telephone. Next to the telephone was the always-open notebook for jotting down notes. She listened to the familiar code name given over the phone. She knew the voice—an Austrian diplomat.

"Go ahead," she said. She listened.

"From an absolutely reliable source…" the voice said. She knew the source, a high official in the Wilhelmstrasse, close to the inner circle around the foreign minister.

"German troops will march into Vienna March 12."

"You're sure?"

"Absolutely. He's seen the plans."

"Please send me all the details at once. I'm giving a public lecture the day after tomorrow. The entire diplomatic corps will be there. And representatives from the German embassy," she said. "I'll release the information then. They'll all be surprised"—and she chuckled briefly—"even the Germans." She listened some more.

"Britain?" she said, skepticism dripping from her voice at the mention of France's increasingly unreliable ally to the north. She said heatedly, "Chamberlain precipitated the current crisis when he said last month that England is not concerned with what happens east of the Rhine." Chamberlain's statement had simply flummoxed her when she heard it. She listened to the voice coming out of the earpiece some more.

"Yes, I know. It was an incredible blunder." She continued listening to the voice crackling over the line.

"Yes, I realize what is at stake. Almost two decades of French diplomacy in eastern Europe have been put at risk by Chamberlain." She listened again.

"When Anthony Eden resigned as foreign secretary and Lord Halifax was appointed to succeed him, well, Berlin saw that as a green light," she explained. The previous week the resolute and principled Anthony Eden had turned in his resignation to Prime Minister Chamberlain. Powerful financial interests dominating the conservative Tory party had won; dissenters to Chamberlain's policy had been silenced. Appeasement was now the unchallenged policy of the British cabinet.

"Yes, all the little countries are at risk," she said. "The dream at Geneva is dying," she added, referring to the League of Nations in Geneva and its ideal of peace through collective security. "Yes, Anthony has been the league's great supporter in Britain." She listened for a few moments. "Good night," she intoned, foreboding in her voice. The telephone line clicked dead.

Théâtre des Ambassadeurs

Wednesday, March 2. Geneviève Tabouis made her way down the crowded aisle of the Théâtre des Ambassadeurs just off the Champs Élysées. She took her seat on the stage. The audience gazed up at the slender woman sitting primly in the chair with her sharp-eyed features and graceful composure wearing a small black fore-and-aft hat, a big silk bow at her collar. The audience knew that Geneviève never disappointed; the auditorium was jam-packed. It had been sold out for days. The master of ceremonies tapped the lectern to quiet the audience. He gave a brief background of Madame Tabouis, describing her many sensational headline-making scoops over the past dozen years as a widely syndicated columnist for the Paris daily L'Oeuvre.

The master of ceremonies announced the title of the lecture as "The Austrian Tragedy." He held his arm out in welcome. Geneviève stood and approached the lectern, turning and smiling at the audience as they gave her a warm round of applause. Austria was on everyone's lips. The fate of Austria was dominating worldwide headlines. Would Hitler march on Austria? He had virtually humiliated the Austrian chancellor Kurt von Schuschnigg two weeks ago at a dressing down administered at the Führer's alpine aerie at Berchtesgaden, the Eagle's Nest. Hitler had demanded the virtual Nazification of the Austrian government. Facing imminent invasion—a German general had shown the astonished Austrian chancellor the invasion plans— Schuschnigg had acquiesced, playing for time.

Geneviève now brought the audience to a state of high expectation. Surely the renowned Madame Tata would deliver something sensational? At the lectern, Geneviève looked out over the audience; the entire diplomatic corps was present including members of the Austrian legation filling the first row. Nearby sat the Italian ambassador, the Ethiopian legation, and even a row of secretaries and newspaper writers from the German embassy.

Geneviève began by providing information about rumors of a high-level meeting in Berlin the previous fall when Hitler laid out his plans for the aggrandizement of eastern Europe. While Hitler rapidly rebuilt the German army, she explained, in Britain Prime Minister Neville Chamberlain spoke about hopeful prospects for disarmament and accommodation with Germany. She traced events leading up to the resignation of British foreign secretary Anthony Eden just two weeks ago. She described how in January came the public revelations of secret Nazi plans for a staged revolt in Austria. The plans called for the Germany army to cross the border to prevent German blood from being spilled by Germans, a trumped-up expression of wounded German nationalism so central to the Nazi message. She explained that the same pretext would be used in the case of the three million Sudeten Germans residing in Czechoslovakia.

Leaning forward on the lectern, Geneviève held the audience spellbound as she explained the midnight telephone calls she had received from Germany and Switzerland at the beginning of February. The furtive late night telephone calls described how Hitler had dismissed the heads of the German army and consolidated all military command in his own person, a command solidified by the personal pledges of allegiance sworn by all German officers to the Führer of all the German people. As a final coup, Hitler had replaced Foreign Minister

Neurath with Joachim von Ribbentrop, then serving as Germany's ambassador to Great Britain.

With the dismissals of the heads of the army and foreign ministry, Nazi power reigned triumphant in Berlin, Geneviève explained. Now the march across eastern Europe would begin. She explained that Austria was the keystone to eastern European security, that "the independence of Austria should be maintained for it is bound up with the independence of Czechoslovakia, and it constitutes the basis for the equilibrium in central Europe."

"Then two nights ago I received a telephone call from an Austrian diplomat and he explained that he knew from an absolutely reliable source," Geneviève explained to the now hushed audience, "that German troops would march into Vienna on March 12—the end of next week." The audience gasped almost as one. They sat stunned. Then heads tilted to their neighbors and hurried whispers were exchanged. Electrifying news.

In a seat near the rear corner of the auditorium sat Carl von Dinckler. He took in the news without a visible stir. *Madame Tabouis has good information*, he thought. *Probably accurate.* He thought the original source had to be in the Bendlerstrasse, the army headquarters in Berlin. *Only they would have detailed plans with timetables*, he reasoned.

Standing in another corner of the auditorium next to some policemen was *l'inspecteur.* He watched Dinckler out of the corner of his eye and came to his own conclusions. *Yes, he was a cool one. So cool that he had to be a trained intelligence agent,* he reasoned. He observed that a regular diplomat would have gasped in surprise at Madame Tabouis's revelation, as in fact the German embassy personnel in the front of the audience had done.

Up on the stage, Geneviève thanked the audience for their attention and then descended and made her way up the aisle, the audience standing and applauding. In the lobby where members of the press and other diplomats gathered around her, she was besieged with questions. Monsieur Osusky, the Czechoslovakian minister, pushed his way to the front and asked to see the message. Geneviève handed it over. He was stunned at the detail.

Geneviève stepped away from the diplomats and was beset by her now scandalized society friends, standing in fashionable dresses and long fur coats. "Ladies, you do me the honor of attending my lecture," she said with a touch of sarcasm. The ladies had been quite cold to her in recent months as Geneviève recounted one sensational scoop after another as European politics rolled toward jarring new uncertainties.

"Geneviève, why must you persist in your unfortunate habit of spreading bad news?" asked Comtesse Hélène de Portes. "My dear, you must be mad! Why, with such talk you'll make the Bourse go down!" she said, referring to the stock exchange, never far from the thoughts of the Paris elite.

Next to her, the Marquise de Crussol asked, "Have you thought of the responsibility you take on yourself by announcing such alarming news? One has no right to frighten people like that." The marquise put on her most affronted look.

Next to Crussol stood another marquise who reproached Geneviève. "Really, Geneviève, my dear, you're becoming absolutely impossible! Whatever you do, please don't talk about all this when you come to lunch tomorrow. My dear friend Senator Caillaux, the leader of the Senate, will be there."

"I would not dream of bringing up the matter, my dear," said Geneviève, who was dismissive of the Senate leader, an aging wunderkind who had brought Popular Front prime minister Blum's government down rather than put the interests of France ahead of his own partisan hatreds. But then that was the Senate, she reflected, a collection of has-been politicians from the provinces. "Dare that I disturb such received opinions from such an eminent politician," she said in her patrician tone, a mocking lilt to her voice.

The three ladies nodded absently at Geneviève while looking around themselves nervously; they were becoming aware of the crowd's warm reception to Geneviève's startling revelations, a reception that suggested the public was buying into the new realities hurtling through time toward them, messages delivered by Europe's leading Cassandra.

"Until lunch, ladies," said Geneviève breezily, and she took her departure.

Alpine Threats

In the Villars-Brancas town house deep in the heart of the Faubourg Saint-Germain, the maid answered the telephone and responded, "No, madame is not here." She listened.

"Yes, this is Mademoiselle Dubois speaking." She listened.

"Is this Frederick?" She paused and waited for an affirmative answer.

"Yes, I have a message for you. Café Les Deux Magots. Four o'clock." She hung up.

In a nearby basement, a policeman put down his earphones and conferred with his colleague. "Sounds like a code word and a rendezvous. Les Deux Magots. Four o'clock."

Les Deux Magots

Carl von Dinckler walked through the thick glass doors of the Café Les Deux Magots in the late afternoon gloom. It had been easy to slip the routine surveillance. He looked around and saw Marie Hélène de Villars-Brancas sitting at a small table in a back corner. He didn't notice the man upfront reading the paper and taking his coffee. He walked over and sat down; he did not remove his overcoat, muffler, or hat. "Comtesse," he said by way of introduction. "So nice to see you today."

"Yes, I feel that way, too. Please, Mimi."

"Yes, of course. We're friends. You have something for me?" he asked, rather brusquely, she thought.

"My source says that General Gamelin spoke with Daladier," she said, mentioning the minister of defense, "and provided a detailed account of the Hitler-Schuschnigg meeting at Berchtesgaden. The general and the minister decided that unlike the Rhineland crisis, this time France has to do something if Germany goes into Austria."

"Anything else?"

"No, he felt you ought to know. Avoid misunderstandings."

"Yes, I agree. Thanks. I'll get this information into the right hands. Anything else?"

"No."

"I better leave. Maybe next time we can talk more." He smiled warmly at her, charm lighting up his eyes.

"I'd like that," answered Marie Hélène. "I really would." Carl stood up and walked out of the café.

Café le Dôme

Carl von Dinckler walked into the bustling café late in the afternoon and looked into the rear corner of the cavernous restaurant. She was sitting there, stirring a small cup of coffee, her overcoat draped over the top of a nearby chair, the brim of a fashionable hat sweeping in front of her forehead. He walked across and sat down, leaving his hat and overcoat on. He hooked his umbrella over the top of the chair on which her overcoat was draped.

"Mimi, nice to see you again."

"You, too, Carl."

"I got your message. Through Thérèse."

"You're worried about my delivering messages through Thérèse?"

"No, I much prefer it to leaving messages at your residence. I would prefer contacting you very discreetly or very indirectly." He looked furtively over his shoulder.

"I see."

"And?"

"The government submitted its resignation last night..."

"Yes, I saw that in the papers this morning...strange...in the middle of a possible diplomatic crisis...to leave caretakers in charge..." said Carl, a slight look of perplexity crossing his face at the disarray in the French government.

"The senior cabinet met this afternoon. The words I was told to tell you were 'no military measures are to be taken.'"

"And Britain?"

"I don't know."

"I better get this to the proper channel right now." He stopped and looked at her, his eyes lighting up in friendship. "Possibly we can share a meal together next time?"

"Yes, I would like that."

"That would be good. Somewhere out of the way. We could have dinner?"

"Yes, I think I know where."

He reached across the table, picked up her hand, and gave it a faint kiss.

"Next time," she said, catching her breath while she thought about the daring of her own idea. She had never shared this hidden place—this very private retreat—with anyone but her maid. "There's a little Russian bistro called Kozlov on the corner at Rue Pierre Leroux and Rue d'Olivet. Go there. Ask for Madame Dubois."

"Not Mademoiselle Dubois?"

"No, madame. That's how they know me. They'll get me. Very discreet, very indirect. No one but my maid knows about it."

"Excellent." He stood up and said, "*Au revoir*." He turned and departed, very businesslike.

Quai d'Orsay

Captain Jacques Morel walked down the hallway on the second floor of the foreign ministry to the Department of Political and Commercial Affairs. He waved to the secretary as he passed her desk and then turned into the office of Thierry Pruneau, his intelligence liaison.

"What was so urgent?" asked Morel with regard to the excited conversation he had had with Pruneau earlier in the morning.

"*Le cabinet noir*," said Pruneau, referring to the foreign ministry's highly regarded cryptanalysis intelligence agency, the "black office" in English, "broke an important cable this morning from Ambassador Welczeck to Berlin. He was in a hurry. They used a low-level code."

"And?"

"France will protest and no more. Cabinet level. That's the message."

"Anything else?"

"Isn't that enough. There's a high-level leak right in the cabinet. Maybe in this building."

"Yes."

"You don't seem unnecessarily bothered by this."

Morel smiled thinly. "I better not say more."

Pruneau bit his lip in consternation but said no more. Morel stood up and departed.

Hôtel Matignon

March 12, Saturday morning. In the small study off the premier's office in the Hôtel Matignon, Chautemps took a seat at the head of the table as Foreign Minister Delbos and Finance Minister Bonnet took theirs. At the other end of the table, Minister of Defense Daladier organized some papers and then provided a summary of events.

"Yesterday, I spoke with General Gamelin and told him that at this time no military measures were to be taken until London was heard from. But that we should be ready to execute those military measures already envisaged conditional upon receiving word from London."

"Yes, we have asked for Britain's collaboration on the Austrian issue," said Delbos, speaking for the foreign ministry. "A common position is much desired." His very posture indicated that he expected no action to come from London. Just more of the English perfidy.

Bonnet carefully listened to the discussion. *What are the military measures envisaged?* he wondered. If Britain had not supported France two years ago on the remilitarization of the Rhineland, why should France expect a different answer this time? Everyone knew Germany was too strong. There could be no question of military hostilities. He looked around the table— the lack of resolve to take action was palpable.

Quai d'Orsay

March 12, Saturday, four o'clock in the afternoon. The aide walked into Secretary General Alexis Léger's large office in the Quai d'Orsay with a message in his hand.

"Message from London, monsieur."

Léger reached out his hand, a sense of weariness across his face. He took the teletype message and began to read. The message was simple: Britain would make a vigorous protest to

Berlin that military occupation of Austria involved serious violations of treaties.

Léger sighed. He looked at the aide and smiled weakly. Unfortunately, this is what he expected—talk and more talk. The aide stood still, waiting for an instruction.

"Thank you," said Léger to the aide. "Please call my limousine. I'm going to the Matignon. The government must be immediately informed. They're meeting."

Palais Bourbon

March 12, Saturday, six o'clock in the evening. In the Salle Colbert, a large private meeting room in the Palais Bourbon, a tall man, slightly stooped and with a droopy mustache, moved to the front of the room. Earlier that day, the stooped man, Léon Blum, had put together a parliamentary majority of the parties of the Left—the Communists, the Socialists, and the Radicals—to form a government to succeed the now departed Chautemps cabinet. But in this time of national crisis, Blum felt that a government of National Union was required to show solidarity in the face of the Nazi threat in central Europe. As the Socialist prime minister of the Popular Front government from June 1936 to July 1937, he had conducted the affairs of state with integrity in the view of almost all observers, a leader able to set aside his own views to represent the wishes of the broad consensus of the political majority, a master of leading unruly coalitions.

Sitting on a front bench, the leader of the conservative centrists, Paul Reynaud, watched Blum move toward the speaking tribune. Reynaud, a great admirer of Blum's intellect if not always of his policies, felt that Blum was the true aristocrat of French public life and deserving of his eminent reputation.

From another seat, conservative journalist and political jeremiad Henri de Kérillis also watched as Blum moved across the floor. An implacable anti-Communist, he nevertheless understood the need for the Franco-Russian pact. He felt that military collaboration with Soviet Russia was the only strategy likely to contain Nazi Germany. As a journalist, unlike many others on the Right, he led a fierce campaign against Hitlerism.

At the speaker's tribune, Blum shuffled some papers, made opening remarks, and then began to speak: "Gentlemen, now is the time for another government of *union sacrée*," said Blum, harkening back to the great sacred union coalitions that governed France during the Great War. "The parties of the Left are in agreement that there should be general unity. Vienna has been taken, and it is evident that the German troops will next seize Prague, and after Prague, Paris! Let us unite to form a government of National Union."

Reynaud watched with a dispassionate gaze for the storm that he knew was coming from the Far Right. Sure enough, Far Right députés jumped up, waving their arms, and shouting, "Down with the Jews! Blum the warmonger!" Pandemonium spread across the room.

Blum, nonplussed, waited and then turned to the leader of the Far Right, former premier Flandin, and said, "If you wish, as a sign of my good faith, you can even choose your own minister of finance."

Flandin stood up, flushed and angry, and answered, "No, we do not want to have anything to do with your Communist government…" He stood there sputtering.

Paul Reynaud saw his opportunity, and he now stood up and stepped out into the open space in front of the tribune. He turned and spoke to all the assembled députés. "It is not Stalin," he said, mentioning the dictator of Soviet Russia, "who enters Vienna today, who will menace Prague tomorrow. It is Hitler…I say today—France must stand united."

A number of députés arose and stepped forward and addressed the députés. They too supported Reynaud's impassioned appeal.

Flandin now stood and spoke again. "Another Popular Front government will only aggravate our relations with the fascist dictators, and worse, displease the Tory government in London."

A Far Right député jumped up and shouted, "War must be prevented at all costs, because war will bring the triumph of Communism." Cheers and clapping accompanied this rant.

Flandin, nodding in agreement, continued, "The time is coming when it will be recognized that we are all in danger from only one thing—Communism. We cannot join a government that includes Communists."

Blum, undaunted, looked up and said, "The country needs the cooperation of the entire working class. You cannot exclude the Communists from a new 'sacred union.' National salvation demands the collaboration of all."

Blum could not believe that the députés would not put the interests of France ahead of partisan rancor. He said in conclusion, "Thank you for letting me speak to you on the needs of the nation this evening. I leave you to your deliberations."

A number of députés stood up and came forward to shake Blum's hand. Henri de Kérillis, speaking across the partisan divide, said, "Monsieur Blum, you are a great Frenchman."

Blum departed from the center of the room and made his way to the door and the hallway beyond, a uniformed usher closing the massive door after him.

After Blum was gone, another député stood and shouted, "Down with the Jews! Down with the warmongers! Down with Blum—hang him on the gallows!" Others nodded and clapped in agreement.

Eventually the vote was taken and Blum's call for a government of national union was defeated by a vote of 152–5. Kérillis was simply stunned. He stood up and walked over to Reynaud, who was saddened but not really surprised. Kérillis said, "Well, all I can say is that it was the most disgraceful parliamentary secret session I ever attended."

"They're acting like children," said Reynaud. The two men walked out of the room and departed the Palais Bourbon into the dark and wintry night.

Café Kozlov

March 12, Saturday, eleven o'clock at night. Carl von Dinckler opened the door to the Café Kozlov on Rue Pierre Leroux and was met with a rush of Russian music and singing. The thronging crowd was making boisterous Saturday night conversation, much of it shouted over the sound of the music. He went up to the small desk by the entrance and spoke to a dark-haired woman with sparkling black eyes and wearing gold earrings like a Gypsy. She wore a traditional long-sleeved embroidered white blouse and an ankle-length black skirt coming down on top of shiny black boots. He asked after Madame Dubois and got an understanding nod and warm smile. "This way," the woman said, and she led him over to a small table in a back corner. "I will get her." She walked across the room and into the kitchen. In moment she came back out, looked over at him, smiled, and nodded. He waited.

Several minutes later, he saw Marie Hélène enter from the kitchen into the dining area. She walked straight over to where he was sitting and sat down without further ado. A waiter came over, and Carl ordered some wine for both of them.

"I'm afraid my news will send you scurrying off. We will have to come here for dinner some other time."

"Yes, the tempo of events is racing."

"The ministry of defense has the Maginot Line manned throughout, but it is exclusively for defensive purposes."

"Yes, that is sensible," said Carl.

"No other military measures are planned," said Marie Hélène, and she paused and looked intently at Carl. "Unless there is a German attack on Czechoslovakia. Jules wanted me to emphasize that."

"Yes, I understand. I'll communicate that clearly."

"Good. There's more. Blum is forming another government, but it's weak, a Popular Front leftover. There was a meeting tonight in the Palais Bourbon, and Blum appealed to the conservative députés for a national unity government."

"And the Right did not go along?"

"Reynaud and other leaders of the Right were sympathetic, but after Blum left, the debate erupted into shouts about not joining the Communists and Socialists."

"Who turned the tide?"

"Flandin," she said, mentioning former premier, foreign minister, and conservative warhorse Pierre-Étienne Flandin.

"Yes," said Carl thoughtfully. He well knew that Flandin had been to Berlin the previous December and had spoken with many of the top Nazi leaders. They gave him the full show. German power had deeply impressed him. In the opinion of the Wilhelmstrasse, Flandin understood the need for accommodation, Weizsäcker had written him. Carl took a sip of wine and added, "Flandin knows the importance of peace."

"Yes, that's what Jules says."

"You're right, though, about the urgency of the information. I must leave and communicate this to my superiors."

"I thought so," she said and smiled while her eyes flashed her bright interest in him.

"Until next time," he said. "And there will be a next time, I promise you. If only for dinner."

"And possibly I can promise more," she said, eyes twinkling, as he stood up to leave.

Avenue de Tourville

March 13, Sunday. Captain Jacques Morel sat at his desk early in the afternoon looking over the signals intercepts of telephone traffic to Berlin from France. There was the transcript of the telephone tap on a German agent calling from Paris to Berlin. The Berlin number was believed to be German military intelligence. The call had been placed at 1:20 a.m. that morning.

The first paragraph in the transcript observed that the French army was manning the Maginot Line throughout, but exclusively for defensive purposes. Morel observed that the paragraph shouted "no action" to anyone reading the information in Berlin.

The second paragraph said that no military measures were expected from France except in case of an attack on the Czechs. Morel understood that this piece of intelligence was of strategic importance. The Germans would get a pass on Austria this time, but any German move on Czechoslovakia might bring forth a French military response. Morel thought that commonsense would dictate that Germany digest its assimilation of Austria before challenging for Czechoslovakia.

Morel leaned back in his chair and thought, Yes, the Germans have a source quite close to the top of the cabinet, a source who was able to get the information out unusually quickly. He was pretty sure about the source, but not how it got to Dinckler so quickly.

There was a knock on the door, and one of Morel's aides hurried in and handed him another page of intercepts. The aide said,

"Decrypt of a message from Ambassador Welczeck to the Wilhelmstrasse that went out this morning."

Morel took the carbon flimsy of the decrypt for his file. He read it: "France will do no more than protest. They are resigned to the Anschluss." Morel waved his aide into a chair across from his desk.

"This is probably based on the same intelligence as the telephone call to Berlin last night," said Morel to his aide. The aide nodded in agreement.

"Austria is over. The contest moves on to Czechoslovakia," concluded Morel. His face fell as he thought of the impossible geographic position in which Czechoslovakia now found itself. It would be surrounded by German military power on three sides. *An almost impossible military problem,* thought Morel. His aide's expression changed to one of concern as he read Morel's thoughts. Morel looked at his aide and put on a positive smile of optimism. He said with playful firmness, "We must keep a proper attitude here. No discouragement."

"Yes, *mon capitaine*," said the aide, and he stood up and departed, his face now resolute.

20. Place Malesherbes

As the guests arrived, they were shown into the drawing room overlooking Place Malesherbes by Arthur, the manservant for Geneviève Tabouis. The elegantly appointed room was rich with antiques from the several reigns and empires of France. Clustered in groups were European diplomats and an assortment of international journalists. Geneviève moved from cluster to cluster, welcoming and chatting.

"For our table today, we are going to have Henri de Kérillis. He is my guest for the first time," she said, mentioning the nationalist député from the wealthy Parisian suburb of Neuilly. "Now Henri and I see domestic politics from quite different perspectives—as you know, I am a great believer in the Third Republic—while Kérillis is contemptuous of parliamentary democracy. But Henri and I are in complete agreement on patriotism and tradition. He is a fierce critic of Hitlerism, and while no friend of Communism, he champions the military collaboration with Russia as one of the few strategic avenues open to France in this troubled time."

"Why does Kérillis believe this when so many others on the Right do not?" asked one of the journalists.

"We both see the Russian alliance as the key to peace."

"How so?"

"If we cannot cement the alliance, then inevitably war will break out."

"There's no other alternative?"

"None that is visible," said Geneviève. "Worse, if war breaks out and there is no alliance, France would be at a horrible disadvantage."

"And Britain?"

Geneviève remained silent and made a light smile. Other faces around the room broke into knowing smiles. Yes, a hard road ahead. Would Britain be there?

Suddenly, there was dead silence. Austrian press attaché Martin Fuchs entered the room. Everyone stood still. Fuchs moved to the center of the room, mildly bewildered, and began to speak in a hollow voice as if he were caught in a bad dream. "Schuschnigg preferred to give in to Germany," said Fuchs, referring to the Austrian chancellor, "rather than abandon his country. He is beginning a long martyrdom." Schuschnigg had been promptly arrested by the Nazis; they had murdered his predecessor Engelbert Dollfuss in 1934 in a failed putsch. Hitler despised all other leaders in the German-speaking world; there could only be one sun in his German universe.

"When will Austria regain her place in Europe?" plaintively asked Fuchs, despair in his voice, bleakness across his face. He looked around the room. Not a head moved, not a lip quivered. No one knew the answer. There is no light when one enters a long dark tunnel.

Again the room fell silent. Henri de Kérillis entered the room.

"Were you at the secret meeting at the Palais Bourbon Saturday night?" asked a British journalist of the French député.

Kérillis nodded in the affirmative.

"Yes, please tells us about it," chimed in an American. The diplomats all looked on inquisitively, too discreet to be anything but polite.

"You want to know how Parliament responded to the Anschluss?" he burst out, worry and exasperation in his voice. "Well, all I can say is that it was the most disgraceful parliamentary secret session I ever attended." Kérillis went on to describe Blum's appeal to the Right députés. "Well, then bedlam broke loose. Shouts, howls, and vile remarks directed at Blum filled the air."

Geneviève nodded in understanding agreement. Two years ago, she had been following Blum's car up a street on the Left Bank when it was attacked by Rightists from a passing parade and he was pulled from the car, and before Geneviève's disbelieving eyes, stabbed and almost killed before some construction workers hauled him to safety. The intensity of blood hatreds on the Right had to be seen firsthand, felt Geneviève.

"What did they say?" asked one of the journalists.

"Down with the Jews! Down with the warmongers! Down with Blum—hang him on the gallows!"

The people in the room stood stunned. Kérillis drove the point home: "This was the way the députés of the Right carried on while the Germans were taking possession of Vienna."

"Why do they feel that way?" asked the British journalist with cool detachment.

"Flandin repeats every chance he gets that we are in danger from only one thing—Communism!"

"But what of the Germans?" asked the American.

"They say war must be prevented at all costs because war will bring the triumph of Communism. The Germans are never considered."

A possibly fatal omission, thought the American.

"Yes," concluded Geneviève, summarizing the conversation, "the opportunity for a national unity cabinet has been missed a second time." Arthur stood at the entrance to the dining room and made a small hand motion. Geneviève turned to the guests and said, "Luncheon is served." She led the group into the dining room with its long table and many chairs and an afternoon of worrisome discussion.

Café Les Deux Magots

In the late afternoon, Marie Hélène threaded her way through the crowded tables inside the café toward a small table in the rear where Carl von Dinckler was sitting reading a copy of the newspaper *Le Temps*. As she approached, he stood up and extended his hand toward the empty chair in a gesture of welcome.

"So nice to see you, Mimi."

"Nice to see you, Carl."

"Possibly later this evening we could meet for that dinner?"

"Yes," said Marie Hélène, slightly taken aback that Carl was putting pleasure one step ahead on the agenda today. "Yes, possibly at Café Koslov."

"That would be very nice." He took a sip of coffee. "Now, about business."

"Monday, Blum invited Monsieur Osusky to the Matignon for a talk. He and foreign minister Paul-Boncour assured the Czech minister that France would honor its treaty commitment to

Czechoslovakia and come to her aid if she were attacked by Germany."

Dinckler nodded in understanding and murmured, "Yes." The Germans knew of the meeting from other sources. Count Welczeck had cabled Berlin Tuesday that Blum had used the words "binding pledge" and crucially added that France would act without waiting for either the League of Nations or Britain. The "period of inaction is to end" wired the ambassador. France under Blum was taking a harder line.

"But will the next French government stick so closely to this pledge?" asked Carl, his question indicating his belief probably not.

"For now, the French government seems committed. They want to reassure Czechoslovakia," said Marie Hélène. She saw that Carl understood France's surface commitment, but she suspected that he did not have insight into the depth of uncertainty plaguing the highest levels of the French government. "Jules wanted me to describe his impressions of the meeting of the National Defense Committee. The generals were very discouraging. France is not ready for war—anywhere. It has no means to go to the aid of Czechoslovakia."

"Yes, but what about Russia?" asked Carl. He let the question hang in the air since it was the one big strategic card France had to play in this geopolitical card game.

"There was a meeting at the Quai d'Orsay with the Russian ambassador yesterday. The Russians wanted to call a conference to discuss ways to stop German aggression."

Carl nodded in understanding. "Yes, your ambassador to Russia urged your government to take up the Russian offer as a way to secure Russian aid to Czechoslovakia."

"Yes."

"That would require France to begin military talks with the Russians to bring the Franco-Russian pact to life," said Carl. French governments had been avoiding this for four years. It was unlikely the French would start now.

"Yes," replied Marie Hélène. "But Jules wanted me to emphasize Foreign Minister Paul-Boncour's words to the Russian ambassador. He said the Russian proposals were 'interesting' and that they would require 'thorough study and painstaking research before they can be given practical expression.'"

Carl leaned back in his chair, took a sip of coffee, and let a smile build across his face as he took the full import of the diplomatic double-talk. "Yes, close collaboration with the Communists is not possible for a French government, even one headed by Blum." In his own thoughts, he mused that the French generals had done their work well; they had scared the government into inaction. He would report that to Berlin. There was little unity at the top of the French government. He had been instructed by the Wilhelmstrasse to keep a close eye on this issue.

"I, of course, want a rapprochement with Germany in the West," said Marie Hélène.

"The old line Prussians, the diplomatic corps, the industrialists…many parties in Germany want that, too," said Carl.

"Good. Now about that dinner?"

"Yes, where?"

"Can we meet at Café Koslov?"

"Yes, let me go back to the embassy and make my report. How about around eight o'clock?"

"I'll be there," said Marie Hélène, a bright smile on her face.

Dinner for Two

Carl von Dinckler arrived at the Café Koslov just before eight o'clock in the evening. Coming through the door, he was again greeted by the hostess with the black luxuriant hair. A bright red cupid's bow was painted on her lips and contrasted with her white powdered cheeks; the dangling gold earrings made for an exotic look. The black hair shined. Yes, a Gypsy. With a flounce of the black hair, the hostess nodded toward a far corner of the little café, and Carl's eyes followed to where he could see Marie Hélène, a black satin cape trimmed with red silk around her shoulders, a large blue jeweled pendant hanging from a silver necklace that gently pushed the dark wool turtleneck sweater into a valley between her breasts, and a black béret on her head. She was sipping a cup of tea and looking at him with a warm smile of welcome. He was enchanted.

A few other couples were scattered about the café; it was quite early for a Left Bank dinner. Carl walked over toward Marie Hélène. She stood up as he approached. He held her by the shoulders and kissed each cheek, whispering, "Good evening. You look simply fetching tonight. A Gypsy aristocrat, perhaps?" She laughed at the compliment as she sat back down. He took a seat across from her.

"You got the information safely delivered?"

"Yes. It will be on its way to Berlin shortly." He reached over and clasped her hand in both of his, sincerity in his voice. "It is important to tell Berlin how strongly the French feel about Czechoslovakia. New arrangements in the East must be worked through step-by-step so the countries in the West can come to fully appreciate that Germany seeks stability in the East so it can pursue peace in the West."

"Yes, I understand. A strong bulwark against Bolshevism must be built in the East."

"French security as much as German security depends upon that," said Carl.

"Jules says the British can't be counted on when it comes to eastern Europe."

"Yes, I'm sure he's right," said Carl, "and we cannot let a Communist army from Russia go and 'save' Czechoslovakia. You would never get them out."

"I understand. Jules says that is one of Poland's biggest concerns."

A waiter came up and murmured, "Madame Dubois...welcome again...and monsieur..." And he looked at Carl.

"We'll have a bottle of good Bordeaux," said Carl, and he looked at Marie Hélène for a sign of approval.

"*Bien sûr,*" she whispered. Of course.

"And may I recommend the special tonight..." said the waiter.

"Yes. We'd be delighted," said Marie Hélène, and she looked at Carl for affirmation.

"Of course," he said.

The waiter took a large candle floating in scented water from a nearby table and set it in the middle of the table. He lit it with a big stick match. He looked at Carl and said, "It makes her eyes even more beautiful." He smiled and left.

"He's right," Carl said. "You're beautiful tonight."

"And you're charming."

"Diplomats are supposed to be."

"Are you really a diplomat?"

"Yes."

"Not a spy?"

Carl laughed. He leaned across the table and said, "Every bit of information I get goes back to the Wilhelmstrasse, to the permanent secretary or the foreign minister. That's what diplomats do."

"I see."

"And work to avoid misunderstandings between two countries, two different peoples."

"And do you get much information from Thérèse?"

Carl laughed. "Oh, that's it, is it!"

"Well, is it?"

"Her husband, baron de Roncée, owns many industrial companies. When I was commercial attaché, I worked to put him in contact with the French subsidiaries of German industrial companies. They were interested in working with him in conjunction with some of the industrial companies in which he has interests in eastern Europe."

"Eastern Europe again?"

"Yes, it's a real interest of ours. Beyond the shouting."

"And the baroness?"

Carl laughed. "Well, I could hardly push her away…you know that…"

"Yes, I guess I do."

"I've never asked about you and…"

Marie Hélène quickly put her hand up to silence Carl. "Please don't."

"OK."

"I want to know if you're interested in me…or am I just another ticket to industrial plants in eastern Europe? Today's romantic conquest leading to tomorrow's acquisition…"

He laughed. "A ticket?" Carl leaned back and relaxed. "I was thinking more like a magic carpet." He turned thoughtful and mused, "A conquest…" He let the words hang in the air.

"Good." She smiled in contentment; she got the answer she wanted. "Let us enjoy our dinner together," she said as she watched the waiter approach with two steaming plates of Russian stroganoff.

The two of them chatted about this and that during dinner. She told him about marrying le comte after the war, and he told her about growing up on his family estate east of Berlin. He let her know that his sympathies were deeply rooted in the Prussian aristocracy and the industrial elite. As they ate, the café filled up. A Russian came out and sat on a stool on a small stage and began to sing mournful ballads while he strummed his guitar, now and again breaking into virtuoso guitar solos of fast-paced rhythm and dazzling chord work, his fingers racing across the frets.

At the end of dinner, the bottle of wine nearly empty, the waiter cleared away the dishes and asked after coffee.

"No, we have other plans, I think," said Marie Hélène. She drilled a look into Carl to silence any comment. He was a bit taken aback at this unexpected development, but remained quiet; she let the waiter walk away.

"My atelier is nearby. We can have a cognac there."

"Yes, I would like that," said Carl. "I didn't know you had a workshop. What do you do?"

"This and that. It is my own. It is in the name of my maid. No one knows I have it. That is why everyone calls me Madame Dubois here. No one knows me in the neighborhood, either."

Carl made mental notes. Yes, she had been correct: very discreet, very indirect. *A hideaway could be very helpful—or a double-edged knife,* he thought. He watched as she looked around, somewhat furtively.

"I want to make sure," she explained.

About what? he wondered.

Satisfied, she stood up. He followed. As he put on his overcoat and hat, she said, "We'll go out the back way. It's through the kitchen."

She led the way, and he followed. He laughed to himself as he wondered just who the spy was here. Outside, they were in a small courtyard. A narrow walkway led back into a block of flats. They walked a short distance and stopped in front of a dark stairwell leading up to the second floor.

"Here," she whispered. She started up the stairs, and reaching a small landing, she got a key out of her handbag and opened the door. She switched on a light as she entered. Carl followed. He looked around; it was a spacious flat, furnished in a modern style, more Bauhaus than Second Empire. On the wall were prints by Picasso and Matisse. An original oil by Modigliani gave a textural feel of modernism to the room, while a Miró splashed color and a sense of serendipity to the surroundings.

"Decadent art," he said. "Not the Führer's favorites." He turned and looked at Marie Hélène with a deadpan expression. "He's an art expert."

She laughed and said lightly, "The exhibition drew record crowds in Munich last year, *n'est-ce pas?*"

"Yes." He walked around and looked closely at the prints and the paintings. He moved to the middle of the room and made a sweeping glance, taking it all in. "Very good, decadent art." He smiled.

She laughed. "I like the eyes in the Miró—a reminder that someone is always watching."

"Was that your concern in the café?" Carl asked.

"A little. As I have taken a leadership role in the Comité des Forges, I've had a sense of being watched."

"Probably true," said Carl matter-of-factly. "The Sûreté is everywhere. That's why we must avoid paper where possible."

"And the telephone?"

"Only for code words and possibly to arrange meetings. Never for information."

"The more out of the way the place the better, correct?" she asked as she batted her eyelashes at him.

"My thoughts exactly," he said as he looked around the room approvingly. "Like here."

"Like here," she repeated. "Let me get you a cognac. You can hang your coat in the hall closet." She walked into the little kitchen. She came out with two large snifter glasses filed with the golden liquid. She handed one to Carl and then walked over and sat down on the long modern couch. He came over and sat next to her. She pulled her legs up under her and sat at an angle facing him, very relaxed, her expression quite interested.

"We must have an understanding…"

"Just one?" asked Carl.

"Thérèse, she can't know, she can't suspect…"

"That means?"

"We're all adults…we live complicated lives…certain complications must continue…"

"I'm a diplomat…I live with complications, contradictions, inconsistencies…"

"Lies…"

"Yes, lies."

"With me, only one honesty, please…"

"Yes?"

"When it's over, just tell me…"

"And I have a thought…too…"

"Yes?"

"The channel to Jules Dugas is important…to my country…I believe to your country…a necessary and required complication…"

"Understand…completely…there's always been a degree of business calculation there…" Marie Hélène placed her glass over on an end table and stood up. She simply stood there facing Carl. He set his glass down and stood up also.

"Now?" he asked.

"Yes," she answered. "I can let you have the big bathrobe in the closet, but you have to promise…"

"Promise what?"

"Nothing underneath," she said with a laugh.

"Do you promise to play by the same rules?"

"Of course." She stood up on her toes and held his shoulders and quickly kissed him on the lips. "I'll be in the bedroom." She walked down the hall and looked over her shoulder and said with a mischievous smile, "Getting ready to play by the rules."

"I have few rules…"

"I was hoping for that…"

Maxim's

126

The incandescent electric lights gave off a bright light through the original gaslight sconces lining the plush red walls brightly illuminating the art nouveau dining room. A table in a far corner provided discreet privacy in a room crowded with dining tables.

Thérèse pushed the veal around in the sauce on the plate, then cut a small piece off and put it in her mouth.

She eats like a well-trained sparrow, thought Marie Hélène. *Keeps her figure, though.*

Thérèse lifted the glass half filled with dark red wine and took a sip. "I'm so glad this dreadful business with Austria is over," she said. "Carl said Jules helped avoid any misunderstandings." She rolled her eyes at the word *misunderstandings* and added with heartfelt feeling, "Please God, no more misunderstandings."

"I really wouldn't know," said Marie Hélène. "I put Jules in contact with some intermediary, and he took it from there. He's very conscious about security."

"Yes, Carl is very closed mouth about what he does outside of his public activities."

"Wise."

"Yes," said Thérèse. "Claude says Czechoslovakia is next," she added, mentioning her husband.

"Really?"

"Yes, we have properties there. Some chemical plants. He worries about them."

"I think the dispute is just about the rights of the poor Germans who live in Czechoslovakia," said Marie Hélène. "Anyway, let's hope so."

"Yes," said Thérèse. "I so want peace. You don't know what it's like." And she looked at Mari Hélène from the vantage point of a young woman during the war years. "You're seventeen...a bride...the rapture of married love, then a beautiful baby boy. While he's at your breast, suddenly you're a widow. The war. The light goes out."

"Well, yes. I was too young," replied Marie Hélène. "But I vividly remember the war. I could hear the cannons when I visited my father's business outside of Nancy. The ambulances...the suffering..."

"Then you're a widow," said Thérèse as she looked off into the distance of her memories, melancholy in her eyes. "You come from a great and old family—your father's *le duc*, a drafty old chateau, lots of family tree, no money. You're a nineteen-year-old baroness. You marry an older man—the only ones left…"

"How did Claude get his baronetcy?"

"My father gave it to him. *Invested* was the word he used. My father had daughters and titles in abundance—dukedoms come with dozens of them. It was cash he was short of."

"Well, I've never heard you complain about Claude."

"Well, no, why should I? He's raised my son like his own. In the early years, it was great. He was younger. Built a great business empire. Lots of vitality. I sang in my twenties…the joy came from deep down, you know where…but let me tell you…" She reached out and picked up the wineglass and took a gulp. "Later, they get older, less interested, fiddle with stocks, then come the years, you know…*faire l'amour à la papa*…" To make love in the slow and unexciting way…

"And?"

"So the opportunity…one more time…the rapture…of pounding youth…"

"Well, yes…"

"Then will come all those other years…I see it coming…like a roaring locomotive in the night…the grandchildren…they crawl up on your lap…*Nana,* they mew…" Thérèse all but slammed the wineglass back down on the table. "I can't stand the thought of it…I want more…now…before it's all over…"

"Carl?"

"Yes," she said emphatically. "Don't look at me that way. I know what turns the covers on a middle-aged woman's bed…it's about access to influence…or chemical plants in Czechoslovakia…or something…but while I have it, I want it…"

"Well, you have him…for now."

"Yes, for now. But war…war…that can take it all away. Like last time."

"We're working for peace."

"Yes, I know. If it would make a difference, I'd sell the whole damn French cabinet...they're for sale every day anyway...why not get some joy out it..."

Marie Hélène smiled. "You've put a very fine description on the current situation, Thérèse."

Thérèse looked over the top of her wineglass and smiled, the brittleness of her expression turning into one of relaxed and easy comfort as her frustrations and anxieties receded like a wave into the primordial sea. "You're a great friend, Mimi."

"Thank you." Marie Hélène looked across the dining room, then put her hand up to her lips, a startled look coming across her face.

"What is it?" asked Thérèse.

"Oh, possibly nothing," said Marie Hélène, regaining her composure. "Over there at that table is Odette..."

"Oh, yes," said Thérèse as she craned her neck around. "That's her. And Baroness von Einem, Abetz's good friend..."

"One of the men is Loys Aubin...a top editor at *Le Temps*," said Marie Hélène, "and the other is Poirier, a man close to a lot of foreign governments...works for *Le Temps* also. I've worked with both of them. They're very understanding of our position...particularly after a contribution..."

"Yes, *Le Temps* is one of us."

"Undoubtedly Odette is lining up political support for her husband's bid to be foreign minister."

"I hear he already has the inside track for it," said Thérèse.

"Then maybe she wants the newspapers to support his program. He's very strong for peace with Germany.... We should be grateful."

"Undoubtedly. If her husband had her ambition, why I dare say he'd be king," said Thérèse with a grand and regal touch.

Marie Hélène laughed at her friend's impertinence. She looked at the foursome across the dining room. "Possibly more than politics is going on?" she ventured.

"Yes, with Baroness von Einem you never know. Possibly she's making new good friends also?" said Thérèse with a chuckle.

"Do you think Odette is maybe making new good friends, too?" asked Marie Hélène with a touch of insouciance.

"I only know she's greedy. The other...who knows...she has the chest for it..."

Marie Hélène roared with delight. "Delicious to think about."

Thérèse nodded and pointed her eyes in the other direction. "Let's duck out the side. I don't feel like saying 'hello' today."

"Good idea." Marie Hélène stood up followed by Thérèse, and the two ladies walked over to a side exit. Outside they noticed a Mercedes limousine with a waiting driver—crisp and efficient.

"Probably belongs to Baroness von Einem," said Thérèse.

Avenue Henri Martin

Geneviève Tabouis walked into the richly decorated drawing room of the modern limestone building on the tree-shaded avenue just a block away from the Bois de Boulogne. She handed her card to the butler. In one smooth motion she turned halfway around and let the white-aproned maid lift her coat off her shoulders. The maid draped the coat over one arm and took Geneviève's hat and scarf with the other; with prim footsteps, the maid walked into the cloak room. The drawing room was alive with the buzzing conversation of politicians, political climbers, and fashionable women, the men speaking self-importantly about the political upheavals going on and the women tossing witty remarks of repartee into the conversational mix. Tomorrow, a massive rejection of Premier Léon Blum's proposed emergency financial program by the Senate was expected. Blum's second short-lived Popular Front ministry would be guillotined by a Senate dominated by reactionaries; once again former Premier Joseph Caillaux led the executioners.

The butler called out her name: "Madame Geneviève Tabouis." The words were drowned out in the muffled cackle of strident and often acrimonious conversation. The butler smiled indulgently at Geneviève, and she replied with an understanding chuckle. She looked around the room and saw the hostess, the marquise de Crussol, speaking laughingly with a group of guests. Her day was coming. Great big blue eyes sparkled with wit on her lovely face, her charming figure a fetching allure stealing away the men's glances. The marquise was the intimate companion of Édouard Daladier, the minister of war, whose political career she tirelessly promoted at her salons, lunches, and dinners. Others could look at the charming marquise he possessed.

Geneviève walked up to the marquise and held her left hand in hers while hugging her with her right arm. She planted a light kiss on the marquise's left cheek. "So nice to see you today, Marie-Louise."

"You, too, Geneviève."

"Your garden is about to bloom," replied Geneviève.

"Yes, a stronger government for France," said the marquise in expectation of Daladier's rise to the premiership.

"We all hope so," said Geneviève with true generosity of spirit. She let her eyes roam around the room and saw Paul Reynaud in rapid-fire exposition on the political events of the day. There were rumors the former finance minister would get a ministry in the new Daladier government. "There's Paul. Let me go hear what he has to say. He's often worth a column all by himself." The other people in the circle made a light laugh at her observation.

Geneviève walked across the room, ears alert to any unguarded comment, eyes fixed on Paul Reynaud. She joined his circle, and he nodded a welcome to her while continuing his fast-paced talk, keeping a half dozen heads nodding by people mostly trying to just keep up. After a few moments, with characteristic impatience, Geneviève interrupted, "Paul, what did you really think of Blum's program?"

"It was solid, Geneviève," Paul replied. "It was a bold and comprehensive program for the economic and financial rebirth of France. Capital would be put to productive use. Credit would be increased, the flight of gold abroad controlled."

"Well, the Two Hundred Families wouldn't want their freedom to profit on gold at the expense of the French public curtailed, would they?" said Geneviève with her waspish sting.

Reynaud smiled but didn't answer.

"What else?"

"Blum proposed a massive increase in rearmament. That would counter the German threat while the expansion of the war industries would stimulate industrial production. Like Roosevelt's New Deal program in America."

"And so it will be defeated tomorrow in the Senate?" said Geneviève, not bothering to hide her scorn.

"Possibly a new government will indeed launch such a program. Daladier has a much wider base of political support."

"Including you?"

"Including me," said Reynaud. "Remember, Geneviève, I supported Blum in the meeting of the Right last month. I put the interests of France ahead of party." He turned and looked around the circle and said, "I always do." Heads nodded in agreement.

Geneviève nodded also. "Yes, Paul. I don't worry about you. It's all the others." Reynaud laughed. "But will Daladier get his program through the Senate?" she asked, doubt in her voice.

"Yes, the Senate dare not defy a big Chamber majority."

She looked over his shoulder and said, "Speaking of worries. I see Georges Bonnet has arrived. I better go catch up with him."

"Let me know what he says," replied Paul as she walked away.

"It will be in tomorrow's column," she said over her shoulder as she headed across the room, the breeze in her voice.

Geneviève came up to the small circle where Bonnet was holding forth. He welcomed her. "Hello, Geneviève."

"Hello, Georges," replied Geneviève familiarly. She listened attentively as Bonnet spoke about the importance of France upholding its treaty guarantee to Czechoslovakia, particularly in light of the German annexation of Austria, an exercise in pure military intimidation. As Bonnet concluded his surprisingly strong statement of support, she nodded thoughtfully. "Brilliantly stated," she said.

Bonnet smiled with satisfaction in light of her approval. "I appreciate the insight you gave me the other night on how Beneš and the other top Czechs see the issues."

"I stay in close touch with the Czech diplomats both here and in London."

"Remember, if necessary, I shall let everything else go in order to protect Czechoslovakia."

Geneviève looked at him and nodded approvingly.

"Remember, Geneviève, you can telephone me at the office, or at my home, whenever you want to, at any hour of the day or night. I am your friend."

The other persons in the circle were impressed with Geneviève's apparent influence.

"On another note," said Geneviève, "how is the new baby?" Georges and Odette had recently adopted a child; Geneviève had attended a baby shower at the Bonnets' residence.

"Oh, Odette just dotes on the child," said Bonnet. The other persons in the circle were impressed with the intimate familiarity Geneviève had with Bonnet, undoubtedly a helpful source for her many startling insights on European politics.

"I will await the announcement of the new list of ministers with optimism, Georges," she said. Looking across the room, she saw Édouard Daladier arrive, a small crowd of people surrounding the minister of war and new premier-to-be; her eyes brightened and she exclaimed, "Ah, the man of the hour. I better go see if I can get a statement."

"By all means," said Bonnet, dismissing her with a smile. He turned to his circle of admirers and continued talking about central European politics.

Geneviève walked across the room. She saw Marie Hélène standing next to Daladier in earnest conversation. She walked up and stood next to Marie Hélène.

"As I explained, comtesse," said Daladier, "part of our response to the Anschluss is an additional hundred and seventy million francs for the Maginot Line."

"Will it extend the line up along the Belgium frontier?" asked Marie Hélène, quite businesslike. "That is the strategic weak spot left unaddressed."

"Of course," said Daladier. "We will start on the extension. But nevertheless funds are always scarce. We have great need for modern aircraft, too."

Daladier turned to Geneviève and said, "Mimi and I were just discussing new programs to strengthen France's defenses."

"A subject always near to my heart and one I deeply support," said Geneviève.

"We find ourselves on the same page today, Geneviève," said Marie Hélène with a light laugh.

"May we always have such comity of views," said Geneviève.

The conversation continued, ranging over a variety of defense issues while avoiding talk about the government Daladier was in the process of putting together.

Chamber of Députés

The dapper little man in a fedora and Saville Row suit held his hand out and guided Geneviève Tabouis toward a seat in the diplomatic gallery overlooking the floor of the Chamber of Députés. Geneviève took a seat. The man, Stefan Osusky, the Czechoslovakian minister to France, sat down next to her and took off his hat. He continued the conversation they had been having on the way into the Palais Bourbon.

"You must have read the article in *Le Temps*, Geneviève?"

"Yes, I did."

"Here let me read from the article. It shocked me to see this in the leading paper of the Paris political establishment: 'Is it necessary for three million Frenchmen, the youth from our universities, our schools, and our factories—our national youth, in fact—to be sacrificed in order to keep three million Germans under Czech domination?'"

"Yes, I know. It is part of a wider campaign in the Paris press to discredit the Czech guarantee," said Geneviève, and she added with tart conviction, "France's solemn treaty obligation."

"My government and I wonder who supports this policy of appeasement?"

"Oh, the policy is being supported by the Two Hundred Families"—the wealthy French elite—"and the industrialists— the Comité des Forges and the others. They control the paper."

"I thought we had more friends in Paris," said Osusky, "and not so many enemies."

"Speaking of friends," said Geneviève, "how did your meeting with Bonnet this morning go?"

"Bonnet assured me that the French government had not changed in its determination to fulfill its treaty obligations to Czechoslovakia." He looked into Geneviève's eyes and added,

"So I expect great things from Premier Daladier's speech to the Chamber today."

"As are we all," said Geneviève. She watched as Osusky pulled out a gold pencil from his pocket and placed an expensive sheet of white paper on a writing pad on his lap. Then the two of them looked out over the semicircular amphitheater of the French parliament, the delegates from the Communist and Socialist parties ranged around on the left side, the Radicals in the center, and the Far Right parties sitting across on the right side from the center of the forum.

Overlooking the six-hundred-seat amphitheater was the speakers' tribune, and above that sat the chair and desk of the presiding officer. Presently Édouard Daladier came in at the head of a file of black-suited men, his cabinet, and they took their seats along the government bench. The Président of the Chamber then called upon Daladier to present his government. Daladier stood up and walked forward and mounted the speaker's tribune. He read out his ministerial declaration. Geneviève already had a copy. She checked off the names as they were read; no surprises here except that the conservatives Paul Reynaud and Georges Mandel had been added to what would otherwise have been an all Radical cabinet. The Socialists, by choice, were out.

Then Daladier set out in broad brushstrokes his government's policies. Coming to central Europe, Daladier said, "We will live up to all the pacts and treaties signed by us, but we shall not refuse to enter into any other amicable negotiations, and therefore it is important at this time that all our national energies be concentrated on the same objectives."

Geneviève took a quick breath. She understood: Daladier's policy was riddled with holes, almost British in its vagueness. She looked down at Osusky's paper; he had written the statement down word for word. The speech concluded, and Daladier walked back to the government bench, applause coming up from the députés. French politics was firmly back in the hands of the center-right, the Popular Front experiment was over.

"Let us go out and have tea, Geneviève," said Osusky. "Possibly you can explain to me why the speech was so much less than I had expected. Bonnet led me to believe that something very concrete would be said. It didn't happen."

"No, it did not," replied Geneviève. "But by all means, let's go have tea." The two stood up and departed the Chamber, Geneviève thinking to herself that the article in *Le Temps* had been coordinated by someone very close to the top, someone close to Bonnet. This was not the two salon aristocrats, Marie Hélène and Thérèse, fronting the propaganda line from the industrialists at a champagne reception. A powerful insider put that story in the paper just before Daladier's speech.

Quai d'Orsay

The message from the French ambassador in Moscow, Robert Coulondre, lay in the middle of the foreign minister's desk. Bonnet read it and then handed it over to Jules Dugas and asked, "What do you think?"

Dugas read the relevant passage out loud: "If the French government intends to make a stand at Prague, it is more urgent than ever to open military talks with the USSR."

Bonnet sagged, his expression limp. "Rather blunt."

"Yes."

"So soon after Austria. What do we do now?"

"We must make strong statements in support of Czechoslovakia. Get Hitler to pause and consider."

"Yes, play for time," said Bonnet. "What about military cooperation with Russia?" He winced at the thought.

"Keep that option open," said Dugas. "The Poles will be in an uproar if we proceed with Russia."

"Yes, I like that—talk about cooperation but do nothing."

21. May Crisis

May 1938. The large room in the Quai d'Orsay was dominated by a vast wooden desk heaped high with dossiers and papers. Two wing tables jutted back from the main desk, giving the ensemble a horseshoe shape. These tables were piled high with even more dossiers. A vast sea of documents from the world of French diplomacy converged on this desk for review by the secretary general of the foreign service, Alexis Léger. He had been a well-regarded poet before becoming a diplomat, a long-serving general in the campaign to create a lasting peace with Germany in the wake of the troublesome Versailles peace treaty. He was the star of the literary salon of the wealthy Comtesse Marthe de Fels in Paris where he gave erudite talks on French foreign policy. In the 1920s, building cooperation between France and Germany had been the order of the day. But the Great Depression brought the rise of a revanchist Nazi state to power bent on expansion. Containment was now the hope.

In front of the secretary general was a dossier containing papers and summaries of the meeting held at the end of April in London between Premier Daladier and Foreign Minister Bonnet with British prime minister Chamberlain and his foreign secretary, Lord Halifax. The document summarizing the meetings was clear; Léger had written it himself. Daladier had explained to Chamberlain that Hitler's goal was the destruction of Czechoslovakia and then Poland and Romania. Then he would turn on the West—Britain and France. Complete German domination of Europe was the goal.

Bothered by the memory, Léger stood up and walked over to the tall window overlooking the River Seine. The trees lining the river were in lush green bloom; Paris was sparkling in the spring sunshine. *Daladier had surely been correct in his vision*, thought Léger. He had feared this trajectory ever since Hitler rose to uncontested power in Germany. The dilemma posed by Czechoslovakia was that if the Western Powers capitulated now they would only precipitate the future war they wished to avoid. *It is the devil's own dilemma*, thought the poet. The people's genuine desire for peace becomes the emotion that carries them to the dark passage of war.

Staring out the window, the secretary general pondered the problem. Daladier had asked General Gamelin to provide him with the precise steps that the French military could take in the event of Germany invading Czechoslovakia. By itself, France could do little, replied the general. Léger understood. Russia was the most important ally in the East, but France had never followed through and implemented the military provisions of its treaty with Russia, the Franco-Russian pact. The remaining alternative, as always, would depend upon Britain.

But Léger had been at the London meeting. He had watched the high-strung Chamberlain chide Daladier on his supposed pessimism. Like many others, Léger concluded that the British prime minister had already written off Czechoslovakia. Chamberlain had told the French that with regard to German aggression on Czechoslovakia he "in all frankness did not see how it could be prevented."

Léger slowly read the conclusion that Daladier himself had written about the London meeting: the British would only join France in common diplomatic action; no military response was contemplated. The British government would ask Hitler to act "with moderation."

Opening another dossier, Léger reviewed more dispatches. The French had hardly left London when their ambassadors reported startling developments to Paris. Foreign Secretary Lord Halifax had assured the Germans that no further military commitments to the French had been made. Ominously, from Berlin came word that the British ambassador has assured the Germans that the Czech question could be settled by Germany and Britain alone; other powers need not be consulted. Well, not the first time the British went it alone, remembered Léger.

Turning to yet another dossier, Léger saw that Henlein, the leader of the Czech Sudeten Germans, had broken off discussions with the Czech government and gone to Germany. Shortly thereafter, Nazi-inspired riots broke out across the Sudetenland. German propaganda shows broadcast lurid tales of Czech terror against poor defenseless Germans. Germany has a sacred duty to protect its kinsmen screamed the Berlin announcers. Reports of German troop concentrations along the Czech border began to reach Paris.

Léger pulled another dossier under his gaze, the result of Foreign Minister Bonnet's talk with the Russian Foreign Minister Maxim Litvinov in Geneva just days ago. Here was a dilemma created by the French themselves. Russia had signed a treaty of assistance with Czechoslovakia, but at French insistence, the treaty only obligated Russia to enter the fray if France moved on its treaty obligation first. The French had not wanted to create a situation where a first move by Russia could automatically embroil France in hostilities in eastern Europe without its own deliberate decision. Thence the trigger clause: France would move first, Russia second.

Bonnet had asked Litvinov what Russia would do if Germany attacked Czechoslovakia. The Russian coolly replied that Russia would honor its treaty commitments to Czechoslovakia. But that answer of course demanded that France move first.

"But how will you come to the assistance of Czechoslovakia," asked Bonnet, "since you have no common frontier with Czechoslovakia? Are you ready to force a passage of your troops and planes through Poland and Romania, if necessary?"

Litvinov replied that France was the ally of Poland and Romania and had great influence with the two countries. Perhaps France could arrange safe passage? Bonnet faced an almost insoluble dilemma. Poland was intractable about preventing Russian troops from crossing its territory.

Léger doubted that Bonnet would put much effort into securing this permission. Bonnet also deeply distrusted the Bolshevik Russians; Léger recalled that Bonnet visibly shuddered at the thought of being allied with the Soviet Union in a war against Germany. Pushing the dossier away, Léger concluded that whatever happened in eastern Europe would depend on Russia. Always had.

Events are moving toward a crescendo, possibly even this weekend, thought the secretary general.

The Ambassador

Robert Coulondre, the French ambassador to Russia, was escorted into the secretary general's office by a liveried usher.

Alexis Léger rose to greet him and then introduced René Massigli, the political director. The three men sat down.

"I have just come from meeting with General Gamelin," said the ambassador. "Before that I met with the foreign minister. He advised me to draw up a proposal to submit to Daladier and himself."

"And so here you are," said Léger with a smile. "What did General Gamelin say?"

"He is very favorable to military talks with Russia."

"Well, that's a start," said Léger. "What are your overall views, ambassador?"

"Simple. If Paris tries to save the peace at any price—appeasement—then France risks being pushed into a future war."

"Yes, we all agree on that." Léger nodded at both gentlemen.

"General Gamelin understands," said the ambassador, "that if concessions are carried too far, Czechoslovakia disappears from the map and then Germany would have a free hand in Poland and then against us."

Léger and Massigli nodded in agreement. That was where the road led.

"It is my conviction," said the ambassador, "that if France and Britain want to halt Hitler, the best place to do it is Czechoslovakia."

"Yes, the Czechs have strong fortifications, a capable army," said Massigli. The ambassador nodded in agreement.

"What is Russia's view on Czechoslovakia?" asked Léger, getting at the heart of the matter.

"I don't think they have any reservations about Prague," replied the ambassador. "The only way to be sure is to have the military talks."

"Another sticking point," said Léger as he raised a difficult subject. "The Poles assure us they will oppose passage by Russian troops across their territory with force."

"Maybe. But from where I sit, I think Paris is attaching too much importance to Poland and not enough to Russia."

"Why do you say that?" asked Massigli.

"The Kremlin does not believe the Poles could maintain a fighting front against the Germans. The Germans would just roll over them."

"Really?" asked Massigli. "I am not sure our General Staff shares that view."

"The Kremlin believes—and they have good information—that for Hitler there are only two fronts—France and Russia."

Léger let out a long sigh. "They're probably right."

"The time has come," said the ambassador with determination, "to make Poland decide for or against us."

"What does the foreign minister say?" asked Léger.

"The foreign minister fully approves opening up the military talks with the Russians," said the ambassador.

"Let us proceed with the proposal," said Léger. The three men got down to work.

Foreign Minister

In a small book-lined study just off the foreign minister's office, Bonnet and Jules Dugas pored over the draft proposal prepared by the Russian ambassador.

"This is going to Daladier's office," said Bonnet.

"It's a strong proposal," said Dugas.

"Yes," said Bonnet, a catlike wariness spreading across his face. "Daladier has barely been in office a month. He will want to look strong and resolute. He has already indicated to General Gamelin that any move by Germany toward Czechoslovakia will call forth a mobilization."

"Indeed, strong action."

"Daladier asked the general for a precise plan of further steps."

"Did the general comply?"

"Yes. But the general did say that what Russia did would be crucial."

"Not Britain?"

"No, not Britain. They can hardly land an army in eastern Europe."

"Nor can we," said Dugas.

"There—the dilemma," said Bonnet. "And now the violent demonstrations by the Sudetenland Germans against the Czech government in the border region. Hitler threatens a violent response."

"The British ambassador in Berlin has ordered a special train to take him away from Berlin. The British are taking a strong position against what they see as Hitler's provocation," said Dugas.

"Quite a change from last month in London," said Bonnet with a touch of irritation.

"The Czech government has ordered up a partial mobilization after an emergency cabinet meeting in Hradčany Castle," said Dugas.

"Yes, a complication," said Bonnet. "I had hoped the Czechs would go further in their concessions to the Sudeteners."

"The Czechs are not going to give up without a fight," said Dugas.

"Daladier will opt for strong action," concluded Bonnet. He sighed. "He has to." He looked at Dugas and said, "You must get word through back channels to Berlin that support for Czechoslovakia is firm and any armed hostilities risk a wider war. This is not Austria."

"Understand," said Dugas. "I will get straight to it."

"Good, I've got to meet the diplomatic correspondents now," said Bonnet.

"What are you going to tell them?"

"That we shall mobilize and protect Czechoslovakia according to the terms of the treaty."

"Well, Geneviève and Pertinax will be pleased."

"Yes, won't they." Bonnet stood up to go meet the correspondents.

Missed Connection

The telephone rang in the foyer of the mansion in the Faubourg Saint-Germain belonging to the family of the Villars-Brancas. The maid picked it up. "Hello?" She listened for a moment and then said, "No, she's not here. She's out at the family estate." She paused. "Yes, the one on the Moselle."

At the other end of the telephone line, Jules Dugas ground his teeth. He remembered. She had told him she would be gone for the weekend and would see him next Tuesday. He thanked the maid and hung up. He paced around the small hideaway office that he shared with Odette Bonnet for their unofficial businesses, which were extensive. He looked at a slip of paper in a file in his desk and then made another telephone call.

"Could I speak with the baroness? It's Frederick," he said to the maid who had answered the telephone. The maid was momentarily confused; this was a different man's voice from the one who usually said he was Frederick. She went and got Thérèse.

"Yes," said the unmistakable voice of Thérèse.

"This is a friend," said Jules. "Frederick."

"Well, yes. Go on," replied Thérèse. She recognized the voice.

"I urgently need to get in touch with our mutual acquaintance. Frederick's other contact is out of town," said Dugas impatiently. Better not say too much over the telephone.

"Yes, possibly I could assist," said Thérèse, a tone of warm cooperation coming over the phone line at the prospect of helping Carl.

"Yes, that would be excellent. The small bistro just down the avenue from Place Victor Hugo"

She listened to the receiver. "Good. In an hour."

Avenue Victor Hugo

Jules Dugas sat at a small circular table in a rear corner with eyes on the front door. He saw Thérèse approach and come through the door. He looked up at her. She saw him and came walking across the room, brushing past the maître d' with practiced ease. Jules stood up. "I'm so pleased you could make it." He held her chair as she sat down.

"Yes, I want to be helpful."

"Here is an envelope," said Jules. "It's open, and you should read it and memorize the message. It would be preferable if you could deliver the envelope in person, but verbally if necessary."

"Yes, I will try," she said. She looked up and smiled at Dugas, a sultry look of expectation coming over her face. "I'm interested in all things involving Frederick—at both ends." He understood.

"Our acquaintance can explain the utmost gravity and seriousness of these communications."

"I understand," said Thérèse. "I will be a faithful messenger."

"Good. If in the future this becomes necessary again, possibly we could meet here?"

"Just let my maid know and I will be on my way."

"Good. Possibly next time I could buy you lunch or dinner?" He looked at her expectantly.

"Yes," said Thérèse, a light smile crossing her face, her expression more than a little bit interested. She rarely missed an opportunity to put an interesting man on the line, an addition to the list of life's romantic possibilities.

"Let me depart first," he said.

"Fine," she said. "*Allez.*" Go.

Berchtesgaden

A weekend of crisis was reaching a crescendo. Adolph Hitler stood out on the broad terrace of his alpine chalet, his hands placed on the balustrade while he leaned forward and gazed out over the valley below, his mind mulling over how and when to strike at Czechoslovakia. He ached for a military confrontation, an opportunity to put the troops on the march. And then there were the Czechs themselves. The gumption displayed by Czech Président Beneš to stand up to him was galling.

Across the terrace, a diplomat representing the Wilhelmstrasse approached Colonel Jodl, a key staff officer on the General Staff and liaison to the Führer. The diplomat explained that the foreign office was besieged with telephone calls from the British, French, and Russian ambassadors protesting the military maneuvers on the Czech border. The Czechs were mobilizing troops. They looked like they would make a fight of it if German troops entered their territory. It was possible that the other allies would come to their aid.

Colonel Jodl asked, "Do you have good intelligence on this? Or is this just the blustering of some ambassadors in Berlin?"

144

"Our best source in Paris, right at the top of the cabinet, says that Daladier will act. He just assumed office; he cannot afford to look weak."

Jodl nodded thoughtfully in understanding and asked, "Your recommendation?"

"The Wilhelmstrasse believes that we must do more preparatory work. Separate the allies from the Czechs, then move. Diplomacy, not invasion, might gain the objective."

"A wise recommendation. I'll take it up with Führer. Wait here and I will get a decision on this."

The representative from the foreign ministry walked over to a far corner of the patio and took a seat and watched as Colonel Jodl approached the Führer. Colonel Jodl explained and the diplomat watched as the Führer's face blackened with rage, an ugly mood coming over his expression, fists clenching and unclenching. The Führer asked a question about Russia, the diplomat could hear the words come across the patio. Colonel Jodl nodded in the affirmative. The Führer cogitated on this, looking darkly at the colonel. Then his manner eased and he turned and gave clear instructions to Colonel Jodl. The colonel gave the Nazi salute and walked back across the patio to the diplomat.

"Return to Berlin and tell the foreign office to inform the Czech minister in Berlin that Germany has no aggressive intentions toward Czechoslovakia. Reports on troop concentrations are without foundation."

"Yes, Herr Colonel," said the diplomat, and he gave the Nazi salute and turned on his heel and departed.

The Führer watched the diplomat depart and then he looked at Colonel Jodl and beckoned him over. The colonel returned, raised an arm in salute, and stood attentive.

"It is my unalterable decision to smash Czechoslovakia by military action in the near future," said Hitler.

"Yes, *mein Führer,*" said the colonel with equanimity.

"By October 1, 1938, at the latest."

"I will see that the plans are prepared," replied Jodl.

"It is my unshakable will that Czechoslovakia shall be wiped off the map," he said, a dark scowl animating his face.

The colonel nodded and raised his arm in salute. He, too, turned on his heel and departed.

Hitler turned and placed his hands on the balustrade bordering the patio and leaned forward, shoulders hunched, gazing out over the valley below, his eyes restlessly searching for unseen answers in the peaks and valleys below him. Another peaceful conquest? He ground his teeth; he saw himself as a man of the sword, not a signer of diplomatic documents. The sword would deliver him to his destiny.

Quai d'Orsay

"Reports are coming in," said Jules Dugas to Foreign Minister Bonnet. "The crisis is easing. The Czech minister has been called to the Wilhelmstrasse to receive assurances."

"Good," said Bonnet. "A policy of firmness has worked...this time."

Dugas nodded in understanding. "Yes, our message got through."

"And the British ambassador in Berlin was firm and resolute. Calling for a special train conveyed concretely that he meant business."

"Undoubtedly the Russian warnings also had a telling effect," said Dugas.

"Yes, indeed. But now something else has come up," said Bonnet. "The British ambassador has called for an urgent meeting. He's never called on a Sunday before."

"When?"

"Right now. He's being shown in as we speak."

There was a knock on the door, and it opened. A liveried usher looked in and said to the foreign minister, "The British ambassador is here."

"Please show him in," said Bonnet as both he and Dugas stood.

Sir Eric Phipps walked in, a nervous little man. *Possibly even more nervous tonight*, thought Dugas, something of a student of British diplomats. Bonnet pointed to an open chair across from his desk, and the ambassador walked forward and sat down. Bonnet and Dugas followed.

"I have a wire from Foreign Secretary Halifax that I am to read to you," said Phipps in a stilted voice. "There are six parts to it."

Both Bonnet and Dugas reached for notepads and pulled out fountain pens. Once ready, Bonnet nodded at the ambassador to proceed.

"That the French government be under any illusion as to the attitude of His Majesty's government...in case of failure to bring about a peaceful settlement of the Czechoslovakia question." The ambassador stopped and let Bonnet and Dugas finish writing their notes. Bonnet looked up and nodded to proceed.

"It might be highly dangerous if the French government were to read more into those warnings than is justified..." Once again the ambassador paused.

"His Majesty's government would come to the assistance of France if she were subject to unprovoked attack by Germany..." The ambassador looked up and across at Bonnet, who was carefully and completely writing everything down.

"Our statements do not warrant the assumption we would take part in joint military action to preserve Czechoslovakia against German aggression..." The ambassador paused and again looked across the desk at Bonnet to make sure that the import of the message was clearly understood. Dugas nodded that he understood.

"Military action is unlikely to prevent Germany from overrunning Czechoslovakia...but would result in a European war the outcome of which would be doubtful..." Once again the pause. Bonnet nodded that he understood. Dugas silently thought to himself that realistically both he and his foreign minister were in agreement with that assessment. The western allies were too weak and too far away to stop Germany from overrunning Czechoslovakia.

"His Majesty's government fully realizes the extent and nature of French obligations to Czechoslovakia but that the French government must keep the above considerations fully in mind..." The ambassador stopped and folded the message and put it into his dispatch case. He carefully locked it.

Neither Bonnet nor Dugas were surprised by the message. They had heard that British prime minister Chamberlain had privately written off Czechoslovakia. But what to say this evening? The ambassador would report back to London almost immediately.

Bonnet leaned back in his chair, steepled his fingers, and looked at Phipps.

"I will put whatever pressure that your government thinks best on the Czechs that you think desirable. The Czechs must behave more reasonably toward the German demands." Bonnet paused and looked at the ambassador.

Phipps replied, "It behooves the Czechs to be more reasonable, for the alternative for them would be total annihilation."

Dugas sat back. Yes, the British ambassador had stated the situation clearly and bluntly.

"I completely agree," said Bonnet. He ruminated for a moment and added, "If Czechoslovakia were really unreasonable, the French government might well declare that France considered herself released from her bond."

Phipps took this in, suppressing a smile. The French position had cracked. Foreign Secretary Halifax's gambit had yielded startling results. He would be most pleased.

"What's more," said Bonnet, "I will speak with the Czech Minister Osusky tomorrow and urge him to return to Prague and tell Président Beneš personally of the vital necessity to act quickly and generously."

"Undoubtedly the chances are now brighter for a peaceful settlement that before," said Phipps. Indeed, a corner had been turned.

"I agree," said Bonnet. "The German government is taking a reasonable attitude here. We will do all that we can to further it along." Bonnet stood up, followed by Dugas and the ambassador. Bonnet walked around his desk and escorted Phipps over to the door and opened it. An usher outside escorted the ambassador outside to his waiting limousine.

Bonnet and Dugas stood in the spacious office. Dugas waited for the foreign minister to sum up.

"With the right compromises, a peaceful solution with regard to the Sudeten Germans is possible. Britain and France must ensure the Czechs see the need for the compromises to come."

"Yes," said Dugas. "New arrangements in the East must be made."

Deuxième Bureau

Captain Jacques Morel sat at his desk. It had been a long weekend of jangled nerves before the crisis had eased. Publicly, the firm positions taken by the British and French governments, combined with veiled threats from Russia, had caused Hitler to back off. Congratulations were going around in Paris.

But just what had caused Hitler to back off? Morel pondered the question this Monday morning. Hitler had not backed away at the Rhineland. Nor had he at Austria. An aide came in and brought decoded messages from Berlin. Morel shuffled through them and pulled one out. He spread it out on his desk. It was from *la bonne source*, a secret informant high up in the Wilhelmstrasse, one close to the hub of deliberations in that opaque bureaucracy. Yes, the good source.

The message was short. Morel read: an informant close to the French cabinet, possibly in the cabinet itself, reported that Daladier would act militarily if Germany moved on Czechoslovakia. Weizsäcker himself vouched for the reliability of the source. The information immediately went to Hitler, reported *la bonne source*.

There, thought Morel. *Just like 1936.* A leak of the most sensitive information right out of the cabinet. The transmission to Berlin, the hurried discussions by the highest officials in the Wilhelmstrasse. Followed by clear action.

Morel leaned back in his chair and thought. It was probably Dinckler. The information probably came from Dugas. Through one or both of the women. Maybe in writing, maybe in code. Unlikely Dugas would pass on this information to Berlin without Bonnet's approval.

So, is this espionage? Treason by a high official? Or is it just a foreign minister keeping a reliable back channel to another government as a way to prevent misunderstandings? Morel pondered the questions. Yes, the delivery of the threat of military action had forestalled German moves on Czechoslovakia, a key objective of French policy. France's interests had been sustained.

Atelier

"The crisis has eased?" asked Marie Hélène as she brought a glass of wine over and gave it to Carl.

"Yes," he said, leaning back on the sofa. He took a sip of the velvety red wine and purred with contentment. She sat down next to him and curled her legs up under herself.

"I'm sorry I wasn't here to take the message," she said.

"Jules met Thérèse at a bistro near her house just down from Place Victor Hugo. She brought me the message in person."

"I bet."

"It's important we do not use telephones unless absolutely necessary," said Carl. "But the information was simply crucial. Berlin told me it may have tipped the Führer's decision."

"Between war and peace?"

"Possibly." Carl sat quietly for a few moments. "You must tell Jules of the information's crucial importance."

"I will," she said.

"This communication channel is of vital importance to both countries," said Carl. Again he paused and collected his thoughts.

"Yes?" she asked, sensing some deeper concerns.

"You must do everything to keep your relationship with Jules intact."

"Everything?" she said with a laugh.

"Yes, everything."

"I believe I am," she replied with a mischievous rise of her eyebrow. "He hasn't asked for anything beyond Tuesdays." She sat quiet for a second and whispered, *"Faire d'amour a la calendrier."* To make love by the calendar.

"Promise?" he said.

"Promise," she answered and then said rather coquettishly, "but you have to promise to do everything to keep our relationship intact."

"Discreetly. I can't risk my relationship with Thérèse," said Carl. "She's the cover."

"Nor do I want you to," she replied. She turned to him. "Speaking of *faire d'amour a la…*"

"Yes, let's," he said as he stood up. "I can spend the night."

"Good. I always like a man with a free day on his calendar," she said with a light laugh.

Morning Light

In the soft gray of the long early morning twilight of the spring day, Marie Hélène slowly stirred as she felt Carl's hands slide over her body ever so lightly, fingers brushing her hair away from her face, lips nibbling on her breast. His hands gently pushed her legs apart, fingers played on the soft skin of her inner thigh, drumming up a soft tattoo as they moved up her leg, a sense of delight spreading across her entire body. She gasped as other fingers wiggled folds of flesh and then spread her moisture around the smooth silky parts. She felt him lean against her body. *Yes*, she thought dreamily, *he is ready...again.*

Even after last night, as she remembered the tangle of frenzied delights as they had gone this way and that. Sated, she had drifted off to an easy sleep. The lingering pleasure was still with her in the morning. And now...again? More fingers, a sharper kiss. She arched her back as her desire rose one more time to welcome his insistent longing.

She marveled as he moved over on top of her as she wrapped her arms around his shoulders and pulled her chest upward into his. She shoved her face into the crook of his neck. Slowly she wrapped her legs around his thighs, pulling his body into hers as he began the pulsing rhythm that put them into one sympathetic motion of desire, a blazing gallop across the bright meadows of her sensual consciousness.

It went on and on, then, suddenly she gasped for breath, shuddered with release, and shook her head from side to side. She lay there feeling his heaving breath on her cheek. He moved slowly inside her. Again? She held on as she felt another wave of desire well up from deep inside and then just as suddenly she shuddered and fell limp in his arms. She lay there like a doll as she felt him slow down. Finally, he stopped, resting on top of her with deep breaths heaving out of his chest, head facing down into her pillow, and he whispered into her ear that they couldn't let it end...regardless...*toujours...tous les deux...*

"*Oui, mon cheri,*" she mumbled. They lay there, entwined, for a few minutes, then he slid down and off her body and rolled to one side. In a few more minutes, he swung his legs off the bed and stood up. He bent down and kissed her forehead.

"I have to leave…before the day takes hold…"

"I understand," she mumbled. She listened as he put his clothes on and heard the door close behind him.

She lay there and felt the beady perspiration on her breasts, the sweat running down her stomach into her thighs, sticky with love. Her legs remained spread out and askew on the bed where they had been when he had rolled away from her. She lay there, the backs of her thighs feeling the dampness of the sheets, limp, spent, sated, wondering where this part of her life would lead, not caring about consequences. There was a warm tenderness of love in her heart for Carl, the feeling of enjoyment of being with the man—but she had known that before with other men—but this…the intensity of the physical emotion of their union just overwhelmed her other sensibilities. Nothing quite like it had ever happened to her before. Jules was fun, but this…my God…

Moscow-Paris

June 1938, Moscow. Robert Coulondre sat in his elegant high-ceilinged embassy office with tall windows behind him open to the summer air. He had slowly realized that he didn't understand Paris as well as a French ambassador should. After the May crisis, he had left Paris with a clear sense of mission to return to Moscow and start the military conversations with the Russians. But for weeks now he had found Paris uncommunicative and uncooperative. What was up?

The ambassador looked across his desk at Colonel Palasse, the military attaché, and said, "Paris attaches too much importance to Poland and not enough to Russia."

"Yes," replied the colonel, "Paris thinks the Russian army is a paper tiger."

"They are mistaken?"

"Quite so. The Russian General Staff doesn't think the Poles could even maintain a front against Germany. The Germans would roll right over them."

"Yes, a previous attaché reported on the strength of the Russian army and got carpeted for his effort. His successor was as docile as a church mouse."

The colonel sat stone-faced.

"And the Czechs?" asked the ambassador.

"Our attaché in Prague says they have a very capable army operating in strong fortifications," replied the colonel. "The fortifications are the key."

"So, if we are going to make a stand in eastern Europe, Czechoslovakia is the place to do it?"

"That is a political decision," said the colonel. He shrugged.

"Yes," said the ambassador. "I just returned from the Czech legation. The minister showed me a copy of a dispatch received from their minister in Paris."

"Yes, Osusky."

"It said the French government will not follow up on the military talks with the Soviets. The government does not want to arouse the anger of the British conservatives."

"Yes, the British," said the colonel.

"So, I'm afraid our efforts to bring Russia into a military coalition to stop Hitler have failed."

The colonel nodded but kept his silence.

"The British have never supported France in trying to build a cordon of allies in eastern Europe to contain Germany," said the ambassador, reflecting on almost a generation of French diplomacy.

"The British look to their navy, not their army," replied the colonel.

"Have you heard rumors that Poland might attack and seize the Teschen part of Czechoslovakia in case of a crisis?" asked the ambassador, changing the subject.

"I have heard the rumors. Poland feels the Paris Peace Treaty should have ceded the land to them, not Czechoslovakia," said the colonel. "More revanchism."

"Yes, the wolves circle," said the ambassador. "I spoke with the Russian foreign minister, Litvinov. He hinted to me that if Poland were to attack Czechoslovakia, then Russia might attack Poland."

"They don't like each other," agreed the colonel.

"No, they don't," said the ambassador. "But it gets worse."

"How so?" asked the colonel, now quite interested.

"I watched Litvinov carefully, like a bride's family watching a bridegroom. I got the strong sense that Russia would not move on Poland without a prior understanding with Germany. The implications trouble me. Maybe the Russians are already talking with the Germans."

"That would end the game in eastern Europe for us."

"Yes, wouldn't it," concluded the ambassador.

22. A Royal Visit

July 1938. In the antique-filled town house overlooking Avenue Foch, industrialists and their wives, or more often than not, well-kept lady friends, stood in circles on thick oriental rugs chatting. White-coated waiters moved around the room serving glasses of champagne as white-aproned maids in black frocks moved from group to group with trays of hors d'oeuvre for the guests. The members of the Comité des Forges were gathered as guests of the baron and baroness de Roncée. Tall French windows were open to the avenue letting the warm breeze waft across the room.

At the head of room, in front of the fireplace, stood Thérèse in a bouffant white dress, trimmed with little bows, and wearing shiny white-and-brown heels. Her hair was piled high on her head, diamond earrings dangled from her delicate ears, and strands of pearls circled her neck. Next to her stood her husband, Claude, a robust and stolid man well into his sixties with machine-gray hair and the hearty self-confident manner of a self-made man. She and her husband were hosting the reception. People liked to say that in the last war Claude had provided the French military with enough munitions to blow Germany up twice over. Unfortunately most of the explosions had just dug up the dirt of northeast France, making an ugly scar from the English Channel to the Swiss border that still had not healed.

Several of the businessmen eyed Thérèse and her still fetching allure. She had great entrée in the corridors of power, they knew. She was the feminine charm that smoothed Claude's many business deals.

In the middle of the room, Marie Hélène stood shaking hands, making small talk and introducing her husband, Henri, le comte de Villars-Brancas, to the guests. Hélène was resplendent in a light blue ankle-length gown with matching sapphire earrings and a large sapphire pendant hanging on a diamond necklace just above her well-presented bosom. Henri, in his early fifties, was all polished charm as he shook gentlemen's hands and inquired after the ladies, most of them simply blossoming with pink-faced delight under his aristocratic manners and beautifully posed compliments. Some of the women wondered why Marie Hélène spent so much time in Paris when there was a gentlemen of such old world charm living a life of ease out on his estate in eastern France.

Standing by one of the windows, a butler turned around and announced to the guests, "Here they come." The guests all crowded out onto the small balconies overlooking one of the most magnificent residential avenues of Paris. Yes, the guests exclaimed as they looked up the avenue. "I see them now," said others. The official procession, which had started at the railroad station in the Bois de Boulogne, was approaching. The king and queen of Great Britain were visiting Paris in the biggest state visit since the war.

First came a mounted troop of cavalry, coffee-colored Moroccan spahis wearing billowy pants, polished black boots, wide red sashes around their midriffs, and red fezlike *chechias* with the Islamic crescent on the front. Next came the Algerian spahis with their wide blue pantaloons and red jackets. The horses stepped high, the columns and rows in precise alignment. Flowing capes came down from the officers' shoulders and lay spread out on the hindquarters of their mounts. Next came a troop of Republican Guards riding chestnut-brown horses and wearing chrome helmets with horsetail plumes streaming from the crowns. Some even wore metal breastplates. Sabers and rifles were near at hand. Following the guards came the open state limousine itself, the king sitting in the rear next to the Président of the République Albert Lebrun. The open passenger compartment was surrounded by two-foot-high panes of bulletproof glass. Republican Guardsmen rode close alongside the limousine screening out potential trouble. Behind the king's limousine came a second limousine carrying the queen and Madame Lebrun.

Along the sidewalks stood thousands of schoolchildren waving Union Jacks and cheering "Vive le Roi!" The king sat in the rear seat wearing an admiral's uniform, gold epaulettes the size of small chandeliers on his shoulders, a gold-trimmed fore-and-aft hat rode above his youthful face, sashes across his chest, medals and stars planted on every square inch of his immaculate tunic. He waved to the right and left, the golden stripes on his sleeve gleaming in the sunlight, his face radiant at the waves of approval coming from the adoring French crowds. In the following limousine, the queen wore a silky white dress with long gloves, her smile blazing away underneath a magnificent hat, her great signature adornment. She waved with genuine good-natured cheer, one of the radiant personalities of the era.

And as soon as it had begun, the cavalcade passed, the cheers echoing from crowds farther up the avenue. Marie Hélène watched the cavalcade proceed up the avenue and then tugged at her husband's arm; they walked over to where Thérèse and Claude were standing.

"So nice to see you again, Claude," said le comte.

"You, too, Henri," said Claude. "Keeping busy?"

"Of course. I'm out on my horse riding over the vineyards every day. A good vintage comes from careful supervision of the vines all summer long. If the owner is not…"

"Oh, yes, I know so well. I walk the factories daily," said Claude with a chuckle. "And the Compagnie de Marne. Keeping it on keel?" he said, mentioning his wife's gigantic family business.

"Hardly," said le comte with a laugh. "I wouldn't know a steam shovel from a bulldozer." What little he had to do with his wife's family company mostly bored him.

"Please tell Claude what you do for our company, dear. It's terribly important," said Marie Hélène, trying to put a bit of heft to her husband's standing. Thérèse leaned in to hear.

"Well, I escort visitors from Paris, those who don't know what the war was like." A pained expression came over his face as old memories came back. "I show them the horrors of Verdun, the impossibility of the defense and offense grinding away the men's lives."

"Yes, a terrible time," said Claude sympathetically.

"Then I give them a tour of some of the new Maginot Line fortifications. Show them the improvements, the necessity of its construction."

"Yes, the voice of experience," said Claude.

"Our future depends upon on it," added Thérèse.

"I hope so. I don't think France could stand the losses of another war," said Henri, his face sorrowful and forlorn.

"We're all working for that goal," said Thérèse with an air of seriousness, "here in Paris." She turned to Marie Hélène. "Aren't we?"

"Yes. Peace."

"And tomorrow night we all attend the grand reception at the Quai d'Orsay and meet the king and queen. The entente with Britain is our rock and our future," said Thérèse with uncharacteristic seriousness about foreign policy. "And then a possible accord with Germany," she said, mentioning her heartfelt goal.

"Germany?" asked Henri with bleak bewilderment. "An accord?"

"At least an understanding," said Marie Hélène. "The reception should be a glittering time," she said, putting an end to the conversation. She turned to Thérèse and said, by way of leave, "Thank you for having us. It was an impressive parade."

Claude watched Marie Hélène and Henri depart and then turned to Thérèse and said, "Let me go over and talk to my colleagues gathered over there. I think I may have some unfinished business with them."

"By all means," said Thérèse. She smiled and walked over to chat with some of her friends. Claude walked over to where a couple of businessmen were huddled in conversation in a corner of the room.

"Yes, I believe there's a deal in the air…about those Czech plants," said one of the businessmen as Claude approached.

"The rumored offering prices are cheap but not unfair," said another. The businessmen were all wondering how to liquidate their interests in Czech industries acquired in the 1920s, often at the encouragement of the French government and with favorable French bank loans. But in 1938, conditions were changing fast.

"Yes, Claude," said one of the men to Claude as he joined the conversation, "the Germans are offering a deal…not a great price…but considering the situation…"

"Yes, I understand. I'm going to speak with my contact at the German embassy. Tell him I'm willing to take the London side of the deal—I hear Prime Minister Chamberlain also owns substantial shares in Imperial Chemical—but that I'd like a sweetener, some I. G. Farben bearer shares in a Swiss account, too."

The other businessmen looked at Claude with surprise. Take some German shares? Highly irregular.

"Sounds shrewd, Claude. Profit on both ends of the deal," said one. The others slowly nodded in agreement. Claude always saw the extra angle.

Champs Élysées

Geneviève Tabouis stood on the upstairs balcony of her brother-in-law's apartment on the Champs Élysées. He was a wealthy industrialist, and waiters and maids circulated among the guests serving champagne and hors d'oeuvres. Geneviève looked up the broad avenue, its leaf-laden trees in the full blush of summer, and saw the horse cavalry circle the Arc de Triomphe, the monumental edifice in the center of the large circular plaza, the Étoile. She heard the crowd's cheers rise to a crescendo as the king saluted the French regimental flags as his limousine rounded the Arc de Triomphe. She called inside, "Here they come."

Guests crowded out onto the small balconies and pushed into the window spaces. Once again, first came the African cavalry, the spahis. Then the clatter of hooves as the Republican Guards thundered down the broad avenue, white sashes making vivid diagonals across their tunics. Motorcycle outriders flanked the horse columns. Once again, crowds were lustily cheering "Vive le Roi" as they pushed the lines of police and Senegalese guards bordering the procession route ten feet out onto the avenue. Then came the second limousine carrying the queen and the crowds shouting, "Vive la Reine."

The industrialists and their wives watched spellbound as the procession trooped by, Geneviève remarking, "Look at the queen's hat. That's almost all people talked about during coronation week last year—her hats." Other guests smiled at Geneviève's name-dropping. She had been an invited guest to the king's coronation in Westminster Abbey the previous year; she was part of the crème de la crème of European society, a confidant of cabinet ministers across Europe.

"We came across the Place de la Concorde on our way here," said one of the industrialists. "It is lined with tanks, big nasty-looking brutes. The king will get a firsthand look at France's military might. Impressive."

"They are going to parade several hundred tanks and fifty thousand troops past the king at Versailles tomorrow, I hear."

"Yes, that's true," said another. "But it's airplanes France is short of. We simply do not produce enough."

"That's the fault of the Popular Front," said another. "Too Bolshoi."

"Or maybe it was capital going on strike. It fled Paris, weakening the franc," retorted Geneviève. She never bought the easy evasions of the wealthy.

"Oh, Geneviève, you can't put France's security interests first when your loyalty is to Moscow two thousand miles away," said another industrialist, repeating the canard about the Popular Front.

"Well, I for one feel there is hope for the future when I see such strong ties between our country and Britain," replied Geneviève, dodging a controversy.

"Why, yes, your own newspaper thundered its headline of a triumphant welcome to the British sovereigns," said another voice.

"Yes, let's trust that the royal trip will be a reminder to Berlin and Rome that we have power that transcends our transient political divisions," said Geneviève to top off the discussion.

"Well, yes," said another voice. "But it was only weeks after his father came to Paris in 1914 that the Great War broke out. Let's hope we have better luck this time."

Quai d'Orsay

Marie Hélène's eyes swept across the vast chandeliered room, deep rugs muffled the footfalls from eight hundred guests, thick draperies hung in elegant arcs from the tops of two-story-tall windows, further dampening the sound of roaring conversation. The reception honoring the king and queen of Great Britain was underway in the Quai d'Orsay, hosted by Foreign Minister Georges Bonnet and his wife Odette. All of Tout- Paris was in attendance.

"Oh, there's Premier Daladier," said Marie Hélène. "We must go pay our respects."

"Whatever you say, my dear," said her husband, Henri de Villars-Brancas. The couple threaded their way through the formally attired crowd of guests toward a corner where the premier was accepting congratulations on the magnificence of the state visit, this great demonstration of the solidity of the entente alliance with Great Britain.

As they came up the receiving line, Marie Hélène held out her hand to the Marquise de Crussol, acting as Daladier's consort this evening. "Oh, Marie-Louise, this is a magnificent reception."

"Yes, Monsieur and Madame Bonnet have outdone themselves with the preparations," gushed the marquise in great appreciation of the success of the reception, not that Odette was one of her favorites.

Just then Premier Daladier reared back in mock astonishment and with a big right hand reached out and grabbed Henri's hand and pulled him forward and swung his left arm over Henri's shoulders and gave him a hug and a hearty welcome. "A truly friendly face from the past." He turned to the marquise and said, "Marie-Louise, I want you to meet Henri de Villars-Brancas. An old comrade. We were in the same regiment during the war."

"Yes, we have the dirt of France under our fingernails," said Henri. "Don't we, Édouard?"

"Indeed we do," said the premier. "Those were the hard days."

"We must not let it happen again," said Henri with a sad fall to his voice.

Daladier swung his arm across the vast reception and said grandly, "That is what the state visit from the king and queen is all about. All hinges on the reaffirmation of the Entente Cordiale."

"And the Maginot Line," added Marie Hélène.

"And the Maginot Line," repeated the premier playfully as he added, "And how are you tonight, Mimi?"

"Delighted to be here."

In a mock whisper to Henri, Daladier said, "No one works harder in Paris to see that work on the Maginot Line is completed. She's our secret weapon for keeping the funding going. The députés can't resist her." Daladier smiled warmly at Marie Hélène.

"Well, I'm gratified she's making her contribution," said Henri. "Resist her? I gather few do, here in Paris," he added with an ironical smile.

Marie Hélène gave him a sharp glance. She was exceedingly discreet, she felt. She looked over her shoulder and saw the line behind her was bunching up. She gratefully said to Daladier, "Thank you so much Monsieur le Président, we must give way to other guests." She nudged Henri along and over toward a champagne refreshment table.

Walking across the room, Marie Hélène said, "Oh, there's Thérèse and Claude."

"Great, another friendly face," said Henri. "These other people," he said as he looked around with a bewildered glance, "are strangers. I don't think they have the dirt of France under their fingernails."

"Well, you had a privileged upbringing, too. Don't be so harsh."

"Privilege ended in the trenches. The misery was very equal."

They walked up to Thérèse and Claude. Marie Hélène and Thérèse hugged; the two men shook hands.

"Didn't know you knew Premier Daladier," said Claude, more than a little impressed.

"Yes, we were in the same regiment during the war."

"Comrades?"

"Yes, he was a good soldier," said Henri. "We all were. The dead? They were the great ones," he said mournfully.

Thérèse reached across and took Henri's hand in both of hers and said in a motherly way, "All of France appreciates the sacrifice."

"Only peace can make it worthwhile," said Henri, doubt resonating in his voice.

"We are all working hard for peace here in Paris," said Thérèse. "Marie Hélène and I work hard with the Comité des Forges to encourage the government to support rapprochement with Germany."

"Yes, I know, but I wonder..." And Henri's voice trailed off.

"Well, I heard that at last night's dinner at the Élysée Palace, the play put on by the Comédie-Française was a great success," said Thérèse in reference to the state dinner hosted by Président Lebrun for the British monarchs. "The younger actresses get their reward tonight," she said with an impish grin and nodded across the room.

Marie Hélène's eyes followed, and she saw Jules Dugas escorting one of the younger *pensionnaires* of the state theater troupe, lovely in a ravishing gown. She smiled and remarked, "Well, the foreign minister's hardworking staff earned their rewards tonight."

"Bet that Odette arranged this," said Thérèse. "She takes a real interest in the boy."

"Well, undoubtedly the boy will take an interest in that girl," said Henri with admiring approval. "Rather striking."

"Yes, he will," said Marie Hélène with an ironical laugh. "Well, he has helped so many people out who have an interest in the government; it only seems fair," she added.

Thérèse gazed at her with admiration: so cool, so detached. *Or did she have some other interest developing?* Thérèse suddenly wondered. Her friend could be too discreet.

"Look across the room. There is Madame Tabouis with her husband Robert."

"Lecturing everyone in sight," added Thérèse with a light laugh.

"Oh look, Leon Bailby, the editor of one of the conservative papers, is going up to Geneviève. This should be interesting," said Marie Hélène. The two couples stood and watched the little drama play out across the room.

Conversations

Pushing his way through the guests, the plump man, arrogant in his opinions, backed by serious money from Rome according to rumors, waddled up toward Geneviève. She stood smiling and said, "Why, Leon, so nice to see you tonight. This is my husband Robert."

The plump man held out his chubby hand and shook Robert's rather bony hand at the end of a long arm. The editor held forth, "Why, Geneviève, I've written a thorough attack on your constant propaganda in support of *bellicisme* against Germany and Italy.

How can we cement friendships with them when all you do is attack them and call them warmongers?"

"I look forward to reading it," said the redoubtable journalist.

"Tomorrow's paper," replied the editor curtly. He nodded at Robert and then proceeded in his ducklike walk toward a group of conservative députés nearby who were mostly enjoying the champagne.

"That will raise your circulation, Geneviève," said Robert.

"Yes, it's an ill wind that doesn't blow someone some good."

Geneviève's eyes brightened, and she said, "Robert, look, here comes Monsieur Osusky, the Czech minister."

"Ah, Geneviève," said Osusky and he grasped her hand in both of his, patting it with warm familiarity. "And who is this handsome gentleman?"

"This is my husband Robert."

Robert held out his hand and said, "Pleased to meet your, Monsieur le Minister."

"Please, Stefan. Czechoslovakia has no firmer friend than Madame Tabouis," he said in all earnestness to Robert.

"Look over there," said Osusky suddenly, his eyes narrowing, a beady look coming across his face. "It is Monsieur Flandin speaking with Lord Halifax."

Geneviève turned and looked. "You're right." Just a dozen feet away, she saw the former prime minister and foreign minister, Pierre Étienne Flandin, huddled with British foreign secretary Halifax in animated discussion, hands gesticulating. Halifax had bumped Eden out of the foreign office to Geneviève's disgust.

"Your favorite ex–prime minister," said Robert with a laugh, "chatting with one of your favorite British ministers."

"Flandin is among the worst of the appeasers," said Geneviève. "And Halifax…"

"Flandin seems to be agreeing with everything Halifax is saying," said Osusky, his keen eye for observation not missing a nuance.

"Yes, one of my apprehensions—an alliance between the wrong elements in Paris and London."

"You dislike Flandin in particular, don't you, Geneviève?" asked Robert.

"Yes, he was foreign minister during the failure to respond to the German remilitarization of the Rhineland two years ago," said Geneviève, remembering with distaste one of the early cave-ins to the Germans. "The first of the failures."

Osusky leaned over and whispered to Geneviève and Robert, "I think I know what they're talking about. Hitler's personal adjutant Captain Fritz Wiedemann was in London just before the monarchs departed. He held private talks with Halifax in Halifax's Belgravia home. There have been rumors about the talks ever since."

"Was Chamberlain there?" asked Robert.

"I believe so," replied Osusky.

"All the snakes were in the grass then," said Robert.

The three of them discreetly watched as Flandin and Halifax talked. Halifax was explaining, Flandin listening and agreeing. Osusky watched and then turned to Geneviève and Robert and said, "I must continue my rounds, the endless trail of the diplomat."

Geneviève and Robert laughed. "Good luck." They watched the diplomat weave his way through the crowd, shaking hands and smiling at acquaintances.

"What do you think, Geneviève?" asked Robert.

"Chamberlain had a personal emissary in Prague last week. I fear they're pressuring the Czechs to give in to Hitler on the question of autonomy for the Germans in the Sudetenland."

"Beneš is tough," said Robert.

"Yes, but the British are playing a hard game."

"Yes," said Robert. "They always do when they're going behind your back. Halifax is one of the really snaky ones."

"We must watch Chamberlain," said Geneviève, real apprehension in her voice. Then she lightened up. "Now let's listen to Yvonne before the entertainment ends," she said, mentioning Yvonne Printemps who was singing in the front of the hall.

"*Avec plaisir,*" he said as his gaze turned to the stage where the svelte and strikingly beautiful French chanteuse was singing the great French folk song "Au Clair de la Lune," or "By the Light of the Moon." The assembled guests were enthralled with the great verve and delightful humor that one of France's premier pop divas brought to this performance before the British monarchs, both of whom listened with wide-eyed pleasure after a day watching tanks trundle past and infantry march out at Versailles. The queen stood there faintly mouthing the words of the song.

Just then a deafening roar from the crowd outside arose. Because of the summer heat, all the doors to the outside were open. The music from the reception mixed with the convivial sound of conversation from hundreds of guests inside the hall and floated on the still air to the ears of the crowd outside. The crowd, sensing that its future well-being was tied up with the alliance with Great Britain, took up great roaring cheers in support of the visiting king and queen. As the night went on, the cheers from the crowd outside mounted in intensity. The crowds pushed into the police cordon on the street below the balcony of the Quai d'Orsay with ever greater shouts calling for an appearance by the king and queen. Huge floodlights from the street below played their lights across the façade of the foreign ministry.

Foreign Minister Bonnet and Odette went up to the British king and queen and conferred, some aides shook their heads in disapproval, but the king moved to reassure them. The king and queen, with their aides discreetly behind them, moved through the doors and outside onto the balcony followed by Bonnet and his wife. The king and queen waved their hands in big arcs above their heads; the crowd roared its approval. Then Bonnet and Odette stepped forward and waved their hands, and the crowd again roared its approval. Bonnet and Odette basked in the public glow. The entire royal visit was a public triumph for his diplomacy; his private talks with Halifax less so. It was difficult to find common ground for an understanding about Czechoslovakia with the British. Someday the crowds would be disappointed.

23. La Banque

Thérèse arrived early for her appointment at the Banque Paris et Londres located in posh Neuilly-sur-Seine. She got out of her limousine and told her chauffeur he could get a cup of coffee at a nearby café. She walked into the lobby of the bank, approached the receptionist, and whispered her name and appointment. The receptionist took her over to a small reception area behind some potted plants and brought Thérèse a cup of tea. She sipped and watched the traffic go in and out of the bank.

Soon the door to the manager's office opened and a heavyset man with crinkly reddish-blond hair swept back from his forehead came out. Below the forehead protruded a large bulbous nose giving him a molelike appearance. *He is almost a caricature of a central European Jew*, thought Thérèse, as she mentally turned her nose up at the man's presence. These expatriate Jews were troublemakers, she believed. The man was clothed in a worn gabardine overcoat. Nevertheless the manager held his elbow, all smiles and pleasing talk. Thérèse caught the words "I. G. Farben." What could that be about? Farben was the big German industrial firm, the firm that had been trying to buy out her husband's factories. The factories were suppliers to the sprawling Skoda arms works in Czechoslovakia. The manager guided the man over to the receptionist, bidding him farewell as if he were a duke. The receptionist stood up and said, "Business over, Monsieur Hirsch?"

"*Ja*," said Hirsch and mumbled something to the receptionist, his French thick with a German accent.

The receptionist replied, "If there is anything you need, please do not hesitate to call me. Your messenger will be here shortly to make the initial deliveries." Hirsch nodded his approval at the arrangement. He put on a trilby hat, pushed his dispatch case up under his arm, made a gracious smile at the receptionist, and took his leave.

The receptionist stood there watching Hirsh leave and then came over to the reception area and said, "Baroness, this way please." She escorted Thérèse up to the manager's door, opened it, and led Thérèse into the dark wood paneled office. The manager stood up.

"Baroness, so nice to see you today," said the manager.

"You, too, Monsieur Zabor." Thérèse sat down followed by the manager. Thérèse reached into her handbag and pulled out a sealed envelope and handed it over to the manager. "My husband insists I watch you count it."

The manager opened the envelope and quickly counted out thousands of francs like a bank teller. "It's all here," he said.

"Yes," said Thérèse. "It goes to Odette personally."

"As always," said the manager.

Thérèse stood up and said, "Thank you." The manager arose and escorted her out to the receptionist. Thérèse walked outside and went over to a small café and found her chauffeur, and the two departed.

La Defense

The long Mercedes limousine flying the pennant of the German embassy drove across the bridge over the Seine River and up into the smoky La Défense region outside of Paris, the factories belching smoke, the smell of sulfur pungent in the air. The limousine pulled into a parking lot near a small office building in front of one of the factories. Carl von Dinckler got out, gave instructions to the chauffeur, and walked up the steps and into the office building. He approached the receptionist and said, "Baron de Roncée, please."

"Yes, he's expecting you, Monsieur von Dinckler," said the receptionist as she stood up and led Dinckler down a hall and opened a door to a corner office. As Dinckler walked into the office, he could see the Seine River through the office windows a half kilometer away. He walked in and found Claude de Roncée standing behind his desk, his hand outstretched in greeting.

"Monsieur," said Dinckler.

"Herr von Dinkler," said Roncée warmly. The two men sat down.

"Have you considered the proposal from I. G. Farben?" asked Dinckler.

"Yes, it's rather low," said Claude, a carefully practiced crestfallen look across his face.

"Czechoslovakia might be a more problematic place to do business in the future," said Dinckler in response. He wanted lots of velvet around the hidden threat.

"Yes, it might," said Claude, not giving anything away up front.

Dinckler could see the baron wasn't likely to move without an incentive; time to advance one square on the chessboard. "Possibly some adjustment in terms might be possible."

"Yes, an adjustment might be acceptable to me and my associates," said Claude.

Dinckler was skeptical of the "associates." He understood Claude owned everything outright. He was not a partner kind of chap. "What do you have in mind?" he asked.

"The exchange for cash in London is OK, but like I said, a little cheap," said Claude. "But considering…and I want to tell you…we believe in Germany…"

Dinckler's eyebrows shot up in amazement. "Yes, Germany does want to forge partnerships with France," he said, barely concealing his surprise. "Not all the French understand that…"

"So, what we would also like—partner to partner—is one share of I. G. Farben stock in bearer shares for each share exchanged for cash in London," said Claude. "The shares can be deposited in our bank in Bern, Switzerland."

Dinckler's face took on a momentary look of skepticism as he considered this proposal, so unexpected, but admirably shrewd. "I think this could be arranged, but I will have to check with the principals first."

"Good. Let me know. Then I will get to you the name of the Swiss bank and manager." Claude knew he had a done deal.

"Good," said Dinckler.

"I can deliver the message through the Comité des Forges," said Claude.

"Yes, that would be fine," said Dinckler. He had many friends on the committee; undoubtedly one of the other industrialists would approach him at a reception with the information.

Claude stood up and held out his hand. "A good deal for both of us, I think."

Dinckler stood up and shook Claude's outstretched hand. "Yes, a good partner for Germany." He turned and departed. Weizsäcker would like the proposal—very creative, achieve an objective while advancing a longer term interest.

Claude stood there and watched Dinckler walk down the hall, saw the receptionist escort him outside, and collected his thoughts. Yes, he could see why his wife liked him.

24. Le Grand Café Capucines

Late August. Geneviève Tabouis walked into the Le Grand Café Capucines, a Belle Epoque brasserie near her newspaper offices in the Opéra district of Paris. The maître d' hurried forward exclaiming, "Bonjour, Madame Tabouis, how are you today?"

"It goes well, thank you, Emil," replied Geneviève. "And my guest? Is he here?"

"Over there," he said as he took Geneviève's elbow and guided her over to a table in a distant corner. As she approached, a black-suited gentleman stood and smiled broadly.

"Geneviève, how nice to see you," the man said.

"You, too, Pierre," she said to Pierre Cot, the Radical politician and former air force minister in the Popular Front government. As she sat down, she said, "You must tell me everything about your trip to Czechoslovakia."

"I saw Beneš, and he told me that they are counting on France," said Cot.

"Does he have doubts?"

"Well, yes," said Cot, concern spreading across his face. "Beneš worries that France will betray him."

"Yes, I'm sure he's been plagued with doubts. Ever since I read the news accounts of Lord Halifax's address to the House of Commons last month, so have I. He said the task is to find a peaceful solution so that the German-speaking population could be granted administrative autonomy within the Czechoslovakian frontiers." She leaned across the table and bore in on Cot. "When the king and queen were here in Paris, I saw Lord Halifax and Flandin talking at the reception in hushed tones. I sensed something was not right."

"Autonomy is just a disguise for dismemberment. That's the real threat to Czechoslovakia," said Cot.

"A death warrant, I would say," replied Geneviève. "What does Beneš want?"

"All he asks is that Daladier be frank with him about what France intends to do."

"And Daladier? Have you spoken with him?"

171

"Yes, I have. Daladier said—and I'm quoting him word for word—that there is no question of our betraying Czechoslovakia. France will fulfill her obligations."

"That's reassuring," said Geneviève.

"What else do you know, Geneviève?" asked Cot, angling for more scuttlebutt from one of Europe's best informed journalists.

"I made the circuit of all the embassies here in Paris. Spoke with my best sources. They confirm that Germany has a lot fewer combat aircraft and air crews than this wave of German-paid propaganda in the Paris papers would have us believe."

"I fear our military intelligence services also overestimate German strength," said Cot, a man with deep inside knowledge of the French ministry of defense.

"Most importantly, the vaunted Siegfried Line is just a shell. It's barely been started," said Geneviève. "So my sources tell me."

"I hear the same thing," said Cot, "but not necessarily from inside our military. They have overestimated German strength on the ground west of the Rhine."

Geneviève nodded in agreement and continued, "All the diplomats tell me that France and Britain have to play their cards well. They must act with the same firmness and resolution they demonstrated in the May crisis. They must show themselves ready to fight." She rapped her palm on the tabletop with determination; the fight was in her voice.

"Yes, everything depends upon that," said Cot. "The Germans are playing a cat-and-mouse game."

"War-threat blackmail I would say."

Ministry of Defense

In the massive ministry of defense building on Rue Saint-Dominique just off Boulevard Saint-Germain, Édouard Daladier sat in his office. He was defense minister as well as premier. Across from him sat General Gamelin.

"And what does the High Command think?" asked Daladier.

"The Germans will have fifty to sixty divisions on the western front facing France right from the start," replied the general.

Daladier's face fell. "I didn't realize the German remilitarization program had progressed so quickly." Fifty to sixty divisions were almost ten times as many as he had been led to believe.

General Gamelin nodded sagely.

"And Germany's western fortifications? The Siegfried Line?"

"The West Wall is not complete but remains a formidable obstacle to any advance by the French army," replied the general.

"Our ability to reach the Rhine River is what makes France a valuable ally to the countries in eastern Europe. If we can't threaten Germany in the West..." said Daladier, and his voice trailed off into doubt and indecision.

"Getting to the river..." mumbled the general and let the thought hang.

"Ten years ago the Rhine was a day's march for the French army," said Daladier. "Now it seems it's an impossible distance away."

"Germany has considerable strength west of the river..." said the general.

Yes, the remilitarization of the Rhineland two years ago, thought Daladier. *That opened the door to the current misfortune.* He pulled his thoughts together and said, "The mobilization becomes even more important...to project a sense of credibility to both Berlin and the eastern European capitals." He paused before continuing. "And possibly Russia."

"I will see to a well-organized mobilization," replied the general.

"Good," replied the premier, ending the meeting.

Café de la Paix

Marie Hélène walked through the thick glass doors and inquired about Thérèse to the maître d', who pointed her toward a banquette down at the far end of the room next to a window overlooking the broad spaces of the Place de l'Opéra.

"So nice you could join me for lunch," said Thérèse.

"Yes, I have business today," said Marie Hélène.

Thérèse looked across the square to the far curb, something catching her eye. A Mercedes limousine was pulling up. *Possibly the same one that had been waiting for the Baroness von Einem outside of Maxim's that day*, thought Thérèse. Somewhat surprised, she saw the man in the worn gabardine overcoat get out. What was his name? Hirsch, yes, Hirsch. Marie Hélène craned her neck around and followed Thérèse's glance.

"That's Monsieur Abetz and the baroness," said Marie Hélène, looking at the couple in the rear of the limousine.

"Yes, of course," said Thérèse, quickly regaining her composure.

"I don't know the other man," said Marie Hélène.

"Nor do I," said Thérèse, feigning disinterest.

"The man hardly looks like someone who would be a friend of Abetz."

"No, he doesn't," said Thérèse absently. *But then what would a man look like who was a courier?* she asked herself. *Nondescript would be better than someone who stood out. A Jew to deliver Nazi money?*

She kept watching Hirsch as he walked down the sidewalk. Then, imperceptibly, he looked like he tipped his finger to his hat as a grubby man shuffled along in a smashed down homburg hat. *The man had the dirty look of a* métèque—*an immigrant*, thought Thérèse. There were so many in Paris these days. The grubby man in the hat kept walking, then stopped, and turned around and seemed to follow Hirsch. *Interesting,* thought Thérèse. Her husband always said follow the money. Was that what was going on today? Was she witnessing some sort of German money connection?

Thérèse turned back and looked at Marie Hélène, asking rather absently, "You said you have business today?"

"Yes, arranging support from the Comité des Forges to the politicians. Another visit to the Banque Paris et Londres. A never-ending chore. The politicians are always needy—more allowance, more allowance, they say."

The Banque Paris et Londres, thought Thérèse. *Interesting, Mimi must also meet the bank manager there. Except Mimi has a different day*, she thought, a smile crossing her face. *Same relationship, different day.*

"What's so amusing?" asked Marie Hélène.

"Oh, nothing," said Thérèse. "It's just Claude has the same experience." The two women continued chatting over lunch.

Hôtel Matignon

In the formal office of the premier, Daladier awaited the arrival of the British ambassador. The British were nervous about the partial mobilization the French had ordered. Soon a formally attired usher in a black tailcoat escorted Sir Eric Phipps into the spacious office. The premier was standing with his hand out to welcome the ambassador. France's number one foreign policy goal was always to maintain the relationship with Britain; everything else hinged on that.

"Let me welcome you, Monsieur le Ambassador." The premier extended his hand indicating the ambassador should take a seat.

"Your Excellency," replied the ambassador as he sat down.

"And what can we do for you today?" asked the premier.

"We have seen indications that you are mobilizing your army in advance of Hitler's remarks to be delivered at the Nuremberg rally in the middle of the month."

"Preliminary measures only," reassured the premier. He noticed that the mouselike ambassador was even more nervous than usual. Previously, the ambassador had represented His Majesty's government in Berlin, where he was known to be in personal terror at the prospect of an outburst of Hitler's anger.

"Yes, we observed last week that the American ambassador delivered remarks that the United States would be unlikely to be drawn into a new war in Europe." Britain and France would face Germany alone.

"I understand," said Daladier. "American public opinion at this time cannot contemplate another war in Europe. The président is very mindful of that."

"We understand that if war were to break out, the Americans would embargo the shipment of airplanes that your government has ordered."

175

"Possibly." Daladier believed other arrangements would be made if hostilities broke out. Roosevelt understood the stakes.

"The Germans have a very powerful air force," added the ambassador.

"Yes, that is my understanding," said the premier. His air force general had told him that if hostilities broke out the French air force would be swept from the skies in two weeks. This opinion weighed heavily on his mind, a consideration that would be ever present in his thoughts in the coming weeks. Air power was the new trump card in international politics. The Germans were rapidly equipping their air squadrons with the new Messerschmitt monoplane fighter plane while French and British squadrons were still largely outfitted with older two-winged biplanes, slow-flying pigeons for the new German hawks to pluck from the sky.

"Well, I'm here today because London is very concerned with what the French reaction might be if German troops crossed the Czech frontier."

"If German troops cross the Czech frontier, then the French will march to the man," said the premier with determined forcefulness.

The ambassador shrank back, his personal fears realized, the concerns of his government confirmed. He replied, "There might be great difficulties if the French army tries to attack the Siegfried Line."

"My chiefs of staff assure me the army is ready," said Daladier succinctly.

"And your internal support?" asked the ambassador, referencing the political divide inside France.

"The people of France know what is at stake. If the Germans take Czechoslovakia, the Germans will then consolidate their strength in the East and turn against France."

"Yes, well then, your government will keep His Majesty's government informed and will consult with us prior to taking any action?"

"France will live up to all its agreements," replied Daladier with firmness. There was silence in the room. He stood up, signaling that the interview was over. The ambassador stood up.

"Thank you, Your Excellency," said the ambassador. The ambassador's wire to Lord Halifax was on the foreign secretary's desk that afternoon.

Daladier watched the ambassador depart and then went back around his desk and sat down. He picked up the telephone and called the foreign minister.

"Georges?" asked Daladier into the mouthpiece. Hearing an affirmative response, he continued. "Phipps just left. He'll be on to London in the hour. Tomorrow I would like you to meet with the ambassador. I want you to pose the fundamental question to Phipps: Germany may attack Czechoslovakia. If so, we will march. Will Britain march with us?"

Daladier listened to the gasp at the other end of the telephone line. Obviously, his bluntness shocked the foreign minister. Daladier listened to the various cavils that Bonnet mounted to his request.

"No, Georges. I want the question asked. Tomorrow." Daladier hung up the telephone receiver on its high-necked cradle. Yes, firmness was the correct policy. Then the doubts came back and nibbled around the edges of Daladier's determination. Particularly the lack of airplanes.

Quai d'Orsay

Georges Bonnet sat at his massive desk, his back to the angled windows in the semicircular portico behind him. He held in his hand the British communiqué issued the previous night in London by the Foreign Office. The authorized statement stressed that Germany should be under no "illusions" and not to believe that it could carry out an attack on Czechoslovakia without facing "the possibility of intervention by France and thereafter by Great Britain."

"...thereafter by Great Britain," Bonnet mumbled to his aide Jules Dugas, repeating the words from the communiqué. Just what Daladier wanted to hear.

"The Paris newspapers are hailing the communiqué in today's papers," said Dugas.

"Yes, they would," said Bonnet, crestfallen at the failure of his most recent appeasement campaign.

"Do you think the British mean it?" asked Dugas.

"No," came Bonnet's tart reply. "But I think we will soon find out. Ambassador Phipps will be here any minute.

Dugas looked around behind him at the closed door and then heard a knock and an usher step inside and say, "The British ambassador…"

"Show him in," said Bonnet as he and Dugas stood.

Sir Eric Phipps walked in and approached the desk, saying, "Your Excellency."

"Please have a seat, Monsieur le Ambassador," said Bonnet. "You know my aide Jules Dugas?"

"Yes, quite well, thank you," replied the ambassador. "I have been requested to read to you the following letter from the foreign secretary. You are welcome to take notes."

Bonnet nodded at Dugas, who pulled out a pad of paper and a pencil from his dispatch case.

The ambassador began to read: "So far as I am in a position to give any answer to M. Bonnet's question, His Majesty's government would never allow the security of France to be threatened…but they are unable to state precisely the character of any future action in circumstances that they cannot at present foresee."

"The same as last May," said Bonnet. The British were avoiding any commitment to Czechoslovakia. Bonnet was right; the communiqué was diplomatic smoke for the newspapers.

Phipps did not contradict him. After a few moments, Phipps stood and said, "Your Excellency, I will take my departure."

"Yes," said Bonnet as he arose with a stagger as if he had lost his strength. Dugas followed. The two men watched Phipps leave.

"Now what?" asked Bonnet.

"Hitler speaks to the Nuremberg rally tonight."

"Yes, let's see what he says," said Bonnet fatalistically, his mind's eye envisioning the red-flagged rally in Nuremberg with its rows of storm troopers and tens of thousands of cheering Germans, the torchlight parades, the pagan-like devotion to war. We're going to stand up to a whole new generation of Germans?

Reaction to Nuremberg

The following morning the foreign minister met with his aide, Jules Dugas, and reviewed Hitler's speech of the night before.

"Well, what did he say?" asked Bonnet.

"More about the Czechs being a pygmy race oppressing an innocent and cultured people, the Germans in the Sudetenland. And conspiracies by Moscow and the Jew devils," said Dugas.

Bonnet nodded sadly at these well-worn words of hatred that were now standard in Hitler's speeches.

"He's asking that the Sudetenland Germans be given the right of self-determination, the right to join Germany," continued Dugas.

"What was the reaction?"

"At Nuremberg, delirium. In Czechoslovakia, something much worse. This morning the Sudetenland Germans rose up, using weapons supplied by Germany, and attacked police barracks, railroad stations, post and telegraph offices, and other public buildings in a half a dozen towns."

"Oh, my God," said Bonnet, and he shrank back into his chair. The fuse had been lit. "The Germans will use the insurrection as a pretext to send their troops across the border...and it will all begin...everything we've worked for...lost..."

"If the Germans cross the border," said Dugas, collecting his words, "France will be obligated to do something."

Bonnet just stared back at him blankly. Do something?

The telephone rang. Bonnet, utterly decomposed, just sat there and looked at the ringing apparatus. Dugas stood up, reached over, picked it up, and said, "Foreign minister's office." He listened for a few moments and then asked, "When?" This was followed by a rather incredulous "Now?" He listened and then slowly put the receiver back into its cradle.

"The British ambassador is entering the building."

Bonnet sat up and collected himself. He said, "Fine. We'll see what he says—now."

In a few minutes, the door to the foreign minister's office opened, and the usher said, "The British ambassador."

"Show him in," said Bonnet as he wearily arose to stand in welcome, followed by Dugas.

"Your Excellency," said the ambassador in perfunctory greeting. Bonnet waved his hand for all to be seated.

The ambassador pulled his dispatch case up onto his lap and opened it. He pulled out a typewritten transcript and handed it over to the foreign minister, saying, "A transcript of Lord Halifax's telegram of last May setting forth that His Majesty's government does not feel automatically obliged to take up arms if France were to resist German aggression in Czechoslovakia." The ambassador had only read the message to Bonnet last May. Obviously the British were strongly signaling their unwillingness to support France on Czechoslovakia.

All the other public statements by the British were eyewash, thought Dugas.

Bonnet quickly read through the transcript: yes, exactly as it had been recited last May. He handed the document to Dugas and then said to the ambassador, "The document will help me in the cabinet debates. I trust the warning still applies?"

"Most assuredly," said the ambassador. He sat back and watched as Bonnet composed his thoughts.

"Peace must be preserved at any price," said Bonnet, his voice rising, his manner verging upon being upset. "Neither France nor Britain is ready for war…Colonel Lindbergh says Germany has eight thousand planes…French and British towns would be wiped out…"

"Yes, the military threats are grave," agreed the ambassador. "And today, if I may ask, there are rumors that your Council of Ministers has decided upon mobilization?"

Obviously, thought Dugas, *the mobilization question explains the ambassador's sudden appearance at the foreign ministry.*

"That's quite untrue. The Council of Ministers decided no such thing," said Bonnet with some vehemence. "It was a limited mobilization. No further measures are contemplated. Peace must be maintained at any price."

"Yes, quite so," said the ambassador, angling for a further statement.

"I am going to speak with the diplomatic correspondents this afternoon. I am going to explain that France rejects any solution involving recourse to arms." Then Bonnet sank back into his chair.

The ambassador sat and watched Bonnet. The foreign minister's shoulders sagged, and his expression turned gray and lifeless. Later in the afternoon the ambassador would describe Bonnet as a defeated man to his superiors in London. Phipps stood and said, "I must be going…"

"Yes," said Bonnet as he stood up hurriedly followed by Dugas, who quickly put down his notes. The two men watched the ambassador depart.

Avenue Foch

The phone rang in Thérèse's town house. The maid picked up the phone and again she heard the man with the unfamiliar voice. She inquired back into the telephone, "Frederick?" She listened some more and then replied, "I will get madame." She set the telephone down and went into the drawing room and approached Thérèse and said, "The other gentleman who says he's Frederick is on the line and that it is quite urgent."

"Fine," said Thérèse graciously, "I'll take the call." She stood up and walked into the foyer and picked up the telephone while waving the maid away. A private conversation. She had many such hushed conversations, the maid knew. The maid walked away wondering about two men and one code word. Strange? Madam had always seemed so conventional in that regard. Two at a time?

"Yes, how nice to hear from you," said Thérèse, recognizing the voice of Jules Dugas speaking in a hushed tone. She listened some more.

"Yes, of course I can do that." Again she listened.

"Really?" Her face betrayed a degree of puzzlement.

"Go straight into the German embassy?" she asked with astonishment.

"What about risks? The Sûreté?" she inquired.

"Surveillance? Yes, I understand that they would watch Carl when he leaves the embassy. They know I meet him?" she said, now truly astonished. The French security services knew about her and Carl. They must know about the hideaway apartment.

"But not us," she said, repeating the assurance. "Secure for now." Undoubtedly he had good contacts in the ministry of the interior; he would know. She understood and was reassured; she was the secret link in the confidential channel.

"Urgent. Yes, I can be there in half an hour."

Place Victor Hugo

The limousine pulled up into a vacant parking space near the steps leading down to the metro station. In the rear seat, Thérèse leaned forward and said to her chauffeur, "I'll be just a minute." She got out of the car and walked over to the steps leading down into the station. She stopped at the first landing, and an older man in a smashed-down homburg hat was standing there. He exactly fit the description she had been told to expect. The man looked vaguely familiar. Then she remembered—the man on the sidewalk—the man who had the rendezvous with the Jew Hirsch. *Strange, did this nondescript man, almost a clochard—a tramp—work for Dugas, too?* She walked up to him, and he nodded to her to open her handbag. She did, and he unobtrusively placed an envelope in it. She turned and walked back up the steps and returned to the car.

"Where to, madame?" the chauffeur asked.

"To the German embassy."

"The German embassy?" asked the chauffeur rather startled.

"Yes, drive straight into the courtyard. I'm expected." She said that with the breezy assurance of someone who usually was. "Then you can return home. I will stay. I have a dinner appointment. My committee work." The chauffeur nodded his understanding. Madame's committee work was handsome and somewhat younger, that he knew. He and the maid kept close tabs on the baroness's committee work. The baron was always appreciative of the information. And no harm was done. Avoid scandal, the baron said.

British Embassy

In the evening, Sir Eric Phipps sat in his study in the British embassy on stately Rue du Faubourg Saint-Honoré quickly writing out his dispatch. He recounted his meeting with the French foreign minister, writing a sentence sure to grab the attention of London: "M. Bonnet's collapse was so sudden and so extraordinary that I immediately went and asked for an interview with M. Daladier."

Phipps continued to write: "I saw M. Daladier…who was gravely perturbed by bloodshed in Czechoslovakia and felt every minute was now precious…I asked M. Daladier point-blank whether he adhered to his policy expounded to me last week…he replied with evident lack of enthusiasm that if the Germans used force France would be obliged also. He said that he had sent two officials to Prague to impress upon M. Beneš the importance of making every possible concession to the Sudeteners…he spoke bitterly of M. Beneš, as did M. Bonnet previously…"

Phipps concluded his dispatch with his observations: "M. Daladier is a different man from the premier I saw last week, and the tone and language were very different…indeed…I fear the French have been bluffing, although I have continually pointed out to them that one cannot bluff Hitler."

Phipps handed the message to his private secretary for transmittal to London. He continued working late into the evening at his desk.

Ambassador's Study

Later in the evening, the private secretary entered the ambassador's study and said, "Premier Daladier is on the telephone."

"Put him through, please," said the ambassador. "Please stand by to take notes. I'll dictate as I go." The private secretary got a pad of paper and sat down. The ambassador picked up the telephone receiver.

"Yes, Monsieur le Président," said the ambassador into the telephone mouthpiece. He listened for a few moments. "Yes, I can take down the message and telephone it personally to the prime minister myself…yes, tonight will be fine…my telephone connection is quite good…"

Phipps nodded to his private secretary to take notes. The ambassador said into the mouthpiece, "Let me repeat as you go so my aide can get the words down exactly..." He paused and listened and then started to repeat, "Matters risk getting out of control almost at once...the entry of German troops into Czechoslovakia must at all costs be prevented because it would confront France with having to fulfill her obligation...by automatic necessity to fulfill her treaty engagement..."

Phipps looked over at his private secretary, who looked back and indicated he had all the words down. Phipps continued to repeat the premier's words, "An immediate proposal for a Three Power meeting between Germany, Britain, and France with a view to obtaining the pacific settlement proposed by Hitler in his speech last night." Phipps listened some more and then concluded the telephone conversation, saying, "Yes, I'll call the prime minister straightaway." He understood: everything must be done to keep German troops from crossing the frontier. Everything.

London

In the prime minister's study at Number 10 Downing Street, the private secretary came in and said, "Ambassador Phipps on the line, sir. He says it's quite urgent."

"Quite so," crisply replied Neville Chamberlain. "Put him on." Chamberlain listened to Ambassador Phipps, his private secretary listening in on another line while furiously taking notes. Chamberlain looked at the secretary who signaled he had good notes. "Thank you, Mr. Ambassador. I'm taking prompt action tonight. We'll be in touch." He hung up the telephone and motioned his aide over.

The private secretary sat down and pulled out his notes. Chamberlain said, "Here, take down this message for immediate transmittal to Chancellor Hitler in Berlin." He paused and collected his thoughts. Then he dictated: "I propose to come to Germany tomorrow by air with a view to trying to find a peaceful solution. Please indicate earliest time at which you can see me and suggest place of meeting." Chamberlain leaned back and said with a degree of self-satisfaction, "There."

Get the framework in place, he thought, *leader to leader.* Then he looked at his private secretary, "Please get it off to Berlin straightaway." The private secretary stood up and left the office.

German Embassy

In the German embassy several blocks away, the *chargé d'affaires,* just back from an unofficial meeting with officials at Number 10 Downing Street, wrote out his telegram to Berlin while the coding clerk stood nearby. He wrote simply: "Prime minister's press secretary informs me prime minister is prepared to examine far-reaching German proposals, including plebiscite, and that Britain would take part in carrying them out, and would advocate them in public." He handed the message to the coding clerk, who hurried out of the office.

The German diplomat leaned back and thought, *The Führer's iron determination is carrying the day.*

Sûreté

The door opened, and *le chef* turned, somewhat surprised at this unexpected visit by *l'inspecteur.*

"What is it?" asked *le chef,* intrigued. They had been waiting for a break. They always came.

"The tap on the apartment of baroness de Roncée has paid off."

"Thérèse? Really?"

"Yes, we caught the word *Frederick.*"

"Yes, the code word for a message."

"Exactly."

"But usually the code word is to arrange for a meeting with the comtesse de Villars-Brancas? Why not this time?"

"She disappears now and again. Here in Paris somewhere. Often overnight. But not to meet Dugas. That's Tuesdays. She meets him like clockwork. We haven't tailed her to find out where—or why. She probably has a little hideaway apartment like Thérèse."

"So in the meantime the source goes straight to Dinckler's mistress?" asked *le chef,* a little disbelieving.

"That's true. The voice on the telephone believes we only have surveillance on Dinckler and that is how we know about Thérèse. He doesn't suspect a telephone tap."

"Of course not. We told the ministry of interior we were not tapping her telephone or any of the cabinet staff. Just the Comité des Forges."

"So they assured him his phone was clean?"

"Yes, that's the way to set it up for a leak from the cabinet. Tell them about the tap on a decoy."

"Of course."

"Nevertheless, why did he go to Thérèse? She is rather obvious."

"Speed. Urgency. Thérèse went straight to the metro station at Place Victor Hugo and descended the steps—we barely got the surveillance in place on time—and picked up an envelope from an older, nondescript messenger. We know him. He's used by the bank to deliver payoffs to the newspapermen and politicians—part of the Abetz propaganda operation."

"And the message?"

"Thérèse delivered it straight to the German embassy."

"The embassy?"

"Yes. She sent her driver home and stayed at the embassy. We didn't see when she left—it must have been surreptitiously—there's a lot of traffic in and out."

"Yes. Interesting. A good day's work."

"Thanks."

Le chef eyed *l'inspecteur*, who was sitting there with a wide grin on his face. "OK, there's something else. Out with it."

"The voice on the telephone. The policeman on the tap was the same one who heard the source from the French cabinet tip off the German embassy in 1936 about the Spanish arms shipment."

With great expectation, *le chef* leaned across his desk and asked, "Yes?"

"The same voice."

"Voilà! It fits," exclaimed *le chef*. "You better go over to the Deuxième Bureau and tell Morel."

"I'm on my way," replied *l'inspecteur*.

Paul A. Myers

Place Malesherbes

Geneviève Tabouis was sipping morning coffee and munching on a brioche while reading the morning papers. She heard a knock on the door and listened as Arthur, her manservant, went and opened it. A messenger handed him a large envelope. He brought it in and laid it on the table next to Geneviève and said perfunctorily, "For you, madame." Packages arrived at all hours of the day and night; telephone calls, too.

"Thank you, Arthur," she said, and she reached over and looked at the envelope. From the legation of one of the smaller east European countries here in Paris. She tore open the envelope, revealing a second envelope from that country's Berlin legation. She opened it and read, increasingly fascinated. It was from her best Berlin source, an individual employed at the Wilhelmstrasse. She read: "Sir Neville Henderson, having delivered the memorandum to Hitler, went to Ribbentrop to explain the British attitude in the matter. After listening to Sir Neville's speech on the determination of the British to support France, Ribbentrop burst out laughing in the British ambassador's face. He seemed perfectly sure that France had no intention of acting at all, and therefore he could mock the British for their serious resolution."

Geneviève set the message down and took a sip of coffee. *Interesting*, she thought. Ribbentrop could see straight into the mind of the French government. He must have very good information.

She turned back to the morning papers. The Russian foreign minister had spoken before the assembly at the League of Nations in Geneva. She read his statement: "We are ready to fulfill our obligations, according to treaty, and to give aid to Czechoslovakia, along with France, to the best of our ability. Our military authorities are prepared to confer at once with the military representatives of France and Czechoslovakia...we believe a meeting of the great powers should be called to agree on collective action should that case be warranted by the march of events..."

She scanned down the statement to the words "if France lives up to her agreements and does likewise." Yes, the rub, the bridge that neither Daladier nor Bonnet wants to cross...a bridge France would have to walk alone...no Great Britain by its side...an uncertain Russia on the other side.

187

Hideaway

On the top floor of an apartment building on a narrow street behind the Madeleine deep in the Right Bank, the last of the afternoon light was coming through translucent linen curtains covering the windows, which were bordered by thick blue drapes hanging from the same brass rods from which the linen fell. Carl lay on the bed and watched as Thérèse stood at the end of the bed and began to dress herself. She pulled a brassiere around her waist and looked down intently as she flicked little hooks into eyes on the clasp. Carl watched as each of Thérèse's ample breasts jiggled as she moved her arms, the nipples dancing in small movements. He was always enchanted by this ritual, a final small frisson at the end of lovemaking. He watched as she put one arm through a strap and tugged the brassiere up, then put her other arm through the other strap. She pulled one cup up and pulled it over her soft white breast, and then the other. She tugged on the straps and wiggled her breasts, setting each one into its well-secured place.

He looked down at her still nude body, the stomach curving down into her darkness, the nice hips, the long legs. *She is all filly*, he thought. And she truly liked to gallop. He smiled at the recollection. She pulled on a pair of knickers, then bent over and pulled a girdle up, gave a grunt, and pulled it up above her navel. She sat down and pulled silk stockings up above her knee and clasped garters. She stood up, pulled a silk slip off the back of the chair, and pulled it over her head. She walked over to a coat rack, took her dress off, and stepped into it. Carl got up and ran the zipper up the back. Then he lay back down. She smoothed the dress over her hips with her hands. Then she took her coat off the rack, put it on, and picked up her handbag.

"Oh, yes," she said. "Claude wanted me to give you this envelope. It's about a bank and a banker. He said you'd know what it meant. Something about the Czechoslovakia business." She handed him the envelope.

"Really? Not from Marie Hélène? That's what I would've expected. Something from Dugas."

"No. From Claude."

Carl reached over and turned on the bedside lamp. He opened the envelope and took out a sheet of paper and read the name of a man and the name of a bank, easily recognizable as a bank in Basel. His recommendations to Berlin on the advantages of having Claude as a French partner had been favorably received. He would see that the I. G. Farben stock was properly delivered. He put the sheet of paper into his suit pocket.

"Yes, I understand."

"He said you would."

"I discussed a business deal with him last week. At his office." *Yes,* he thought, *I understand Claude's message, and his choice of messenger.* He knew. Well, Thérèse was the decoy, the bright bauble to attract the attention that was always on him away from the other business, the secret channel with Marie Hélène.

Quai d'Orsay

Geneviève Tabouis was ushered into the Rotunda Drawing Room, the foreign minister's magisterial office of kinglike proportions. She was seated by the usher. She looked across the vast wooden desk at Georges Bonnet who was seated just in front of the oval rotunda with its three large windows overlooking the well-tended park behind. She could see Bonnet was out of sorts. Normally self-controlled and shrewdly calculating, he was fidgety and nervous this day.

"Yes, Geneviève," he said hesitatingly.

"Monsieur le Minister," began Geneviève.

"Georges, Geneviève, Georges," said the minister with minor impatience at Geneviève's formality; larger troubles had his mind in turmoil. "We've been friends for a long time."

"Yes, but I've come today to say that I can't support in my column where our foreign policy seems to be going. I can never support the idea of the Sudetenland being incorporated into the Reich. It would destroy Czechoslovakia." Geneviève and other diplomatic journalists like Pertinax felt strongly that a crossroads had been reached. Geneviève glanced down at her notes. She looked up and saw that Bonnet was in near panic at her words. Exasperation was on his face...his mind frustrated by the impossibility of trying to control French public opinion with half the Parisian papers against him...led by one of his oldest and dearest friends...

Bonnet stood up and paced before the two-story tall windows, the three-century-old chandeliers sparkling above him. He turned and said to Geneviève, his voice tremulous with worry, "But, Geneviève, do you know what war is like? War with bombs?" Whatever else could be said about Bonnet, he had seen arduous frontline duty in the trenches of the Great War."

Bonnet looked up at the ceiling, then turned and walked over and stood by the tall window, his shoulder brushing the heavy folds of the tapestry-thick drape, and looked out the window and stared at the Seine River below.

"If war comes," he said forlornly, "that is where I shall wind up."

Startled, Geneviève sat in her chair, collecting her thoughts, and calmly replied, "If war comes, you will probably end up like all the rest of us. Perhaps, if the worst comes to the worst, you will be hit by a bomb. But why should you throw yourself into the Seine?"

"I won't throw myself into the Seine," he said. "If war comes, there will be a revolution, and the people will throw me into the river." His voice rose almost to a scream.

Geneviève stood up, embarrassed by this breakdown in nerve.

Pulling himself together, Bonnet said, "Believe me, my dear Geneviève, we feel exactly the same about Czechoslovakia. I want to save the country. I am even going to Geneva to talk with Litvinov—but don't be surprised if the Russians fail us, too!"

Geneviève hid her astonishment at the statement; it was contrary to all she understood about Russia's recent assurances on Czechoslovakia. She gently said, "The Russians have said they would support Czechoslovakia three different times this year—in March, June, and most recently just a couple of days ago. Possibly you could explore these assurances while you are in Geneva?"

Bonnet looked at her bleakly and nodded in understanding.

"Good luck on your trip to Geneva, Monsieur le Minister," she said and turned and departed, dark thoughts crossing her mind as to why France had to rely on the weak resolve of Daladier and Bonnet.

25. Mounting Crisis

Lord Halifax came into the prime minister's office at Number 10 Downing Street. The prime minister stood and said, "I want to give you a briefing on my meeting with Hitler at Berchtesgaden. The cabinet will meet within the hour."

Halifax sat down and asked, "Is a deal taking shape?"

"Yes, we got down to business straightaway. I told Hitler that I recognized the need to detach the Sudeten areas, but that I would first have to get cabinet approval and of course bring the French along."

"He understood?"

"Yes."

"What's next?"

"I proposed another meeting in a few days and in the meantime asked that Germany refrain from any military action."

"And?"

"He agreed to both."

"Your impression of Hitler?"

"In spite of the hardness and ruthlessness I saw in his face, I got the impression that here was a man who could be relied upon when he had given his word."

Lord Halifax took this in and found it very reassuring. British policy would work, not just today, but well into the future.

"And about the French?" asked the prime minister.

"I have here a letter from Phipps," replied Halifax. Halifax pulled out the letter and began to read: "Bonnet repeated to me this morning that he and the French government would accept any plan advocated by the prime minister…and impose it upon the Czechs; if the latter were recalcitrant, they would be told that France would disinterest herself from their fate…I feel pretty certain that the French will by no means resort automatically to arms, even if German forces cross the Czechoslovak frontier…"

"Good," pronounced the prime minister. "The French will be here tomorrow."

The French

Premier Daladier and Foreign Minister Bonnet walked into the British cabinet room as Prime Minister Chamberlain and Foreign Secretary Halifax stood to greet them. After a round of introductions, the statesmen and their aides took their seats.

Chamberlain proceeded to brief the French visitors on his recent trip to Berchtesgaden stressing that "the situation was much more urgent and critical than I supposed." He continued to say that he favored accepting Hitler's demand for self-determination for the Sudeteners.

Nothing surprising here, thought Daladier. He had been well briefed on the prime minister's meeting with Hitler. Nevertheless, with a firm tone in his voice, he explained, "Germany's real aim is the disintegration of Czechoslovakia and...a march to the East. Romania will be next...the result: Germany will soon be the master of Europe and then will turn on France and Britain."

Chamberlain listened politely and replied, "I raised that question with the German chancellor at Berchtesgaden about whether the return of the Sudetenland would be his last territorial demand or whether he was aiming for the dismemberment of the Czechoslovakian state. The Führer gave me his assurance that this was his last such demand—he wanted no Czechs in the German Reich, he said."

"Does he mean that?" countered Daladier.

"I carefully watched him, and I believe that he can be relied upon to keep his word unless something unexpected happens."

"Let the minutes show that I disagree," said Daladier, glancing down the table toward a private secretary.

The prime minister nodded in acknowledgment of Daladier's point but continued to argue the importance of taking Hitler up on the agreement.

Daladier replied by affirming that France would honor her commitments to Czechoslovakia if she were attacked by the Germans, but he collected his thoughts into carefully chosen words. He wanted to pose the dilemma to the prime minister in such a way that a solution might be discovered that would lead to a way out of the predicament.

Daladier spoke directly to the prime minister: "The problem is to discover the means of preventing France from being forced into war as the result of her obligations, and at the same time to preserve Czechoslovakia and save as much of that country as is humanly possible." Some part of Czechoslovakia was now on the bargaining table.

The prime minister smiled his broad self-confident smile as he saw the way forward: avoid a German military attack on Czechoslovakia while delivering the Sudetenland territories to German control. Czechoslovakia would be made to relinquish the lands in question; the French would acquiesce in the policy.

Daladier watched and waited for Chamberlain to make the next move. Chamberlain did not disappoint. "A formula. All territory where the Sudeteners comprised more than half the population will be ceded to Germany."

"And Czechoslovakia itself?" asked Daladier.

"An international guarantee of the new boundaries…against unprovoked aggression…in which Great Britain will participate…"

The French premier nodded in acquiescence. The talks were unfolding as Bonnet had foreseen, possibly better than he had hoped.

"Of course," the prime minister added, "the new assurance is conditional on the Czechs abrogating all their treaties of mutual assistance with France and Russia."

Bonnet quickly grasped Chamberlain's thinking—the two western democracies would be out of the Czechoslovakian business for good. Longer term, there might be some negative consequences with Russia, but those were hard to gauge.

The meeting was concluded with the firm resolution of the parties that Czechoslovakia would be compelled to accept terms.

Quai d'Orsay

The Parisian press was shooed by the ushers into a small room just outside the doors to the foreign minister's office.

There they waited for Bonnet to finish his meeting with M. Osusky, the Czech minister to Paris.

"What did you hear from London, Geneviève?" one of the journalists asked.

"A program of concessions has been decided upon. Details to follow," replied Geneviève.

"Yes, the devil's always in the details," replied another journalist.

Suddenly the gilded doors to the foreign minister's office swung open. The journalists swarmed to look inside the office. In a few moments, they saw the Czech minister come forward. Geneviève was shocked at his pale appearance, his unsteadiness on his feet as if he were drunk. Seeing the journalists, he stopped and composed himself, bringing himself to an erect posture, and walked forward to the assembled reporters. He stopped and stood there, his fists clenching and unclenching, his face turning purple, and said in a strangled voice: "Gentlemen, you see before you a man who has been condemned without having been given a hearing."

He motioned toward Geneviève, who hurried over and caught hold of his arm and helped him out of the room toward his waiting limousine. She followed him into the rear seat of the car. After the car had departed the courtyard of the Quai d'Orsay, Osusky slumped back against the cushions and held out the paper he had been clutching in his hands. Geneviève took it and quickly scanned the words. It was the Franco-British document informing the Czechs of the concessions Paris and London were demanding that Prague give to Hitler in the face of Nazi intimidation.

"It is nothing less than a death warrant for Czechoslovakia," exclaimed Geneviève.

Osusky sadly nodded.

The two of them rode in complete silence to the Czech legation. In the vestibule of the legation, they were met by Osusky's private secretary. They went into the minister's office, and Osusky called for his secretary and started to dictate a message.

Turning to Geneviève, he said, "I am going to try to make Beneš see that he is lost, and Europe with him, unless he makes every effort to resist the terrible intimidation that the French and British are using to force us into accepting the partition of our country. There is not a minute to lose, as your minister, M. Lacroix, and the British minister, will meet with our foreign minister shortly. And this will be the end. I know that."

"The Russians have not been heard from yet. Possibly Beneš will be able to counter the proposal?"

"No, Britain and France will not only refuse to support us if Germany attacks us, but they will burden us with the whole responsibility for starting the war."

Geneviève sat silent.

"Yes, Geneviève, I lost all my illusions this morning."

They chatted for a few more moments and then Geneviève took her leave. Outside the legation, she heard a newsboy cry out, "Read Colonel de la Roque's article," mentioning the well-known right-wing political leader.

Geneviève bought a copy and read the article: "France is the only nation capable of accomplishing this great feat of arbitration. We are faithful to our noble traditions in this hour, and worthy of our great destiny. The role played by France during the past three weeks will be extolled in the future, and this chapter will be one of the most brilliant in our history." Geneviève sighed with resignation. *So much for naught*, she thought.

Walking toward the Quai d'Orsay, Geneviève walked into a small bistro and went to a rear table and sat down. It was time to take up the only weapon Geneviève had: her pen. A waiter brought a cup of her favorite tea. She pulled out her pad and headed a blank page with the title "war threat blackmail," a shorthand concept she had popularized to describe Hitler's mode of operation. Then she stared at the blank sheet of paper.

What had gone wrong? She and a few other journalists with inside sources on Germany had exposed the facts of Germany's lack of military strength at every opportunity; she had hammered away at the weakness of the Reich week after week. The Siegfried Line was inadequate for defense; the Germans only had men under arms equal to Czechoslovakia when mobilized; the Czechs had formidable defenses that would be hard to crack; the Germans were unprepared on both the western and eastern fronts; the German General Staff was opposed to going to war at this time.

Most importantly, in both France and Great Britain, where her name was on page one of newspapers almost every day due to syndication, her credibility was sky high. She had the assistance of a person in Berlin who had been able to supply her with information of startling importance. She had been able to print accounts of frenzied discussions at the top of the German government between Hitler and his generals, often within a day or two of when the conversations had taken place.

She collected her thoughts and then jotted down notes for the column she would dictate to a stenographer at the newspaper office later that afternoon, a column recounting and recapping what she knew about the course of the crisis.

She looked up and saw one of the top journalists for *Le Temps* take a seat at a small table upfront near the window. He was one of the foot soldiers in Bonnet's defeatist propaganda campaign, the constant smoke screen of lies and deception spread by the French government. She kept her head down and continued writing. The journalist seemed to be waiting for someone. She kept an eye on him.

Presently an older and somewhat decrepit-looking man came in wearing a crushed down homburg hat. He sat down opposite the polished journalist and pulled a large envelope out of his inside overcoat pocket and handed it across to the reporter, who slipped it into his pocket. The journalist ordered a coffee for the decrepit-looking man from the waiter, who brought it over. The journalist stood up and said he had better depart. He patted the old man on the shoulder and left.

Geneviève wondered, *Information or money?*

Place Malesherbes

Geneviève sat at her dining room table and watched Arthur pour coffee into her guest's coffee cup and set out breakfast rolls. Hubert Ribka was the editor in chief of the leading Prague daily paper. More importantly he was the "Gray Cardinal" for Président Beneš, the confidant entrusted with important communications.

"Please tell me," began Geneviève, "what the reception was like in Prague when they received Osusky's dispatch?"

197

"At Hradčany Palace, it was high drama that night. After meeting with his ministers, Beneš walked out looking like an old, old man. He had aged ten years in a few hours."

"Yes, Osusky was crushed, too."

"He had to bow before the wishes of France and England and accept this plan of theirs, although it deprives us of our defenses, and delivers us up to Germany."

"Tell me the reaction of the Czech people."

"Well, the Czechs are confident in their army and air corps, and in particular the motorized divisions. So their reaction in Prague was violent and they tore down the French flag and swore to defend the country in spite of the British and French."

"And the politics?"

"Well, the two agrarian ministers," said Ribka, referring to ministers from a major conservative party, "favor capitulation."

"Yes, my sources say several of the Prague bankers have met secretly at a villa with the agrarians outside of Prague to force a capitulation."

"Yes, they say they'd rather be occupied by Hitler than defended by Voroshilov," said Ribka, mentioning the Russian defense minister.

"Russia?" asked Geneviève. Always the question: would Russia come to Czechoslovakia's aid?

"Beneš met with the Russian ambassador. He assures Beneš of Russia's support, but Beneš questioned him closely on all the contingencies. There can be no resistance by Czechoslovakia if there is any equivocation...by Russia..."

"Yes, Russia is only obligated to help Czechoslovakia if France honors her commitment first," replied Geneviève thoughtfully. Too much wiggle room here. "A tough decision."

"We Czechs," said Ribka, "are doing a good deal of thinking these days. We have not forgotten, you know, that Spain, too, went to war..."

Geneviève nodded. A painful experience, a cautionary example...Spain...to plunge one's people into the abyss of war...the death and destruction always many times larger than first expected...maybe it's better to give in and hope for the best...

The two continued talking. Geneviève explained that a strong feeling of solidarity with Czechoslovakia was rising among the French public as the Czech government resisted the Franco-British demand for concessions presented to Osusky several days ago. Daladier had been forced to react, she said. The premier was mobilizing several more classes of reserves to active duty and sending them to man the Maginot Line in eastern France. Just then, Arthur entered the room and said to Geneviève, "It's time."

She turned and said to Ribka, "I have to go now. I have a farewell to make."

Gare de l'Est

Arthur drove the large touring car through the teeming traffic clogging the approaches to the huge train station in eastern Paris. Young soldiers were everywhere.

"You can let me out over there," said Geneviève. "I will only be ten minutes."

The car swung over, and Arthur hurried around and opened the door. Geneviève scurried out and joined the throng heading for the open doors under the massive façade of the majestic train station. Inside the cavernous station, troops were being assembled by officers and sergeants and then marched down the long concrete platforms to waiting railway carriages. Geneviève was moved by the heartbreaking good-byes between families and soldiers; deeply impressed by the dignity of the marching soldiers. She was struck, in this era of the Popular Front, that troops were singing both the "Internationale" and the "Marseillaise" with a vigorous sense of patriotism.

Finding the correct platform, she worked her way down past the luggage carts and the squads of soldiers, looking up at the lampposts at the signs hurriedly taped up until she came to the one matching the slip of paper in her hand. She walked along the carriage, searching with her eyes into the open windows, until she exclaimed, "Francois." Her twenty-one-year-old son, *un sous-lieutenant*, leaned out of the window, very pleased, and said, "*Ma mère.*" Geneviève stood on her tiptoes and held her son's hands in hers and said her motherly good-byes.

A soldier standing next to François told her reassuringly, "Well, we had to fight Hitler someday, so why not now?"

It was a question Geneviève would rather not have to answer as she thought of her son out on the French frontier facing Germany. She smiled reassuring at the young soldier but said nothing. As train couplings clanked and wheels creaked, the carriage made a jolt. Geneviève let her son's hands go as she stepped back from the carriage, now slowing moving forward foot by foot, then meter by meter, down the track. She stood there waving at the receding figure of her son leaning out of the window as the carriage emerged into the sunlight outside the station and the train started to bend around the first curve of its journey to eastern France.

She turned and walked back down the long concrete platform and then across the reception area underneath the large blackboard listing the departing and arriving trains. She pulled up with a start as she watched Carl von Dinckler casually strolling through the throngs of milling soldiers, looking this way and that. Well, nothing illegal about that. Possibly a good omen—a report might go back to Berlin that French troops with solid morale were entraining toward the eastern border with Germany. Outside she found her car and then Arthur drove her hurriedly across Paris to the foreign ministry for a press briefing.

Arriving at the Quai d'Orsay, Geneviève hurried down the corridor of the majestic building toward the pressroom. Outside the minister's office, she encountered her adversaries, chatting and smoking, the defeatists of the Bonnet circle. There were a couple of ranking députés from the parliament's Foreign Affairs Committee, various officials, several bankers. *The whole clan*, she thought. Jacques Chastenet, one of the editorial directors of *Le Temps* and the ringmaster of the propaganda campaign, came up to her. "What happened to you? You look as if you had just been to a funeral."

"On the contrary," she said. "I have just witnessed a wonderful spectacle of youth and valor. I have just left the Gare de l'Est."

"Well, why shouldn't those young men be brave?" said Chastenet with a cynical sneer. "What have they got to lose?"

"Nothing," she snapped. "They have not gone off to defend their own fortunes and privileges."

Chastenet threw away his cigarette, anger in the throw of the hand, contempt in the flick of the fingers. The other journalists smiled up their sleeves. *They always do*, thought Geneviève. A corrupt sense of privilege stalked these corridors of power, purchasing the politics of whatever government ruled the day, unmindful of the future consequences.

Quai d'Orsay

Late at night in the foreign minister's office, Bonnet and Dugas were impatiently awaiting the bad news from Prague. The French minister in Prague, Victor de Lacroix, was telegramming an account of how the Czech cabinet rejected the Anglo-French proposals on the Sudetenland. The Czech response said "that to accept them would put Czechoslovakia sooner or later under the complete domination of Germany."

Bonnet was steamed at this intransigence. Czechoslovakia was rejecting Hitler's demands. An usher brought the telegram in, and Bonnet snatched it out of his hands and said in dismissal, "Thank you." The usher quickly retreated.

Bonnet read through the telegram with increasing exasperation. Bonnet exclaimed to Dugas angrily, "The Czechs are trying to put me on the spot—they want me to go on record that France intends to renege on the security guarantee."

"It's the Czechs' duty to agree to the proposals, not try to shift the blame to France," said Dugas with disgust in his voice.

"Here," said Bonnet, handing the telegram to Dugas, "you know what to do with it."

Dugas took the telegram and hurried out of the office.

Bonnet reached across his desk and picked up the telephone and said to the operator, "Daladier, please." The call went through, and Bonnet said, "Monsieur le Président, you had better come over. We're drafting a reply to our minister in Prague."

Dugas returned with what appeared to be a fresh telegram and handed it to Bonnet. He read through the doctored telegram and pronounced it "excellent." Bonnet said to Dugas, "You better get Léger. We'll need him for the drafting." Dugas departed.

Several minutes later, Dugas returned with Léger. Bonnet showed Léger the telegram and outlined what he thought the reply should be.

"Yes, Monsieur le Minister," said Léger. "I have received word from the British foreign office that the British minister in Prague has told Halifax that a solution must be imposed."

"I quite agree," said Bonnet.

Lèger took the telegram and a pad of paper over to a nearby desk and began composing a message to the French minister in Prague for delivery to the Czech government.

A few minutes later, Daladier and his aides arrived. The men grouped themselves around Bonnet's desk. Bonnet was now standing so that Daladier could sit at the desk in the middle of the circle of men. Sharp discussion bounced around the desk followed by agreement that Léger's message met the needs of the situation. Bonnet looked at the clock; it was half past midnight. He handed the message back to Léger and said, "Please telephone the message to our minister."

Léger looked at the foreign minister. A telephone call? Bonnet's gaze bored in on Léger. The secretary general shrugged and walked across the room to a small desk with a telephone and made the call. He started to read the message, "France and Britain have set forth the only proposal, which under the circumstances can prevent the Germans from marching into Czechoslovakia…if the proposals are rejected by the Czech government…they must assume responsibility…and Czechoslovakia must understand that France has the right to draw its conclusions in the case of such a rejection…"

The telephone line went across eastern France, across Germany, to Prague. In Germany, the listening post made a transcript of the telephone conversation. A German officer looked at the transcript, blinking with unbelief. In the clear? A typed transcript was sent to Berlin.

In Paris, Bonnet summed up, saying, "Yes, the responsibility for any German attack is now on the Czechs…where it belongs."

26. Munich

The British prime minister took a seat in the conference room overlooking the Rhine River in Godesberg, Germany. An aura of smug optimism accompanied the British delegation; they had just accomplished in a couple of days the near impossible set of demands upon which the Germans had insisted. Chamberlain was sitting straight-backed in his black broadcloth jacket, stiff in a high-necked wing collar, the black tie knotted at his throat, an image of Victorian rectitude out of the previous century. He was ready to present to Hitler all that the Führer had requested and be done with the crisis; he looked forward to returning to London. The day before the Czech government had accepted the Anglo-French plan; the Czech government had resigned, and a Czech general had formed a new government to implement the plan.

Hitler took a seat across from Chamberlain. He wore his Nazi party brown blazer with black pants and presented a more relaxed and contemporary image than the stiff-necked British prime minister.

Getting the Anglo-French plan approved had not been easy in any of the allied capitals. In Paris, three ministers—Paul Reynaud, Georges Mandel, and Paul Champetier de Ribes—had resigned from the cabinet before Daladier compelled them to withdraw their resignations and remain at their posts.

In London, Winston Churchill had resoundingly condemned the proposals as "the complete surrender of the Western Democracies to the Nazi threat of force. Such a collapse will bring neither peace nor security to England or France."

Nevertheless, Chamberlain explained to Hitler that all that Germany had asked for had been accomplished. An eyewitness was struck by the personal self-satisfaction in Chamberlain's demeanor.

"Do I understand," said Hitler, "that the British, French, and Czech governments have agreed to the transfer of the Sudetenland from Czechoslovakia to Germany?"

"Yes," replied Chamberlain with a smile.

"I'm terribly sorry," said Hitler. "But after the events of the last few days, this plan is no longer of any use."

Surprise sprang across Chamberlain's face, his head traveled from right to left across the room, and then a slow-burning anger came over his demeanor. Disappointment and puzzlement played out on his face as he sat quiet for a few moments. Then slowly he began a discursive explanation of all that British statesmanship had accomplished to accommodate the Führer's demands.

Hitler sat listening unmoved. He replied to Chamberlain, "The Sudeten area must be militarily occupied by Germany at once." He pushed a map showing the territories to be ceded across the table to Chamberlain. Chamberlain could quickly see that the areas went far beyond the areas in the Franco-British plan.

Chamberlain turned and conferred with his aides. He looked across the table at the Germans. Nothing was forthcoming. He slowly rose. "We best return to the Peterhof," he said, referring to the hotel at which the British delegation was staying. The conference broke up, the British with a deep sense of foreboding.

Hotel Dreesen

The following day, after a flurry of letters, the British again met the Germans in the Hotel Dreesen for a final meeting late at night. The two delegations sat down, and Hitler pushed a memorandum with the accompanying map across the table.

"Why, this is nothing less than an ultimatum!" exclaimed Chamberlain.

"No, it isn't," replied Hitler.

"Yes, it is. It's a diktat."

"No, it isn't," emphasized Hitler. "Here, look, the document is headed by the word *memorandum*."

An adjutant entered the room and handed a message to Hitler. He looked at it and handed it to the interpreter. "Read this to Mr. Chamberlain."

"Beneš has just announced over the radio a general mobilization in Czechoslovakia."

The conference erupted into a back and forth over who had mobilized first. The talks continued past midnight.

Weary, Chamberlain silenced the table and looked at Hitler. "Is this your last word?"

"Yes, it is."

"My efforts have failed. All the hopes with which we brought to Germany have been destroyed."

Hitler was somewhat taken aback. He paused and stared at Chamberlain and said, "You are one of the few men for whom I have ever done such a thing. I am prepared to set one single date for the Czech evacuation—October 1—if that will facilitate your task." He grabbed a pencil and went over the memorandum himself and changed the dates.

A mild look of surprise came over Chamberlain's face. A very small concession, but possibly a start. "Although we are not in a position to accept or reject the proposals, we will transmit them to Prague," said the prime minister.

The British stood and returned to their hotel. The following morning, they departed for London.

London

The prime minister returned to his office after the cabinet meeting. It had not gone well. The cabinet had rejected the Godesberg memorandum. Very frustrating. The foreign secretary joined him in his office with more bad news.

"The French and Czechs have rejected the Godesberg memorandum," said Halifax.

"So what do the French propose to do?" asked Chamberlain.

"They're calling up more reservists. Their mobilization is starting to resemble a full mobilization."

"Oh, my," said Chamberlain.

"Ambassador Phipps reports seven more French divisions reached the border this morning. That makes fourteen divisions to reach the frontier in the past two days."

The resemblance to August 1914 was becoming clear; the fuse was being lit.

"The ambassador reports that Monsieur Flandin called on him to say that the peasant classes being called up are all against the war.

He says that all that is best in France is against war, almost at any price. He says it is only being encouraged by a small, but noisy and corrupt, war group." Phipps's use of the word *corrupt* had raised more than a few eyebrows in the foreign office— British diplomats don't call foreigners "corrupt." It's bad form.

Avenue Foch

The telephone rang in the foyer. The maid answered. She recognized the voice and replied, "Let me get her, monsieur."

Thérèse came to the telephone. "Yes, so nice to hear from you again."

She listened to the voice coming out of the earpiece. "Yes, the same as last time. I understand. Half an hour." She hung up and spoke to her maid. "Please get the chauffeur. I have to go out. I'll be back late." More important information for Berlin, information that would help secure a peaceful resolution of the current crisis. *Well, I am doing my part*, Thérèse thought.

Deuxième Bureau

Captain Jacques Morel was sitting at his desk trying to piece together the conflicting evidence about German strength behind the Siegfried Line, the vaunted West Wall. He had a nagging sense that the Deuxième Bureau was greatly exaggerating German strength in the West that it presented to the French High Command. But hard evidence about German strength was elusive; there were shadows everywhere east of the border. If called upon, would the French army be able to break through and reach the Rhine River? During the 1920s, it had been a simple motor march by the French regiments down to Mainz. If the same occurred in 1938—if France could reach the Rhine in a matter of days—then Germany would be done for.

In his mind, he thought through what a likely scenario would look like. Most likely, he thought, a French army on the Rhine would put the Red Army in Warsaw if not on the Vistula River, the border with Germany. The Russians, unlike the British and French, believed the Polish army was a paper tiger,

206

a bunch of dimwits who would ride their horses with sabers drawn into roaring tank formations. With Russians on their border, and the French on the Rhine, the Nazi government would be overthrown and a new government in Berlin would sue for peace. No second war in Europe. *Worth the risk?* he wondered.

An aide came in and said, "Here's a decrypt of a message from the German embassy to the Wilhelmstrasse."

Morel took the message and read it through: Foreign Minister Bonnet was threatening to resign over the cabinet's rejection of Hitler's latest demands. The German embassy counseled patience: let appeasement forces do their work. French resolve would crumble under British pressure.

Morel leaned back and ruminated: the information had to come from the very top of the French government. The advice indicated someone who had great confidence in their insight into the French cabinet. Only one person in the German embassy fit that bill: Dinckler. And the Sûreté had just told him that Dugas was the French source in the cabinet feeding Dinckler.

Morel turned to the aide and said, "See that the Sûreté gets a transcript of the message."

"Oui, monsieur," replied the aide and departed.

London

Premier Daladier and Foreign Minister Bonnet and their aides walked into the cabinet room at Number 10 Downing Street. Introductions were made, and the participants sat down. Jules Dugas sat at Bonnet's right.

Prime Minister Chamberlain provided a rundown on the meeting with Hitler at Godesberg. Chamberlain expressed doubt about the military strength of France and explained that he had no illusions about British strength. Other British voices seconded the prime minister's opinions. These circumstances dictated further appeasement felt the British. Daladier pushed back, sharply and frequently, on each point.

"The French government," began Daladier, "unanimously rejects the Godesberg proposals because our cabinet realizes that Hitler wishes not so much to take over three and a half million

Germans as to destroy Czechoslovakia by force, enslaving her, and afterward realizing the domination of Europe, which is his object."

Chamberlain then spoke in an effort "to remove French misunderstandings" about Hitler's Godesberg proposals, "explaining" that Hitler wanted to send in troops immediately "only to preserve law and order."

Daladier disagreed and said that the Godesberg demands "amounted to the dismemberment of Czechoslovakia and the beginning of German domination over Europe and that the France would not accept this."

Taking a different tack, Chamberlain asked, "What do you propose to do next?"

"Our next step should be to say to Hitler that he should return to the Anglo-French proposals," countered Daladier.

"And if Hitler refuses?"

"In that case each of us will have to do our duty."

"I think we shall have to go a little further than that," said Chamberlain. He had seen in person Hitler's implacable intransigence.

"I have no further proposal to make," concluded Daladier.

Chamberlain continued, "We better not fence about this question...we need to get down to the stern realities...Hitler said this was his last word...he would take military measures...what would the French attitude be in that event?"

"The French government will fulfill her obligation," replied Daladier.

"But how? Does the French General Staff have some plan?"

Daladier now fielded a "running fire of questions" from Chamberlain and the British about how France would fight.

Daladier faced the British and replied, "I believe that after the French troops have been concentrated, an offensive should be attempted by land against Germany...and it should be possible to attack by air..."

Disbelief was on the faces of the British. Attack Germany?

Daladier leaned across the table and challenged the British on the great weak point in their thinking—that appeasement today would sate Hitler's lust for conquest tomorrow. The premier asked, "At what point are you prepared to stop? How far will you retreat?"

Chamberlain brushed this argument aside and argued that Hitler would not go back to the prior proposal and that he would not accept an international commission. He got to the nub of his argument: "What would we do if faced with a German invasion of Czechoslovakia?"

The prime minister then spoke to the double-barreled question of how could the French save Czechoslovakia by waging an effective war against Germany. "M. Daladier has indicated that the French plan is to undertake offensive operations...and also to bomb German factories and military centers...we wish to speak quite frankly and say the British government has received disturbing accounts of the condition of the French air force...and we would ask what would happen if a rain of bombs descended upon Paris..."

Daladier replied in a confident manner, the determination of a French leader in his voice, "I am always hearing of difficulties. Does that mean that we do not wish to do anything? Is the British government ready to give in and to accept Hitler's proposals?"

Daladier looked directly across the table and asked, "Mr. Chamberlain has indicated that Hitler has spoken his last word. Does the British government intend to accept it?"

Chamberlain replied that it was not really for either the French or the British government to accept or reject the German proposals, but for the Czech government. He concluded that "he did not think it was for the British government to express an opinion, but for the French government to decide."

With the meeting winding down, Chamberlain asked Daladier if General Gamelin could attend the following day's talks; the prime minister had been thoroughly briefed on the indecision pervasive at the top of the French High Command. Daladier readily agreed, and the meeting adjourned.

The General

General Gamelin arrived the following morning at the French embassy in London. He was briefed by Daladier, who was visibly discouraged by the British fear of Hitler. Daladier had seen it in the eyes of the British ambassador in Paris, Phipps, who was in physical fear of Hitler. Hitler had defeated one British diplomat after another in their own minds. Gamelin also gathered that Daladier had his doubts about Bonnet; he was cautioned not to bring Bonnet into his discussion. Gamelin has long ago sized up Bonnet as the defeatist in the cabinet. Now on the spot, Gamelin felt that he himself was "the victim of a very painful affair, which originated in the intrigues of M. Georges Bonnet."

Arriving at Number 10 Downing Street, Daladier went in and spoke with Chamberlain privately for a few minutes. Daladier found that Chamberlain had had a change of heart during the night. Based on Daladier's firm stand the previous evening, the prime minister now believed that the French would honor their commitment to Czechoslovakia if the Germans invaded. In that event, the prime minister concluded, Britain would stand by France.

The two leaders talked, and Chamberlain told Daladier that he was dispatching his confidential adviser Sir Horace Wilson to Berlin that morning to meet with Hitler and deliver a letter appealing one last time for a direct negotiation to arrange for the peaceful takeover of the Sudetenland by the Germans.

"If Hitler's response is negative," confided Chamberlain, "then Wilson is to read him my letter that says that if France becomes actively engaged in hostilities with Germany, then the United Kingdom would feel obliged to come to her aid."

Daladier could see that there had been an enormous change during the night in British policy. Chamberlain explained that London had long believed that a firm declaration in 1914 might have forestalled Germany from attacking France. A similar set of circumstances seemed to prevail now.

The two men then asked Gamelin to join them. Using maps and briefing papers, Gamelin proceeded to give his estimate of the situation. The general noted that the French would have one hundred divisions plus excellent fortifications. In contrast, the Germans lacked good fortifications and their army was smaller and had many deficiencies. The Czechs had thirty divisions and strong fortifications; the Germans would have hard going breaking through in any invasion.

"Can the Czechs hold out?" asked the prime minister.

"If they retreat into Moravia, certainly they would continue to exist as a fighting force."

"Germany. Its strengths?" asked Chamberlain.

"Certainly a superior German air force," replied Gamelin. Always a sticking point in the minds of both the French premier and the British prime minister.

"As to Italy..." continued the general.

Chamberlain broke in and said, "If we march, Italy won't march." He was as dismissive of the Italians as the Russians were of the Poles.

Gamelin agreed that was likely. He was thanked by the two leaders, and Chamberlain asked him to confer with the British chiefs of staff. Gamelin departed to talk with the British chiefs.

The British generals felt their army was not ready for war. The navy felt itself prepared. Gamelin was interrupted by a telephone call from his chief of staff in Paris. He took the call and listened, making notes. He turned and spoke to his British hosts.

"Marshal Voroshilov contacted my staff," he said, referring to the Russian defense minister, "and the Soviets now have thirty infantry divisions, a mass of cavalry, numerous tank formations, and the bulk of their air force ready to intervene in the West."

The British whispered among themselves. Gamelin could see that the British were horrified at the thought of Russia invading and passing through Poland—a British ally—to come to the aid of Czechoslovakia. The new realities were disturbing so many of the old understandings.

Gamelin finished talking with the British chiefs and rejoined the French delegation. The French then met with the British delegation, and Chamberlain repeated the message that he had shared privately with Daladier earlier. Chamberlain made a show of giving the assurance in writing to Daladier. The French departed for Paris. Daladier had accomplished far more than he dared to hope.

Berlin

Two British diplomats and the prime minister's special emissary Sir Horace Wilson sat in Adolf Hitler's office in the Chancellery. Four hours hence Hitler was going to address the German people on the Czech crisis by radio from the Berlin

Sportpalast, a giant auditorium. Chamberlain hoped the personal delivery of his message by Wilson would induce Hitler to moderate his demands in the upcoming speech to the German people.

Wilson began by telling the German leader that the Czechs had rejected the German demands made at Godesberg. Hitler jumped to his feet and shouted, "There is no sense at all in negotiating further." The aroused dictator shouted and screamed, "The Germans are being treated like niggers! On October 1, I shall have Czechoslovakia where I want her! If France and England decide to strike, let them! I do not care a pfennig."

Wilson shrank back from Hitler's fury; the three British diplomats were speechless. Intimidated by Hitler's outburst, Wilson put off reading Chamberlain's special message that Britain would support France in the event of hostilities broke out. An inexperienced diplomat failed to deliver the prime minister's most important instruction. The browbeaten British diplomats retreated back to their embassy. Representatives of the world's most skilled diplomatic corps had bobbled the job.

Hitler proceeded to deliver his speech inside the great hall in Berlin to thousands of delirious Germans promising that he would have the Sudetenland four days hence—on October 1.

Back at the embassy, Wilson telegrammed his failure to Chamberlain. Early the next morning, Chamberlain wired back that Wilson must return that morning and deliver the message to Hitler. Chamberlain had given his word to the French.

Place Malesherbes

At nine thirty in the evening, Geneviève Tabouis sat listening to Adolf Hitler spew out his hatreds and threats over the radio from the Sportpalast in Berlin. The German leader hurled venomous insults at "Herr Beneš" declaring that war or peace was in the Czech president's hands. She felt this was simply another example of Hitler's war-threat blackmail.

Interestingly, she heard Hitler, taking a break from his frenzied shouting, assure the audience that this was his last territorial claim in Europe. He dismissively said, "We want no Czechs."

The telephone rang, and she went into the foyer and picked up the receiver and sat down at the little desk. "Yes?" she asked into the mouthpiece. She recognized the voice; an important diplomat in London was on the line.

"At this very moment," the voice said, "a secretary at the foreign office is giving out to representatives of the four big news agencies in London the following communication: 'If, in spite of all the efforts of the prime minister to prevent it, Czechoslovakia is the object of an attack by Germany, France will be obliged to go to her aid, and Great Britain and Russia will immediately back up France.'"

Geneviève wrote the communiqué down word for word. "Are you sure?"

"It is in Lord Halifax's own handwriting."

"It will appear in my column tomorrow morning. I'll be telephoning in the story shortly." She listened some more and then hung up. She worked on her notes, and the telephone rang again. She picked it up. Almost dumbfounded, she exclaimed, "Georges?" Foreign minister George Bonnet was on the line."

"Geneviève, I wanted to personally warn you about the British communiqué. It has not been officially confirmed. It's suspect."

"Thank you, Georges. I'll check it out," replied Geneviève, and she hung up.

Geneviève made several more phone calls and found that other members of the French press had been instructed to treat the London communiqué as "most suspect." One source told her that one of Bonnet's close personal friends at a leading Paris paper had written an article accusing the communiqué of being a Soviet deception: "One cannot help suspecting that this communiqué was written for the sole purpose of increasing the tension between France and Great Britain and Germany, and to play the game of the Soviets, who are crying for war."

The atmosphere of lies surrounding Bonnet is becoming overwhelming, thought Geneviève. She went with her story.

Berlin

At noon the following day, Sir Horace Wilson and the other British diplomats returned to the German chancellor's office. Hitler was calm and explained that all he was interested in was whether or not Czechoslovakia accepted or rejected his demands. He got up and paced his office and turned and faced the British and, clasping his hands in front of him, said with relish, "If they are rejected, I shall destroy Czechoslovakia." He repeated the threat several more times. The British diplomats realized with shocking dismay that Hitler looked forward to armed intervention; he wanted to see his tanks roll.

Faced with this provocation, Wilson stood up from his chair, cleared his throat uneasily, and said, "I have one more thing to say, more in sorrow than in anger, that if hostilities break out between Germany and France, then the United Kingdom will come to the aid of France." The British diplomats waited for the outburst they were sure was coming.

"I can only take note of that position," said Hitler heatedly. "It means that if France elects to attack Germany, England will feel obliged to attack her also." Hitler was posing Germany as the victim.

Wilson moved to refute the argument by saying that he did not know if "in fulfilling their obligations France would attack Germany."

Hitler broke in and raised his voice to a shout, "If France and England strike, let them do so! It is a matter of complete indifference to me! Today is Tuesday. By next Monday, we shall be at war."

Wilson shrank back from the bluntness of Hitler's statement. Collecting himself, he moved to leave a positive option on the table, saying, "A catastrophe must be avoided at all costs. I will try to make those Czechs sensible." The British diplomats departed.

Hitler watched them leave and contemplated his next step.

Place Malesherbes

Geneviève Tabouis sat at her dining room table sipping morning coffee looking through the papers. The semiofficial *Le Temps*, the mouthpiece of the establishment, carried a front-page letter from former premier and foreign minister, Pierre-Étienne Flandin, the leader of an important center party in the Chamber of Députés. The headline screamed, "You Are Being Deceived," and the text went on to say, "People of France, you are being deceived! A cunning trap has been set...by the Popular Front politicians and...by occult elements to make war inevitable..."

Geneviève suspected the reference to the occult referred to her. She glanced at one of the right-wing papers and saw, "Madame Tata has the magic key that opens all the diplomatic dispatch cases...and she sees the secret messages in her trances...in which she sees what will happen before it happens..."

Well, that is one way to look at it, she thought. Her sources from both Berlin and London had been unusually accurate. Day after day, the morning papers carrying her column with these history-making revelations flew out of the news kiosks.

Arthur came in and told her that posters carrying the message had been plastered all over the walls of Paris during the night. The propaganda campaign was now in full swing.

"Really?" inquired Geneviève. "All over Paris?"

"Yes, but the police are taking them down as we speak," replied the servant. He set more newspapers down on the table.

Ah, yes, she thought. There it is, the reaction to the publication of the British communiqué. She read through the gleeful account in the leading rightist paper: "The group of dirty liars who have printed this news in various papers...these scurrilous camp-followers of the warmongering gang who have dared to give out this alarming news, ought to be ferreted out, arrested, and brought to judgment. No punishment would be too severe for a crime such as theirs."

The papers on the Right didn't like Geneviève and Pertinax publishing the truth about the British communiqué that Bonnet had so assiduously tried to suppress. Geneviève knew that journalists pitching the Bonnet line were paid well by foreign powers to write these lies.

Les Deux Magots

Carl von Dinckler walked into Les Deux Magots café and headed toward the back corner. Marie Hélène was sitting there stirring a coffee. Dinckler sat down and said, "I got your message."

"It's very urgent," Marie Hélène said. She leaned across the table and whispered, "I just picked up the envelope."

"Envelope?" asked Carl.

"Yes, Jules said there wasn't time. Too much information, too important. Details about the mobilization. And this morning's cabinet meeting—Bonnet and two other cabinet members want to go with Hitler's demands."

"Yes, that's critical."

"I'll slip it over to you under my scarf."

"Fine."

"Here it is."

"Good. I got it." Carl slipped the envelope inside his overcoat and into a pocket. He looked at her with smoldering intensity. "I'd like to see you."

"Me too."

"Tonight?" asked Carl, and added as an afterthought, "If you're free."

"I can't. Tonight is Tuesday."

Dinckler sighed and took a breath, resignation in his voice: "Understand. I probably won't be able to break free until after the first of October."

"I understand, too," she said. "Then the days will be for you."

"Except Tuesdays."

She laughed and said, "Except Tuesdays. Remember, you said a 'necessary complication' in our lives."

"Yes, I just didn't think I'd get so possessive."

"I'm glad you let that emotion overtake your clocklike thinking, Herr Diplomat."

"Yes, the work. It never ceases." He added as an afterthought, "The quest for peace."

Wilhelmstrasse

State Secretary Ernst Freiherr von Weizsäcker sat in his office and read the telegram just in from the ambassador in Paris. The flimsy was marked in red letters "Very Urgent" across the top of the scrolllike message that had been torn from the teletype just minutes ago. The French had mobilized sixty-five divisions and would have them deployed on the German frontier by the end of the week. Weizsäcker drew back; the French would outnumber the Germans on the frontier by almost ten to one. Did the French understand the magnitude of their advantage?

The German diplomat pondered this news. What would the French do with this predominance in strength? The German military attaché in Paris wrote that the French will launch an immediate attack from Alsace-Lorraine with an axis of advance centered on Mainz, the big German city on the Rhine River and gateway to the plains of Germany.

And Italy? What was the German ally doing to draw French strength to the Italian border? The attaché reported: nothing.

Weizsäcker turned to a second telegram from the Paris embassy. A source close to the top of the French cabinet reported that at this morning's cabinet meeting Foreign Minister Bonnet and two other ministers strongly supported yielding to Hitler's demands. Daladier was wavering in the face of ordering a general mobilization.

Weizsäcker leaned back in his chair. How would this play out? Undoubtedly Bonnet would use the British to make the case for meeting Hitler's demands. But could it be done before October 1? Weizsäcker didn't doubt that Hitler would order the army across the border on October 1; he was spoiling for a fight.

But if fighting broke out, would the French use their vast strength?

Berlin

Early in the evening, Adolph Hitler sat at his desk in his study working on his letter to Prime Minister Chamberlain. Bad news about army mobilizations in Czechoslovakia and France, and even the mobilization of the British fleet, had been coming in all day. The British? Mobilizing their fleet?

The German chancellor worked with an aide to get the translation moderate in tone. He wanted the appeal to Chamberlain to work. The aide felt the Führer was stepping back from the brink.

Hitler read over his missive: "My proposals are not intended to rob Czechoslovakia of every guarantee of its existence and German troops will stop at the demarcation lines. I will negotiate details with

217

the Czechs and am prepared to give a formal guarantee for the remainder of Czechoslovakia. I must leave it to your judgment whether, in view of these facts, you consider that you should continue your effort…"

"This will do," said Hitler to his aide. "Send it off to London."

Hôtel Matignon

Premier Daladier sat at his desk and looked at the draft of the speech to be broadcast to the French people if, as he felt increasingly certain, war became inevitable. The crucial sentence stared up from the white sheet of paper: "to explain to the French people that despite all our efforts for peace we had to intervene in the face of German aggression."

There was a knock on the door, and an usher opened it and announced, "The Air Minister is here to see you."

"Send him in," said Daladier as he rose to greet the minister.

Guy La Chambre entered the office with a dispatch case and took the proffered chair across from the immense desk of the premier. The two men were close friends and enjoyed each other's confidence. La Chambre opened his dispatch case and brought out a memorandum of several pages and handed it across the desk, explaining, "General Vuillemin spoke with me yesterday about the state of our air force. It was a bleak warning. I asked the chief of staff to put the warning in writing. Here it is."

"Has General Gamelin seen this?" asked Daladier.

La Chambre hesitated and stammered to explain.

"No, of course not," said Daladier, completing the minister's answer. "Let me read it." Daladier sat back and started reading through the document.

"Let's see," said Daladier, "the air force has about seven hundred planes, and the air force chief of staff says they're not much good."

"Yes, the modernization program is behind." Daladier had worked with La Chambre on Plan V, an ambitious program to modernize French aircraft factories and quintuple monthly aircraft production over those of the previous Popular Front government. Budgeted spending for the air force had been more than doubled; the spending was focused on production of new state-of-the-art fighter aircraft. Task one was to secure French air space from German incursion. In the meantime, a thousand advanced fighters had been ordered from America. Daladier understood all of this. But the airplanes were not here now. Across the border, the Germans were deploying their modern fighters. They had stolen a march.

"Indeed. Yes, I understand; the Germans have deployed their new monoplane fighters, and ours are just starting to come off the production line," said Daladier. The new German Messerschmitt Bf 109 had set the world speed record the previous November and was considered the finest fighter in the world. The Deuxième Bureau estimated the Germans had a staggering five hundred of these fighters deployed in frontline squadrons ready to fight.

"Our deployment of new fighters is at a much lower rate than the Germans, I'm afraid," said the air minister.

"And the British?"

"We estimate planes from Britain would arrive late. They would number in the dozens, not the hundreds," said the minister. "The British contribution to the battle for European airspace would be too few, too late."

Daladier sighed. "Yet our mobilization of the army has gone very well. Nevertheless, General Vuillemin says the air force would not be of much assistance once offensive operations commenced."

"I'm afraid that's correct."

"Can an army fight effectively today without good air support?"

"That's problematic."

"And then there would be the German air attacks on our war production," said Daladier as he read from the document, "and massive and repeated enemy air attacks on the great centers of population." The annihilation of the Spanish Basque town of Guernica a year and a half before by the German Condor Legion was on everyone's mind. The artist Pablo Picasso's stunning mural of the brutal air attack was the talk of the Paris Expo the previous year where it had hung in the Spanish Pavilion virtually in the shadow of the Eifel Tower. To subject Paris to the terrors of air attack with a completely inadequate air force was a frightening reality for the premier.

Daladier waved the paper around. "So as I understand this report, a heavy burden. In a couple of hours, Prime Minister Chamberlain is going to address the British public by radio."

"Do you know what he is going to say?" inquired the air minister.

Daladier pulled another piece of paper out of the pile on his desk and said, "Our ambassador in London reports the prime minister is expected to say that Czechoslovakia is too small an issue to go to war over...that he sees little that he can do in the way of further mediation..."

The air minister felt deep sympathy for the immense burdens on Daladier's bulllike shoulders as he contemplated the horrible choices faced by the premier. Important principles of the very first importance of international statesmanship would collide with the utterly dreadful consequences that a modern war would bring.

Number 10 Downing Street

The prime minister sat at his desk and listened to advice from various advisers on the radio speech he had just addressed to the kingdom. There seemed to be no path out of the maze. It was all a great puzzle. There was a knock on the door, and a private secretary came in and handed the prime minister a letter. "From the German chancellor, sir." Chamberlain quickly opened the letter and read it through.

"Hitler's offering to negotiate...what's more he's willing to give a formal guarantee for the remainder of Czechoslovakia."

"That's the way forward," said Halifax. Other heads in the room nodded. *A way forward, thank God!* they thought.

"Let's get a reply off straightaway," said the prime minister. "Tell Hitler I'm ready to come to Berlin myself and discuss arrangements..."

Berlin

In the German chancellery, the British and French ambassadors frantically tried all morning to present proposals to Hitler but were left cooling their heels in the anteroom. The day would be called "Black Wednesday" by allied diplomats. The deadline to the German ultimatum to the Czechs expired at two that afternoon. After that hour, the ambassadors feared, Hitler would launch his armies across the border into Czechoslovakia. The British ambassador finally got Göring to intercede, and the German number two man got the French ambassador an appointment. The French diplomat made it into the Führer's office at noon brandishing a crudely drawn map showing large chunks of Czechoslovakia that Foreign Minister Bonnet was prepared to cede to Germany. Hitler's aides noticed that the Führer was impressed with the generous markings on the map.

Suddenly, the door opened and another aide rushed in to tell Hitler that the Italian ambassador was in the anteroom with an urgent message from Mussolini. Hitler got his translator and went out and met the Italian diplomat, who shouted, "I have an urgent message to you from the Duce!" The ambassador delivered the message telephoned to him just an hour before by Mussolini in Rome. The Italian added, "Mussolini begs you to refrain from mobilization." Hitler's time limit on his ultimatum to the Czechs was now only two hours away.

"Tell the Duce," replied Hitler, "that I accept the proposal." Hitler smiled warmly; it had all fallen into place before he even saw the British ambassador.

A few minutes before the two o'clock deadline, Hitler dispatched invitations to London, Paris, and Rome for a conference at Munich at noon the following day.

House of Commons

In London, Hitler's invitation had not yet arrived. It was three o'clock in the afternoon, and Prime Minister Chamberlain sat at his seat on the Treasury Bench of the House of Commons. An aide came up and whispered in his ear, his head nodding in the negative, and then retreated. All that day the prime minister had awaited a reply from Hitler to the letter he had dispatched the previous evening. Nothing. Ambassadors had been banging on Hitler's door all morning. No success. Nothing had been heard. Finally, word came that Mussolini's proposal had been accepted by Hitler. But what did that mean? A breakthrough? Chamberlain rose and stepped forward and addressed the House of Commons:

"Whatever view honorable members may have had about Signor Mussolini, I believe that everyone will welcome his gesture…for peace…which has caused Hitler to postpone mobilization for twenty-four hours…"

The sitting members politely greeted this news. The interminable problem continued in all of its indefiniteness. Was this a breakthrough? Or something else? An aide came up and handed the prime minister a note. He looked down at it, and his face broke into a broad smile.

"That is not all. I have something further to say to the House. I have now been informed by Herr Hitler that he invites me to meet him at Munich tomorrow morning. He has also invited Signor Mussolini and Monsieur Daladier. Mussolini has accepted, and I have no doubt Monsieur Daladier will accept. I need not say what my answer will be…"

All members on both sides of the ancient hall of the Parliament jumped to their feet, shouting in a mad hysteria. A wild throwing of paper ensued, and many members' cheeks were streaked with tears. A voice shouted, "Thank God for the prime minister!"

Chamberlain stood at the podium, his owllike visage smiling as he slowly turned his head from side to side taking in the massive display of delirium at the prospect of peace. Smugness and contentment radiated from his dark eyes; in his heart, he had always known he was right.

Number 10 Downing Street

The prime minister sat chatting with the foreign secretary. A private secretary came and said, "A telegram from our minister in Prague. A communication from Président Beneš." The prime minister raised his eyebrows at the foreign secretary. *What is this?*

The prime minister read aloud, "I beg Mr. Chamberlain to do nothing at Munich that could put Czechoslovakia in a worse situation than under Anglo-French proposals…I beg therefore that nothing may be done in Munich without Czechoslovakia being heard..."

"To be expected," said Lord Halifax.

"I already sent Président Beneš a telegram that I shall have the interests of Czechoslovakia fully in mind." Chamberlain smiled contentedly. Duty done. What came after in Czechoslovakia was mostly a French problem.

"I'll get a message off to the Czech foreign minister later tonight," said Halifax, "advising them to have a suitable representative, authorized to speak on their behalf, available to go to Munich on short notice tomorrow."

Wilhelmstrasse

The jovial Reichsminister Hermann Göring entered Minister Konstantin von Neurath's spacious office. Neurath was now a minister without portfolio in the Nazi government with Hitler's appointment of Ribbentrop to the position of foreign minister. Nevertheless he was the pro; no one ever accused Ribbentrop, a former champagne salesman, of professional attainments as a diplomat. State Secretary Ernst von Weizsäcker joined the two men with a pad of paper and pen.

"Let's get the compromise plan down," said Göring with a hearty laugh at the word *compromise*, "on paper and off to Rome."

"Let's be very specific about what we want," said Weizsäcker as he started to write.

"I quite agree," said Neurath. "This proposal will probably be adopted almost word for word if our information from Paris is correct."

"Our London ambassador agrees," said Weizsäcker. "Chamberlain is in no mood to quibble. If he resists, Daladier will stand by himself..."

Neurath added, "If he even makes the effort..."

The three men worked away steadily at the written document.

"Let me go get the translator," said Weizsäcker as he stood up and left the office. He returned shortly with the translator, who translated the document into French, the international diplomatic language. Weizsäcker read it over and said, "Telephone it to the Italian ambassador."

Austro-German Border

Mussolini arrived in the early morning on his special train from Rome at the German-Austrian border. Waiting there was Hitler's special train, which had also traveled all night from Berlin to arrive at the border by dawn. Mussolini went over and boarded the Führer's private railcar for a meeting with Hitler. The two dictators met to formulate a common plan of action at the upcoming conference with the British and French, which was scheduled to start in Munich later that day.

The Führer's train pulled away from the station in a cloud of steam, officials standing along the platform saluting with raised forearms in the Nazi salute. The train barreled north toward Munich. The two dictators stood around the large map table with Hitler explaining to the Duce how he intended "to liquidate" Czechoslovakia. The depth of the German planning was impeccable; the German military might marshaled for the invasion impressive.

"Either the talks beginning today must be immediately successful," Hitler cautioned, "or I will resort to arms." Mussolini could see that Hitler relished the prospect of armed conflict, of watching his motorized troops roar into action, but the Italian dictator felt a war at this time would be one for which he was not yet ready. He would push hard in today's meeting the proposal telephoned to him last night by his ambassador in Berlin as he boarded his train in Rome. His ambassador said the proposal had top-level backing from just below the level of the Führer.

"Besides, the time will come," Hitler grandly pronounced, "when we shall have to fight side by side against France and England." Mussolini, chest puffed out, jaw jutting forward, agreed.

Munich

In Munich, the four leaders entered a large conference room in the Führerhaus on the Königsplatz in the center of Munich, a series of massive art deco buildings built to celebrate the ascendancy of the Nazi party in the city of its birth. The leaders took seats around a circular table in no particular order; a mood of goodwill hovered over the table as the four leaders started talking. Chamberlain and Daladier seemed agreeable. Mussolini decided to get down to business.

"In order to bring about a practical solution to the problem," said the Duce, "I wish to make the following proposal." He read out his proposal. Hitler and the other Germans in the room listened in stony silence. Chamberlain and Daladier listened attentively to what came to be known as the "Italian proposals."

Chamberlain responded, saying that "he also welcomed the Duce's proposal and declared that he himself had conceived of a solution on the lines of this proposal."

Daladier chimed in to say that he "particularly welcomed the Duce's proposal, which had been made in an objective and realistic spirit."

Chamberlain's special adviser Sir Horace Wilson found the Italian proposals to be a "reasonable restatement of much that had been discussed in the Anglo-French and Anglo-German conversations." Wilson's key task later in the evening was to explain the eventual agreement to the Czechs.

The British and French ambassadors to Berlin echoed similar sentiments.

Chamberlain then moved that a representative of the Czech government should be present. Daladier mumbled lukewarm support, mentioning that while no obstructionism by the Czech government would be tolerated, a Czech representative who could be consulted might be an advantage.

"I am not interested in an assurance from the Czech government," thundered Hitler. "I will not have the presence of any Czechs." Chamberlain and Daladier slowly retreated under Hitler's intransigence.

Chamberlain finally got Hitler to agree that the presence of Czech representatives in the next room would be allowed. The Czech representatives were sent for and arrived later in the afternoon where they cooled their heels in ignorance of the discussions going on in the next room—talks that were settling the fate of their country.

The discussions continued well into the afternoon, Hitler hurling demands like thunderbolts and Chamberlain giving way. In contrast, the high-handedness of Hitler's behavior was galling to Daladier, who had no trust in Germany and understood the war-threat game of blackmail being played. France's ranking diplomat, Secretary General Alexis Léger, watched the boiling frustration rise in Daladier; he now understood why he had replaced Bonnet on the French delegation. Daladier would never personally be able to explain the terms to the Czechs; that task would fall to Léger. Twice during the afternoon, after outbursts from Hitler, Daladier stood up and went into the other room, steaming with frustration and anger. Each time Reichsminister Göring followed him out and soothed his feelings while assuring the French premier that he would smooth out the rough edges of the diktat. Both Göring and Daladier had been frontline soldiers and commanders in the Great War. Göring understood the inner steel that had infused the young frontline commanders that carried the burdens of combat in the last war. He was able to calm the French premier down. Nevertheless, Daladier hated taking it; one body blow after another all afternoon long.

Early in the evening, a British diplomat entered the room next door where the two Czech representatives waited and started to outline the terms of the agreement being reached in the other room. He was simply softening the Czechs up for what was to come later from Sir Horace Wilson. The current proposal was much harsher than the earlier French-British proposals to which the Czechs had reluctantly agreed.

"Do not the Czechs get to be heard in the negotiations?" asked one of the Czech representatives.

The British diplomat smoothly rebuffed the Czech appeal, adding that "you could not understand how hard it has been to negotiate with Hitler."

Several hours later, the clock moving toward midnight, Sir Horace Wilson came into the room and met with the two Czechs and explained the main points of the program while giving them a new map of the Sudetenland areas to be evacuated at once. The two Czech envoys attempted to protest, but Wilson cut them off and said he had nothing further to say. He left the room. The Czech diplomats stared at the door. The coup de grace had been administered.

The two Czechs turned to the remaining British diplomat who replied, "If you do not accept, you will have to settle your affairs with the Germans absolutely alone."

"And the French?" one of the Czechs asked.

The British diplomat slowly said, "They are disinterested."

The two Czech diplomats were crushed; this was most likely the end of their country. Their sovereignty was being given away at a bargaining table at which they did not even have a chair.

An hour past midnight, Hitler, Chamberlain, Mussolini, and Daladier signed their names to the Munich Agreement. The German army would begin its march into Czechoslovakia the following day and complete its occupation of the surrendered lands ten days afterward. With the Italian proposals, Hitler had achieved all the goals initially denied him two weeks prior in the Godesberg talks.

After the Second World War, German diplomats testifying at the Nuremberg trials explained the ruse that had been played on the British and French leaders, leaders who more or less willingly walked into this deception.

With the ink drying on the agreement, the Germans and Italians departed. Journalists outside the building watched Hitler descend the steps with "the light of victory in his eyes," while Mussolini strutted down the stairs with the cocky sureness of being on the winning side of the most important negotiation of the 1930s.

Back in the conference room, the Czech envoys were brought in. Chamberlain made remarks, and the agreement was given to the stunned Czechs.

Addressing Daladier and Léger, one of the Czech diplomats asked if they expected an answer from the Czech government to the agreement. Daladier, noticeably nervous, stepped back and said nothing. Léger stepped forward; he had been rehearsing his remarks in his mind all afternoon and into the evening. He was the professional diplomat. He said that "the four statesmen had not much time and that no answer was required from the Czechs since the plan was considered as accepted." A fait accompli.

The two Czechs looked at the French with astonishment. The 1924 treaty lay on the conference room floor, a key piece of European collective security trampled by considerations of "peace."

"Your government," curtly explained Léger, "has until three o'clock this afternoon to send its representative to Berlin to sit on the commission."

Chamberlain stood listening to the explanations, yawning almost continuously. The business was over.

British diplomats handed the Czechs slightly corrected maps. The Czechs felt like debauched women. The Czech envoy later cabled his government in Prague, "Then they were finished with us. We could go."

Two hours later outside the Hotel Regina where the British delegation was staying, Premier Daladier descended the steps after saying his good-byes to Chamberlain. A western journalist observed that he looked like "a completely beaten and broken man."

Another journalist asked the French premier, "Monsieur le Président, are you satisfied with the agreement?" The premier, tired and weary, blinked at the question and continued silently down the steps and stumbled into his waiting limousine. The night was over.

Hitler's Apartment

The following morning, Chamberlain traveled to Hitler's private apartment in Munich for one final meeting, unbeknownst to the French or anyone else. Chamberlain entered the apartment carrying his ubiquitous umbrella and gave it and his hat to a valet. He opened the discussion with a long and rambling monologue somewhat to Hitler's annoyance—what was all of this about? Among other things, Chamberlain implored Hitler that in the event of any Czech intransigence he "would not bomb Prague with the dreadful losses among the civilian population which it would entail."

Hitler, stunned, replied, "I always try to spare the civilian population and confine myself to military objectives—I hate the thought of little babies being killed by gas bombs."

Reassured by Hitler's goodwill, Chamberlain talked in a jaunty manner along this line for what an increasingly morose Hitler felt was forever. Then before the astonished Hitler, Chamberlain pulled out a piece of paper from his pocket on which he had written a joint agreement that he hoped they would both sign and immediately publish. It would be politically helpful to him at home, explained the British prime minister. A German translation was hastily prepared, and Hitler read through the several paragraphs:

"We regard the agreement signed last night…as symbolic of the desire of our two peoples never to go to war with one another again…and resolved that the method of consultation…will contribute to the peace of Europe."

Hitler looked at Chamberlain, then looked at his aide, and with a certain reluctance, signed the document and handed it to Chamberlain. *Be done with this man*, he thought. A pleased expression broke over Chamberlain's face, and he warmly thanked the Führer. Chamberlain and his aides departed, satisfied with their work during their two days in Munich.

Hitler watched them go and turned to an aide and said derisively, "If ever that silly old man comes interfering here again with his umbrella, I'll kick him downstairs and jump on his stomach in front of the photographers."

Le Bourget Airport

The sleek modern two-engine Air France airliner carrying Premier Daladier and Secretary General Léger back to Paris approached Le Bourget Airport. Looking out the window, Daladier could see huge crowds at the airfield and the highways leading to it. He felt a deep sense of bitterness at having abandoned a faithful ally and sensed he would face an angry reception from the Parisian crowds. He asked the pilot to fly around the airport one more time while he prepared some remarks. Then the plane descended on the field and taxied up to the art deco terminal building. Daladier emerged to the delirious cheering by the crowds flooding across the concrete embarkation area. He descended and stepped up to a radio microphone arranged by Radio France and addressed the nation:

"I return with the profound conviction that this accord is indispensable to the peace of Europe. We achieved it thanks to a spirit of mutual concessions and a close collaboration."

The premier stepped back from the microphone and started to shake hands with the many notables in the reception committee. To

General Gamelin, he whispered, "It wasn't brilliant, but I did everything I could."

As Daladier moved down the reception line, Gamelin whispered to an aide, "*C'etait fini*—it's finished. Germany has won a new victory and a great one."

Daladier came to Paul Reynaud. The bantam minister stepped forward and in a low voice needled the premier, who was also the defense minister, "Where are you going to find thirty-five new divisions now?" Reynaud had put his finger on the weak point of the dismemberment of Czechoslovakia; France may have gained time but lost a powerful military ally with a large armaments industry—the Skoda arms works was the third largest in Europe—and a capable, highly motivated army sitting right on the flank of Germany.

A waiting limousine pulled up, and Daladier got in. The vehicle pulled away and started down the highway to downtown Paris, the street lined by cheering crowds. Astounded by the cheering crowds and wary of this moment of fleeting public satisfaction, Daladier leaned over and said to an aide, "*Les cons*—the fools—if they only knew what they were cheering."

Heston Aerodrome

Outside of London, Chamberlain landed at Heston Aerodrome and descended from the airliner bringing him back from Munich. He walked up to a radio microphone and broadcast a speech to the British public while standing before a multitude of desperately grateful British people. Chamberlain said:

"The settlement of the Czechoslovakian problem…is…only the prelude to a larger settlement in which all Europe may find peace. This morning I had another talk with the German chancellor, Herr Hitler, and here is the paper which bears his name upon it as well as mine…I would just like to read it to you: We regard the agreement signed last night…symbolic of the desire of our two peoples never to go to war with one another again."

Chamberlain held the document out in his right hand waving it before the crowd. It was not the Munich Agreement, as many supposed, but rather the joint declaration that he had signed with Hitler just that morning in the Führer's apartment, a scrap of paper that those German officials present at the signing felt was of little importance.

Later that day, another approving crowd, delighted to have been delivered from the evils of another war, crowded the small street outside Number 10 Downing Street. Chamberlain came out and addressed the adulatory crowd, saying, "My good friends…a prime minister has returned from Germany bringing peace with honor. I believe it is peace for our time…"

Paris

Former premier and foreign minister Pierre-Étienne Flandin telegrammed congratulations to the four leaders who had participated at Munich. Hitler wired back to Flandin: "I am grateful for your efforts…on behalf of an understanding and complete collaboration between France and Germany…" At the Quai d'Orsay, Bonnet and Dugas read the German chancellor's wire with satisfaction and as a signpost toward their next diplomatic goal—a peace agreement with Germany.

"I was surprised that Chamberlain had been farsighted enough to get a written peace agreement with Hitler before departing Munich," said Bonnet.

"Yes, Chamberlain stole a march on us," said Dugas. "Daladier simply does not believe in a peace agreement with Germany. He refuses to see the potential."

"Well, I'm sure it is the Franco-Russia pact that stands in the way of Berlin making a similar agreement with France," said Bonnet.

"We must develop a strategy to work around it," said Dugas.

"Please start work on it," said Bonnet. "But overall, we're in a strong position."

Indeed, with regard to the public euphoria surrounding Daladier's return to Paris, Bonnet was also riding a crest of popularity since he was seen as the chief architect of the Munich Agreement even though he had not attended. He observed that the press "presented the Munich Agreement as a success for the skillfulness and the firmness of French diplomacy…and that France was beyond reproach."

Paris's largest paper quoted the foreign minister: "There is one criticism which I refuse to accept, and that is that France was not loyal to her signature. France's signature is sacred. Czechoslovakia wasn't invaded, was she?"

Place Malesherbes

Geneviève Tabouis sat at her desk in her study, her beautiful Persian cat Lotus drowsing on her lap, as she sipped coffee and read the morning newspapers. Yes, she murmured to herself as she read *Le Matin*: "Peace is won. It is won over the crooks, sellouts, and madmen." She thought the catalog of villains was backward, but then Paris seemed to be on the far side of the looking glass these days.

Turning to *Le Temps*, she read, "It is a relief that a few farsighted and courageous leaders had triumphed over the 'war party.'" Yes, always the war party and she was its high priestess. She continued reading the papers from London and the wire reports in the English-language Paris press. What became apparent was how completely the Soviet Union had been excluded from the talks settling Czechoslovakia's fate. Fear of Communism trumped fear of loss of freedom. The degree of miscalculation stunned her.

She stood up and walked into the kitchen and said to Arthur, "Please get the car. We're going out this afternoon."

An hour later, Geneviève's touring car was making its way up Rue de Grenelle to the *hôtel particulier* that housed the Russian embassy. She had an appointment with the ambassador. Russian diplomats both here and in Geneva liked Madame Tabouis because she got the quotes down exactly as they said them. The message delivered was always clear, which further made Geneviève a "must read" in the capitals of Europe.

Ushered into the ambassador's office, she took the proffered chair and sat down opposite Monsieur. Souritz and made her greeting. The brusque Soviet ambassador got straight to the point: "They didn't consult us even about the drafting of the communiqué demanding concessions from Czechoslovakia.

The first news we got about the conference we read in *Paris-Soir*."

"They didn't even consult the Czechs according to my sources," added Geneviève with a strained smile.

"Yes, but then they said that we had agreed to the proposals that we never saw," said the ambassador, visibly steamed. "This lie was inexcusable, and a complete reversal of the true facts for, as you know, since March we have made no less than six different offers of collaboration to the Quai d'Orsay and the foreign office, without ever receiving a reply. I intend to make categorical denials in the press of the French and British statements."

"Yes, the record must be set straight."

"Why, the Quai d'Orsay has even tried to establish the fact that we had 'authorized Daladier to act for the Soviets at Munich, and that Paris and Moscow were in constant touch with London during the whole crisis.'"

"My Moscow sources confirm this," she agreed. Geneviève had the inside scoop about what French ambassador Coulondre had wired back to Paris from Moscow.

"All of this, naturally, has weakened the Franco-Russian pact. It is, in fact, on its last legs."

"My source in Moscow," said Geneviève, looking down at her notebook, "says that your foreign minister took note that the Western Powers deliberately kept Russia out of the negotiations...my poor friend, he said...what have you done? You have opened the way to a fourth partition of Poland."

The Russian ambassador sat stony faced and said nothing. Geneviève presumed she had the statement exactly correct.

"My source says that a new partition of Poland could only take place with the collusion of Russia and Germany." She looked up from her notebook and asked, "Is the Soviet Union going to return to an entente with Germany?"

The ambassador sat stone still and said nothing. Geneviève made a slight smile. She glanced down at her notes and read out loud the conclusion reached by her source at the Quai d'Orsay, based on what the French ambassador had cabled back to Paris: "From France, the Soviet Union now expects for the moment nothing more." The silence from across the desk reinforced the message.

She stood up, as did the ambassador. He escorted her to the door, saying, "Yes, our pact is on its last legs. It is sick!" She would duly report these words in her column; she wondered if the right people would get the message.

Outside, Geneviève got into the rear seat of her touring car while saying to Arthur, "Now, on to the Chamber. They are voting today to ratify the Munich Agreement." The limousine pulled into traffic and turned a corner and headed several blocks over to the Palais Bourbon, the seat of the Chamber of Députés. Geneviève hurried inside and headed for the press gallery.

On the stairs going up, she met Pertinax. The two journalists continued to the press gallery and took their seats overlooking the amphitheater that was the Chamber. "I am afraid," confided Geneviève, "that today's vote will be an exhibition of the very weaknesses that have brought about this shameful submission to Hitlerism."

"Yes," said Pertinax, "we are witnessing a breakdown of our political system that can be compared with nothing else in our entire history."

"Almost all the députés who were for resisting Germany have been beaten down by the government with the help of the bankers, businessmen, and Rightist press," she said with disgust.

Pertinax asked her, "What do you hear from the East? Do they have confidence in France?"

"I am in contact with all the capitals. But I hear the same thing from Poland, Romania, Yugoslavia—not much."

"Yes," said Pertinax in a falling voice. He had heard the same thing.

"They'll all scramble to make the best deal they can with Berlin," said Geneviève with the unerring eye she had for the next move on the European diplomatic chessboard.

They sat and watched as Daladier mounted the tribune and spoke to the assembled députés: "If we had gone to war to aid Czechoslovakia, how do we know that Czechoslovakia's integrity would have been maintained, even then?" He then answered his own question unconvincingly.

"Very lame," whispered Geneviève. Pertinax nodded and kept taking notes.

They watched the vote taken as it was recorded. The Communists almost to a man voted no. A few Radicals sat in abstention. All the rest voted for the government.

"There, only Kérillis voted against Munich," said Geneviève, speaking of the non-Communist députés. "All the rest went along."

"Except over there," said the observant Pertinax. "One Socialist député voted no."

Geneviève gave a harrumph. The two turned their eyes back to the tribune where Daladier pronounced his conclusion: "I have no regrets." The gavel came down, and the session was adjourned.

Geneviève descended down the long stairs and went outside and across the square where she found Arthur and her car. "One more stop, Arthur. The Czech legation."

She got in the rear seat, and Arthur navigated the touring car across the avenues of the Left Bank and pulled up in front of the Czech legation. A doorman came out from behind the iron gates and opened the door, and Geneviève alighted. She pulled her long fox fur overcoat around her to ward off the evening chill and walked into the legation. Inside she handed her overcoat, scarf, and hat to a maid while a private secretary escorted her into a sitting room.

Inside the sitting room, Geneviève sat next to a warmth-giving fireplace and waited. Presently the door opened and she stood up. The butler escorted Edvard Beneš into the room. She walked over, both hands outstretched, and said, "Président Beneš."

He hugged her and then held her back by the shoulders and said, "No more, I'm afraid not. I had to resign."

"I'm so sorry to hear that, Edvard."

"My life was threatened," he said. "You know, they are murderers."

"Yes, I know," said Geneviève. "And Paris?"

"I went to see Daladier," said Beneš, and his voice broke. He looked at Geneviève plaintively and said, "Daladier refused to see me. He does not dare face me."

"Yes…" she mumbled in reply. *Possibly Daladier has some private regrets*, she thought.

"May I get you some tea?" asked Beneš.

"Yes, that would be nice," said Geneviève. "Where are you going after this?"

"On to London. I've been there before," he said, mentioning his experience with London during the First World War. "The government in exile...the émigré activities...keep the flame...all that stuff."

27. Place du Palais Bourbon

Daladier may have not had any regrets, but he did embark on an ambitious program to strengthen his government and bolster France's defenses. Great changes were in the air as Thérèse came into the luxurious apartment of the Comtesse Hélène de Portes across from the Palais Bourbon. She walked over and said hello to the hostess. The comtesse was simply brimming with good humor now that her paramour was again holding high office. Reynaud had been moved from the justice ministry to the finance ministry. Hélène de Portes could see her glamorous destiny unfold before her.

Thérèse looked around for Marie Hélène. She wasn't there, not that she said she would be. But Paris was brimming with political gossip. Odd that she would miss it. Thérèse got a glass of champagne and walked over and stood near the windows and peered out at the square below in the late afternoon light.

It was a busy day, she thought. In the morning Dugas had called; he had urgent information for Berlin. She had gone to the rendezvous at the metro station and picked up an envelope from the nondescript man in the smashed down homburg hat. She had delivered it to the German Tourist Office over by the Madeleine as Carl had instructed. He had given her the address as an alternate. He said he was getting ready to depart for Berlin; important work about the German-French peace agreement was getting underway, he said.

Looking around the drawing room, teaming with politicos and fashionably dressed women, Thérèse drifted over to where Paul Reynaud was holding forth. Reynaud was just taking up his duties as finance minister in the Daladier government.

"We," said Reynaud, and he nodded across the room at Daladier standing in the middle of another conversation circle, "are providing the military with an additional twenty-five billion francs, almost tripling the defense budget. We are going to dramatically increase the size of the airplane plants and start producing some of the most modern fighter planes in the world."

Appreciative murmurs buzzed among the listeners. France was on the move.

Thérèse listened and then walked over to where Daladier was similarly holding forth. He was earnestly speaking with a group of députés and others, his expression deadly serious. She hovered on the edge listening to the conversation.

"The new aircraft production from our own plants should add two thousand modern frontline fighters to the air force."

"Is that enough to counter the Germans?" someone asked.

"Good question," replied Daladier. He dropped his voice. "But I've ordered a thousand modern planes from the Americans. They will arrive next summer."

"How will you pay for them?" asked another individual, astounded at what a thousand planes would cost.

"We"—Daladier nodded across the room at Reynaud—"are coming up with an innovative financing package that will get around the American Neutrality Act." The Neutrality Act required arms to be paid for with cash. But Daladier was working with the Americans on a financing package that would involve mortgaging French colonial territories in both the Caribbean and the Pacific to pay for the armaments. Very ambitious, very daring.

Then with a scowl of determination on his face, Daladier said, "If we'd had three thousand aircraft, there would not have been a Munich." The other members were startled by the determination in Daladier's voice. Thérèse watched and thought to herself that Daladier was going *belliciste*—warmonger. But her husband Claude had told her that there would be big contracts in France for assembling the American airplanes once the shipments got to France. The planes would come in crates and need to be assembled and tested. He and his industrial group wanted some of the contracts. He had asked her to work with Marie Hélène on securing favorable consideration from the ministry of defense. Everyone knew Mimi had the inside track with defense contracts.

Thérèse walked across the room to the entranceway and gave her champagne glass to the butler, got her overcoat, scarf, and hat from the maid, and left.

Outside she found her limousine and got in. She leaned forward and told the chauffeur, "Avenue Foch." The limousine drove across the square and turned on Boulevard Saint-Germain and headed up the tree-lined boulevard in the late twilight. Coming down the other side of the street, she thought she saw Marie Hélène's limousine coming. It looked like there was a man in the rear seat next to her. "Pull over," she said to the chauffeur.

As the car stopped at the curb, Thérèse got out and walked back down the sidewalk; she watched the other car go down the boulevard. Two blocks before the German embassy, it pulled over to the curb. A man got out, looked back into the rear seat, and gave his good-byes to the woman, and then he closed the door and stood on the sidewalk. He watched the limousine pull away. Thérèse recognized immediately the profile: Dinckler.

Thérèse looked around at the early evening darkness—the time of day whispering its cruel message—a time not for business but for love. She knew. She was crushed. How could Marie Hélène do this? Her best friend? This wasn't business. She was pretty sure she had taken care of whatever remaining business Dinckler had in Paris before leaving for Berlin that morning when she delivered the letter from Dugas. This wasn't about peace; this was about betrayal.

Tears rolled down her cheeks, the powder on her face blotting, the mascara streaking. Carl was hers. She took a handkerchief out of her handbag and dabbed at the eyes and wiped her cheeks. She got a grip on her emotions, squared her shoulders, and then walked over and got back into her limousine. She softly said, "Avenue Foch."

Wilhelmstrasse

Carl Friedrich von Dinckler was escorted into the office of State Secretary Ernst Freiherr von Weizsäcker by the stern-faced, efficient secretary.

"Ah, Carl," said Weizsäcker as he stood and shook Dinckler's hand in greeting. "Did you just get in from Paris?"

"Yes, I took the night train."

"We got the information you sent yesterday about Bonnet and the French cabinet. Very good."

"Thank you. The source is impeccable."

"As has been all your Paris work," said Weizsäcker in warm tones. "Everyone here in Berlin—at the highest levels, I assure you—is pleased with the important information you provided during the Munich negotiations. As I discussed with you last year, diplomacy rather than military force was able to gain the strategic objective."

"The French cabinet was deeply divided at the top," said Dinckler.

"Yes, the Führer has a sense of how to seize the opportunity in these situations. Eastern Europe's ability to challenge the Reich has been fragmented, fractured, and weakened."

"Russia?"

"Good question. Our embassy in Moscow reports Stalin is drawing his own conclusions."

"The French and British excluded the Russians from consideration more than I would have thought," said Dinckler. "There have always been loud voices in Paris to activate the military provisions of the Franco-Russian pact. Those voices were ignored."

"Yes, Madame Tabouis and that claque."

"Yes, the French journalists are very loud, very shrill," said Dinckler.

The state secretary looked over Dinckler's shoulder and out through his open door toward the hallways and offices of the foreign ministry and sighed. "She has very good sources." He suspected some were in this very building.

"Yes, possibly too good," said Dinckler.

Returning to business, the state secretary said, "Yes, the embassy reports the Russians are reconsidering their foreign policy and that Stalin will be more favorable to Germany in the future and much less so to France."

"Yes, the French lost Czechoslovakia and burned their bridge to Moscow."

"Well said. A double loss. Our Moscow embassy believes there will be favorable opportunities for a new and wider German economic agreement with the Soviet Union. That means critically important raw materials…"

"To go with the new arms plants acquired in Czechoslovakia."

"Yes, getting those factories out of French ownership was good work, and well, responding to that French owner's request for the I. G. Farben shares, that was like cutting warm butter…doing our work for us…"

"Possibly in the future we will want reliable French partners…"

"Yes, indeed. This year has seen a remarkable run," said Weizsäcker with pleased confidence. "Now, Foreign Minister Ribbentrop would like to present the Führer with a Christmas present, so to speak—a Franco-German peace pact. Accordingly, we have brought you back from Paris to work with our staff on an appropriate agreement to be signed by the two foreign ministers in Paris, the pact that you say Bonnet is eager to have."

"I would say 'envious,'" said Dinckler. "Bonnet was very envious of the pact Chamberlain took back to London."

"Yes, initially the Führer was dismissive of the agreement with Chamberlain. But once we saw on the newsreels the prime minister wave the document around at the aerodrome upon his return before the cheering crowds, we saw the power of its propaganda value. Goebbels doesn't miss things like that."

"So something similar to the Chamberlain agreement?"

"Yes, exactly. Something Bonnet can wave around. We assume Daladier will not."

"Correct. But Bonnet craves publicity and attention…"

"And it is not as if our own foreign minister, Ribbentrop, would not appreciate a turn on the world stage under the spotlight…solo…"

"So, a simple document and a grand state visit," said Dinckler.

"Exactly. Lots of champagne."

"I think this should be rather easy to accomplish."

"Sometimes, Carl, I think you make all of this look too easy," said Weizsäcker with paternalistic affection. The two families had been close for centuries, a cousinhood too complex to unravel.

Avenue Foch

The telephone rang in the foyer. The maid picked it up. She heard the familiar voice and the words "Monsieur Frederick." She went and got madame.

"Hello," said Thérèse. Yes, it was Jules Dugas. She had been waiting for the call.

"Yes, a lunch would be fine," she said. "Yes, late lunch would be very suitable." She listened, and a slight smirk crossed her face. She had expected the invitation; she imagined that Dugas had rarely been turned down.

"No, I don't think the restaurant on the Champs Élysées would be appropriate," she said and paused, adding, "This time." She let the future hang open.

"Suggest? Why, you could come to my house. Late Sunday afternoon."

She listened some more and answered, "No, we will be quite alone. The servants will be gone; it's their day off. Remember, the Popular Front reforms."

The voice came through the earpiece with a chuckle, then pleasant and amiable. She replied, "Quite private. You can come through the back way." Then she outlined instructions to finding the rear entrance.

"Yes, when you get back from the convention in Marseilles...I do look forward to it," she said, a dark sparkle in her eye. Carl had been gone for a long time now. And there were some things she wanted to know.

Marseilles

Geneviève Tabouis sat in the press gallery watching the Radical Congress. A titanic battle of words got underway as Édouard Herriot, long-time Radical warhorse and Président of the Chamber of Députés, launched into a heated defense of traditional French foreign policy with its emphasis upon alliances in eastern Europe anchored by a grand alliance with Russia.

Geneviève watched Herriot, a former professor with a strong intellect and legendary virility, battle the appeasers in the Radical Party. She thought back over the years to when the League of Nations still offered hope. She had been a great friend of Herriot, and he had been a frequent guest at her apartment explaining French policy to foreign journalists and visiting diplomats, his great wit delighting the visitors. Often, she had sat at his right hand during many interviews with journalists, and if the word *maitresse*—mistress—had had been whispered about her, well, as long as it was softly said and discreetly mentioned, no harm. She smiled to herself at her memories, and remembered his many friendships in the salons of Paris.

Yes, back in the days when French foreign policy had purpose and direction under Foreign Minister Barthou, so sadly cut down by an assassin's bullet right here in Marseilles in 1934. She remembered that dinner party at her apartment she gave for Barthou, one of many where he sparkled. He had looked around the table, after several glasses of wine, and said to her sotto voce, which everyone heard, "Geneviève, I believe I have slept with every woman at the table except"—and he held his wineglass out toward a young woman at the far end of the table—"that one." Geneviève smiled at the recollection. The women at the table looked around at one another with laughing eyes and suppressed smiles; the husbands smirked under raised eyebrows. The great statesmen had been in his element. Yes, back in the years when French diplomacy was leading the way toward a better Europe, and optimism put the sharp edge of vivaciousness to life. *Now begin the hard years*, she thought.

Geneviève turned her eyes back to the podium below. Daladier vehemently defended the new policies brought about by the Munich Agreement. Daladier said, echoing words previously spoken by Chamberlain, "Let France look to her own empire, and give up worrying about what goes on beyond the Rhine." The Radical politicians who believed in collective security were dismayed, but the appeasers carried the day. The Congress gave a vote of approval to Daladier's policies and congratulated Daladier and Bonnet "upon their energy and spirit."

The following morning, Bonnet gave his own defense of the Munich Agreement. He was followed by Herriot, who again defended traditional French policy centered on the Franco-Russian pact and collective security. Pierre Cot, the Radical air force expert, took the rostrum to defend collective security and appeal for resistance to German aggression. Suddenly, demonstrators flooded the convention floor, and with shouts, hisses, and boos, drowned out Cot's speech, and completely disrupted the order of the convention. The demonstration broke up the convention leaving the Radical Party divided on both foreign and domestic policy. Geneviève wrote in her notebook: "No common meeting ground on any matter whatsoever." The center of French politics no longer held.

On the train going back to Paris, Geneviève talked with various Leftist members of the Radical Party. One of them bitterly complained, "The disturbance was organized by the Marseilles gangster Carbone. He was hired by the old bulls, the corrupt claque around the Chautemps brothers. They bring nothing but corruption and contempt on to the head of the Radical Party." Geneviève mentally made a note; yes, she had seen Jules Dugas there. He was the long-time Chautemps "fixer" who watched over Bonnet, and was rumored to be close to the dirty politics—the use of underworld methods—that hovered around the edges of the Chautemps group. Yes, the demonstration could easily have been his work. That's what fixers do.

Another Radical politician complained, "There is systematic coercion everywhere today, and it paralyzes all efforts toward a stronger policy."

Avenue Foch

Thérèse waited in the servants' dining nook near the rear entrance late Sunday afternoon. She was wearing a high-waisted dressing gown with a tight bodice, putting her figure on alluring display. *It is time to have a good time*, she thought. She stood up as she heard someone come up to the door; she went and opened the door, and Jules Dugas stood there in slacks and a sweater.

He handed her a bouquet of flowers and said, "A gift from Marseilles. It's still springtime down there."

"Yes, I know. We visit there often. My husband got his start there; he was just off the boat from Corsica."

"I trust he's not in Paris," said Jules with a good-natured laugh.

"No, he is with his factories in the east of France," she said with a smile. "Here, come in. We can go into the drawing room and have a glass of wine. Some fruit if you are hungry."

"Yes to the wine. No to the fruit. I had lunch on the train."

"The convention in Marseilles was a success?"

"Yes, quite so. There are always some rough edges, but they were overcome."

"Fix rough edges, that's what you do?"

"Yes, that's what I do."

"For the Bonnets?"

"Yes, and for the Radical Party. It's been my home."

The two of them moved into the drawing room. Thérèse poured two glasses of chilled white wine and gave one to Jules, who took a seat on a couch. Thérèse sat down a couple of feet away and half turned facing him, her body suggesting intimate familiarity.

"Tell me," she said, "about Marseilles."

"The Munich Agreement was overwhelmingly approved. We now move on to our grand initiative."

"Which is?"

"That's what the envelope to Dinckler was all about. Monsieur Bonnet would like to finally get the Franco-German peace agreement down on paper and signed. Just like Chamberlain did his last morning in Munich."

"Did you give Carl any last-minute information just before he left?" she asked. "I would have been happy to deliver it. Have a chance to say good-bye."

"No, everything was in the envelope."

"Yes, I see," she said rather thoughtfully.

"You seem bothered by something," said Jules, looking at her inquiringly.

"No, it's just he's been away a long time."

"Well, maybe I can dispel any lingering loneliness," he said with brio, the self-assured confidence on full display. The wealthy, slightly older woman had been one of Jules's specialties; he had been in many a Parisian boudoir during his political ascent.

"Yes, I'm sure you can," said Thérèse with a coquettish smile. Jules felt he understood her like a well-worn playing card.

"Well, my understanding is that Dinckler will be back with a draft agreement that we can all review and then make final arrangements for a signing ceremony."

"Here in Paris?"

"Yes, hopefully before Christmas."

"A real peace agreement?" asked Thérèse, a truly hopeful tone in her voice.

"Yes, what we've been striving for all these many months."

"That would be very nice," she said. She also thought it meant Carl would be back. She hoped so. The thought warmed her spirit. Nevertheless she had a guest right here, at her invitation, who was very much caught up in the excitement of now. She felt a tingling of expectation, a soft rush where she really liked to feel a rush. She stood up and set her wineglass down.

"Come," she said as she held out her hand, palm down. He stood up. She took his hand and said, "This way." They walked down the hallway.

Propositions

Later, in the darkness, she lay in bed, the sheets and covers in mad disarray. She could still feel his heat. They had gone on all afternoon and into the evening. He was very inventive; she smiled at the memories. She watched him silhouetted in the window as he buttoned up his shirt and pulled his sweater over his head. He looked over and smiled at her in the darkness. She lay there, not quite exhausted. Possibly he had been without a woman for a while. That or maybe this was a dimension of his political success that she had not appreciated before. She never saw him lack for feminine company at a salon or reception.

Wearily she got up and walked over and put on her dressing gown. She quickly cinched the waist strap and then stood and brushed her hair into place with her hands. He came over and took her hand, and they walked out of the bedroom and toward the rear entrance. She hugged his arm and reached up and kissed him on the neck as they stood by the rear door.

"We could more meet often, if you like," he said. "Thursdays, possibly?"

"I think not now, I'm too...what can I say...but yes...we'll get together..."

"Well, fine. Maybe we can have that dinner down on Champs Élysées some afternoon or evening...in an upstairs private room...a very discreet rendezvous..."

"Yes, possibly...I would like that...a lot," she murmured. *Yes, possibly a repeat*, she thought to herself. She hugged his arm close to her and then let it go.

"Oh yes, I hate to bring it up…but Odette wants the monthly retainer from Claude's companies to increase…she's increasing the fees for our political services…there are many hands out…many mouths to feed…to pave the way…"

"Yes, I understand," said Thérèse. She expected this, but possibly not today. She sighed inwardly and thought to herself that indeed it was a very brazen business.

"It's all part of being a grande dame, I'm afraid," said Jules sympathetically.

"Yes, I'm sure it is. I wasn't going to bring it up, either," she said, her voice trailing off, "but Claude and his group are very interested in getting part of the airplane contracts…"

"The American airplanes?"

"Yes."

"I will put the word in to Daladier's political aide."

"Claude wanted me to work with Mimi…"

"Excellent choice. She knows her way through the ministry. We'll have it covered from both ends."

"Yes, I'll speak with Mimi about it…"

"We always accommodate Claude, you know that."

"Yes, it's all so businesslike."

"I truly like you, Thérèse, or I wouldn't be here." He squeezed her hand and turned and left.

Luxembourg Gardens

In the weak sunshine of a late autumn morning, Marie Hélène entered through the iron gates of Luxembourg Gardens and started to walk up the gravel path toward a point overlooking the pool where children sailed their toy boats. Thérèse had wanted to meet with her before going on to lunch. Marie Hélène was sure Thérèse was highly expectant as Carl was expected back any day now. She was, too. Jules was expecting big things with Dinckler's return. Said it would be almost as big a thing as the visit by the British monarchs the previous summer. As Marie Hélène approached, Thérèse stood up and held out her hand. She gave Marie Hélène a desultory shake and sat down.

"I want to get something clear, Mimi. I'm deeply hurt."

"Hurt?"

"Yes, it's about Carl. You're having an affair with him."

"I think I'm going about business with him. Jules wants a confidential link. I deliver information to Carl."

"You're having an affair with him," said Thérèse adamantly. "I know. The last day Carl was in Paris I delivered the information to him…and then later in the early evening I saw you with him."

"Giving him more information," quickly countered Marie Hélène.

"Not so. Jules said I gave him all the information that was delivered that day."

"Jules?"

"Yes, Jules. Two can play this game. I had, shall we say, a meeting with Jules."

"Really," said Marie Hélène, somewhat surprised at this development but not surprised that Jules was on the prowl. And until Carl had come along, Thérèse had mostly been a wandering star. "Well, he is a man that likes to keep an open calendar. I long ago came to accept that."

"Yes, he offered me Thursdays…"

"Well, we could have been sisters in *faire d'amour de le calendrier*," she said with a sardonic laugh. "I gather you didn't take his offer."

"No…I wanted something better…this time…with Carl…"

"He's yours, Thérèse. I would never try to take him from you. Jules urged me to do it…said the Germans don't trust someone unless…they like to have something on you…"

"And it doesn't bother you? Being blackmailed?"

"Blackmail? It's not blackmail; it's just business. That's what we do here in Paris, Thérèse. Don't you understand that?"

"Business? I'm tired of business. Just this once," she said wistfully. "Something special…for me…"

Marie Hélène stood up and said, "I'd better be going. But let's please try to work together, Thérèse."

Thérèse stood up and said, "Yes." The two women took opposite paths out of the gardens.

Paul A. Myers

28. The Return

Carl von Dinckler sat on the bed in his shorts in the late afternoon twilight in Thérèse's hideaway apartment sipping a glass of champagne, his gift for this reunion with Thérèse. He had called her straightaway upon his return to Paris from Berlin. Now she stood over by the window in a silk slip, her breasts voluptuously pushing the silk forward, the cleavage an enticing invitation, the hips pulling the material taut across her derriere.

"I have to know, Carl," she said.

"What?"

"Why did you have an affair with Mimi, my best friend?"

"Affair? It was business; she has been delivering information to me from Dugas."

"Not the day you returned to Berlin. I saw you with her on Boulevard Saint-Germain."

"Oh."

"Remember, I delivered the information to the tourist office at your request that morning."

"Well, maybe there was more," Carl said diffidently.

"There wasn't. I asked Jules Dugas."

"You did?"

"Yes, two can play this game. He's with Mimi on Tuesdays. Most of the rest of the week he is free."

"So you got him on a free day?"

"I had to know."

"OK, so what? I'm not betrothed to anyone…yet?"

"No, I understand that…but I wanted something special with you…I had hoped…"

"It's not like she didn't throw herself at me…or rather I should say Dugas pushed her at me…said the Germans wouldn't trust the information if she didn't…"

"Oh yes, easy opportunity as duty…at least with Mimi it's usually easy opportunity for easy fun…"

"It's not like that…Dugas really controls her…"

"Maybe…you said betrothed…what does that mean?"

250

"As you know, in the Wilhelmstrasse the number two official is Ernst Freiherr von Weizsäcker. The Dincklers and the Weizsäckers have been intermarrying for centuries...Weizsäcker has nieces...when I return to Berlin next time...the families expect..."

"So, that doesn't change Paris."

"No, but in German 'freiherr' means baron...and in France you're a baroness, the daughter of a duke, you know the family codes...family first...family last..."

"Yes, I do. And I wish you the best in your future marriage in Berlin...but we're in Paris...now."

"Yes...and I am as true to you as my duty allows...that's all I can say...things are expected of me..."

"If I weren't so fond of you..." Thérèse finished her champagne in a gulp. She walked over to the bed and stopped and pulled her slip over her head. She stood before Carl. He set his glass down and reached behind her and took a buttock in his hand and pulled her toward him and buried his face in her and gently kissed her most privately, her fingers running through his hair, a slow moan of satisfaction rising in her throat.

Quai de la Tournelle

Jules Dugas leaned on his elbow in bed and looked at Marie Hélène standing naked in the early morning twilight coming through the window in his flat high above the Seine River. He loved looking at the soft turn of her rear end, the slender hips, and the little nipples sticking out from firm round breasts. Last night's lovemaking had been memorable, intense and abandoned, like a coiled spring slowly unwinding.

"It's a beautiful view here, the twin towers of Notre Dame, the flying buttresses, the town houses on Île Saint-Louis."

"Yes, it is."

"You told Thérèse too much."

"I didn't mean to."

"She knew...I told you I would do anything for you...I understand the importance of getting the right information into the right hands...that's how these governments work...and money...but I didn't want to betray Thérèse...not this way..."

"Well, Carl is back...I'm sure he'll make it right with her..."

"Did the information help?"

"A great deal. Carl brought back a Franco-German peace agreement...Bonnet presented it to the cabinet yesterday afternoon...it is everything we hoped for...our secret little highway is delivering a big public benefit to the people of France and Germany..."

"Well, I suppose that is reason for celebration..."

"Big celebration...we'll be having a signing ceremony at the Quai d'Orsay with Foreign Minister Ribbentrop...a state visit...and a big reception at the German embassy...Tout-Paris will be there...except for the Jews of course...particularly after what happened last week..."

"Yes, the troublemakers...that assassination of the third secretary at the German embassy last week was dreadful," she said, mentioning the assassination carried out by a disgruntled young Jewish man protesting the inhumane treatment of his parents in a German concentration camp. Her first thought when she heard the news had been: what if that were Carl? She was sure Thérèse had the same thought.

"It was worse than you think. It set off a massive retaliation against Jews all across Germany...shops destroyed...the incident is being called the Crystal Night because of all the broken glass on the streets..."

"And our government?"

"Bonnet barely got the peace agreement through the cabinet...the Jewish cabinet members said it would look bad at this time...some others agreed...finally those around Chautemps came forward and pushed it to a favorable vote...but it was close..."

"Thank God. We must get a peace in the West signed. All that we've worked for."

"Yes, it is on the way."

"I look forward to it."

"Good, I was expecting you to accompany me to both soirées."

"I'd love to. Celebrating peace is second only to..." Marie Hélène returned to bed and pulled back the covers and got in and snuggled up next to Jules and let her fingers run over his body.

"Again?" he asked with a touch of weariness. "You are turning from a woman into…"

"An insatiable goddess of passion, you mean." She giggled and pulled him over on top of her. "Goddesses have the power."

With Pleasure

Later in the morning, Jules took Marie Hélène home to her family town house on his way to the Quai d'Orsay. The taxi stopped outside the big wooden door, and Jules turned to her and said, "I didn't want to bring it up until now, but Odette wants more retainer from the Comité des Forges and from your family company, the Compagnie de Marne. She says the cost of arranging all the support for the new peace agreement is high…"

"Yes, I suppose so," Marie Hélène said with a tinge of disappointment.

"Bonnet really supported you on getting the additional funding for the Maginot Line in Daladier's supplemental appropriation. Reynaud wanted to spend it all on airplanes and tanks. Daladier insisted…"

"Yes, Compagnie de Marne owes all of you a great deal…you have been loyal supporters…"

"And you of us."

Marie Hélène's expression brightened, she smiled, and she said with a sultry tone in her voice, "*Avec plaisir, monsieur.*"

The cab driver held the door open. She kissed Jules good-bye and got out of the taxicab. She stood on the sidewalk and watched the cab pull away and drive down the street. Jules looked back through the rear window. She smiled and waved.

Yes, she thought. *Women always pay a high price when they want to live a low life.* She laughed to herself. It was her mother who repeated that message to her when she was a girl. She remembered. She owed her mother a lot—in particular her beauty. Her mother had been the most beautiful girl in her village. Nevertheless she had yearned to get out on her own and explore the excitement of being a young woman in Paris. And she had. The pleasures were wonderful, and besides, her father could afford it. She turned and went over and rang the bell to the entrance to the family town house.

A Betrayal in Europe

29. Salon de l'Horloge

Under a gray sky and a chill breeze in early December, the long black Mercedes limousine, motorcycle outriders in front and back, moved away from the entrance of the Hôtel de Crillon and crossed the immense Place de la Concorde. The limousine traversed the Pont de la Concorde as steel-helmeted members of the mobile guard and the police lined the streets in a double row, one rank facing the roadway and the other facing out to keep away the crowds that were not there. The limousine turned and drove slowly up the quay alongside the Seine River toward the French foreign ministry. Arriving, it swung through the gates and stopped at the entrance to the limestone edifice.

At the top of the steps stood Georges Bonnet, Secretary General Alexis Léger, and several aides and liveried ushers in welcome. The German foreign minister, Joachim von Ribbentrop, and Ambassador Count von Welczeck got out of the limousine, followed by an interpreter, and walked up the steps and shook outstretched hands. The party quickly moved inside.

Moving toward a conference room prepared for the meeting, secretaries arranged along the walls with steno pads at the ready, Ribbentrop turned and noticed Bonnet's personal study and said, "That will do." He walked in followed by a somewhat surprised Bonnet and the others. Ribbentrop took a seat in front of Bonnet's desk, turned, and looked over his shoulder and spoke to his interpreter, "If you could wait outside with the others..."

Count von Welczeck took a seat next to Ribbentrop while Léger stood behind Bonnet's shoulder. Ribbentrop, smiling and amiable, came straight to the point. "We are about to sign a joint declaration. Now we want from you a full recognition of the implications in the Munich agreement. In other words, we wish you to formally agree to our having 'a free hand in central Europe.'"

Bonnet smiled, looked up at Léger, and replied to Ribbentrop. "The secretary general and I were discussing before your arrival that we would like to arrange for an international guarantee for the remaining fragment of Czechoslovakia." Bonnet smiled and added, "Of course, what you are asking of France is not possible just now."

Ribbentrop shrugged his shoulders good-naturedly and replied in a pleasant tone, "Well, we'll leave the matter open then. It can be taken up with the Führer later." He stood up and looked around at the office with interest and then said, "Let's proceed to the signing ceremony." The four men filed out.

A Signing Ceremony

Several minutes later, another limousine swung through the gates of the Quai d'Orsay and came to a halt on the far side of the Germans' Mercedes. An usher walked over and opened the rear door, and Geneviève Tabouis alighted. She was wearing a long black fore-and-aft hat, a long dark fox fur coat, and a dark wool muffler around her neck. She had a large handbag on her arm. The usher escorted her over and up the steps and pointed with his left arm and said, "Salon de l'Horloge."

"Yes, I know the way," breezily replied Geneviève. She walked over and gave her coat, muffler, and hat to another usher and then proceeded down the hallway.

In the spacious and ornate Salon de l'Horloge, the Clock Room in English, a large crowd of people had assembled to watch the formal signing of the Franco-German pact. Geneviève looked around and sighed and thought of the many path-breaking agreements that had been signed in this majestic room, almost a temple to modern diplomacy. She looked around further, and in one corner, she saw a large crowd around Otto Abetz, who had accompanied Ribbentrop from Berlin to Paris to manage the affairs of the German Press Association. She made a sidewise grimace.

Abetz, looking past his circle of admirers of the German Press Association, saw Geneviève and broke away and crossed the room, smiling and friendly. "Geneviève, so nice to see you again." Geneviève nodded politely but remained glacial. "Oh, don't be that way," chided the German official.

"That's the way I feel."

Abetz made a playful frown and said, "Perhaps you can tell me, Madame Tabouis, why the police segregate us every time we make a move in Paris."

"Would you like the crowds to throw rotten eggs at your minister?" she said tartly.

"No, but that would not happen, I am sure. The truth is, the French government is afraid that the crowds would cheer our minister and the other Germans. The French people are anxious to welcome us."

"There might be a difference of opinion on that."

Abetz made a playful frown at Geneviève's reply.

"And what about all the anti-French demonstrations in Rome," asked Geneviève, changing the subject, "the territorial demands by the Italian parliament. Does Germany really support Italy's claim to Corsica?"

Abetz smiled as he saw the safe ground ahead. "Of course not, Madame Tabouis. Herr von Ribbentrop has disavowed all support for those claims." Abetz then went into a detailed exposition of the German position. Geneviève wrote it all down.

"Thank you, Herr Abetz. You have been most helpful," said Geneviève. "I'll quote you on that."

Just then, floodlights were thrown on, bathing the room in bright light. The polished tabletop where the declaration awaited signatures glistened under the glare. Bonnet stepped forward and summarized to the press that the pact involved the two countries agreeing to consult with each other in the future. The two ministers stepped forward and signed the document, Ribbentrop signing in his distinctive green ink, which drew something of a perplexed look from Bonnet. The two ministers turned around, faced the cameras, and shook hands.

Bonnet stepped forward and said, "We are following President Roosevelt's lead in being 'good neighbors.'"

Ribbentrop stepped forward and agreed. "Yes, good neighbors," he said, beaming like the champagne salesman he had once been—one who had just made a big sale.

A waiter brought up glasses of champagne and handed them to each foreign minister. Other waiters hurriedly passed out glasses of champagne to guests around the room. Then the two statesmen turned to each other, clinked glasses, and made a toast to the "No War" agreement just signed.

Léger scurried around the room handing out the communiqué to reporters, the press release highlighting the "good neighbor" phrase.

Over at the side of the room, Geneviève scribbled her impressions into her notebook, closed it, and shoved it into her handbag. Léger came up and handed her a communiqué with downcast eyes.

"It's not your fault, Alexis," she said.

"There's a larger duty..." he mumbled. "It's been like that ever since Munich."

She stuffed the communiqué in her handbag. She looked around the room at the beaming officials, and then watched as liveried footmen ushered Premier Daladier, Bonnet, Ribbentrop, and other high officials into the adjacent Salon de la Rotonde where sixteen chairs had been set out at a long table.

The doors to the room closed as Geneviève watched the statesmen take their seats. Discussions of major concern to the two countries were scheduled to begin immediately. She looked across the room and caught Abetz's eye. She smiled, made a small wave of farewell to the German official, and turned and walked toward the hallway leading to the front entrance.

In ten minutes, Geneviève Tabouis was at her newspaper office dictating her story to a stenographer: "Herr Ribbentrop in his first days of conversation had occasion to repeat several times that his government is not disposed to support the Italian position in the Mediterranean."

She went on to declare that questions about Italian territorial claims in the Mediterranean and the issue of Jews being allowed to take property and money with them when they left Germany would be the subject of tomorrow's talk. She explained that Bonnet would raise the issue of the Jews and their property at the request of British prime minister Neville Chamberlain, who keenly felt the impropriety of such confiscation of private property.

As always, Geneviève had leading insights gleaned from key insiders into what was going on behind the floodlights of the press conferences and the closed doors of diplomatic conference rooms.

Dinner at the Quai d'Orsay

The limousine pulled up in front of the entrance to the Quai d'Orsay in the cold chill of the December night. An usher opened the rear door, and a middle-aged man wearing evening dress stepped out, turned around, and presented his hand to a lady scooting across the seat. The lady put one leg out and then the other. She stepped out and stood up while pulling her long wrap around her, tugging at her scarf, and presenting her arm to her escort. She beamed and, with radiant eyes sparkling, said, "Robert."

"Geneviève," he said affectionately.

The couple walked across the drive, dodging around other limousines where couples were decamping, and walked up the steps. The man presented an invitation to one of the ushers and said, "Robert and Geneviève Tabouis."

"This way," said the usher. He stood and waited as the lady and the gentleman handed their overcoats, mufflers, and hats to an attendant at the cloakroom. Then the usher escorted the couple down to the Salon de l'Horloge, which was now arranged as a large reception room. Couples were scattered about in small groups talking, some in German but most in French.

"I recognize most of the officials, cabinet members for the most part," said Robert.

"Yes, most of the cabinet, but not all," said Geneviève. She made a mental note.

"There are enough industrialists here to have a second Industrial Revolution."

"Yes, the Comité des Forges is well represented." She nodded toward one group and said, "That's Marie Hélène de Villars-Brancas, comtesse de Villars-Brancas, of the Compagnie de Marne. She's a leading presence at the Comité des Forges. She's with Jules Dugas, the *chef de cabinet* for Bonnet. It's his dinner tonight."

"She's strikingly attractive."

"Yes, isn't she? But I'm afraid Jules has turned her head."

"Well, a pretty one to turn."

Geneviève laughed. "I've heard over the years that below that pretty head there's a body that burns..."

"We French are supposed to appreciate that..."

"Over there," said Geneviève, "is Thérèse Mathilde de Roncée, baroness de Roncée. She's with the second secretary of the German embassy, Carl Friedrich von Dinckler. I believe he's one of her pets."

"Well, a handsome pet," said Robert.

"They always are with Thérèse," said Geneviève with a knowing smirk. Then Geneviève noticed that Thérèse was making a hard, daggerlike stare at Dugas as if he were an unwanted guest at a garden party. Strange? Then as suddenly as it occurred, the storm left Thérèse's face and she turned to Dinckler and made a charming witticism to which her circle responded with a light laugh.

"Yes, I'm aware of the family name, von Dinckler. Distinguished."

"Yes, but possibly the most duplicitous of the Germans. One picks up the scent of the trail...the money from French subsidiaries of German companies to the big French papers...mostly *Le Temps* and that ilk...money to Odette, Bonnet's wife...and I have long suspected that Dinckler is the puppet master, the master string puller, but the trail always goes cold in the streets leading to the German embassy. The secret stays hidden."

"Even with your sources..."

"My source at the Wilhelmstrasse says there is someone deep in the embassy orchestrating the policy subversion at the top of the French government, someone right here in Paris...it has to be him...but I've no proof."

Robert knew she probably had deeper secrets but would never say and decided to change the subject: "Why is he with the baroness if he's such a clever spy? She's ten years older than him."

"She's a close friend of the comtesse de Villars-Brancas...and her husband is an important industrialist."

"So a diplomat sleeping with a baroness on intimate terms with the comtesse...who is sharing a bed with...why, that would put him in position to read the French foreign minister's very thoughts, wouldn't it?" said Robert.

"Once he got past the distractions…"

"Well, you tell me the really good ones always do. So, just the man I'd like to meet!" Robert took his wife's arm and led her over toward Dinckler.

"Thérèse, you look stunning tonight," said Geneviève as she came up.

Thérèse beamed. "You, too, Geneviève. That looks like a Molyneux creation you have on," she said, referring to Geneviève's gown.

"Yes, I wore one of his gowns to the coronation and then last summer to the state dinner for the king and queen. Monsieur Molyneux was so pleased he gave me this gown. Said I was a billboard."

"I would say a beautiful model," offered Dinckler gallantly.

"I of course promised Monsieur Molyneux I would give him the most favorable of news coverage," said Geneviève with a laugh.

"Favorable coverage from Madame Tata? Well, well, one of the rare and lucky ones," parried Dinckler.

"Possibly," admitted Geneviève. "But gazing into my crystal ball, I see that we live in an era of dark events."

"Possibly as we achieve a new peace," said Dinckler, spreading his arm across the assembled guests, "new light will appear to illuminate any remaining dark events."

"Well said," said Robert.

"Well, I love the dress," said Thérèse.

Geneviève shook Thérèse's hand and smiled. Ever correct, she turned and said, "Herr Dinckler, my husband Robert Tabouis."

"Yes, Radio France, I believe?" said Dinckler.

"Quite right. Do you keep yourself informed on even those of us toiling in the lower ranks?" said Robert.

"The spouse of Madame Tabouis would be of special interest. She is rumored to be well connected in Berlin."

"I've heard those rumors, too."

"Why, I understand even the Führer reads Madame Tata," said Dinckler, somewhat to Robert's astonishment.

"Well, you must know. You undoubtedly are well connected at the top of the Wilhelmstrasse, too," said Robert.

"Possibly not as high up as Madame Tata," said Dinckler with a sly and knowing smile.

"All an exaggeration, I assure you," said Geneviève congenially.

A man came up in white tie and tails, a large tricolor sash across his chest, medals in a row across his chest, and good-naturedly said, "Geneviève." Then he turned and held his hand out to Robert. "And, Robert. So nice you could join us this evening."

"Thank you, Monsieur le Minister," said Robert deferentially to Georges Bonnet.

The foreign minister's wife Odette swept up, a woman of bosomy proportion in a beautiful gown bedecked with jeweled necklaces and shimmering bracelets. She held out her hand and said, "Geneviève, so nice you could come tonight. I don't get to see you as much as we used to."

"Georges's foreign policy keeps me very busy."

"Yes, you don't seem to have the same enthusiasm for the foreign policy of peace as the other journalists."

"True, but there are a few of us still left."

"Too many I should say," said Odette.

"Oh, there's Alexis. I must go say hello," said Geneviève, begging off from what could get quickly tiresome.

Robert nodded to Dinckler and Bonnet and followed his wife a half dozen steps to where Alexis Léger was standing arm in arm with the elegant Comtesse Marthe de Fels, of whose literary salon he was a shining star. The two were speaking with Countess Madeleine de Montgomery, utterly fetching in a long gown accentuating her long legs and beautiful ash-blond hair. The wealthy Montgomery was the editor of a leading fashion magazine.

"Alexis, feeling better tonight?" asked Geneviève while nodding at Comtesse de Fels, a lady of high intellectual refinement.

He looked at her with a dry expression and said, "Marthe and I are admiring the irony of circumstances tonight—the brazen fist trying to pass itself off as a polished glove."

Geneviève laughed. "Poetic." She looked at Countess de Montgomery and asked, "Minou, what do you think?"

"Of course, we're pleased to be here, basking in what little irony there is at a German reception," said Minou. "One wants to see the German retinue in person, even if only for one night..."

"One night?" asked Geneviève mildly perplexed.

"Yes, just one night, because unfortunately I had to decline my invitation to the reception at the German embassy tomorrow night."

"You did?" asked Geneviève. "I thought I was one of the few to not be invited...except of course the Jewish cabinet ministers. You declined the German embassy?" asked Geneviève, sensing a story.

"Yes, I telephoned my regrets to the German embassy today. You see, I told them that I had already invited Monsieur Osusky of Czechoslovakia for dinner," she said, referring to the Czech minister.

"Very apropos," said Geneviève with a hearty laugh.

"Yes, I read Blum's blistering account in *Populaire* about excluding the Jewish cabinet members," said Minou. "This is all an empty ritual, I'm afraid. There's no peace here."

"Can I say 'leading hostess'?" asked Geneviève, the story already forming in her mind.

"Yes, that would be appropriately discreet," said Minou. She glanced across the room and saw the bemedaled German ambassador, Count von Welczeck, approach. "Oh, I think someone is going to give me a talking-to." She put a wicked smile on her face. "No mischievous deed goes without its spanking."

"Countess," said the ambassador as he came up.

"Count," said Minou with exaggerated deference.

"I keep asking our social secretary why I never get an invitation to your house for one of your famous receptions," said the ambassador in excellent French.

"But, *mon cher ambassadeur*," said the countess, "every time I get ready to send you an invitation, I find that your government has just annexed another European country belonging to a friend of mine."

Geneviève laughed, Alexis kept a straight face, and Robert smiled benignly.

"But, *ma chère comtesse*, think of today's agreement. This is a time to celebrate new understandings."

"Only if they lead to new and better futures—for my many friends in Czechoslovakia, for instance," said Minou.

Taking a deep sigh and looking around the room for escape, the ambassador said, "Possibly it is time for me to pay my respects to the foreign minister." He nodded in the direction of foreign minister Bonnet and added acidly, "And his charming wife."

Like the sexual temptress that she could be, Minou leaned forward and folded herself around the ambassador's arm, holding it close to her lithe body, her perfume enveloping his senses, and in a sultry voice whispered—while blowing hot breath into his ear—"I understand…the charming wife."

As the ambassador awkwardly untangled himself from Minou's grasp, Alexis suppressed a smile while holding out his hand and saying with diplomatic gravitas, "Ambassador."

The ambassador bowed slightly toward Geneviève and nodded at Robert and Comtesse de Fels and then turned and walked over toward the foreign minister. Geneviève watched the German diplomat present himself to the French foreign minister and then reach out and give Odette's hand a kiss with real old-school flair.

"I hardly know them anymore," said Geneviève to her husband. "He's so craven, and she's so crass."

"Yes, bad policy and sycophancy don't go well together."

"Speaking of sycophancy," said Geneviève, and she nodded toward Abetz a dozen steps away. Standing beside him was Abel Bonnard, formally attired, various accoutrements establishing his membership as one of the Immortals in the Académie Française.

"If Abetz is infiltrating the Académie, he's found the perfect door opener," said Geneviève.

Robert looked Bonnard over closely. "Look, Abel's wearing the pendant of the Académie around his neck," he said, mentioning the richly enameled decoration hanging by a green-and-white ribbon around his neck that is bestowed on sitting members.

"And the beautiful decoration of the Académie on his chest," said Geneviève wistfully. "Yes, the Far Right has penetrated the last bastion of French distinction."

"One might say that bastion fell when they admitted Bonnard. His novels scandalize without being redeemed by the art of insight."

Geneviève laughed at her husband's wit. "Listen, here they come," she added.

As Abetz and Bonnard walked by, Bonnard said to Abetz, "When you are ambassador...representing the Reich..."

"Yes, and when you have your ministry..."

Bonnard clasped his hands with childish joy and exclaimed, "We must instill in the children the values of the high culture of *la patrie*." The fatherland.

Geneviève smirked at her husband. "See what is becoming of *la belle* France."

"No longer the République," observed Robert. "*La patrie*. The republican lights are going out."

30. L'Étoile

In the damp December morning, with gray overcast hugging the rooftops, a limousine pulled up to a curb on one of the side streets radiating out from L'Étoile, the big square at the top of the Champs Élysées surrounding the massive Arc de Triomphe. Marie Hélène got out of the limousine, pulled on her gloves, and pulled her fur coat tight around her. A few moments later, another limousine pulled up and parked across the street. Thérèse got out of the rear of the limousine. She looked around, and somewhat startled, saw Marie Hélène. Regaining her composure, she let herself make a small wave. Marie Hélène waved back and then with her arm motioned for Thérèse to come join her. The two women were heading to the same place.

Thérèse crossed the street and walked over to Marie Hélène. "We must stay friends, Mimi. I know that."

Marie Hélène nodded in agreement.

"But I was so upset. You don't know what Carl means to me, to my life," said Thérèse with a plaintiff tone in her voice.

"I think I do," said Marie Hélène. "Rest assured. I'm never going to take him away from you, Thérèse."

"It's an obsession. A last chance at what love was once like…before the war took it all away."

"I understand."

"Do you? For you it's all just part of a dangerous game, *une liaison dangereuse*, a game I think you like playing."

"Possibly," admitted Marie Hélène. "Jules wants me to keep the channel open to the Germany embassy. Carl is the key, he says. Jules says that peace hangs on our efforts."

"Yes, we want that and something else, too," said Thérèse. "At least Claude. He wants me to work with you on getting help with the ministry of defense so his industrial consortium gets some of the contracts to assemble the new American airplanes."

"Of course. That's what we do here, Thérèse, charm the political power for money."

"Can you help me, Mimi?"

"I think you've already helped yourself," said Marie Hélène with an ironical lilt in her voice. "Jules Dugas is the key."

"He is? For defense contracts?"

"Yes, he's really Camille Chautemps' boy and Chautemps is the power behind the throne in the cabinet."

"I see."

"Jules likes you."

"Yes...I like him, too." She made a deep sigh. "I understand him also."

Marie Hélène laughed. "And I'll help at the defense ministry."

The two women walked up the sidewalk toward the Étoile, encountering a double line of steel-helmeted mobile guards.

"We are here to see the ceremony," said Marie Hélène, presenting a rare engraved invitation. The guard motioned to a superior, and an officer came over.

The officer looked at the card and then said, "Let them through." He turned to the two women. "May I suggest you watch from over there. You can't actually approach the Arc. No one is allowed."

"Understood," said Marie Hélène. The two women walked over to a good vantage point on the edge of the broad square.

Over on a stairway leading into a nearby building stood three men. *L'inspecteur* gave a nudge to *le chef* and pointed to the two women.

"Yes," replied *le chef.* He pointed out the two women to Jacques Morel standing next to him.

The two women looked down the Champs Élysées and watched as the black limousines came up the avenue, the sidewalks screened by a double file of mobile guards and police. The limousines came to a halt at the edge of the square. Foreign Minister Ribbentrop got out of the leading limousine.

"Look at that," said *l'inspecteur* with a touch of amazement in his voice. Ribbentrop was wearing the black uniform with the silver insignia of a general of the SS, Hitler's elite Praetorian Guard.

"Incredible," said Morel. "Right in the center of Paris."

"Yes, and Foreign Minister Bonnet trotting alongside," said *le chef* with uncharacteristic disgust at the obvious toadying.

From a limousine toward the rear of the group, Jules Dugas got out and walked up and joined Ribbentrop and his party. The party walked over to the eternal flame burning in the center of the space under the Arc de Triomphe. Dugas spoke briefly with the officer of the guard.

German Foreign Minister Ribbentrop wearing his SS uniform signing the Golden Book at the Etoile. Foreign Minister Bonnet standing behind him without hat.

The officer of the guard waited until Ribbentrop had centered himself before the tomb of the Unknown Soldier. Behind the uniformed foreign minister came Carl von Dinckler and several other men with a huge wreath adorned with ribbons in the Nazi party colors.

The French officer came to attention, raised his sword, and called out to his men, "Present arms."

Rifles flashed into an upright position in front of each soldier's chest.

Ribbentrop took a step forward and placed the wreath on the tomb of the Unknown Soldier. He stepped back and gave a military salute.

"Order arms," barked the French officer. The soldiers brought the rifles down alongside their right legs.

Ribbentrop walked over and signed the Golden Book. Foreign Minister Bonnet stood behind him bareheaded in this solemn moment. Then Ribbentrop turned on his heel and went back to his limousine followed by his party.

Dugas turned to the police commander and said, "Don't let any of the press photographers near the site. Absolutely no photographs."

"Understood."

"After the limousines have returned to their hotel," said Dugas, nodding down the wide avenue, "then remove the wreath and take it to Invalides."

"Yes, monsieur," said the police commander.

Dugas walked over to the commander of the army guard and said, "Well done." The crisp formality had been just right. He turned and walked back to his waiting car. He looked over and saw Marie Hélène and Thérèse but did not acknowledge them. They watched him walk without any sign of recognition.

"Cold out here this morning," said Thérèse.

"Yes," said Marie Hélène. "A very cold peace, I'm afraid."

"Yes, maybe France is going to need those airplanes after all."

"I still have hopes that a strong defense will lead to peace," said Marie Hélène.

Thérèse sighed and shook her head in the negative. "I think something is coming to an end here. Germans in black uniforms standing before the eternal flame…"

Across the broad square, the three French intelligence officials watched the women talk. As the two women walked away, l'inspecteur said, "All the pieces to the Paris-Berlin channel were here this morning."

Le chef let his eyes follow the women across the square and said thoughtfully, something having caught his eye, "Madame de Roncée seemed distracted by something."

"I'll keep an eye on that," said l'inspecteur. "Possibly there is a jealousy among the ladies."

Le chef nodded in agreement and said sagely, "Possibly the women are in a competition for one of the men?"

"But which one?" asked l'inspecteur.

"Undoubtedly events will reveal the answer," said le chef. Then he looked at Morel and changed the subject, asking, "And which country on the chessboard is the next target for the taking?"

"The rest of Czechoslovakia, then Poland. As long as Hitler doesn't think France will go to war, he will keep taking," said Morel.

"And Bonnet keeps delivering that message through Dugas to Berlin," said *l'inspecteur*.

"And so Hitler will keep taking," said Morel.

"And we can only sit and watch," said *l'inspecteur* with deep resignation, "waiting for something to turn up."

"The game continues," said *le chef* cheerfully. "It always does." He looked at the two women now leaving the square, smiled, and said, *"Cherchez la femme."*

The other two men laughed. Then the three men walked down the steps and returned to their offices.

31. Avenue Malakoff

Geneviève Tabouis entered the ultra-contemporary flat with the spacious rooms overlooking Avenue Malakoff in the wealthy sixteenth arrondissement. Its owner, the Countess Madeleine de Montgomery—known to all as Minou—was the wealthy editor of one of Paris's trendiest women's magazines, heiress to the Noilly-Prat fortune. The flat had glistening white walls and curtains, long purple couches along the walls unlike anything seen in a Paris drawing room. The spacious rooms were broken into smaller spaces by wide screens of Chinese lacquer with finely drawn scenes of stylized gardens. The passages between rooms were heralded with black-and-gold bronze Venetian pages standing sentry while the corners of the rooms were set off by huge bouquets of white flowers. The gloom of winter darkness outside the windows was broken by light from a multitude of colored candles. Geneviève smiled to herself and thought that the flat was a decade or two ahead of the avant-garde. She walked over to the hostess and said, "Minou, I enjoyed your performance with the ambassador the other night at the Quai d'Orsay. The only bright spot in a dreary week."

"Thank you, Geneviève," replied Minou. "I fear the Germans are up to no good, something beyond bad manners and clumsy diplomacy."

"That's my constant anxiety, too," said Geneviève. "I have a sense of foreboding." She looked over Minou's shoulder and saw Marie Hélène and Thérèse chatting with each other across the room. She excused herself and walked over to say hello.

"Good afternoon, ladies. I so enjoyed the opportunity to speak with you at the dinner at the Quai d'Orsay the other night," said Geneviève by way of greeting.

"Thank you, Geneviève," replied Thérèse. "Carl enjoyed his exchange with your husband. It's so rare to see him actually joke about anything official."

"Yes, diplomats are charmingly dull. Except maybe on the end of a telephone line late at night when they really have something to say."

Marie Hélène nodded and smiled with self-satisfaction. There was nothing dull about her thoughts about Carl today. He had sent her beautiful red flowers this morning with a note—*ce soir*. At the parting outside the restaurant yesterday, there had been an air of deep sincerity she had never seen before. There was a certain tremulousness in his voice when he whispered in her ear, "I love you." Her knees had gone weak. She had been in a state of expectation all day. She barely heard Thérèse speak.

"But if the diplomats don't talk, dull or otherwise," said Thérèse, "then peace must come by more devious means." She looked around the room, and her eyes alighted on Jules Dugas. She caught Jules' eye and a smile flashed across her face. Returning to the conversation, she collected her thoughts and said, "I need to leave. Bankers are coming for dinner."

Marie Hélène said, "I'll be in touch later."

Thérèse nodded good-bye to the two women, turned, and walked out of the apartment. Across the room, Jules Dugas watched. He made polite excuses to the two young actresses from the Comédie Française he was chatting with and followed Thérèse out to the landing above the stairwell.

"Thérèse?" he called out after her.

"Yes?" she said, turning around, a look of anticipation on her face.

"With regard to our letter," said Dugas, a touch of supplication in his voice. "Your firm needs to pay the increased retainer for the services we're providing your family's many enterprises…and have been…"

"Yes, I spoke with Claude. He agrees subject to…the American airplanes…"

"Yes, I've put the word into the ministry of defense. Claude's group will be part of the assembly team," said Jules, referring to the industrial group that will assemble the new airplanes arriving from America by ship.

"Thank you…I know it's just business…" said Thérèse.

"Thérèse, business is business…but you're more than business…if you're free…"

The slow smile of the coquette crossed her face. "Thursday, perhaps…"

"Champs Élysées…the restaurant…"

"Late in the afternoon…"

"Yes," she said, now accepting a future where she would be many men's plaything—like it always had been before Carl…but with Carl she now realized she had just been used…like all the others…an introduction…a contract…

Jules reached out and picked up Thérèse's hand and gave it a soft kiss. He smiled. Her husband Claude and his industrial group would be a handsome source of income. He watched her as she turned and continued down the stairs and outside to her limousine. He went back and got his overcoat and hat and followed Thérèse out into the gloom of the December afternoon. He looked forward to Thursday—something special, perhaps. The prospect of money and pleasure always buoyed him up.

Inside the apartment, Marie Hélène saw Jules leave. Her day was now clear. She had checked in with the Café Koslov earlier in the afternoon—a message was waiting for her.

She looked at the two young actresses, now standing alone in a corner. *Though not for long*, she thought. Soon Abel Bonnard approached the two and said, "Your playmate has left. Will there be others?"

The two actresses giggled, hands over their mouths, heads bobbing in affirmative, their eyes alight with mischief.

"And who might they be? Députés? Members of the cabinet perhaps?"

"Oh, we could never tell," said one.

"Let's play a game. Nicknames…surely you have nicknames for your favorites?"

More giggling, hands quickly put over mouths, stolen glances at each other…

"Come on now…"

"Eyes."

"Eyes?" asked Bonnard.

"He likes to watch," said one of the actresses.

Bonnard looked at the two with an appraising eye and took a shrewd guess, asking, "*Ensemble? Together…*"

The two laughed and bumped shoulders together in delight at the game. Bonnard smirked. They giggled. He continued, "And if you're bad?"

The giggling rose to a pitch, then one reached over and held the other's shoulder and whispered in her ear.

"Now you can tell me, your uncle Abel…"

One young lady leaned over and whispered to him, "The riding crop."

Abel reared back and put his hand over his mouth in mock shock. "Does he hurt you?"

"Oh, no, we hit him…but not very hard…where he likes it…he coos like a baby…"

Abel said sweetly, "You two are so full of charm…let me get some more champagne…we have so much to talk about…for literature…possibly a play…a classic French farce…on the stage…for you two…"

The two actresses nodded eagerly in agreement, and Bonnard hailed the waiter to bring more champagne. To be the inspiration to a French play…a great farce…on the Paris stage…written by a leading member of the Academie Française…

Marie Hélène smiled and thought that possibly the actresses will like what Bonnard writes about them in his low bedroom farce more than her embarrassed memories of being rolled over on the soiled sheets depicted in the lurid pages of one of his scandal novels…promising the inside look at life at the top in Paris. She shrugged her shoulders and turned and surveyed the room.

She watched as Hélène de Portes approached Geneviève and Minou. She heard Geneviève say to Minou, "Ah, a contrary wind approaches."

"Geneviève, it is an ill wind that doesn't blow someone some good," said Minou with good humor. "I will leave you to the gale," she said as she stepped away and headed toward another group of guests, leaving Geneviève to cope with the rough-edged conversation of Madame de Portes. Marie Hélène decided to go listen to the comtesse and Geneviève engage in their verbal fencing.

"Geneviève," said Hélène de Portes, "how could you bring up the Jewish problem in your column when the Germans are here trying to make peace? You know they're troublemakers."

"Who? The Jews or the Germans?"

"Oh, you're impossible, Geneviève," said the comtesse with a pout.

"Besides," said Geneviève, "it was the British prime minister who raised the issue. I only reported it."

"The same thing," said Hélène dismissively.

"At least the reception at the German embassy for Herr Ribbentrop was a great success. Everyone was indeed very well mannered," sniffed Portes.

"And in Italy the trains run on time," said Geneviève, "at least so the English say."

"Well, I don't know about trains in Italy, but at least Paul had a chance to talk things over with the Germans," said the comtesse, referring to her lover Paul Reynaud.

"Did Paul get to speak with the German hosts," Geneviève asked with an impish smile on her face, "after the Prague ham or before the pâté-de-fois-gras from Strasbourg?" She was quoting off *la carte,* the printed menu at the German embassy, which had scandalized Tout-Paris with its insultingly titled items. The Germans' perverted sense of jejune humor astonished the French guests, who found the Germans to be mostly humorless Nazis. And this after having received engraved invitations in German instead of in French, the host language. No manners at all.

"Just a little attempt at humor," said the comtesse. "Not something the Germans are good at."

"We agree on something," crisply responded Geneviève.

"Nevertheless, a successful meeting. They even laid a wreath at the tomb of the Unknown Soldier. So touching. Overall, the agreement is a step toward peace," said Portes, reciting the conventional wisdom.

Marie Hélène broke into the conversation. "Yes, I saw it. I was at the Étoile."

"You did?" asked Geneviève. "I cannot believe he wore his SS uniform to place a wreath on the tomb of the French Unknown Soldier."

"Why?" asked Hélène de Portes. "A soldier paying respect to a soldier."

"The SS are hardly soldiers. They're Hitler's personal bodyguards. Keepers of the fanaticism," said Geneviève. "They wielded the knives in 1934, the Night of the Long Knives—butchers in shiny black boots." She made a brief shiver as she thought back to the barbarity of how Hitler had consolidated his Nazi party power over the blood-soaked corpses of his Brownshirt allies.

"He was wearing the black uniform," said Marie Hélène. "I saw it. And the Death's Head emblem on the cap. It looks like he's from a sinister world."

"Nazi Germany is," said Geneviève.

Hélène de Portes rolled her eyes, the matter was of no significance to her, and continued her argument. "And as to the Jewish troublemaking, if we listened to the Jews, we would already be at war. That's all they want."

There is some truth to that, thought Marie Hélène.

"Well, there's Paul speaking with the Polish ambassador," said Geneviève, taking the opportunity to change the subject. "Paul will tell us what the future holds."

The Poles? Another group of troublemakers, thought Marie Hélène. Both Jules and Carl thought that. Thérèse had airily dismissed the Poles; she thought they were at best a bunch of stable boys.

"Poland's future? Let me go hear the good tidings right from the horse's mouth," replied Geneviève as she took the opportunity to step away from the argumentative Hélène de Portes.

She crossed the room and came up to group of people surrounding Reynaud and the Polish ambassador, Lucasiewics. As Geneviève approached Reynaud, Marie Hélène followed her and stood next to her.

"Ah, Mimi," said Geneviève in a whisper to Marie Hélène, "Paul always provides a frank opinion."

"Yes, he is for a strong defense."

"Did you enjoy the dinners and receptions surrounding the Ribbentrop visit?"

"Very much so," replied Marie Hélène. "Jules feels that every positive step toward peace must be taken. No stone left unturned."

"And those steps are leading to peace?" asked Geneviève skeptically.

"Jules says positions must be tested by diplomacy," replied Marie Hélène. "France's interest is peace in the West."

"And war in the East will not affect the West?"

"The East? I don't know. It's the West I care about. No one believes more in a strong defense in the West than Compagnie de Marne," said Marie Hélène with frank determination.

"Yes, Compagnie de Marne has been paid handsomely to build that defense," said Geneviève lightly.

"We believe in it," said Marie Hélène with a touch of heat.

The two women turned toward the center of the circle where Paul Reynaud now took center stage of the conversation, saying to the Polish ambassador, "You celebrated Czechoslovakia's misfortunes too hastily. It won't be long before the Germans get after you."

Blood rose in the face of the Polish ambassador, a diplomat both smart and quick-tempered. "Never," he exclaimed. "Germany will not dare. We're stronger and more intelligent than those Czechs. And, besides, you see that they're leaving Czechoslovakia alone now."

"By March," said Reynaud, "Germany will have devoured Czechoslovakia. And in August, she'll attack Poland."

Faces around the circle registered astonishment at the bluntness of Reynaud's prediction, though none doubted its accuracy. Marie Hélène crinkled her nose and frowned. *More bellicisme from a leading belliciste,* she thought. *No wonder he is one of Geneviève's favorites.*

Geneviève glanced at Marie Hélène and caught her eye. The journalist raised an arched eyebrow over a faint smile and whispered, "Possibly true. War approaches."

Marie Hélène turned serious and said, "We will be ready in the West...the defenses...the new airplanes..." She held her hand out to Geneviève and said, "Until later." She turned and departed.

Time for Carl, she thought. He understood her...her life...a love that could only be enjoyed in fleeting moments and never captured in the amber of commitment...but a love that had its own destiny…captured in the chords of a Gypsy guitar…on a Paris night…

32. Sûreté

Le chef looked up as he heard a knock on his door. *L'inspecteur* opened the door and walked in. "What is it?" *le chef* asked.

"I have more on baroness de Roncée and comtesse de Villars-Brancas."

"Yes?"

"The butler at Madame de Portes's apartment said that he overhead Dugas arrange an assignation with Thérèse. Said it sounds steady."

"Good. And the comtesse?"

"We tailed her from Madame de Portes's salon. She has a small hideaway apartment behind a Russian bistro out in the Seventh. Dinckler met her there."

"An interesting pas de deux."

"Exceedingly so."

"Anything else?"

"The baroness is now working to help her husband Claude win some contracts for assembling the new American warplanes when they arrive. Dugas is the contact."

"Well, business as usual."

"She's also asked Marie Hélène to help get the airplane contracts through her numerous contacts at the ministry of defense."

"Yes, understandable. And the comtesse?"

"She's angling for more contracts on the extension of the Maginot Line along the Belgian border."

"Normal," pronounced *le chef.* "And Dinckler?"

"Well, obviously, he now knows about the airplanes."

"That was to be expected."

On the desk the telephone rang and a white light blinked above a button on the base of the apparatus. *Le chef* punched the button below the blinking light and picked the telephone up in his hand. It was his secretary.

"Yes?" he asked.

"*Le chef de cabinet* is on the line," said the voice of his secretary.

"This early?" His eyebrows arched up in astonishment. A phone call from the minister's chief of staff. He looked at *l'inspecteur* and made a face. Authority was making a request. He listened some more and then let out a low whistle. "The minister personally?" He raised his eyebrows to emphasize the question for *l'inspecteur*'s benefit.

"Now?" His face took on a look of well-practiced bureaucratic resignation. "Has he given you a name?"

"No," said *le chef* as he repeated the secretary's answer. "Well, put the man on."

"Yes, monsieur," his secretary replied, her faint voice coming out of the receiver. He waved with his hand for *l'inspecteur* to listen as he held the telephone in the center of the desk, the earpiece pointing up.

A gruff, somewhat elderly voice came on the line. "You're a hard person to get hold off." This person obviously took his connections to the top for granted.

"Yes, it's intended that way," said *le chef*. "Whom do I have the pleasure of speaking with this morning?"

"We spoke before, last fall," said the voice.

"Yes, we did. How goes it, Claude?"

Claude didn't miss a beat. "It's about Thérèse."

"And?"

"I know about the German, Dinckler. My agents know a lot. I keep an eye on Thérèse. Would be a fool not to."

"Yes. And what about Dinckler?"

"Met him in person several times. He was always straight with me."

"Really?"

"Got me out of Czechoslovakia."

"Before or after?"

"Before you say," repeated *le chef*. *Dinckler is playing a smart game*, he thought. "Yes, I'm sure he was always straight with you. Diplomats are trained to present themselves that way."

"And I know about Jules Dugas and Marie Hélène. And now Dugas and Thérèse."

"Yes, and what's your interest in Dugas?"

"Can he deliver? I know he's a real political fixer. Supposedly works for Bonnet, but that's a front. He's babysitting Bonnet. He's been part of the Chautemps mafia from back in his days with the Paris prosecutor's office."

"Yes, he's close to all the old bulls at the top of Radical Party."

"And Odette, she's—what do we say—on intimate terms with several bigwig newspaper people. If she's not splitting sheets with them, she's a least divvying up the boodle with them."

"There has been influence peddling at the highest levels."

"There are lots of double games going on. And Mimi's been in both beds at both ends of the double game for a long time. And now Thérèse."

"You have quite good agents."

"In my position, it pays to know who's nosing around the property."

"And your question this morning?"

"Two questions. First, can this guy Dugas deliver on the contracts I want or is he just playing Thérèse along? We're shelling out good money. It's more than just about Thérèse having a good time. I hate to pay a staffer that kind of money; I like to go straight to the top."

"Well, Bonnet is something of a straight arrow. His wife wears the pants over there."

"So it's Dugas then. Can he deliver?"

"He can deliver," said *le chef.*

"Fair enough. Second question. I understand Otto Abetz and the Comité France-Allemagne. Not my kind of guy, but..."

"Yes..."

"What's the deal with him and Dinckler? He and Abetz can barely stand each other. I've watched him; Dinckler's heels never click when he shakes Abetz's hand."

"Interesting," laughed *le chef.* "But yes, you are correct. Two rival operations in Paris. Abetz works for Ribbentrop in Berlin— he's all Nazi. Dinckler works for Weizsäcker and the old line Prussian crowd. We believe there are two competing power factions in Berlin."

"Whaddaya know. The aristocrats don't like the Austrian housepainter," snorted Claude. "And you think the Prussians might knock over Adolf?"

"There are those rumors."

"And you would have a telephone line straight to the new government in Berlin?"

"That's our thinking."

"And Dinckler's the link?"

"Possibly."

"Smart," said Claude with a tinge of admiration in his voice. "You government guys aren't always as dumb as you look."

"I'll take that as a high compliment," said *le chef*. "And your wife?"

"She just wants to be loved. A woman gets to a certain age; they want to pass through the flame one more time…"

"Yes…"

"When I was younger…"

"Understood," said *le chef* sympathetically. He listened for a few more moments and then hung up with the words, "Good luck with the airplanes, monsieur."

33. Place de l'Opéra

Geneviève Tabouis worked late into the evening of New Year's Eve at the offices of *L'Oeuvre*. The shouts and celebrations from revelers on the streets below were a faint murmur beyond the closed windows. She was rewriting the final chapter for her new book *Blackmail or War*. Her pencil tip glided over the sentences as she read:

"If France fails to readjust her foreign policy and to base it upon the Franco-Russian pact, she is condemned to go from concession to concession, then from capitulation to capitulation, until the day comes when Hitler...

"Without powerful allies in the East, she will be helpless, and will uselessly sacrifice her young men...

"Peace was not created at Munich on September 30, 1938..."

Finished with her work, the clock struck midnight and the year 1939 began on the festive streets of Paris. Geneviève set her work aside, put on her overcoat and scarf, plumped a warm hat on her head, and descended the stairs and walked out onto the Place de l'Opéra. She strolled along the sidewalk with the jostling crowd. Restaurants were brimming with revelers, champagne corks were popping, glasses clinking, little toy horns tootling. Never could Geneviève remember Parisian crowds being so deliriously gay.

Reaching Boulevard de la Madeleine, Geneviève spotted an empty taxicab and hailed it. She was tired; it had been a long day, a tiring year. In minutes the cab had her back at Place Malesherbes. She rode the lift up and entered her apartment. Her beautiful Persian cat Lotus slinked out of sight, its tail down.

Geneviève walked into her workroom and saw that her lovely Louis XVI looking glass had fallen from the wall and its glass had shattered. She sat down on her chair and looked across the small room and contemplated the smashed glass and wondered about the year to come.

End

Postscript

On March 15, 1939, Adolph Hitler sent German troops to occupy the remainder of Czechoslovakia. Six weeks later in Berlin, Hitler broadcast on international radio an attack on the international press and singled out by name Geneviève Tabouis: "As for Madame Tabouis, that wisest of women, she knows what I am about to do even before I know it myself." Madame Tabouis's speaking engagements in France and Britain soared.

As the summer of 1939 progressed, the Russians moved diplomatically away from France and Britain and secretly began negotiating with Germany. On August 23, 1939, German foreign minister Ribbentrop and Soviet foreign minister Molotov stunned the world by signing in Moscow the Russo-German Nonaggression Pact. Hitler had achieved an alliance with Stalin; twenty years of French diplomacy was vanquished. A week later on September 1, Germany invaded Poland. With the expiration of a British ultimatum demanding German withdrawal from Poland, Britain and France entered the war against Germany on September 3. The Second World War had begun. Stalin followed with his own invasion of Poland on September 17. Hitler and Stalin divided Poland between them per a secret protocol attached to the Nonaggression Pact.

With its eastern flank secured by its alliance with Russia, the German army turned west and in May 1940 attacked France near the Belgium border, broke through French defenses, and defeated France in a lightning six-week blitzkrieg. The result was an armistice tantamount to surrender in June 1940. Former premier Camille Chautemps was a key proponent of the armistice and an architect of bringing Marshal Henri Pétain to power. Days later in Vichy, the French parliament voted the Third Republic out of existence.

As the French government collapsed, Geneviève Tabouis was warned that she was on a Nazi arrest list. Days later she stood on the deck of a British destroyer outside the harbor of Bordeaux. She looked above her head at the slowly rolling deck of the British merchant ship *Bellaria* and, steeling her resolve, hoisted herself up the swinging ladder and headed off to exile, her family left behind in occupied France. When she arrived in Britain, her good friend Winston Churchill urged her to go on to America to add her voice to those urging President Roosevelt to come to Britain's aid. She did not return to France until after the war.

Alexis Léger was deposed as secretary general of the foreign ministry in May 1940 during the cabinet upheavals accompanying the military collapse of France. He followed Geneviève Tabouis up the ladder onto the *Bellaria* and headed for a long exile in the United States, where he remained after the war. In 1957, he was given a villa in Provence by admirers, and he began to split his time between France and the United States. He continued as a poet and was awarded the Nobel Prize for Literature in 1960.

During World War II, Ernst Freiherr von Weizsäcker was transferred to the Vatican in 1943 as ambassador. In the wake of the failure of the July 1944 plot against Hitler, he declined to return to Germany, fearing arrest. Many of the conspirators were old-line Prussian aristocrats. The pope gave him political asylum in the Vatican. After the war, he was prosecuted as a war criminal by an American military tribunal at Nuremberg in what was termed the Ministries Trial (the "Wilhelmstrasse Trial") and served three years before being released after a review of his case by the American high commissioner; the Americans were consolidating power in a new West German republic. He was defended at trial by his son Richard. Decades after the war, Richard became president of Germany, serving from 1984 through the reunification when he became the first president of a reunified Germany.

On May 8, 1940, with the war against Germany going badly, a slashing debate got underway in the British House of Commons on the premiership of Neville Chamberlain. David Lloyd George, the steel-willed prime minister who led Britain to victory in World War I, made the telling criticism, "The prime minister must remember that he has met this formidable foe of ours [Hitler] in peace and in war. He has always been worsted." Chamberlain resigned two days later.

Some Sources

Bernier, Olivier. *Fireworks at Dusk: Paris in the Thirties*. Boston, Little Brown & Co, 1993.

Jackson, Peter. *France and the Nazi Menace: Intelligence and Policy Making, 1933-1939*. Oxford. Oxfod University Press, 2000.

Lazareff, Peter. *Deadline: The Behind-the-Scenes Story of the Last Decade in France*. New York. Random House. 1942.

Pertinax. *The Gravediggers of France*. New York. Doubleday, 1944.

Shirer, William L. *The Collapse of the Third Republic: An Inquiry into the Fall of France in 1940*. New York. Simon and Schuster, 1969.

Tabouis, Geneviève. *They Called Me Cassandra*. New York. Charles Scribner's Sons, 1942.

New York Times archives, 1937-38.

Image of Ribbentrop at the Etoile from the Internet. Public domain.
.

Editorial Services

CreateSpace—Editorial evaluation and line copyedit. Excellent services at an economical fee.

About the Author

Paul A. Myers lives with his wife in Corona del Mar, California. When not writing, he works as a sole practitioner CPA. He has written five historical novels and one satirical novel about the 2012 Greek financial crisis, a maritime history, several travel profiles, and a memoir about service as a soldier in Vietnam.

Paul A. Myers on the *terrasse* at Café Les Deux Magots in Saint-Germain-des-Prés on Paris's Left Bank.

See author's webpage at myersbooks.com.
Email author at myersbooks@gmail.com.
Follow on Facebook at myersbooks and Twitter at @myersbooks

Also by Paul A. Myers

Novels

Greek Bonds and French Ladies (a satire)
A Farewell in Paris
Paris 1935: Destiny's Crossroads
Paris 1934: Victory in Retreat
Vienna 1934: Betrayal at the Ballplatz

Travel profiles

French Sketches: Cap d'Antibes and the Murphys
French Sketches: Cap Ferrat and Somerset Maugham
French Sketches: Monaco, Onassis, and Prince Rainier
History

Other

North to California: The Spanish Discovery of California 1533–1603
Clerk! The Vietnam Memoir of Paul A. Myers

All titles available in e-book editions.

23911993R00168

Made in the USA
San Bernardino, CA
04 September 2015